MURDER
ON THE
MINNESOTA

Also by Conrad Allen

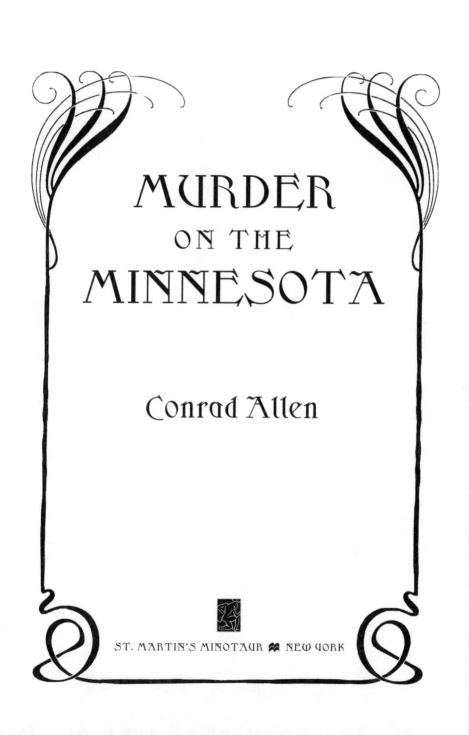

MURDER
ON THE
MINNESOTA

Conrad Allen

ST. MARTIN'S MINOTAUR ⚲ NEW YORK

www.minotaurbooks.com

ISBN 0-312-28092-0

First Edition: January 2002

10 9 8 7 6 5 4 3 2 1

To Carrie McGinnis
with many thanks for
the patience, wise counsel,
and editorial expertise

MURDER
ON THE
MINNESOTA

ONE

They were being driven along Fifth Avenue in a hansom when he broke the news to her. Genevieve Masefield sensed that he had something important to divulge but she did not press him. One of the first things she had learned about George Porter Dillman was that he could not be rushed. He liked to take his time. Accordingly, their conversation moved at the same leisurely pace as the cab. With the sun glinting off its harness, the bay mare pulled them along at a gentle and unvarying trot. Genevieve peeped out from under the broad brim of her straw hat to admire the mansions they passed and to enjoy her fleeting fantasies of ownership.

"I like that one," she decided, pointing a finger.

"You have good taste, Genevieve."

"It's such a gracious house."

"I agree," he said, "but it would come at a gracious price."

She gave a sigh. "There's always a catch."

They made a handsome couple. The tall, slim, elegant Dillman was immaculate in a pale gray suit, his straw boater angled to display his striking features to the best advantage. Genevieve wore a dress of white lace and a pair of white lace gloves. A slender young woman with a natural beauty, she exuded a sense of good breeding that was at variance with her origin as the daughter of a London draper. Each complemented the other. Anyone seeing them together would assume from their easy familiarity that they had known each other for a long time. In fact, Dillman had met her only nine months earlier on the maiden voyage of the *Lusitania*. It had turned out to be a fateful encounter.

The hansom rolled on through the traffic until it reached the Flatiron Building. Genevieve sat forward and craned her neck to look up at what was reputedly the tallest building in the world. When they came to the point where Fifth Avenue and Broadway merged, she gaped afresh at an imperial edifice of red brick, white tile, and terra cotta.

"What's that, George?"

"Madison Square Garden."

"It's enormous!"

"Oh, we have bigger buildings than that in New York."

"It looks so *foreign*."

"The Spanish influence. Inspired by Seville, I'm told."

"Look at that tower. It could have come from a cathedral."

"Well, I guess that Madison Square Garden is a cathedral of sorts," he observed dryly. "The tower is almost three hundred and fifty feet high. It was the architect's crowning achievement."

"He must be so proud of it."

"He would be, Genevieve, if he were still alive. Unfortunately, he was shot dead in the Roof Garden restaurant."

Genevieve was shocked. "He was murdered?"

"Yes," he explained, settling back in his seat. "It caused a huge scandal. Stanford White was a successful society architect. He was shot in the head at point-blank range."

"By whom?"

"The jealous husband of a young lady who claimed that White had seduced her when she was barely sixteen. She was not his only conquest, it transpired. Stanford White had a rather lurid private life. The press had a field day uncovering it."

"What happened to the killer?" she wondered.

"He's in a mental institution in Fishkill. The first trial collapsed so they had a second one earlier this year. Harry Thaw—that was his name—was declared insane so he avoided the death penalty. Was there nothing about it in the English newspapers?"

"Nothing that I saw."

"I'm surprised. It dominated the front pages over here. I would have thought that some of your reporters would latch onto the English connection."

"English connection?"

"Yes, Genevieve," he said with a smile. "Incredible as it may seem, Harry Thaw had an aristocratic brother-in-law. No less a person than the Earl of Yarmouth."

"Goodness!" she exclaimed. "An *earl*?"

"Don't be fooled by that title. In spite of his blue blood, he was nothing but an unemployed New York actor when he met Thaw's sister. The story goes that the Earl of Yarmouth was arrested for debt on the morning of his own wedding. They had to pay off his creditors for him."

Dillman was an excellent guide, patient, knowledgeable, and keen to show her the sights. Genevieve was very grateful. Though she had visited New York City a number of times, she had never had the chance to take a proper look at Manhattan. Working for the Cunard Line was a pleasurable duty but it limited her free time. No sooner did she and Dillman dock in one ship than they were being assigned to another for an eastbound crossing. It suddenly struck Genevieve that her friendship with George Porter Dillman had developed, for the most part, on the treacherous waters of the Atlantic. It was a welcome change to spend more time with him on solid ground.

"Heavens!" said Genevieve as another dwelling caught her eye. "That's not a house at all. It's a veritable palace. An imitation French château."

Dillman grinned. "Wait until you see the Vanderbilt mansions."

"Why?"

"They're even more grandiose. There are three of them on Fifth Avenue. My favorite is the one on the corner of Fifty-second Street. It cost every bit of three million dollars."

"I know the Vanderbilts like to splash their money around."

"Ostentation is all part of the game," he said disapprovingly. "The house was built by William Kissam Vanderbilt at the behest of his loving wife, Alva. Apparently, it's a cross between the Château de Blois and a Renaissance mansion at Bourges. They also own a summer resort in Newport, Rhode Island. The Marble House is even more sumptuous than their residence here."

Genevieve was impressed. "You seem to know a lot about them, George."

"I was once a dinner guest of the Vanderbilts."

"Were you?"

"Not that they would remember me," he admitted, "and it was not to the Marble House that I was bidden. It was to the other Vanderbilt mansion in Newport. An Italian palazzo of alabaster and gilt. It was built by Cornelius the second for his wife, Alice. They called it the Breakers. You'll get some idea of its size when I tell you that it needed almost fifty servants to run it."

"How do you know?"

"Because I was there on that bizarre night when the Vanderbilt ballroom was filled with the uniforms of a historic British regiment. Take my word for it," he said, his eyes sparkling nostalgically. "I was wearing one of those uniforms."

She was astonished. "You?"

"Along with all the other actors who were hired for the night. Cornelius the second had delusions that he was the Prince of Wales. His dear wife humored him by mounting this elaborate charade. It was very realistic. The attention to detail was remarkable." Dillman chuckled. "I bet you didn't know that I once served in the British army, did you?"

"No, George."

"It was my first job as an actor. It gave me a taste for it."

"You say that Mr. Vanderbilt had delusions?"

"His mind was quietly crumbling, poor fellow."

"Think of the expense involved," she said, shaking her head in wonder. "His wife must have loved him to go to all that trouble on his behalf."

"She was devoted to him, Genevieve. And there are far worse people he could have imagined himself to be than the present King Edward. Anyway," he went on with a fond smile, "that was the social highlight of my life. I had dinner with the Vanderbilts in a splendid red uniform."

"Where did all their money come from?"

"That's the interesting thing."

"Why?"

"The original Cornelius Vanderbilt started out as the captain of a ferry between New York and New Brunswick. From that humble beginning, he built up a fleet of freighters, then developed a transatlantic steamship line." Dillman gave a shrug. "After that, he moved into railways and made an even bigger fortune. Transport, Genevieve," he noted, wagging a finger. "That's where the Vanderbilt millions came from, and I think there's a lesson in it for us."

"Us?"

"Of course," he replied with mock seriousness. "We're in the transport business as well, remember. We may be minor employees of the Cunard Line at the moment but, if we follow Vanderbilt's example, we'll end up ruling the oceans of the world."

Genevieve laughed. "If only it were that easy!"

"What would you do with all your money?"

"I wouldn't waste it on a palatial mansion, I know that."

"So how *would* you spend it, Genevieve?"

She became pensive. "I'd travel the globe," she said at length.

"I was hoping you'd say that," he confessed, taking his cue,

5

"because it brings me to the reason I wanted to show you something of New York today. I was seizing the opportunity while it still exists. If you agree to my suggestion, you won't be seeing this city again for quite some time."

"Why not?"

"You'll be far, far away from here."

"Will I?"

He gave a nod. "How would you like to have a rest from crossing the Atlantic?"

"A holiday?"

"A working holiday, Genevieve. Aboard the *Minnesota*."

She frowned slightly. "That's not a Cunard vessel, is it?"

"No, it belongs to the Great Northern Steamship Company."

"I've never heard of them."

"That's not surprising," he conceded. "They're a very small company. I just happen to have a friend who works for them and he's asked me to do him a favor."

"What sort of favor?"

"The *Minnesota* has problems. I won't bore you with the details now. Suffice it to say that the ship needs some eagle-eyed detectives on its next voyage. I agreed to help."

"But you have commitments to the Cunard Line."

"I've spoken to them about that," he said, flicking a speck of dust from his sleeve. "They're perfectly happy to give me leave of absence. We've been sailing between here and Liverpool since last September, Genevieve. Our faces are getting a little too familiar. If we're seen too frequently on Cunard liners, people will start to work out that we can't really be bona fide passengers."

"That would be disastrous."

"Exactly. Lose our cover and we limit our effectiveness."

"So what's the answer?"

"Venture into new territory with the *Minnesota*."

"Where does she sail?"

"The Pacific." He smiled as her face lit up. "First port of call is Japan, then we cross to mainland China. We'll be carrying freight as well as passengers. In fact, that's one of the reasons they want us aboard. It will be a real challenge for us, Genevieve."

"I can see that," she said, trying to absorb the shock. "I assumed that we'd be back in England by the end of next week. Instead of that, you're talking about Japan and China. I can't seem to get my mind around the idea."

"I'm sorry to have sprung it on you like this."

"It's certainly a tempting offer."

"But not one you have to accept," he stressed. "I've signed on for the next voyage of the *Minnesota,* but you're free to work on a Cunard steamer, if you prefer."

"Without you?"

"I'm afraid so, Genevieve."

"But we operate so much better as a team."

"Of course," he said with enthusiasm. "Your class and my know-how make a great combination. What do you think? Are you ready for a trip to the Far East?"

"When do I have to decide?"

"Pretty soon."

"So what you're offering me is a fait accompli," she said reproachfully as doubts began to crowd in on her. "You're putting a gun to my head just like that man in the Roof Garden restaurant."

"No!" he protested.

"You make a major decision yourself, then ask me to take it or leave it."

Dillman was defensive. "That's not how it is at all."

"Then why not give me more warning?"

"I only made a definite commitment yesterday."

"After you'd spoken to Cunard," she reminded him. "You should have told me that this was in the wind, George. It's unfair to go to our employers behind my back."

"You've always let me negotiate with them in the past."

"This is different. I had a right to be told everything at the outset."

"The offer came out of the blue, Genevieve."

"That doesn't mean you have to conceal it from me. I thought that this ride today was in the nature of a treat," she said, waving an arm at the passing houses. "But it was simply a trick. A way of softening me up so that I'd be more amenable to your plan when you finally disclosed it to me. It was a means to an end."

"The end was to acquaint you more closely with New York."

"Before you whisk me off to the Far East."

"Don't you *want* to visit Japan and China?"

"Of course," she said, "but not necessarily on these terms."

"You seemed to like the notion at first."

"That was before I realized you'd made secret arrangements."

Dillman was contrite. "Genevieve, I'm sorry," he said, squeezing her arm. "Maybe I was a trifle high-handed. It was wrong of me. I should have confided in you at an earlier stage. Listen," he continued, "forget about me and my offer. The *Carmania* sails for Liverpool on Monday. You can sail with her."

'Stop it!" she said with exasperation. "You're doing it again."

"Doing what?"

"Trying to make up my mind for me."

He flashed her a smile. "Would I dare to do that?"

"Yes, George, and you know it."

"All I'm doing is to offer you a choice."

"When you've already made yours."

"I told you, Genevieve. I'm doing a favor for an old friend."

"And what about me?" she asked with controlled vehemence. "I thought that I was your friend as well. Don't I qualify for a favor?"

"Calm down," he soothed. "You can have as many favors as you wish."

"The one that I'd value is some plain, old-fashioned honesty."

"I *am* being honest," he argued earnestly, "and I bore you in mind throughout. When the offer was first put to me, I said that I'd only consider it if you could work with me on the *Minnesota*. It was a conditional acceptance."

"Except that you forgot to mention it to me—until now."

Dillman took a deep breath. He realized that a hansom was not the ideal place for an argument. Raised voices seemed inappropriate in the gentle rocking motion of the cab. The pleasure of sitting in close proximity to Genevieve was vitiated by the anger he had provoked. His calculations had gone awry. Expecting her to be delighted with the news, he was instead facing a broadside of criticism. It taught him that he did not know Genevieve Masefield quite as well as he thought. The lesson was sobering.

For her part, Genevieve was torn between delight and annoyance. The prospect of a voyage to the Far East conjured up romantic images in her mind, but they were blurred by the circumstances surrounding the offer. What hurt her most was that Dillman was now suggesting that they might work apart when his support was the only thing that made her function as a private detective. Trained as an operative in the Pinkerton Agency, his experience was a vital component in their joint success. Without him, Genevieve would be struggling. There was a more important consideration, and it was one that caused the sharpest pangs. When she first agreed to work for the Cunard Line, she did so largely in order to be close to a man for whom she conceived a real affection. That affection had deepened over a series of voyages. Did it mean so little to him that he could discard her without any visible compunction?

Dillman read her mind. "I want you to come with me, Genevieve," he said.

"Do you?"

"I hate the thought of our being apart."

"I wish I could believe that."

"Can you have any doubts?" She searched his eyes for reassurance. "I was too hasty. I see that now. I should have shown you the courtesy of discussing this with you at the outset. I regret it bitterly."

"So do I, George."

"Please don't let it come between us. It won't happen again."

"What guarantee do I have?"

"My word."

"I thought I already had that," she replied sadly.

He lowered his head for moment, accepting her rebuke without complaint. The afternoon tour of New York had met with an unforeseen obstruction. Dillman wondered how he could remove it. He looked up at her again.

"It was my turn to have delusions," he said.

"Delusions?"

"Yes. I didn't think I was the Prince of Wales with a British regiment at my command. Mine was a more ridiculous fancy. I believed that I knew what you wanted."

"So you kept me in the dark."

"Foolishly."

"I'm old enough to make my own decisions, George."

"I accept that. What a mess!" He sighed. "Neither of us ends up getting what we'd choose. I sail off to Japan alone and you board the *Carmania* without me." He was in need of reassurance now. "Is that what will happen?"

There was a pause. "How long will the *Minnesota* be away?" she asked.

"Several weeks." He saw her wince. "It takes the best part of a fortnight to reach Yokohama. And there's the small matter of getting to Seattle in the first place. That will involve a very long and tedious train journey. It will be even longer and more tedious without you, Genevieve."

"Is that all I am?" she teased. "An amusing distraction on the train?"

"Of course not!"

"Are you sure?"

"Absolutely sure."

"Will you miss me?"

"Painfully."

"What would you do to persuade me to go with you?"

"Anything," he vowed. "Anything at all."

She was touched by the obvious sincerity in his voice. Genevieve disliked arguments as much as he did, and there had been very few of them in the past. This was a new situation, a disagreement that was central to their relationship. They had reached a turning point, and she was uncertain how to proceed. Genevieve was aware of a paradox. Wanting him to view them as an inseparable team, she nevertheless clung to her independence. She agonized in silence. Togetherness and personal pride exerted conflicting claims upon her.

"Let me tell you what I need before I can even consider this venture," she announced, watching him carefully. "I want your solemn promise that you will never again take me for granted. It's humiliating, George."

"I understand that. It won't happen again."

"Do you promise?"

"With all my heart."

"Good," she said, relaxing. "In that case, I have only one more question."

"Do you?"

His hopes flickered. Genevieve bestowed a conciliatory kiss on his cheek.

"What sort of clothes will I need to pack for the Far East?" she asked.

TWO

It was the most exhilarating journey she had made in her entire life. Genevieve Masefield was so fascinated by the scenic beauty that unfolded around her day after day that she had no time to notice the jolting of the cars, the noise of the locomotive, the clouds of black smoke, the discomfort of the seats, the chatter of her fellow passengers, the shortcomings of the food, or the interminable length of the ride. For someone who had only ever seen English countryside through the window of a train, America was a revelation. Prairies, mountains, rivers, lakes, and forests competed for her attention. The sky was a continual object of wonder, changing in color and appearance as they surged along beneath its vast awning. What overwhelmed Genevieve was the sheer scale of everything. Bridges were massive, tunnels were endless, and the occasional viaduct completely dwarfed its British counterparts. Herds of cattle ran into thousands, buffalo thundered in profusion across the plains, wheat fields stretched to infinity. Even the towns they passed and the stations at which they stopped were sources of intense curiosity to Genevieve. Crossing the continent was one big adventure.

George Porter Dillman was equally impressed by it all, but more phlegmatic in his response. Though it was his first trip from one coast to another, he had some idea of what to expect and was able to give Genevieve some useful information at every stage. Each new state produced a brief history, each new city unleashed a fresh supply of amusing anecdotes. Dillman was a good listener with a retentive memory. The journey gave him the chance to retell some of the many stories he had picked up about different parts of his native country. Seated opposite him, Genevieve was an appreciative audience. She was never bored. They were a hundred miles from their destination before she asked the obvious question about the vessel on which they were to sail.

"Why is it called the *Minnesota?*"

"I guess it's because that's where her owner lives," he replied. "No less a person than the celebrated James J. Hill."

"You'll have to excuse my ignorance," she said. "Who exactly is James J. Hill?"

"A railroad king. He built the Great Northern on the heels of the Northern Pacific Railroad. Both of them end in Seattle. We're traveling over his tracks right now. Mr. Hill is a farsighted businessman. The prize at stake for him was trade with China, so he had the two ships built to further his interests."

"Two?"

"The *Minnesota* and the *Dakota.*"

"No need to ask why he chose *that* name. It's the neighboring state."

"Jim Hill is a hero in Dakota," said Dillman. "His railroad really opened the state up, North and South. Actually, he was a Canadian by birth but he found more scope for his genius south of the border."

"He sounds like an enterprising man."

"I take my hat off to him. He's a man with real vision."

"Have you ever met him, George?"

"Unfortunately, no," he admitted, "but I did get to see him

when the *Minnesota* was launched. And his daughter, for that matter."

"His daughter?"

"Miss Clara Hill. I felt so sorry for her."

"Why?"

Dillman gave a sympathetic smile. "Things didn't go quite to plan, Genevieve. It must be all of—what?—five years ago now. April 16, 1903. I doubt if Jim Hill and his daughter have forgotten that date either."

"What happened?" she asked.

"I had an invitation to the launch at Groton, Connecticut. Now there's another example of his vision," he noted in passing. "Since no yard in New England was big enough to build the two giant vessels that were projected, Hill constructed an entirely new yard. Groton was a good choice. He bought a forty-acre shorefront property with a solid rock foundation that ran down to deep water. That's where the fiasco occurred."

"Fiasco?"

"Launching a ship is a difficult job at the best of times," he explained. "When the vessel is over twenty thousand tons, it's both difficult and perilous. So much can go wrong."

"I'm sure."

"They had serious problems with the *Minnesota*. What a day! Everyone was there for the occasion. I was one of a crowd of thousands on land, and thousands more were watching from boats. Every member of the Connecticut state senate turned out. It was a proud day for the Hill family."

"Did it all end in tears?"

"Not exactly, Genevieve, but it came close to that. I can see Clara Hill now," he said reflectively. "She looked quite beautiful. She was wearing a maroon coat, a sable boa, and a flower-trimmed hat. But when she tried to crack a bottle of champagne across the bow, nothing happened. A frantic message came up from the yard superintendent and her father rushed off at once."

"What was the matter?"

"The men couldn't shift the timbers holding the ship. A hundred of them were swinging huge wooden rams without making any impression. I can imagine what Mr. Hill said to them. He speaks his mind. Meanwhile, of course," he continued, "his daughter was shivering in the cold on that platform. She stuck it out bravely for an hour, then retreated to the shelter of the shipyard fence. All we could hear up above were the deafening thuds as the men hammered away relentlessly at the timbers. We began to wonder if the ship would ever be launched."

"And was it?"

"Eventually," he confirmed. "Another hour went by, then the word came up from below. By this time, Miss Hill had been fortified by hot coffee from her father's railroad parlor car. She rushed back to the platform, smashed her bottle without ceremony, and the *Minnesota* slid gracefully down the ways and into the water."

"What a relief!"

"That was the general feeling."

"How did you come by the invitation to be there?"

"I was once in the same business, remember," he said wistfully. "Of course, we only built yachts up there in Boston. They were tiny by comparison with an ocean-going liner. But you make lots of friends in that world. One of them was involved in the construction of the *Minnesota,* and thought I'd be interested to take a look at her."

"Did you ever imagine that you'd sail in the ship, George?"

"No, this is a real bonus."

"I could say the same."

"In what way?"

"Well," she said, glancing through the window as another glorious vista beckoned, "I never expected to see any of this. To be frank, I didn't so much come to America as flee from England. Just look at it, will you?" she urged, indicating the view with a hand. "My mouth has been wide open since we left New York." Genevieve turned back to him. "If I'd known it would be this beautiful, I might have come sooner."

15

"I'm glad you crossed the Atlantic at precisely the time you did," he said fondly. "Otherwise, I might never have had the pleasure of meeting you."

"The pleasure is mutual."

They exchanged a smile, then lapsed into silence for a while. Genevieve studied the landscape again before shifting her gaze to the cloud formations above it. Minutes passed before she became aware that he was watching her. There was a contented expression on his face, but it was edged with concern.

"What's the matter?" she asked.

"Nothing," he said evasively.

"I know that look in your eyes, George. Something is troubling you."

"Slightly, perhaps."

"Go on."

"Well," he confessed after a pause, "I just hope that I'm not dragging you into something that we'll both regret. It won't be a case of five days on a Cunard liner this time. We'll be at sea far longer, and the trip may be fraught with danger."

"Danger?"

"We're not just there to look out for thieves and cardsharps, Genevieve. That's the easy bit. The main reason they want us onboard is to safeguard the cargo. They have a strong suspicion that someone is concealing smuggled goods inside legitimate freight."

"What sort of goods?"

"That's the problem," he said, shaking his head. "They're not entirely sure. It's going to be a tricky business, make no mistake about that. We're looking for something when we don't even know what it is."

"Do we have any leads at all?"

"None that I know of, Genevieve, but we'll be briefed more fully when we get aboard. One thing is certain. These people are professionals. A great deal of money is involved here. Be warned," he emphasized. "When the rewards are that high, they'll stop at nothing to avoid detection."

"I'll be very careful," she promised.

"You'll need to be—and so will I."

"What about the sister ship?"

"Sister ship?" he echoed.

"The *Dakota*," she reminded him.

"Ah, yes."

"Do they have the same problems aboard that?"

"Not anymore, I fear. That's the other thing I should warn you about."

"What?"

"Hazards at sea," he said. "The Pacific is a hungry ocean, Genevieve. It swallows ships in one frightening gulp. The *Dakota* ran aground on a submerged reef forty miles from Yokohama. It was a total loss. When that kind of thing happens, the biggest vessel in the world is utterly helpless."

They reached Seattle with hours to spare before the *Minnesota* sailed. It was only when she alighted at the station that Genevieve realized how exhausting the train journey had been. Her limbs were stiff and her neck ached. When they were ready to embark, they parted company so that they could appear to be traveling separately. Dillman had learned from experience that they were more effective if they were not recognized as a couple. Individually, they could go places and elicit information that would have been impossible under other circumstances. While accepting the wisdom of the arrangement, Genevieve regretted that she would not see as much of Dillman on the voyage as she would have liked, but she had the reassuring feeling that he would always be there in an emergency.

As soon as she entered the customs shed, she saw that this would be a very different assignment. During her work on transatlantic liners, she dealt almost exclusively with American or European passengers. The *Minnesota* carried a much more cosmopolitan population. Asiatic faces abounded. There were Chinese, Japanese, Koreans, Filipinos, and even a few Siamese. The simplicity of their clothing made her feel ridiculously overdressed. Genevieve could not understand a word of their rapid conversations, but those who glanced in her direction showed an immediate deference. Of the white passengers, a large majority were American, disparate accents suggesting that they came from all over the continent. It would not be quite so easy for Genevieve to adopt her usual camouflage by joining a group of her compatriots. That could prove a hindrance. On the *Lusitania* and its like, she blended in perfectly. Here, she saw, she would tend to stick out.

When she came out onto the landing stage and caught her first glimpse of the ship, she stopped in her tracks. Without quite knowing why, Genevieve was profoundly disappointed. Though smaller than the twin flagships of the Cunard Line, the *Minnesota* was a daunting sight. Over two hundreds yards in length, it loomed over the harbor like a gigantic black whale. What set it apart from the ships on which she normally sailed was the fact that it was also a freighter, capable of carrying a cargo of thirty thousand tons as well as substantial amounts of water and coal. The last of a consignment of flour was still being loaded into the hold. To her eye, the *Minnesota* lacked distinction, and Genevieve put it down to the fact that it had a single funnel at its center. The Cunard flagships had four stacks apiece. Only three of them were functional, but a fourth had been added for reasons of symmetry. Four stacks suggested power and gave a vessel definition. Genevieve felt that there was something missing from the *Minnesota*.

Yet it had one revolutionary feature that gave it an advantage over its rivals. A deep, melodious, American voice at her elbow obligingly pointed it out to her.

"I bet you've never seen one of those before, have you?" he said.

"One of what?" she asked, turning to face a big, broad-shouldered man in his thirties with an attractive woman on his arm. "I was looking at the funnel."

"Forget the funnel. Every steamship has one or more of

those. Take a look at that winch," he advised, pointing a finger. "That's one of thirty-seven aboard, and every one of them is electric. Isn't that something?"

"I suppose it is," agreed Genevieve.

"Listen to that accent, Horry," said the woman with a smile. "Don't you love it?"

"You know me, honey," he replied. "I adore anything English. Oh," he went on, touching his hat politely in greeting. "Allow us to introduce ourselves. Horace and Etta Langmead. We're from Chicago."

"I'm pleased to meet you," said Genevieve, exchanging brief handshakes with them. "My name is Genevieve Masefield. You've already guessed where I come from."

Langmead grinned. "We worked that out before you even spoke."

"Is it that obvious?"

"Delightfully so. Is that Miss or Mrs. Masefield?"

"Miss, actually."

He was surprised. "Really? You mean, you're not married yet? What's wrong with the guys over there? Are they all blind or just plain stupid?"

"You're being personal, Horry," said his wife. "Excuse him, Miss Masefield."

Genevieve smiled tolerantly. "No offense taken."

They set off toward the vessel and their respective porters, who had waited patiently in their wake, now trailed behind them with their luggage. Genevieve took an instant liking to the newcomers. Horace Langmead was a handsome, confident, well-dressed man who was affable without being presumptuous. His wife, Etta, was a plump, dark-haired, vivacious woman with expressive dimples in her cheeks. From their air of prosperity, Genevieve suspected that they must be first-class passengers, an impression reinforced by the sight of their trunks. She had made her first friends, and she sensed that the Langmeads would be pleasant traveling companions. Her early reservations about the *Minnesota* began to fade.

"Are you going to Japan or China?" wondered Etta Langmead.

"Both," said Genevieve.

"Wonderful! So are we. Do you hear that, Horry?"

"Loud and clear," he said.

"Have you been to the Orient before, Miss Masefield?"

"No," said Genevieve, "this is my first time."

"It's the same for me," admitted Etta with quiet excitement, "though my husband has been to Japan and China many times."

"Strictly on business," he added.

"What's Japan like?" asked Genevieve.

"Much too good for the Japanese."

Langmead gave a confiding laugh, then stepped back so that the women could go up the gangway first. When their tickets were examined, they were escorted to their cabins by stewards. The Langmeads had been given one of the eight luxury suites on the boat deck, but Genevieve was conducted to a cabin on the promenade deck. Like all the first-class accommodation, it was on the outside of the vessel, and she had a first view of the Pacific Ocean through one of the portholes. Large, comfortable, and well appointed, the cabin could be electrically heated in colder weather. Genevieve was very pleased with what would be her home for several weeks. She settled in at once by unpacking her trunk and hanging up her clothes in the fitted wardrobe. As the hour of departure neared, she went out onto the promenade deck to join the other passengers at the rail.

It was odd. Crowds of friends and well-wishers lined the quayside, but Genevieve felt no sense of occasion. She had been spoiled. Having sailed on the maiden voyages of both the *Lusitania* and the *Mauretania,* she knew what it was like to leave port in a blaze of glory. As she reflected on those early experiences, she could still hear the celebratory roar of the thousands who had gathered in Liverpool to send them off, and the symphony of sirens from the flotilla of vessels on the

River Mersey. Fireworks had lit the night sky. History was in the making. Nothing like that was happening now. Genevieve was not traveling on one of the acknowledged greyhounds of the seas. She was on a routine voyage of a ship whose average speed was a modest fourteen knots. Dillman had warned her that there might well be danger aboard. She gave an involuntary shiver. Something told her that the trip would not be as enjoyable as she had first imagined. Genevieve was on a vessel full of total strangers, making a journey into the unknown.

The sound of commotion brought her out of her reverie. She looked down to see a violent altercation taking place at the foot of the gangway. Two members of the crew and a porter seemed to be involved, but the central figure in the argument was a tall man in a black suit and hat. His voice rose effortlessly above the hubbub. Gesticulating angrily, he finally cowed the others into submission. It was only when the man removed his hat to look up at the ship that Genevieve caught sight of his telltale white collar. The truculent passenger with the booming voice was a clergyman.

Dillman wasted no time in unpacking his luggage. No sooner had he been shown to his cabin on the upper deck than he set off on a preliminary reconnaissance of the ship. The *Minnesota* had a luxury and elegance that were necessary to attract passengers on lengthy voyages to the Orient. Considerable money had evidently been spent on the fixtures and fittings. He was particularly impressed by the covered promenade on the upper deck, allowing him to circle the superstructure in its entirety. Windows existed on all three sides, an unusual feature in a liner of that type. A large saloon was decorated with style and furnished with care. Aft of the saloon was a grand staircase with paneled walls. Ascending the steps until he reached the promenade deck, Dillman came out into a corridor that led to the library. Chords on a piano reached his ears and, through an open door, he saw that someone was playing the instrument in what was called the Ladies' Boudoir. He smiled when he read the name. The place was out of bounds to him, but Genevieve Masefield could enter at will and might gather some useful gossip in the female sanctuary. He wondered if she could also play the piano.

After a brief visit to the boat deck and the bridge deck, he worked his way back down through the vessel until he reached the orlop deck. Given over to freight and food stores, it was inaccessible to unauthorized personnel. Dillman resolved to explore the area at the earliest opportunity. In order to do his job properly, he was determined to see every inch of the *Minnesota*. As he made his way back up the stairs, there was a long blast on the siren to signal departure. Lines were cast off, cheers went up from the onlookers, then tugs pulled her clear of land and out into Puget Sound. Dillman was too seasoned a sailor to feel the need to be on deck at the critical moment. He decided to return to his cabin to unpack. When he reached the upper deck, however, he was met by a strange sight. Two stewards were in animated discussion farther down the passageway. One of them, with a cabin trunk on a trolley, seemed to be reprimanding the other, keeping his voice low and relying on graphic gestures to reinforce his argument. The second steward, a Mexican, eventually conceded defeat and went into the cabin. Moments later, two passengers came out through the door. The first was an elderly man of middle height with gray hair slicked back neatly over his head. His companion was a tall, stringy clergyman in his forties with rimless eyeglasses balanced on a hooked nose. Their conversation was altogether more civilized. When the older man offered an apology, the clergyman waved it away and beamed tolerantly. The Mexican steward emerged from the cabin with various items of baggage. After shooting him a look of disgust, the other steward wheeled the trunk into the room, followed by the clergyman.

The elderly passenger strode toward Dillman with a quiet smile.

"Age before religion," he said. "I guess I'm in luck."

"What was the problem?" asked Dillman.

"Oh, some confusion over the cabins. I asked specifically for one with a private bath, but the steward put me in there by mistake." He glanced over his shoulder. "His English is a little shaky. He didn't understand when I complained."

"His colleague was giving him quite a roasting."

"It's all sorted out now, thanks to Father Slattery."

"I'm surprised to see a priest in first class," observed Dillman. "The Church is always preaching poverty. How can our friend afford a cabin on this deck?"

"He can't," explained the other. "But he obviously had a loyal congregation. Father Slattery is a Catholic priest, off to do missionary work in China. Anticipating the hardship he might face when he gets there, his congregation decided that he would at least travel in comfort. They clubbed together and bought him a first-class ticket."

"That was very kind of them."

"Yes, they must be sorry to lose him." He used a key to unlock a door, then stood back so that the Mexican steward could take his luggage in. "Unfortunately, my Spanish is no better than his English. Do you think I should give him a tip?"

"If it was an honest mistake."

"It was," said the other, taking a dollar from his pocket. "Actually, I think it was the chief steward's fault for assigning me to the wrong cabin in the first place." When the steward came out, he slipped the money into his palm and sent him off. He extended a friendly hand toward Dillman. "I'm Rutherford Blaine, by the way. It looks as if we're going to be neighbors."

"George Dillman," said the other, noting the firmness of his handshake.

"How far are you going, Mr. Dillman?"

"All the way. It's a round trip."

"I wish I had your stamina."

"What about you?"

"Tokyo," said Blaine. "When I'm done there, I head straight back home on another vessel. Marie doesn't like me to stay away for too long."

"Marie?"

"My wife."

"She's not traveling with you?"

"Not on this trip."

Dillman was about to ask his new neighbor if he had been to Japan before when the clergyman stepped out of his cabin. A disgruntled steward came after him and stalked off down the passageway. Blaine was amused.

"I think the congregation forgot to provide their priest with a tip."

Slattery walked toward them. "I feel as if I'm on the brink of a great adventure," he declared. "Don't you, Mr. Blaine? It's exhilarating." He thrust a bony hand at Dillman. "Liam Slattery."

"This is Mr. Dillman," said Blaine.

"Welcome aboard, Father," said Dillman as they shook hands. "I understand that you're a missionary."

"Wherever God calls me, I must go."

"He obviously wants you to travel in style."

"I always find luxury a little embarrassing."

"It never embarrasses me," said Blaine. "I revel in it."

"You have a hedonistic streak, sir," chided Slattery.

"No, Father. I have a touch of arthritis, that's all. It appreciates a soft chair and a comfortable bed. Luxury somehow keeps the twinges under control."

"Prayer might do the same for you, Mr. Blaine."

"I've never found that."

"Are you a practicing Christian?"

"Of course, Father."

"Roman Catholic, I hope?"

"Baptist."

Slattery was appalled. "What a pity!"

"Each man follows God in his own way," said Blaine, pushing open the door of his cabin. "Do excuse me, gentlemen. I have to unpack my cases."

Father Slattery watched him go, then switched his attention to Dillman. Eyes glinting under bushy eyebrows, he appraised him shrewdly. There was a fearlessness in his gaze that the detective had to admire.

"You're a brave man, Father Slattery," he commented.

"Am I?"

"Catholic missionaries have suffered badly in China. I remember reading the reports of the Boxer Rebellion. Some terrible outrages were inflicted on your colleagues."

"We're used to persecution, Mr. Dillman."

"Do you have no qualms?"

"None whatsoever," said Slattery boldly. "The situation in China has improved markedly in the past couple of years. Even if it hadn't, I'd still answer the call."

"Have you been abroad before?"

"No, Mr. Dillman. My life so far has been spent in America. In San Francisco, for the most part. It's a beautiful city with a rich Catholic heritage."

"So I understand."

"I leave with great regret, but my future is elsewhere."

"Good luck with your missionary work," said Dillman, putting his key into the lock of his cabin. "I wish you every success in China."

"Oh, I'm not waiting until I get there, Mr. Dillman."

"What do you mean?"

"My work starts right here."

Dillman was surprised. "Onboard the *Minnesota*?"

"Of course," said Slattery with a broad grin. "There are over fifteen hundred passengers on this ship, including a large number of Chinese. Why wait for weeks until I reach China when I can begin the search for converts here?"

"No reason at all, I suppose."

"My first move will be to take services aboard."

"But the ship already has a chaplain."

Slattery was disdainful. "An Anglican," he said with unconcealed disapproval. "I see to the needs of those who follow the true religion. Tell me, Mr. Dillman," he went on, moving in closer. "Are you, by any chance, a Catholic?"

"No, Father."

"May I ask why not?"

"I don't have time to explain at the moment."

"Later, then," said Slattery firmly. "We'll discuss the matter at length."

"There's nothing to discuss."

"Oh, yes there is. Your spiritual salvation."

"That's been taken care of, Father Slattery."

"I doubt that, my friend. We need a proper debate."

"But it's quite unnecessary."

"I insist, Mr. Dillman," said the priest, squeezing his arm. "I insist."

Turning on his heel, Slattery went back to his cabin and disappeared inside. Dillman was slightly dazed, wondering why an invitation to a theological debate sounded so much like a threat.

THREE

It's great to see you again, George," he said, pumping Dillman's arm. "I wasn't sure that you could make it in time. It's a heck of a train ride from New York."

"I survived, Mike."

"What about your partner?"

"Genevieve is as tough as they come," said Dillman with an affectionate smile. "Don't worry about her. She took the journey in her stride without complaint."

"I look forward to meeting the lady."

Mike Roebuck was the purser on the *Minnesota*. Still in his thirties, he was a cheerful man of medium build with rugged features and a roguish grin. He and Dillman were old friends who had not seen each other for a number of years. It was a happy reunion. After exchanging banter for a few minutes, Roebuck spread his arms.

"What's the verdict, George?" he asked.

"That purser's uniform lends you real distinction."

"I wasn't talking about myself, you idiot. What do you think of the *Minnesota*?"

"I like what I've seen of her, Mike."

"She's a tidy ship," said Roebuck proudly. "Best I've ever sailed on."

"I'll enjoy finding my way around."

"Let me give you some help."

The two men were in the purser's office, a neat, rectangular cabin with a large desk at its center. Charts and framed photographs covered the walls. A faint whiff of polish hung in the air. Roebuck indicated the drawing that was laid out on the desk. It was a detailed plan of the vessel.

"This is just what I need," said Dillman, poring over it with interest.

"There's another one underneath, giving you a cross-section."

"Excellent. Can I borrow these, Mike?"

"Be my guest."

"What's this?" asked Dillman in surprise, spotting a name on the drawing. "Am I seeing things or does it actually say Opium Den?"

Roebuck grinned. "We don't call it that, George, but that's what it amounts to. Let's face it. You sail to and from China, you're going to carry a lot of Chinese passengers. The guy who designed the ship reckoned that they ought to have a space set aside for them." He jabbed a stubby finger at the drawing. "There it is."

"I'll enjoy studying this," said Dillman, straightening up.

"What else do you need?"

"A look at the manifest."

"I had a rough copy made for you," said Roebuck, opening a drawer to extract a small sheaf of papers. "As you'll see, we've got a mixed cargo. There's a full passenger list as well and various other bits of information. Here you are, George," he said, handing the papers to Dillman. "You'll find everything here except the shoe size of the captain. Oh, by the way, he wants to meet you."

"What sort of man is Captain Piercey?"

"A veteran sailor. Runs a tight ship. I think he's a first-rate skipper."

"Does he mind having us onboard?"

"Heck, no!" exclaimed Roebuck, clapping him good-humoredly on the shoulder. "Captain Piercey is delighted to see you. So am I, George. And not simply because we go back a long way together."

"How did you get on to me in the first place?"

"Your reputation went before you."

Dillman was astonished. "All the way to Seattle?"

"Word travels," said Roebuck. "One of our officers served on the *Mauretania* for a while. We were talking about security with him when your name suddenly popped up. Tom Colmore gave us glowing reports of what you did during the maiden voyage."

"I had a lot of help," said Dillman modestly.

"From what I hear, you and your partner saved the day. And it wasn't an isolated case. According to Tom, you're their number-one man. You've had a string of successes on Cunard ships. That's why we were so keen to poach you."

"Borrow us, Mike," corrected Dillman. "We're only on loan. When this voyage is over, we go back to the transatlantic service."

"What if you fall in love with the magic of the Orient?"

"I never allow distractions."

Roebuck laughed. "You always were a single-minded son of a gun." His face slowly hardened. "Okay," he said, sitting on the edge of the desk, "let's get down to serious business. We've got problems, George. We have strong reason to believe that somebody is smuggling right under our noses. We can smell the stink, but we can't quite work out where it comes from."

"What alerted you?"

"A name that kept appearing on our passenger list. Mr. Rance Gilpatrick. He's a real menace. The cops have a file inches thick on him but he's far too clever to be caught. His sidekicks always take the rap."

"Is he aboard now?"

"Oh, yes. Gilpatrick has one of the premier suites on the boat deck."

"Does he travel alone?"

"No, George," said Roebuck with a roll of his eyes. "He always brings his wife. Except that the lady who's sharing his cabin today is not the same one we had a few months ago. The time before that, there was a different one again. He seems to have an endless supply of Mrs. Gilpatricks. The guy must breed them."

"Maybe he's a bigamist."

"I don't think any of these unions have been blessed in the sight of the Lord."

"Like that, is it?"

"Judge for yourself, George. The last 'wife' was thirty years younger than him."

"No law against that."

"But there is a law against falsifying passports."

"So why hasn't he been picked up?"

"His documents always seem genuine," admitted Roebuck. "He gets through customs without a hitch and we never challenge him. We prefer to have Rance Gilpatrick where we can keep an eye on him."

"What do you think he's smuggling?" asked Dillman. "Narcotics?"

"Possibly, but that's not his main interest. We think he's into another highly lucrative market—silk. Last time we docked in Yokohama," he explained, "we had Gilpatrick trailed by a detective. He followed him to a dealer who specializes in silk. There was only one drawback, George."

"Drawback?"

"Before he returned to the ship, our man was beaten up in an alleyway by a couple of Japanese thugs. He was half-dead by the time they found him."

"I get the message, Mike."

"Pass it on to your partner. Things may get rough. Needless to say," Roebuck went on, "we couldn't link the assault to Gilpatrick in any way. And since the current wife rejoined the ship with a couple of silk kimonos, he appeared to have made a legitimate purchase from the dealer."

"In other words," concluded Dillman, "he knows that you're on to him."

"He revels in the fact, George. That's what makes it so galling. Gilpatrick is taunting us. It's simply a game to him, and he always seems to win."

Dillman pondered. "I'll change the rules slightly," he said at length, flicking through the sheaf of papers. "But there's something you forgot to give me, Mike. I need a list of crew members."

"There's over two hundred and fifty of them."

"Give me the name of everyone aboard—including the ship's mascot."

"You'll have it."

"One more thing," said Dillman. "Who's the assistant purser?"

"Pete Carroll."

"How tall is he?"

Roebuck was baffled. "About your height, I guess. Similar build."

"Good. Does he have a spare uniform?"

"Why do you ask?"

"I may need to borrow it," said Dillman.

On the first evening at sea, dinner was a relatively informal affair. First-class passengers converged on the dining saloon on the upper deck. Lined with mahogany and lit by an array of glittering chandeliers, it had a grandeur worthy of a luxury hotel. Genevieve Masefield was glad that she had made the acquaintance of the Langmeads. They not only invited her to join their table, they introduced her to five other passengers they had managed to befriend since coming aboard. It soon became clear that Horace and Etta Langmead were compulsively gregarious. They collected people.

One of them was a red-faced old man with a walrus mustache that concealed his upper lip and a bald head that positively gleamed. Joseph McDade had strong opinions.

"Teddy Roosevelt is a disaster!" he declared, smacking the table for emphasis. "We don't want that damned cowboy as our president."

"The American electors disagree with you, Mr. McDade," said Horace Langmead.

"Only because he pulled the wool over their eyes."

"I think Mr. Roosevelt has his virtues."

"Well, they're outweighed by his vices, Mr. Langmead. And, boy, does he have enough of those!" He turned to Genevieve, seated beside him. "What do you think, Miss Masefield? How do you rate our so-called president?"

"I can't make a fair judgment, Mr. McDade," she replied tactfully. "I know too little about him."

"We have the opposite problem. We know too much about the guy."

"Joe, dear," said the pale Blanche McDade, sitting meekly on the other side of her husband. "Maybe this is not the best time to talk politics."

McDade ignored her. "Have you heard about his latest act of madness?"

"No," said Genevieve.

"He's sent our entire fleet—sixteen battleships in all—on a trip around the world. It's lunatic!" insisted McDade. "The chairman of the senate committee on naval affairs condemned the notion. His colleagues disliked it. Every sane mind in Congress was against it. But does that stop Teddy Roosevelt? Oh no! He trampled over the opposition as if he were leading his Rough Riders in a cavalry charge in Cuba. It was shameful."

"President Roosevelt is his own man," said Langmead reasonably. "You have to give him that, Mr. McDade. Nobody tells him what to do."

"Well, I wish that someone would," retorted the other. "It's all very well adopting a big-stick policy, sending the U.S. fleet on a journey of almost fifty thousand miles so that we can impress everyone with our naval power. But what happens while they're away?" he demanded, plucking at his mustache. "We could be invaded by Japan or Russia or, worse still, by China. Has our imbecile president never heard of the Yellow Peril?"

"This conversation belongs in the smoking room," suggested Henrik Olsen with a diplomatic smile. "We don't want to bore the ladies, Mr. McDade."

McDade bristled. "I wasn't boring anyone."

The waiter arrived to pour wine into their glasses and provide a welcome pause. Genevieve looked around the table. With the exception of Joseph McDade, she had a set of amenable companions. The Langmeads were turning out to be a delightful couple, generous and extroverted, and Blanche McDade, albeit subdued by her forthright husband, exuded a quiet intelligence. Genevieve hoped to talk to her on her own at some stage. The other woman at the table, Fay Brinkley, was even more interesting. She was an attractive woman in her thirties with a poise that indicated a high social position. Traveling alone from Washington, D.C., Fay Brinkley was on her way to Shanghai to visit a brother in the colonial service. Seated next to her was the diminutive figure of Henrik Olsen, a white-haired Norwegian banker who was celebrating his retirement by making extended visits to America, Japan, and China. Olsen was there to enjoy himself and did not want his evening marred by a tirade from McDade against the incumbent president.

Genevieve found the eighth person at the table the most difficult to assess. David Seymour-Jones was a tall, rather gangly man in his early forties with a full beard and a shock of red hair. Though his jacket was expensive, it was too large and badly creased, giving him a slovenly air. Seymour-Jones was an enigma. His face was impassive and his eyes gave nothing away. Genevieve could not make out if he was shy or simply cowed by the bluster of Joseph McDade. As conversation broke out again around the table, she turned to the silent Englishman.

"I understand that you're an artist," she began.

"Of sorts, Miss Masefield."

"What do you paint?"

"Anything and everything," he said softly. "I have a particular passion for the fauna and flora of Japan. But don't confuse me with a real artist," he went on with a self-deprecating smile. "You won't ever find my work hanging in the National Gallery or the Tate. All that I do is to record what I see. I keep a sort of pictorial diary."

"Purely for private use?"

He shook his head sadly. "Even we bohemians have to eat occasionally, Miss Masefield. My earlier work in Japan was published last year and they want to bring out a second book in due course."

"That's wonderful!" she said with sincere approval.

"It does enable me to soldier on. Along with my other little enterprise."

"You have another iron in the fire?"

"Of necessity," he explained. "I collect curios and artefacts to sell to museums back in England. The problem is that I hate parting with some of them. Have you ever felt the sheer joy of possessing something beautiful?"

"I'm not sure, Mr. Seymour-Jones."

"Well, I have. It gives me the most indescribable pleasure. I've hung on to certain items until the very last moment." He looked at her quizzically. "What do you know of Japan, Miss Masefield?"

"Precious little," she admitted. "Though I did see *The Mikado* at the Savoy."

He managed a first grin. "That's a travesty of the real thing, I'm afraid. Gilbert and Sullivan have no understanding at all of Japanese culture. Besides, wherever they're set, their operas are essentially about England."

"I'd have to agree with you there."

"What's your interest in Japan?"

"Oh, I'm a tourist, Mr. Seymour-Jones. A wide-eyed traveler."

"I knew that you two would get along," said Etta Langmead, easing herself into the conversation. "Have you discovered any mutual acquaintances back in England?"

"Not yet," replied Seymour-Jones.

"You will, I'm sure. Where are you from, Miss Masefield?"

"London," said Genevieve.

"And what about our artist?"

"I was born in Cambridge, Mrs. Langmead," said Seymour-Jones, reaching for his wineglass. "But I've spent a lot of my life abroad."

"Seeking inspiration, I daresay."

"Something like that."

"You're a restless spirit."

"I suppose that I am, Mrs. Langmead."

"What's your favorite country?"

"The one that I'm in at any given moment." He sipped his wine and turned away to escape her amiable interrogation.

It was a delicious meal. The more time passed, the more pleasure Genevieve took from her companions. After his earlier outburst, Joseph McDade was more restrained, saving his energies for the rich food and fine wine that were set in front of him. When he did contribute, he entertained the whole table with anecdotes about the problems of running a copper mine. Blanche McDade came out of her shell to toss in a supportive comment from time to time, and Fay Brinkley turned out to have an uncle who was involved with the copper industry in Arizona. Connections were gradually made between all eight of them. Even Henrik Olsen, the natural outsider, found points of contact with the others. By the end of the meal, they were confirmed friends. Only David Seymour-Jones held aloof from the pervading togetherness. While the other men adjourned to the smoking room for a cigar, he mumbled an excuse and went off to his cabin. Blanche McDade also felt the need of an early night. When she withdrew from the table, the other three women were left alone.

As the self-appointed hostess, Etta Langmead thought an apology was in order.

"I'm sorry about that, Miss Masefield," she said. "I hoped that you might be able to bring him out a little. Mr. Seymour-Jones seems so detached."

"English reserve, Mrs. Langmead."

"You don't suffer from it."

"Is that a compliment or a criticism?"

Etta giggled. "Oh, a compliment. That's why I put you next to him."

"He was pleasant enough company."

"But he hardly *said* anything."

"That doesn't mean he wasn't enjoying himself," remarked Fay Brinkley, rising from her seat. "Mr. Seymour-Jones may have been on the quiet side but I fancy that there was a lot going on beneath the surface."

"That was my impression," said Genevieve, getting up.

"Oh, well," decided Etta, joining them as they headed for the exit. "Perhaps he'll improve on acquaintance. We met him on deck when we were about to sail. He was doing the most brilliant sketch of the harbor. I saw it over his shoulder. I just had to tell him how wonderful it was. He seemed so lonely and neglected. That's why I invited him to join us. Artists are usually such intriguing people. Oh!" she exclaimed, coming to a halt as she remembered something. "Silly me! I've left my purse at the table. Do go on, ladies. I'll join you in a minute."

While Etta Langmead scurried back into the dining room, Genevieve fell in beside Fay Brinkley. She was glad of a moment alone with the older woman.

"I do admire your self-control," she told her.

"Self-control?"

"I could see how much you disagreed with Mr. McDade when he was making those disparaging comments about President Roosevelt. But you never once lost your composure and started an argument."

"What was the point?" said Fay. "Prejudice of that kind is impervious to reason."

"Mr. McDade does tend to rant."

"His poor wife was squirming with embarrassment."

"I noticed."

"Yet she's very loyal," noted Fay. "Blanche McDade must have heard those stories about the copper mine a hundred times, yet she still pretended to be interested."

"What did you make of the others?"

"Mr. Olsen was sweet, and the Langmeads are a charming couple. They work as a team. I liked that about them." She lowered her voice. "Though I do think that Mrs. Langmead is wrong about our artist. He wasn't as detached from it all as he looked."

"Oh?"

"I was sitting opposite him. I had a perfect view of Mr. Seymour-Jones."

"What do you mean?"

"Only this," confided Fay. "There was a more important item on his agenda than good food and conversation. I could see it clearly in his manner, and in the way he kept shooting those sly glances."

"I saw no sly glances."

"You weren't supposed to, Miss Masefield. They were aimed at you."

Genevieve was startled. "At me?"

"Of course. Who else? In my opinion, David Seymour-Jones doesn't have an ounce of English reserve. The reason he was so silent is that he was considering what to do about it."

"About what?"

"You, Miss Masefield. He's smitten." She arched an eyebrow. "Surely, you realized that? You've made a conquest."

George Porter Dillman dined at a table for four that was set in a quiet corner. He was grateful to be well clear of Father Slattery, who was dominating his dinner companions on the other side of the room as if occupying a pulpit. Even from that distance, he could hear the priest's voice in hortatory vein. Dillman preferred the company of Rutherford Blaine, a relaxed, urbane man with a dry sense of humor. Also at the table were the Changs, a Chinese-American couple who were returning to their native country for a vacation. Small, neat, and unfailingly polite, they wore Western dress and spoke faultless English. Li Chang was very proud to be an American citizen, but he had risen from humble origins.

"Do you know what my father did?" he asked.

"No," said Blaine pleasantly, "though I guess he was an immigrant."

"He was, sir. Over forty years ago now."

"What did your father do, Mr. Chang?"

"He worked on the Central Pacific Railroad." Chang looked from one man to the other. "Have you heard about how it was built?"

"With great difficulty, I should imagine," said Dillman.

"That's an understatement," added Blaine smoothly. "The Central Pacific was engaged in a fierce battle with the Union Pacific. They were both determined to be the first to offer a transcontinental service. Correct, Mr. Chang?"

"Yes, sir," said Chang. "But it wasn't a fair fight. The Union Pacific went over land that was largely flat and had a supply chain back to the east. My father's company, the Central Pacific, was coming from the west, so it had to bring most of its materials and its locomotives around Cape Horn. Have you any idea how many miles that is?"

"Twelve thousand," answered Dillman promptly.

Chang was surprised. "You've sailed around the Horn, sir?"

"No, but I've met many people who have. Go on with your tale, Mr. Chang."

"The Eastern gangs were mostly Irish and defeated Southerners," said the other, "but the Western crews came largely from China. There was an old joke that the Union Pacific was built on whiskey, while the Central Pacific was sustained by tea." He shook with mirth and they smiled obligingly. Chang's face darkened. "Whiskey and tea are different," he continued sadly. "When the two crews finally passed each other, a war broke out. They fought with fists, pick handles, stones, even gunpowder. My father lost an eye in one battle." His wife put a comforting hand on his arm. "That's why I worked so hard to improve myself, you see. My father was only a coolie on the railroad, but I studied to become an engineer. I help to build railways on a drawing board."

"What with?" asked Dillman gently. "Whiskey or tea?"

Chang laughed again and his wife grinned beside him. They were an amiable pair, and Dillman enjoyed talking to them. Blaine was more interested to hear about China, plying them with questions and asking them to speculate on the future of their homeland. The Changs had divided loyalties. Born in the East, they had both been brought up in America and saw that as their true home. Though he spoke lovingly about Peking, Li Chang readily admitted that he would not have prospered quite so well there.

"Are you on vacation as well, Mr. Dillman?" said Chang.

"Yes," replied Dillman. "I'm fulfilling a lifetime's dream."

"And you, Mr. Blaine?"

"I'm going to Tokyo on business," said the other. "I buy and sell."

"What will you buy in Japan?"

"Whatever takes my fancy, Mr. Chang. No whiskey, perhaps, but plenty of tea."

The remark set the Changs off again and they laughed in unison. While taking a full part in the conversation, Dillman was also keeping an eye out for his prime suspect. The purser had given him a description of Rance Gilpatrick, but the detective saw nobody who fitted that description. He decided that

Gilpatrick was either dining in his cabin with his current mistress or concealed somewhere in the mass of bodies. From where he sat, he could pick out Genevieve and was reassured to see how easily she had won acceptance in her little circle. When he noticed her leaving the saloon, he checked his watch. They had arranged to meet later on to compare notes, but there was still an hour to go. The Changs were tiring visibly. Excusing themselves from the table, they shook hands with both men before slipping away. Blaine turned to Dillman.

"Nice people," he observed.

"Delightful."

"Don't let me hold you up if you want to go to the smoking room."

"That's okay, Mr. Blaine," said Dillman. "I don't smoke."

"Sensible man. Neither do I. Nasty habit." He sat back in his chair. "In that case," he said affably, "would you care to join me in a brandy?"

"Thank you."

"My one indulgence. Brandy at bedtime."

"As long as we agree on a plan of escape."

"Escape?"

"Yes," said Dillman, glancing across the room. "It looks as if Father Slattery is running out of parishioners. If he descends on us, we need to have an excuse ready."

Blaine smiled as he let his gaze drift across the room. Slattery was in his element, holding forth with a finger raised in admonition. Only two of nine guests at his table were still there, trapped by the glare of his eyes like rabbits caught in the light of strong lamps.

"I can see why his congregation clubbed together on his behalf," said Blaine. "I bet they couldn't wait to get rid of him. You have to feel sorry for China, don't you? They give us all that excellent tea, and we give them someone like Father Slattery." He summoned a waiter and ordered two glasses of brandy. "So, Mr. Dillman," he resumed easily, "we've heard Mr. Chang's life story. What's yours?"

"Oh, it's not nearly so interesting."

"No one-eyed father?"

"And no pitched battles on the railroad."

"You said that you came from Boston."

"That's right," agreed Dillman. "I was groomed for the family business. We build ocean-going yachts for rich people who hear the call of the sea. It was very exciting at first and, of course, I had the opportunity to sail a great deal myself."

"I had the feeling that you were an experienced sailor."

"The sea is my first love. Unfortunately, it was displaced by another."

"A lady, perhaps?"

"Yes, Mr. Blaine," he confessed, "but not in the way you might assume. The lady in question was an actress in a play I saw at a theater in Boston. And I wasn't so much entranced with her as with the whole idea of acting. She *moved* me. Simply by standing on a stage and declaiming lines written by someone else, the lady had the most profound impact on me—and on the rest of the audience. It was quite unnerving."

"What did you about it?"

"I had this overpowering urge to be an actor. I longed to be up on that stage with the rest of them. Of course, I was much younger then," said Dillman, "and much more impressionable. But the feeling was so intense. I wanted to belong to a profession that gives so much pleasure by working on people's emotions."

"How did your father take the news?"

"He was livid, Mr. Blaine."

"In his shoes, I'd have been the same."

"He did everything he could to stop me from leaving the firm but I felt I just had to strike out on my own. My father warned me that I'd be penniless inside a year, but he was quite wrong." He smiled ruefully. "It only took six months."

Blaine was amused. "We all have to suffer for our art," he said. "But you have the looks for an actor, Mr. Dillman. I'd have thought you'd do well in the profession."

"Acting takes time to learn. I gradually improved."

"And are you established now?"

"I get by."

"You must do, if you can afford a first-class cabin on the *Minnesota*."

"I came into some money," said Dillman airily, eager to halt any further probing into his life. "It enables me to see something of the world. So I intend to forget about everything else and simply enjoy myself."

"Surrender to the experience?"

"Exactly, Mr. Blaine."

"I envy you. Ah!" he said, looking up as the waiter arrived with their brandy. "We can both surrender to this experience." He gave a nod of gratitude to the waiter, then lifted his glass to rub it gently between his palms. "Brandy is my idea of nectar."

When his glass was warmed slightly, he raised it in a silent toast to Dillman, then took a first satisfying sip. Dillman was about to taste his own brandy when he became aware that they were being watched. It was an uncomfortable sensation. Out of the corner of his eye, he caught a glimpse of someone who was standing beside a potted palm. They were under surveillance, and he resented the fact. When Dillman suddenly looked around, however, the man had vanished.

"What's the matter?" asked Blaine.

Dillman turned back to him. "Nothing," he replied, sipping his brandy.

"Were you searching for someone?"

"No, no."

"Do you know anyone else aboard?"

"Only the gentleman in cabin number twenty-five."

Blaine grimaced slightly. "By the time we get to Japan, I have a horrible feeling that everybody on the ship will know Father Slattery. Our missionary intends to spread the Word of God far and wide."

"He fully expects to make converts."

"I'm one of them. He converted me out of one cabin and into another."

Dillman put his glass down. "Does Mrs. Blaine never travel with you?"

"Not when I'm on business. It would be too unfair on Marie. Japan is a beautiful country that deserves to be explored at leisure. No wife wants to be left in a hotel room while her husband goes off to deal with his business associates. Marie would hate that."

"Have the two of you ever had a vacation in Japan?"

"Not yet," said Blaine with a note of regret. "But we will. I've promised her."

"Everyone who's been there speaks highly of it."

"I'm sure that you will, Mr. Dillman."

"How long are you staying?"

"A few days, that's all."

"You go all that way to spend such a short time there?"

"It's the journey that matters," said Blaine, lifting his glass again, "not the destination. I'm a student of human nature. That's why I always enjoy voyages."

"Yes," said Dillman thoughtfully. "I suppose that people's true character does emerge when they're at sea. I'm not quite sure why. Perhaps it's because they've left the security of land. They experience a sense of freedom and release."

"That depends on their nationality."

"In what way, Mr. Blaine?"

"Well," argued the other, "we Americans might feel that sense of release, but I've never noticed it in anyone from Europe. Take the English, for instance. Whenever they set sail, they seem to become even more English, if you know what I mean. They cling to their social rituals and withdraw into themselves."

"Not all of them."

"There are honorable exceptions, I guess."

"Indeed," said Dillman, thinking of Genevieve Masefield. "I must confess to a soft spot for England. I suppose you'd call me an unrepentant Anglophile."

"Why is that?"

But the question went unanswered. Before he could say another word, Dillman saw a dark shadow fall across the table. He looked up in dismay to see Father Slattery looming over them, grinning broadly as if he had just bumped into two old friends.

"Good evening, gentlemen!" he said effusively, sitting down without invitation. "You don't mind if I join you, do you?"

FOUR

Genevieve Masefield found the evening both enjoyable and informative, but she made sure that she was back in her cabin well ahead of time. She slipped off her gold earrings and removed her pearl necklace, then put them both away in their respective cases. They were much more than cherished presents. Along with the rest of her jewelry, they were essential items in her disguise as a first-class passenger, visible symbols of wealth that could hold their own with the adornments worn by other women. Blanche McDade had been covered in jewelry, wearing rings on most fingers and a gold bangle on her left wrist. On the front of her dress was a gold brooch in the shape of a leaf. An expensive pair of earrings and a diamond necklace completed the display. It was a paradox. The most timid and reticent woman at the table wore the most ostentatious jewelry. Genevieve suspected that she had done so at the insistence of a husband who was eager to show off some of the gifts he had lavished on his wife. Etta Langmead had worn far less jewelry, and Fay Brinkley had worn none at all, save for a gold clasp halfway up her left forearm.

When she heard a tap on her door, she knew that it was

bound to be him. Whatever his faults, George Porter Dillman was unerringly punctual. He believed that lateness was often nothing more than lack of consideration. His theatrical training had also served to make him a good timekeeper. A late entrance on stage was unprofessional. Genevieve opened the door to admit him, then checked the passageway to ensure that nobody had seen him enter. Dillman looked around the cabin with approval. Closing the door, she waved him to a seat but remained standing. He gave her a warm smile.

"It's very snug in here," he observed. "Well up to Cunard standards."

"I'm really starting to like the *Minnesota*."

"You may change your mind when you hear what I have to say, Genevieve."

"Why?"

"I'll come to that," he said, savoring the pleasure of being alone with her again. "First, tell me how you got on."

"Pretty well, George."

"You seemed to be part of a congenial group of people."

"I was," she agreed. "More or less, anyway. Mr. McDade was rather trying at first, and David Seymour-Jones was not exactly a sparkling conversationalist. Otherwise, I had a very pleasant evening."

She described what had happened and told him how she had warmed to Fay Brinkley. Nobody had been more friendly toward her than Etta Langmead, but it was the dignified Fay who made the deepest impression on her and with whom Genevieve sensed a bond. The two of them had agreed to have a private meeting the next day. Though she talked about David Seymour-Jones, she made no mention of his romantic interest in her, largely because she doubted if it really existed but also because she was unsure of Dillman's reaction. It was strange. He had never exhibited the slightest sign of jealousy before, yet she found herself drawing back from a disclosure that might put him to the test. She talked about everyone she had met. He was pleased by what he heard.

"I watched you from time to time," he said. "You were one of them."

"I felt it, George."

"Winning people's confidence is vital."

"What about you?" she asked. "When I was leaving the saloon, I saw you at a table with three other people."

"One of them was Rutherford Blaine, and the others were Mr. and Mrs. Chang."

He explained who his companions were and what he had learned from them. Dillman was annoyed that his private conversation with Blaine had been interrupted by the Catholic priest. Genevieve remembered the man clearly.

"I saw him coming aboard. He was having a loud argument with someone."

Dillman sighed. "That would be Father Slattery."

"Is he really so obnoxious?"

"No, he's just so convinced that he's right about everything. He's a true zealot, and there's no margin for error in such people. Mr. Blaine is a much more complex and interesting man. I like a hint of human fallibility in my friends."

"Is that why you chose me?" she teased.

"I rather hoped that we'd chosen each other, Genevieve."

"Am I fallible enough for you?"

"I'll reserve judgment on that," he said with a laugh.

"How did you get free from that Father Slattery?"

"Mr. Blaine came to my rescue there. He's a mild-mannered man, but he can be very assertive when he chooses. In the nicest possible way, he told Father Slattery that we had some confidential matters to discuss, then eased him gently on his way. It was over in seconds. I'm still not quite sure how he did it."

"Was the priest offended?"

"On the contrary," recalled Dillman. "He was full of apologies when he backed away. He met his match in Rutherford Blaine. However, the danger is not completely past, I fancy. Father Slattery is determined that he and I should get together."

"Why?"

"He thinks I'm a potential convert."

"You, George?"

"I must have an aura of spirituality."

Genevieve suppressed a smile. "That's not what I'd call it."

Dillman turned to more professional concerns. After telling her about his visit to the purser, he passed on the detailed description he had been given of Rance Gilpatrick. Genevieve was pensive. She went swiftly through the long list of people she had noticed in the dining saloon.

"I don't think he was there, George," she decided. "If he's as distinctive as he sounds, one of us would have picked Mr. Gilpatrick out. But I know someone who's bound to bump into him sooner or later."

"Who's that?"

"The Langmeads. They have a cabin on the boat deck as well."

"They'll be neighbors of Gilpatrick. Keep in touch with them."

"I don't have to," she said with a smile. "Etta Langmead has adopted me."

"Care to swap her for Father Slattery?"

"No, thank you!"

Genevieve sat down and crossed her ankles. Dillman had given her a fairly full account of his dealings with the purser but she felt that he might have held something back out of consideration for her. She pressed for more detail.

"What sort of a man is this Rance Gilpatrick?" she asked.

"The worst kind, Genevieve. He uses people. According to Mike Roebuck, he's guilty of almost every crime in the book. Gilpatrick has worked his way up the coast," said Dillman. "He started in Los Angeles, moved his business interests to San Francisco, then branched out further north. He owns saloons in Tacoma and Seattle, apparently. And he has a finger in dozens of other pies."

"You mentioned something about silk."

"That's only the purser's guess, but I think he could be right. It's a very profitable trade. Do you know much about silk, Genevieve?"

"Only that I can't afford to buy enough of it."

"Is that a hint?"

"I'd never be so calculating!" she said with mock indignation. "In answer to your question, all I know is that the finest silk comes from China and Japan."

"Only not on this vessel," he explained. "The Canadian Pacific Line seems to have something of a monopoly. Their ships have special holds, fitted with side ports for speedy loading. Because silk is so costly, the insurance premiums are correspondingly high, so speed is essential. It's important to get the stuff back quickly, loaded onto a train, and sent off to Chicago or New York. But, of course," he pointed out, "if your cargo of silk is not declared, you don't have to pay a cent in insurance. You can ship the stuff back by means of a slower vessel."

"Like the *Minnesota*."

"A bale of silk will fetch eight hundred dollars on the open market. Smuggle thirty bales back to Seattle, and you might clean up the best part of a quarter of a million dollars."

"I hadn't realized there were those kinds of returns."

"Rance Gilpatrick aims high."

"What gave the purser the idea that he was dealing in silk?" She saw him hesitate. "Come on, George, I want the truth. Don't keep anything from me."

"Fair enough," he said with a shrug. "The last time they docked in Japan, Mike Roebuck had him followed by a detective. Gilpatrick went to a silk dealer. Before the detective could get any firm evidence, he was beaten to a pulp." Genevieve swallowed hard. "Gilpatrick doesn't take prisoners."

"Are they sure he was responsible for the attack?"

"The purser doesn't believe in coincidences. Neither do I."

There was a long pause. "You did warn me there might be danger," she said.

"True, Genevieve, but at least we know where it's coming

from. Every other time we've sailed together, crimes have been committed and we've had to search for the culprit. It's the other way around now."

"We already have our suspect."

"Rance Gilpatrick. All we need to establish is the nature of his crime."

"Supposing that he *is* buying silk," she asked. "Does he pay for it in cash?"

"That's the question I've been asking myself. It's not impossible that he's involved in some kind of barter. He may have goods aboard that somehow don't show up in the manifest. Gilpatrick exchanges them for the silk."

"How? Everything is checked so carefully by customs."

"They can't open every crate and box, Genevieve. There are always cunning ways to smuggle goods. Look at the antiquarian bookseller we caught on the *Lucania*. His consignment of rare books turned out to consist largely of bootleg liquor. He took me in completely at the start."

"And me," she conceded.

"Suspect everyone. That's the golden rule." Dillman stretched himself. "Well, it's been a long day," he said, rising to his feet. "I'll let you get some sleep."

"Before you go, can I ask you a personal question?"

He grinned. "That depends how personal it is."

"Did you vote for President Roosevelt?"

"That's a secret between me and the ballot box."

"In other words, you didn't."

"As a matter of fact, I did. I respect the man. Why do you ask?"

"Mr. McDade had nothing but contempt for him," she said, remembering the virulence of the man's scorn. "He seems to hate the idea of having anything at all to do with the rest of the world. That includes Britain, by the way. He thinks an American president should think only of America."

"That's an all too popular view, I'm afraid," said Dillman wearily. "The doctrine of splendid isolation. I'm dead against it myself. If I'd turned my back on the rest of the world, our paths would never have crossed."

"He got so angry about President Roosevelt."

"People do, Genevieve."

"You don't, obviously."

"He's trying to build bridges with other nations. That's a sensible policy, in my opinion. Since we have to share this planet, we should make an effort to get on together."

"Mr. McDade would disagree. I'm glad that your Mr. and Mrs. Chang were not sitting at our table. He said some very unkind things about Chinese immigrants."

"There's a lot of resentment against them on the West Coast."

"Why?"

"It's the natural distrust of the foreigner, Genevieve. Let's be honest," he went on with a twinkle in his eye. "You probably distrusted me at first."

"I still do."

They traded a laugh and then she got up to open the door, peering out to see if the corridor was empty before giving him a signal. Dillman gave her a farewell kiss and slipped out. As he headed for the stairs, he reflected on a productive evening and decided that he would spend an hour studying the plans of the ship before he turned in. A perusal of the manifest would also be included. He wanted to know the precise details of the cargo that they were carrying. It was the freight that was slowing the vessel down. Standing at the rail of a Cunard liner, he always got an immediate sense of speed and power. The *Minnesota* was a little more pedestrian, but that might work to his advantage. It would allow him and Genevieve far more time to detect any crime that was being committed.

The crucial thing to remember was that they were on the vessel for a specific purpose. Conviviality was very seductive. In the company of friends, it was easy to lose concentration. They had to remain alert. Rance Gilpatrick was no stranger to violence, and Dillman was certain that he would have a confederate or two aboard. One of his first tasks would be to identify everyone associated with the man. Instinct told him that Gilpatrick's circle was not confined to the passenger list. If he was smuggling on the scale envisaged, he would need inside help. It opened up a new line of inquiry. Turning it over in his mind, Dillman descended the stairs and made his way toward his cabin.

When he came into the passageway, a warning bell sounded inside his head. Someone was there. The uneasy sensation he had felt in the dining saloon shot through him again. It was eerie. Though the passageway was empty, he was sure that he was being watched. Making an effort to appear relaxed, he strolled to the door of the cabin and let himself in. Why was someone keeping an eye on him? Did he have an unknown enemy? Had his cover been exposed? Dillman found it worrying. He listened at the door for a long while until he thought he heard footsteps outside. He moved quickly but there was nobody there when he opened the door. Yet he sensed that someone was nearby. Hurrying to the end of the passageway, he looked around the corner and was just in time to see a man disappearing up a companionway. Dillman gave chase, but the man had too much of a start on him. Emerging on the promenade deck once more, Dillman searched first in one direction, then in another. It was all in vain. His phantom shadow had melted away into the night.

"It's good to see that someone takes our advice," said Mike Roebuck, making a note of the items and issuing a receipt. "If everyone put their jewelry in the safe, we'd lower the risk of theft considerably."

"I thought I'd kill two birds with one stone," said Genevieve. "George told me that you wanted a word with me."

"I do, Miss Masefield. I like to be able to put a face to a name."

"Well, here I am, Mr. Roebuck."

"So I see."

"Have you employed a female detective before?"

"No, I can't say that I have."

"Then you're way behind the times. According to George, women were used in the early days of the Pinkerton Agency. They proved their value again and again."

"I don't doubt it," said Roebuck, studying her with interest. "People like you can reach places that no man would dare to enter. You inspire more trust as well. Looking at you, nobody would think for a moment that you were a detective."

"That's my main weapon."

"It's going to be needed on this voyage."

"I gathered that."

"How did you come into this racket?" he wondered.

"I met George Dillman on the maiden voyage of the *Lusitania*."

"What were you doing on that?"

"I thought I might have seen England for the last time," she confessed. "I had this weird notion that I'd settle down in America and start a new life."

"Was there something wrong with the old one?"

Genevieve was evasive. "I felt the need for a change, that's all."

"Then George came along and altered your plans for you."

"He can be very persuasive, Mr. Roebuck."

"You don't need to tell me that," he said with a chuckle. "We've known each other since we were teenagers. I used to work in his father's boatyard during vacations. Oh, yes. George Dillman has a silver tongue. He can charm birds out of a tree."

"He's also an excellent detective."

"That's why he's here."

"He taught me everything I know."

"Judging by your record, you were a prize pupil. The Cunard line must miss you."

"I hope so," said Genevieve. "It might encourage them to raise our fee."

Roebuck laughed. When he had been told that Dillman had a female partner, he did not quite know what to expect. Various images had flitted through his mind, not all of them flattering. Confronted with Genevieve herself, he was taken aback. She was far more poised and beautiful than he had anticipated. He sensed the inner toughness to which Dillman had referred. Genevieve was not the kind of woman to dissolve into a fit of vapors at the first sign of trouble. She was resilient.

"How much has George told you?" he asked.

"Everything, Mr. Roebuck."

"Did he mention what happened to your predecessor?"

"He was beaten up when you reached Japan. Have no fear. I'm not going into this with my eyes shut. I know the risks, and I'm prepared to take them. We've been in tight corners before," she said, stating a fact rather than boasting of an achievement, "but, as you see, we lived to tell the tale."

"George is a lucky man."

"We need luck in this business."

"That's not what I meant, Miss Masefield."

"We're here to do a job," she said crisply. "That's all that matters."

He became solemn. "I agree. Now, this is my suggestion. Rance Gilpatrick is far too wily a character to take chances with, but his latest 'wife' is a different matter. Her name is Maxine Gilpatrick—at least, that's the name she's using. We haven't seen her before. She's new, less suspicious, easier to get at. I think that you should target her."

"That was George's feeling as well."

"Don't make it too obvious. If at all possible, find a way to get acquainted with her. Who knows? She might just let something slip."

"I hope so."

"You have a kind face. Women will confide in you."

"Men confide in me as well," she said wryly. "Unfortunately, they always seem to confide the same thing, so the conversations tend to be short."

Roebuck grinned. "You have to pay a price for your beauty, Genevieve."

"I found that out a long time ago."

"I'm sure. Well," he said, spreading his arms, "any way I can help you?"

"I don't think so."

"What has George asked you to do?"

"Concentrate on the first-class passengers."

"I'd go along with that. You'd look a bit out of place in steerage."

"They must have their share of crime down there, Mr. Roebuck."

"Oh, sure," he agreed. "But it's petty stuff. What can you steal from people who sometimes don't have much more than the clothes they stand up in? Steerage belongs to the small fry, Miss Masefield. We're hunting a killer shark named Rance Gilpatrick."

Dillman got his first look at Rance Gilpatrick that morning. After an early breakfast, Dillman went up to the bridge to introduce himself to Captain Piercey and to listen to his comments about security onboard ship. The two men got on well. Aware of Dillman's interest in marine architecture, the captain showed him around the bridge, then pointed out the salient features of the vessel. It was when the detective made his way down to the boat deck that he encountered Gilpatrick. The latter was unmistakable. He was a big, bulky man in his fifties who had paid an expensive tailor to disguise his spreading girth beneath a well-cut waistcoat and jacket. His face was large and flabby, with a neat mustache beneath the prominent nose and side whiskers that had been dyed black to banish the traces of gray. It was the eyes that Dillman noticed first. Though his face bore a contented smile, Gilpatrick's eyes were cold and watchful. They missed nothing.

Rance Gilpatrick was promenading around the boat deck with his putative wife on his arm. A woman of medium height, Maxine Gilpatrick was in her early thirties, but her Junoesque proportions made her look older than she really was. She had the kind of glamour that hinted at a career as a showgirl. Her flamboyant clothing turned most heads, and she clearly enjoyed creating an impression. As they walked past him, Dillman had little time to make an accurate assessment of her, but he sensed a proprietary air about Maxine. It was almost as if Gilpatrick were on her arm and not the other way around. Dillman wondered if they were, after all, legally married.

Not wishing to draw attention to himself, he made no attempt to trail them. Instead, he made his way down through the ship toward the orlop deck, intending to take a closer look at the freight now that he had permission from the captain and a set of keys. Dillman got no farther than the main deck. It was a bright morning and the sun was reflected on the curling waves. Most passengers had been tempted out to take a walk or to lie in deck chairs. One of them had a more serious purpose. When Dillman reached the main deck, he saw the man less than ten yards away. Father Slattery was in his element. Crouching down, he was talking to a group of Chinese who were seated on a bench. The priest was not haranguing them at all. His voice was low and persuasive. Dillman could see the effect he was having on his little congregation. They were entranced by what he was saying. This was a new side to Father Slattery. In place of the urgent Christian with the bellicose manner was a gentle shepherd in search of a flock. Dillman had to accept that Slattery might well turn out to be a gifted missionary in China.

Hauling himself upright, the priest shook hands with everyone on the bench, then turned around. Before he could escape, Dillman was spotted. Slattery descended on him.

"Good morning!" he said, grasping Dillman's hand between both of his own. "I didn't expect to see you down here among the steerage passengers."

"I was having a gentle tour of the whole vessel, Father Slattery."

"Would you care for some company?"

Dillman was firm. "No, thank you."

"Too early in the day to discuss your beliefs?"

"Far too early, Father Slattery."

"Then let me give you some advice," warned the other in a conspiratorial whisper. "Don't get too close to Mr. Blaine. They're charming but untrustworthy."

"Who are?"

"Baptists."

"But Mr. Blaine and I were not talking about religion."

"When you break bread with a Baptist, you're *always* talking about religion even if you didn't realize it. They're as subtle as snakes. They try to influence you."

"Isn't that what you're doing as well, Father Slattery?" asked Dillman.

The priest beamed. "I have an excuse. It's my job." He looked around the crowded deck. "The Chinese are a simple people. It will be a challenge to work among them, but it will be a rewarding one." He indicated the bench nearby. "My friends over there were delighted when I pointed out that there were no class distinctions in heaven. God expects nobody to travel in the cramped conditions of steerage. His love embraces all of us. Everyone shares the luxuries of first class in heaven."

"That's a comforting thought," said Dillman, about to leave.

"You haven't told me what church you attend yet."

"My parents were devout Episcopalians."

"Good!" said Slattery, rubbing his palms together gleefully. "That's promising."

"Is it?"

"Of course, Mr. Dillman. Baptists are beyond recall, but Episcopalians are more accessible to rational discussion. It means that we can have some wonderful arguments."

Fay Brinkley thought she saw something twinkling on the distant horizon. She sat up.

"What's that?" she asked.

"Where?" Genevieve looked in the direction in which her companion was pointing. "I'm not sure," she said when she picked out the glinting object. "It must be another ship."

"That's reassuring. We seem to be so completely alone out here."

"The Pacific is a vast ocean."

"Yes, Genevieve. It's a little frightening at times."

"I wouldn't have thought that anything frightened you, Fay."

"Oh, lots of things frighten me," admitted the other.

"Such as?"

"The idea of dining with Mr. McDade again."

Genevieve laughed. "That's not frightening—it's terrifying!"

The two women were reclining in deck chairs in a sheltered corner of the promenade deck. Their friendship was slowly blossoming, and they were now on first-name terms. Fay Brinkley was turning out to be a woman of accomplishments. She had published three volumes of poetry, edited a political journal, and been involved in the campaign for women's suffrage. Genevieve was certain that other facets of her talent would emerge in time. Fay now began to probe on her own account.

"What made you decide to leave England in the first place, Genevieve?"

"Oh, the usual thing."

"A disastrous romance?"

"I'm afraid so," admitted Genevieve. "A broken engagement. To be honest, there was nothing to keep me in England. My parents had recently died and, since I was an only child, there was no close family. So, instead of moping over what had happened, I elected to see something of the world instead."

"A wise decision. You don't strike me as the type who mopes."

"I'm not, Fay. Besides, when I'd called the whole thing off, I was more relieved than upset. I felt that I'd had a lucky escape."

"So it was you who terminated the engagement?"

"Comprehensively."

"Why was that?"

"My fiancé did something that I found quite unforgivable."

"I wish that more young women had your resolve," said Fay, "but they don't, alas. One of the failings of our sex is that we have too great a capacity for forgiveness. We put up with things that ought to be rejected wholesale. Look at Blanche McDade," she went on. "I suspect that her entire marriage has been an act of willful toleration. What woman of spirit would let an oaf of a husband dominate her in that way?"

"She must have loved him once, Fay."

"And now she's financially dependent on him. The familiar story."

"Is that why you never married?"

"But I did, Genevieve. When I was too young to know any better."

"How long did it last?"

"Little over a year. Disenchantment set in during the honeymoon."

"Oh, I'm sorry."

"There's no need to be," said Fay cheerily. "Everyone benefited in the long run. My ex-husband is now happily married to a doting second wife. She's borne him four children and doesn't seem to mind the fact that he spends most of his free time playing golf or smoking cigars at his club. Somehow that way of life didn't appeal to me."

"I can see that."

"My parents were horrified at first. They did everything they could to prevent me from leaving. Divorce was anathema to them. It carried a stigma that, quite frankly, I've never felt."

"Fear of divorce is a powerful thing," said Genevieve. "Especially in England. It keeps unhappy marriages together. Rather than face the social embarrassment, some men and women endure the most awful misery in the name of holy matrimony."

"Were your parents happy?"

"Not exactly, Fay. They never argued in front of me, mark you. On the other hand, I can't remember them sharing any real joy together. My mother seemed to accept that as the way it had to be."

"Fatalism."

Genevieve was rueful. "She schooled me to look nice, speak politely, and be agreeable. It never occurred to her that women were put on this earth for other reasons than simply making themselves attractive to men."

"What would she do if she saw you now?"

"Disapprove strongly."

"Not necessarily," said Fay. "In her heart, your mother might envy you."

"I think she might at that. She never had the chances that I did."

"It's not the chances, Genevieve. It's the courage to take them when they come along. You know the value of seizing opportunity."

"I haven't done it as successfully as you, Fay."

"Oh, there's been a lot of failure mixed in with my success," confessed Fay. "One thing I can say, however. I'd much rather be where I am now than raising four children and listening to my husband snoring all night." She turned to appraise Genevieve. "What do you picture yourself doing in a year's time?"

"I really don't know, Fay."

"Does that worry you?"

"No," said Genevieve. "It doesn't. Actually, it rather excites me."

Fay Brinkley nodded in approval and gave her arm an affectionate squeeze. The conversation continued. They were enjoying each other's company so much that they did not realize that they were under observation. Standing some distance away, David Seymour-Jones had a clear view of the couple as he used a pencil on his sketch pad. He looked shabbier than ever and wore a battered straw hat. Though he was watching two women, only one of them appeared on the white paper.

When he had finished the portrait, he tore it out of the pad, examined it critically, then took a deep breath.

Genevieve was listening intently to Fay when he came up to accost her. After a mumbled apology, he thrust the piece of paper into her hand, lifted his hat in farewell, then shuffled quickly away. Genevieve stared down at the flattering portrait of her.

Fay Brinkley was amused. "I did warn you, didn't I?"

FIVE

Something was wrong. George Porter Dillman's years as a detective on land and sea had sharpened his instincts considerably. As he checked the freight in one of the holds, he sensed that it was not quite what it purported to be. At face value, it all tallied with the manifest. Boxes, barrels, sacks, cases, and other containers had been neatly docketed after examination by the customs officials. Every item bore a label that carried details of its contents, its weight, its country of origin, its sender, and its intended recipient. In stacking the cargo, the crew had made maximum use of space. Fragile items had been handled with great care and stored in protected areas. Dillman took a last look around the hold. Flour was the principal export, but there were other foodstuffs there as well. He wondered why he felt so uneasy about the consignment. Though it appeared to be perfectly in order, he was nagged by the thought that something was amiss. The name of Rance Gilpatrick inevitably popped into his mind.

When he had locked the door after him, he made his way along a narrow passageway on the orlop deck. It was a far cry from the luxury of the first-class areas. Concessions to comfort simply did not exist here. There were no thick carpets and paneled walls. Expensive lampshades had been replaced by bulbs that gave minimal light. No framed paintings added color and interest. It was a part of the vessel that was purely functional. It smelled faintly of oil. His footsteps echoed on the metallic floor and his shoulders brushed the bare walls. The roar of the engines was amplified. He could feel their vibrations. Deep inside the hull, Dillman was just as intrigued as he would have been on the bridge deck. Maritime design fascinated him. As he made his way toward the lower orlop deck, he studied the construction of the vessel, noting features that would have been invisible to the untrained eye.

It was when he stopped to look down a companionway that he was conscious of a problem. Someone was lurking nearby. For the third time in twenty-four hours, he knew that he was being watched. Initially concerned that he had been deliberately trailed throughout the ship, he soon dismissed the notion. There was no sense of menace this time. He was not so much being followed as observed. It was as if he had stumbled upon someone's territory. Dillman took immediate action. Walking along to the next junction, he turned to the right and continued on his way for several yards. Then he came to a halt, swung round, and retraced his footsteps as quietly as he could. He waited patiently at the junction of the passageways. Seconds later, he heard stealthy movement. A head peeped furtively around the corner. Dillman did not hesitate. He reached out to grab the man by the neck and pulled hard. His captive let out a shriek of protest.

"No hurt me, sir!" he begged.

"What are you doing down here?" asked Dillman.

"Nothing, sir."

"You're lying."

"No, sir. I do no harm."

"This part of the ship is out of bounds."

"Yes, sir. I get lost." The man turned away. "I go now."

Dillman tightened his grip. "You're staying here until we've sorted this out."

He was holding a pale, thin, frightened Chinese man in his twenties. It was clear that the newcomer was not a member of the crew, and equally obvious from his manner that he was no legitimate passenger. Dillman had seen the same expression of terror on the face of every stowaway that he had caught aboard a ship, but the others only had to endure five days in hiding on a transatlantic voyage. This man was hoping to remain undetected for very much longer. When his captive began to sob and shiver, Dillman felt sorry for him. It was only a ruse. As soon as the detective relaxed his hold, the man tried to push him away to make his escape. Dillman was far too quick for him, grabbing both of his wrists and tugging hard. Letting out a yell of pain, the man found himself slammed against the wall. Dillman towered over him.

"What's your name?" he demanded.

"Wu Feng, sir."

"Do you have a boarding ticket?"

"I lose it, sir."

"In other words, you're a stowaway."

"No, sir," bleated the man. "I come down here by mistake."

"You got onboard the *Minnesota* by mistake, my friend," said Dillman calmly. "The Great Northern Steamship Company takes a dim view of people who try to travel on their vessels without paying. It's a crime, Mr. Feng, as you well know. How did you manage to sneak onboard?"

"I have ticket, sir. It go missing."

"You're lying again."

"No, sir!"

"Don't waste my time," said Dillman, fixing him with a stare. "I'm employed on this ship as a detective and one of my tasks is to search for stowaways. I've seen too many of them to be fooled, Mr. Feng. You look, sound, and act like a stowaway because that's exactly what you are, isn't it?" Feng's head dropped to his chest. "I'll ask you a second time. How and when did you manage to get aboard?"

"I have to go home, sir!" declared the other, looking up at him.

"Then you should have bought a ticket."

"I go to China."

"Yes, I already worked that bit out. What I don't understand is how you got past the crew at Seattle. They control access to the vessel very strictly. You dodged them somehow, didn't you?" Feng shook his head. "Are you alone?"

"Yes!" insisted the other, nodding vigorously. "I alone."

"Then you'd better come with me," said Dillman, taking him by the arm.

"Wait!"

"Do I have to march you out of here by force?" Dillman read the look in his eyes and understood. "You're not alone, are you?" The stowaway sagged. "Okay, Mr. Feng. Let's stop playing games, shall we? Who else is with you and where are they hiding?"

"I alone," whimpered the man feebly. "I alone."

"Tell that to the master-at-arms," said Dillman. "He won't believe you either."

The Langmeads continued to widen their social circle. When Genevieve Masefield joined them for luncheon, she found herself being introduced to a Japanese couple, Tadu and Hisako Natsuki, and an English couple, Bruce and Moira Legge. The eighth member of the party was one that Genevieve had hoped to avoid throughout the voyage, but she concealed her dismay well when she was placed next to Father Liam Slattery. She was glad to lose the McDades and to be spared the embarrassment of meeting David Seymour-Jones again, but the priest was a new source of worry. His bustling evangelism had already upset crew and passengers alike. Genevieve did not wish to become his latest victim. She wanted the pleasurable company of Fay Brinkley, not a Catholic homily at short range. Tadu

Natsuki was a short, sleek man in his thirties with an engaging manner and a polite smile. His wife, a plump but not unattractive woman, contributed little to the discussion beyond smiles and nods of assent. The Legges were so eager to be liked that they both talked too often and too loudly, as if by compulsion. Nearing fifty, Bruce Legge was a balding man with a failed attempt at an Imperial beard. His wife, Moira, had a glass eye that disfigured an otherwise beautiful face.

Father Slattery was on his best behavior at first, allowing the others to set the pace of the conversation and concentrating on the job of methodically loading food into his mouth. Moira Legge felt the need to display their social credentials.

"In which part of London do you live, Miss Masefield?" she asked.

"Chelsea," said Genevieve.

"Really? We had a house in Cheyne Walk, didn't we, darling?"

"Yes, dear," said her husband. "A fine property."

"But rather too small for our taste," continued Moira Legge, spearing some lettuce with her fork. "We entertain on a large scale, you know. That's why we moved to Belgravia. We gained three more bedrooms, a huge wine cellar, a splendid garden, and a dining room worthy of the name. We can seat over twenty guests with ease."

"It sounds like a heck of a big house," said Horace Langmead admiringly.

"We hate to skimp, don't we, darling?"

"Yes, dear," said Legge. He turned to Genevieve. "Do you know the Braydons?"

"I'm afraid not, Mr. Legge," she replied.

"What about the Unwins? They live in Chelsea as well."

"It's a large district."

"But everyone knows Toby Unwin," said Moira with a brittle laugh. "He and his wife give the best parties in Chelsea. At least, they did in our day, didn't they, darling?" Legge grunted his assent. "Surely you've heard of Toby Unwin?"

"No, Mrs. Legge."

"How strange!"

"I'm not fond of parties."

"Why ever not? Bruce always claims that they're the stuff of life."

"I'll say!" agreed her husband.

"Toby's parties were legendary."

"What about the Finch-Howards?" said Legge, stroking his beard. "They're typical Chelsea denizens. Ever come across them, Miss Masefield?"

Genevieve shook her head politely. The Legges continued to bombard her with names, but she recognized none of them. She was also anxious to get off the subject of her London life, especially as she had now renounced it so completely. When one more question was hurled at her, she saw a way to terminate the cross-examination. Moira Legge's glass eye glinted accusingly at her.

"Who on earth *did* you know in Chelsea?" she asked.

"Lord Wilmshurst," said Genevieve.

"Oh!"

"I was very much part of his circle."

It worked. The Legges were sufficient snobs to be impressed by someone who rubbed shoulders with the aristocracy. They had not quite reached that level themselves. Now that Genevieve had been placed above them in the social hierarchy, they backed off at once. She was heartily relieved that they had not pressed her for any details of her acquaintance with Lord Wilmshurst. It was the broken engagement to his son, Nigel, that had precipitated her flight from England on the *Lusitania*. Her brief connection with the Wilmshurst family was something about which Genevieve did not care to be reminded. It had been a painful experience, and the memory still rankled.

Father Slattery decided to take a more active role in the conversation.

"Are you ever troubled by guilt, Mrs. Legge?" he wondered.

"Guilt?" repeated Moira.

"Yes."

"Guilt about what, Father Slattery?"

"Your patent lack of concern for fellow human beings. It's so blatant." He looked around the table at each person in turn. "What about the rest of you?" he wondered. "Any hints of remorse among you? Any troubled consciences?"

"Don't get too religious on us, Father," said Horace Langmead amiably. "We just want to enjoy a pleasant meal, that's all."

"Exactly, Mr. Langmead. We're engaged in thoughtless self-indulgence."

"I was simply eating a salad," said Etta Langmead.

"Yes," challenged Slattery, rounding on her, "but did you stop for a moment to think how many millions of people do not have the blessing of food on their table? It's easy for us to recite the Lord's Prayer and ask to be given our daily bread because we can take it for granted. Does it never occur to you that, while we gormandize here, a large section of the world's population is starving?"

"You ate as well as any of us," said Natsuki politely.

"Oh, I don't deny it, sir. Mea culpa. I'm as guilty as you are, Mr. Natsuki. More so, in the sense that my appetite is greater than yours. But I have an excuse, you see. I go to a life where rigor will be the order of the day." He waved an arm at the table. "I'll never get near food of this quality again. This is my last opportunity to partake of such a delicious meal. While I eat, however, I suffer. Each mouthful is accompanied by the realization that I'll see nothing but empty bellies in China."

Moira wrinkled her nose. "Need we talk about such things?"

"Of course, Mrs. Legge. It's our duty."

"It may be your duty, Father Slattery," said Etta Langmead pleasantly, "but we're not Catholic priests. Naturally, we feel compassion towards those less fortunate than ourselves, but that doesn't mean we should go without food."

Slattery wagged a finger. "Denial is good for the soul."

"That depends on what you mean by the soul," suggested Natsuki.

"I'll be happy to discuss that subject at length, sir."

"Only not now, Father," insisted Langmead, trying to divert him. "There's a time and place for everything. Even you must accept that."

"Oh, I do, I do."

"In Japan," said Natsuki, "we have a different idea of the soul."

"A misleading one," countered Slattery.

"We do not feel misled."

"What's your religion? Shintoism, I suppose."

"We are proud to admit it," said Natsuki, touching his wife's arm.

"Nobody should take pride in their ignorance. I've spent a lifetime trying to enlighten people, to rescue them from their misguided beliefs."

"Tolerance is a virtue," said Genevieve, stung into comment by the priest's grinning complacence. "Because you serve one faith, Father Slattery, it doesn't entitle you to insult the religion practiced by Mr. and Mrs. Natsuki."

"I go along with that," said Etta Langmead pointedly.

"So do I, honey," added Langmead.

Slattery's face was a picture of innocence. "I insulted nobody."

"You did, Father. We all heard you."

"Then you misunderstood me, Mr. Langmead."

"Oh, I see. So I'm misguided as well, am I?"

Etta raised a hand. "Don't get upset, Horry."

"I'm not upset, honey. I'm just trying to calm things down a little."

"Please," said Natsuki with an appeasing smile. "Do not speak up on my account. Let us forget it. There was no insult. We talk about something else."

"There!" declared Slattery, banging the table for effect. "The typical action of a man who has lost an argument. He retreats from the field."

Natsuki's eyes flashed. "I retreat nowhere, sir."

"But it might be a good idea if you and I did, Father Slattery," said Langmead as he felt his wife's warning kick under the table. "Why don't we take a stroll?"

"Because I'd rather stay here," said Slattery doggedly. "You invited me."

"Not to have a doctrinal dispute."

"We're having a slight difference of opinion, that's all, Mr. Langmead."

"I think we all know what yours is, Father Slattery," ventured Bruce Legge.

"It was a golden rule at Toby Unwin's parties," announced Moira, clapping her hands like a child. "No religion and no politics. They ruin everything. That's why Toby's parties were so successful. They were dedicated to harmless fun."

"There is nothing harmless about fun," decreed Slattery.

"You weren't there," she retorted.

"Thank goodness!" murmured Legge.

Slattery hit his stride. "We should have higher ideals in life," he argued. "Were we really put on this earth to eat, drink, and waste our energies in pointless frivolity? Of course not. As ever, the Bible is our surest guide. God created us in His own image for a particular purpose." He glanced at Natsuki, who was sitting bolt upright. "That includes you and your wife, Mr. Natsuki. God is not limited by geographical boundaries."

"Your God is not ours," Natsuki reminded him.

"He would be if you had the sense to let Him into your life."

"I feel that we should respect other cultures," said Genevieve reasonably.

"Not if they are based on fundamental error, Miss Masefield."

"That's a very unkind observation, Father Slattery."

"Truth sometimes is unkind."

"Have you ever *been* to Japan?"

"No," he replied airily, "but that doesn't invalidate my point. I've never been to Africa, but I know that it's full of ignorant savages."

"We are not ignorant savages in my country," said Natsuki.

"Yet you're very resistant to change. I've read the reports from our Catholic missionaries there. They struggle to make an impact on the Oriental mind. Japan is very hidebound," asserted Slattery, blithely unaware of the effect he was having on the others. "That's what happens when a country is isolated for so long from the rest of the world. It loses touch with reality."

Horace Langmead tried to wrest conversational control from him, but Slattery would not yield it. Opposition only served to inflame his lust for argument. Genevieve saw the reactions of her companions. Etta Langmead was gritting her teeth and vowing never to share a table with the priest again. Bruce and Moira Legge suffered in silence. Hisako Natsuki sat there with a fixed smile while her husband resorted to the occasional defensive remark. Though never less than polite, Natsuki was finding the indiscriminate attack on his faith very hurtful. Genevieve sensed that the wounds were deep. She did her best to deflect Father Slattery from his theme, but he surged on as if in his pulpit, six feet above contradiction. What annoyed the others was that he continued to enjoy his meal so much while he spoke, swallowing food between sentences and washing it down with liberal quantities of wine. It was perverse. In taking away their appetites, he seemed to have increased his own.

Suddenly, much to their relief, the diatribe was over. Father Slattery rose to his feet without warning and dabbed at his lips with a napkin before setting it down beside his empty plate. He exuded bonhomie.

"Please excuse me," he said, distributing a smile around the table. "I have a service to take later on and need to prepare myself. It's been so good to meet you all. The meal was a positive delight."

Cheered by the prospect of getting rid of him, Horace Langmead shook him by the hand, then waved him off. Shoulders hunched in apology, he turned to the others.

"I'm so sorry about that," he said gloomily. "We made a hideous mistake. When we first met him, he was charming."

"I thought he'd never stop talking," moaned Etta.

"Or eating."

"Yes, Horry. And he had the gall to lecture us on world starvation."

"Fancy being a member of his congregation!" said Bruce Legge.

"No, thank you," moaned his wife. "When he stood up like that, I thought, for one horrible moment, that he was going to take a collection."

Langmead chuckled. "If it meant sending him on his way, I'd gladly have contributed." He turned to Genevieve. "You had the worst of it, Miss Masefield, sitting next to him. That foghorn of a voice was right in your ear. He was quite insufferable. Is that what celibacy does to a man?"

They laughed at the remark, but each one of them was still deeply upset. Father Slattery had deprived them of the enjoyment they would certainly have had without him. Luncheon had been an extended ordeal. The Langmeads kept apologizing for inflicting the turbulent priest on the others, and Bruce Legge tried to lighten the atmosphere by telling some feeble anti-Catholic jokes. Genevieve's attention was caught by Tadu and Hisako Natsuki. Where the others had been irritated by Father Slattery, they had been hurt at a deep level. Natsuki was talking to his wife in Japanese. His voice was low and his manner restrained, but Genevieve sensed the crackle of real anger. She wished that she could understand what he was saying.

Mike Roebuck had worked on passenger vessels too long to be surprised by anything. Stowaways were a predictable hazard. The purser sighed with resignation.

"How many of them were there, George?" he asked.

"Two. Wu Feng and his father."

"Hiding on the orlop deck?"

"Yes," said Dillman. "Heaven knows how they got down there! Steerage is uncomfortable enough but at least you get a bunk, even if you have to share a cabin with complete strangers. The Fengs were sleeping on the bare floor. They had virtually no luggage."

"What about food and water?"

"Barely enough to survive on."

"They must be desperate."

"They were, Mike. They implored me not to report them."

"Poor guys!" commented the purser. "What a way to travel! Most stowaways sneak aboard, then mingle with the steerage passengers during the day to cadge food from them. It sounds as if these two would have spent the entire voyage without any natural light. What was their story?"

"They hated America."

"Then why go there in the first place?"

"The usual hopes of making good. They hadn't counted on antagonism."

"Hostility to immigrants is growing all the time."

"They found that out, Mike. First week they arrived, the old man was beaten up in Seattle. He still has the scars to prove it. Wu Feng couldn't earn enough to keep the two of them, so they decided to go home."

"By means of a free trip on the *Minnesota*."

"That was the idea," said Dillman, "but it would never have worked. Sooner or later, one of us was bound to find them down there."

"They're lucky. Fifty years ago, skippers weren't so considerate. They'd have thrown stowaways overboard like any other unwanted cargo. Wu Feng and his father would have had to swim to China." Roebuck touched the peak of his cap as an elderly female passenger went past. "Where are they now?"

"With the master-at-arms."

"He'll sort them out. Thanks, George. You did well."

73

"It's all part of my job."

"We want you hunting bigger game than a pair of fleeing Chinamen."

They were standing at the rail on the upper deck. When Dillman tracked him down, the purser was listening to a catalog of complaints from a Mexican passenger whose grasp on English was very insecure. Mike Roebuck had been grateful to be rescued by the detective. Dillman told him about his thorough search of the ship.

"Have you spotted our prime suspect yet?" asked Roebuck.

"Yes, Mike. Your description was as accurate as a photograph."

"Rance Gilpatrick's photograph ought to be on a wanted poster."

"In effect, it is."

"Was he alone?"

"No, he had the new lady in his life on his arm."

"What on earth do they see in that fat old fraud?"

"Wealth and power always attract some women."

Roebuck grinned. "Is that why I lose out with them?"

"You're too honest to make your fortune the way Gilpatrick did. Besides," said Dillman, "he's living on borrowed time. When we catch him, his wealth and power will disappear in a flash."

"So will his supply of wives."

"Yes, they'll run for cover. The present Mrs. Gilpatrick didn't have the look of a woman who'd stand by him if he went to prison."

"Maxine might turn out to be his weak spot."

"That's what I suggested to Genevieve."

"I know, George, and I'd reached the same conclusion. I asked your partner to snuggle up to Maxine Gilpatrick in the hope of finding something out." He gave a wistful smile. "What a treat! If Genevieve Masefield snuggled up to *me*, I'd tell her everything."

"Including the fact that you're married?"

"Don't spoil my dream!"

"How did you get on with Genevieve?"

"Extremely well. She's a very special lady."

"It takes nerve to do the kind of work that she does."

"She looks as cool as a cucumber."

"Genevieve will prove her worth on this voyage," said Dillman fondly. "She always has in the past. Nobody ever suspects her of being a detective. Especially the men. They're too busy being dazzled by her charm."

"It worked on me, George. I freely admit it."

Dillman gazed thoughtfully at the undulating expanse of the Pacific.

"Let's hope that it works on Maxine Gilpatrick as well," he said.

Genevieve Masefield was happy to see Fay Brinkley again. Separated during luncheon, they met again in the Ladies' Boudoir and exchanged notes. Fay listened sympathetically to Genevieve's tale of woe.

"What rotten luck!" she said. "I had the opposite experience. Everyone at my table was very nice but excessively dull."

"Oh, Father Slattery wasn't dull," conceded Genevieve. "Just annoying."

"Why did the Langmeads invite him?"

"They're still trying to work that out, Fay."

"Let's make a point of dining together this evening."

"Yes," agreed Genevieve, "as far away from Father Slattery as possible."

"It's a deal!"

"I was so embarrassed on behalf of Mr. and Mrs. Natsuki."

"They probably dismissed him as another brash American. Anyway," said Fay with a knowing smile, "let's put him aside, shall we? I want to hear about the other man in your life."

Genevieve was caught off-guard. "What other man?"

"Our lovestruck artist."

"I'd forgotten him."

"Well, I don't think he's forgotten you, Genevieve. Mr. Seymour-Jones has an obsessional look about him. Once he commits himself, he does so to the hilt."

"Oh dear!"

"You should be flattered."

"Well, I'm not, Fay."

"Wouldn't you like to enjoy a mild flirtation?"

"No," said Genevieve. "Especially not with David Seymour-Jones."

"Underneath that bohemian exterior, he's personable enough. And you saw that portrait he drew of you," noted Fay. "It was a declaration in itself."

"It's not one that I sought or wanted. Why choose me?" asked Genevieve with quiet exasperation. "I've done nothing whatsoever to encourage his advances."

"Try looking in a mirror."

"What?"

Fay nudged her playfully. "Oh, don't pretend to be so naïve. With a face and figure like yours, you attract men by the dozen. I suspect that you've coped with it pretty well until now. David Seymour-Jones is hardly a serious threat to your virtue."

"I know, Fay, but I wouldn't like to hurt his feelings."

"We're all bound to break a few hearts along the way."

"Not deliberately."

"So what will you do?"

"Keep out of his way." She glanced around. "I may be in here rather a lot."

"Why?"

"Ladies only. It's the one place on the ship where I'll be safe from Father Slattery and David Seymour-Jones. I can keep religion and romance firmly at bay."

"One of them will still find a way to get to you," teased Fay.

It was an ideal place for a meeting with a friend. The chairs were comfortable and arranged in a way that allowed complete privacy. Seated in an alcove, Genevieve and Fay had a good view of the rest of the room. There was a scattering of women in the boudoir, exchanging gossip, making plans for the evening, reading magazines, or simply enjoying the melodies that someone was playing on the piano. Genevieve basked in the restful atmosphere. It was a comfort to have a friend like Fay Brinkley in whom she could confide. The American had a worldliness that was noticeably lacking in all the other women Genevieve had so far encountered. Etta Langmead, Moira Legge, and Hisako Natsuki were extensions of their respective husbands, women who had no independent life of their own. Blanche McDade was kept in an even darker shadow of a man. Fay would never settle for being a mere accessory on a man's arm. It was one of the many things about her that appealed to Genevieve.

The room gradually emptied until only a handful of women remained. Fay excused herself. Genevieve stayed to finish her cup of tea and to reflect on the long conversation she had enjoyed. She realized with a start that the music had stopped. Genevieve was disappointed. Even though she had only heard them intermittently, the soothing melodies in the background had been a delight. She got up and made her way to the piano. Sitting on the stool, she played a few chords, then looked around to see if anyone objected. Nobody even turned a head in her direction. Genevieve played on, starting with the "Moonlight Sonata," relieved to discover that her fingers still retained much of the skill they had developed during long years of piano lessons. Her confidence slowly grew and she plucked a waltz from her memory. After working through her repertoire, she glanced down at the music in front of her and read the name of Stephen Foster. Humming to herself, she played the first verse of the song. When she started the second verse, she discovered that she had company.

> Beautiful dreamer, out on the sea,
> Mermaids are chanting, the wild Lorelei.
> Over the stream . . .

It was not the voice of an amateur, singing the familiar words out of sentimental impulse. The woman was a soprano with perfect pitch, hitting each note with the ease and conviction of a true professional. As the voice soared on, Genevieve felt a hand on her shoulder, encouraging her to play the rest of the song. She was keen to oblige. Acting as accompanist to someone with such obvious talent brought out the best in her. Everyone in the room turned to listen with appreciative smiles. When the final chord was played, they broke into spontaneous applause.

"Thanks, honey!" said the woman. "That was great."

"You have a wonderful voice," said Genevieve, getting up to look at her.

"I trained as an opera singer but fell by the wayside."

"It was a pleasure to play for you."

"We must do it again some time."

"I'd like that."

"You from England?"

"How did you guess?" She offered a hand. "I'm Genevieve Masefield."

"Pleased to meet you," said the woman, ignoring the hand and kissing her on both cheeks instead. "My name is Maxine Gilpatrick."

George Porter Dillman was on his way to the dining saloon that evening when he was intercepted by the purser. Roebuck took him aside to pass on some astonishing news.

"We have a Good Samaritan onboard," he said.

"What do you mean?"

"Do you remember those stowaways you found?"

"How could I forget them?" asked Dillman.

"They're stowaways no longer. Someone bailed them out by paying their fare."

"Who was it?"

"A Catholic priest called Father Slattery." Dillman was taken aback. "Yes," Roebuck went on, "it surprised me at first. I mean, who cares about stowaways? Apparently, this Father Slattery has been scouring the ship for repentant sinners. He asked the master-at-arms if we had any bad boys in custody and heard about the Fengs. He took pity on them at once."

Dillman was touched. "He paid both their fares?"

"Out of his own pocket. They've only got bunks in steerage, but that's a big improvement on spending the voyage under lock and key. Father Slattery is on his way to join a Catholic mission in China."

"I know, Mike. I've met him."

"What's he like?"

"He's a prickly character."

"He must have a good heart as well," said Roebuck.

"Oh, he does. I've seen him in action."

"He's given two penniless Chinese a first taste of Christianity."

"What will happen to Wu Feng and his father?"

"Nothing, George. They're off the hook."

"No punishment for sneaking aboard the ship illegally?"

"The master-at-arms didn't want to let them off scot-free, but Slattery talked him into it. He's a persuasive guy. Besides," he continued, "I fancy that being caught by you was punishment enough for the Fengs. They've had their scare."

"So it seems. But I've got glad tidings for you as well, Mike."

Roebuck smiled hopefully. "You've caught Gilpatrick redhanded?"

"Not exactly," said Dillman, "but we've made a slight breakthrough. Genevieve has, anyway. I had a note from her to say that she's made friends with Maxine Gilpatrick. Genevieve is dining at their table this evening."

"How did she manage that?"

"By playing a piano."

"Piano?"

"That's all she said in her note. I'll get the full details when we meet up later."

"I can't wait to hear them!"

Roebuck went off, leaving Dillman to continue on his way to the dining saloon. Dress was much more formal on the second evening afloat. The men wore white ties and tails, while the women took the opportunity to put on their most fashionable dresses. Silk and satin hems brushed the floor. Stoles were draped around shoulders. Jewelry was much more in evidence, and the ship's hairdressers had clearly been kept busy. When he entered the saloon, Dillman was immediately aware of the pervading scent of perfume. A small orchestra provided music for the occasion. The novelty of the first day was behind the passengers. They could now luxuriate in the vessel's facilities and concentrate on developing new friendships.

Dillman was at a table for six. Though dining once again with the Changs and with Rutherford Blaine, he acquired two additional companions. Angela Van Bergen was a garrulous woman from New York in her early forties. On her way to Kobe to join her husband, she talked ceaselessly about his business affairs, their fondness for Japan, their regular vacations in exotic corners of the globe, and their plans for retirement. Mrs. Van Bergen had a life that was so supremely organized that it was barren of real adventure. Willoughby Kincaid, by contrast, led a much more freewheeling existence. The sixth person at the table was a tall, well-built man of middle years with a black mustache as the focal point of a once handsome face. In appearance and manner, Kincaid was a perfect English gentleman, but Dillman detected a faintly dissolute air about him. At all events, he was a more entertaining companion than Mrs. Van Bergen. While she paraded her love of Japan in front of the others, Dillman struck up a conversation with the Englishman.

"What brings you to this part of the world, Mr. Kincaid?" he asked.

"Restlessness, sir."

"I don't follow."

"Nature equipped me with itchy feet, Mr. Dillman," said the other. "I like to keep on the move. When I first left my native shores over twenty years ago, I did so in a jingoistic spirit. I wanted to explore every inch of the British Empire."

"What happened?"

"I fell in love with the whole idea of travel. Why restrict myself to our imperial domains when there are so many other wonderful places to see? I'm never happier than when I'm in transit. I'm a rolling stone who was educated at Eton."

"You obviously have no wife and family to hold you back."

"No, Mr. Dillman. I prefer to travel light. What about you?"

"Oh, I'm not married either."

"Another lucky bachelor, eh? Able to take his pleasures where he finds them." He gave a throaty chuckle. "I had a feeling that we were two of a kind." He leaned in close to Dillman. "What did you think of Seattle?"

"I had very little time to see anything of it, Mr. Kincaid."

"Pity. It's a lively town. You'd have liked it."

"Would I?"

"Rather!" said Kincaid with enthusiasm. "It's grown a lot in recent years, but there's still a rough-and-ready feel to it. Seattle knows how to give a man a good time."

"That wasn't always the case," noted Dillman. "Seattle prospered because it was the gateway to Alaska. When they struck gold in the Klondike, the town was booming. In those days, it was known more for its brawling than its hospitality. Money was flooding in, but there was one item in short supply."

"Women?"

"Exactly, Mr. Kincaid—though not the kind that you may have in mind."

Kincaid beamed. "Women are all one to me. Infinitely desirable creatures." His eye fell on Mrs. Van Bergen. "With one or two exceptions, that is. But do go on, sir."

"There was a man called Asa Mercer, who was president of the university. He must have been a venturesome individual," said Dillman, "because he traveled all the way to the East Coast to round up a collection of virginal young ladies, eleven in all, who were ready to marry some of the good citizens of Seattle, sight unseen."

"Now that's the kind of assignment that would have appealed to me," said Kincaid, eyes gleaming. "Driving a wagon full of virgins across the continent."

"They made excellent wives for the pioneers. On his second trip back east, Mercer found almost fifty women, some of them Civil War widows. To show how highly he rated the ladies, he married one of them himself."

"Fatal mistake. He was throwing away his freedom."

"He was helping to build Seattle."

"Then he deserves full credit for that."

Willoughby Kincaid was an observant man. Though the ship had only been at sea a couple of days, he had already made several friends and could identify others by name. As he pointed out various people to Dillman, the detective was impressed by his range of acquaintances and by his tenacious memory. Kincaid seemed to forget nothing.

"I'm an explorer, Mr. Dillman," he explained. "I explore the hearts and minds of people who engage my interest."

"Is it a rewarding hobby?"

"Very rewarding. One is always learning something new."

The arrival of the main course marked a natural break in the conversation. Mrs. Van Bergen seized the opportunity to deliver another one of her monologues.

"Of course," she said with a condescending smile, "my husband and I make an annual visit to England. We probably know London as well as you, Mr. Kincaid, even better in some respects. It's our second home. We go to the theater and the opera and we're invited to so many bridge parties. Bridge is a game at which I really excel," she boasted, revealing a row of large, uneven teeth. "That's why I'm always in demand as a partner, especially when we play for money. Yes, when we're in England, it's one long and delightful social event. My husband has so many friends in high places, you see. We dine out virtually every night. They know us by name in all the best restaurants. We've met several aristocrats and, at a ball we attended last year, we even caught a glimpse of King Edward. Such a handsome man, I think, and so unmistakably *royal*. We've heard the rumors, naturally, but I don't believe a word of them. People who link his name with scandal are just being mischievous. Don't you think so, Mr. Kincaid? It's too bad of them. They should have more respect for their monarch."

Kincaid shrugged. "Some of them feel he has willfully forfeited that respect, Mrs. Van Bergen. Do you know what his latest peccadillo is?"

Kincaid enjoyed telling her, provoking gasps of disbelief. Mr. and Mrs. Chang listened with wide-eyed curiosity, and Blaine was mildly amused. They were grateful to Kincaid for taking over the conversational reins from Mrs. Van Bergen. Her monologues could be interminable. Dillman, too, was relieved to escape the grating sound of her voice. Glancing across at Genevieve, he was pleased to see how relaxed she was in the company of Rance and Maxine Gilpatrick. She looked striking in a blue silk dress and an array of jewelry. At a table for twelve, she was clearly the central figure. What interested Dillman was the fact that, apart from Genevieve, the Gilpatricks, and another woman, everyone at the table was of Chinese or Japanese origin. They were uniformly deferential to their host, and he was lording it. It was almost as if the corpulent Rance Gilpatrick were holding court.

They had reached the dessert before Dillman heard the whisper in his ear.

"Magnificent, isn't she?" said Kincaid.

"Who?"

"The lady you've been looking at all evening."

"There was nobody in particular."

"Come off it, old chap. Every red-blooded man in the room has been stealing glances at her. I have, I know that. So has Blaine. Even our little Mr. Chang let his gaze stray in her direction. Why should you be any different?"

"Well," admitted Dillman, "it is difficult not to notice her."

"There's nothing to rival an English rose."

"You could be right, Mr. Kincaid."

"Her name is Genevieve Masefield."

Dillman turned to him. "You *know* the lady?"

"Not yet," said Kincaid smoothly, "but I intend to repair that omission very soon. As I told you, Mr. Dillman, I'm an explorer. And frankly, I can't think of a more enchanting subject for exploration." He sipped his wine. "Can you?"

SIX

Studying himself in the full-length mirror, Rance Gilpatrick adjusted his waistcoat, then pulled out his gold watch to check the time. Maxine came up behind him.

"What did you think of her?" she asked.

"Who?"

"Jenny Masefield, of course."

"She's more of a Genevieve to me."

"Did you like her?"

"I loved her," said Gilpatrick, slipping his watch into his pocket as he turned to face her. "What man wouldn't? She's got the face of an angel. Mind you, I wasn't so impressed by that friend of hers."

"Fay Brinkley?"

"Why did she have to horn in?"

"Jenny had promised to dine with her this evening."

"Well, I could have done without her at the table. Fay Brinkley was a little too knowing for my taste. She was one of those clever women that I detest most," said Gilpatrick with asperity. "Next time you invite Genevieve, make it clear that she comes without baggage."

"Fay Brinkley was pleasant enough."

"Not when you looked her in the eyes." He moved to the door. "See you later."

"Where are you going?"

"To talk business."

"But I haven't finished yet," she complained, squaring up to him. "Which is more important to you—me or your business associates?"

"You, Maxine," he said, stroking her arm. "You know that."

"Then why are you deserting me like this?"

"I won't be long, honey. Wait up for me."

"But there's something to discuss first."

Gilpatrick looked blank. "Is there?"

"You've forgotten already," she said angrily. "When I raised it at the table, you were all in favor of it. Now, you can't even remember what it was."

"Remind me."

"I want to sing, Rance."

"You spent your whole life singing."

"I'm not talking about work in your saloons. That's all in the past now. I'm not strutting around a stage and wiggling my ass for a crowd of noisy drunks anymore. I had aspirations at one time," she said with a forlorn smile. "I wanted to sing opera."

Gilpatrick cackled. "Thank God you didn't try it in one of my saloons!"

"Don't laugh at me!" she warned.

"I'm not laughing, honey."

"Yes, you are. Take me seriously for a change."

"Nobody could take you more seriously, Maxine," he said, planting a kiss on her forehead. "Surely I've proved that by now. If you want to sing, go ahead and sing."

"You'll need to speak to someone first."

"Will I?"

"There!" she exclaimed. "I knew it. You haven't been listening to me."

He looked at his watch again. "Maxine, they're waiting. I have to go."

"Not until we've sorted this out. I asked Jenny and she thought it was a great idea. So did you when we were having the meal." Determination shone in her eyes. "I want to give a recital of songs in front of an audience. Fix it for me."

"They already have entertainment onboard."

"They can have some more."

He was uncertain. "I'll try, honey, but I can't promise anything."

"Fix it," she insisted. "When I sang again this afternoon, I felt inspired. My voice is still there. The other ladies loved me." She grasped his arm. "It's what I want to do, Rance. I need to perform. Jenny Masefield will be my accompanist."

"Is she good enough?"

"She's better than any of the pianists in your saloons."

"That was different."

"She and I can work together. I know it. All we need is the chance."

Gilpatrick rubbed his chin. "Leave it to me," he said at length.

They were in their cabin on the boat deck. No sooner had they retired there after dinner than Gilpatrick was ready to go out again. Maxine never pried into his business dealings. All that concerned her was that she was the beneficiary of them. But she needed something to divert her on the long voyage, and the notion of a public performance excited her beyond measure. She was wearing a long black dress that emphasized her figure, and her hair was encircled by a diamond tiara. Other items of jewelry were artfully placed. Maxine crossed to examine herself in the mirror.

"How do I look?"

"Terrific!" he said.

"But I was almost invisible beside Jenny."

"Don't you believe it, honey!" he lied. "I hardly noticed her."

"She has such class, Rance."

"Genevieve is from England. They breed thoroughbreds over there. But it's all on the surface, Maxine. As a woman, you leave her standing."

"Do I?"

"Trust me," he assured her with a grin. "I should know."

"I just wish I had that poise."

"You've got it. That was the first thing I spotted about you."

"Was it?" she said, turning a cynical eye on him. "That's not how I recall it, Rance. I didn't even get the chance to show any poise before you moved in on me."

"You complaining?"

"I'm just setting the record straight."

"Good." He kissed her again. "Now I must get off to that meeting."

"Don't forget your promise."

"Promise? Oh, that," he said, raising a flabby palm. "Don't worry, Maxine. I'll arrange it. You want to get up on a stage again, I'll make sure it happens."

She snuggled up to him. "You can be so sweet when you try."

"I *am* sweet, honey. I don't need to try."

"How long will you be?"

"An hour, at most."

Maxine blew him a kiss. "I'll be waiting for you."

"I'm banking on it." He opened the door, then paused in the doorway. "You know, the more I think about it, the more I warm to the idea. Maybe you and this Genevieve Masefield should give a performance together. You'd get to know her better."

"That's part of the attraction."

"Why? She's not exactly your type."

"So what? I like Jenny and she likes me. Isn't that enough?"

"Yes," he said pensively. "I guess it is. You got some kind of bond with her. Work on the friendship. It'll be as much for my benefit as yours."

"Your benefit?"

"Of course."

"I don't understand."

"Miss Masefield is an interesting lady," he explained. "She's got looks and brains. That's rare in a woman. Very rare, in fact. And she has definite class. It pours out of her. But there's something that's not quite right about her."

"What do you mean?"

"I can't put my finger on it," he admitted. "I just know it's there."

"You're wrong," said Maxine. "She's as genuine as they come."

"We'll see, honey. Get to know her properly, that's all I ask. I still think that Genevieve Masefield is too good to be true." He waved a farewell. "Find out why."

When Dillman arrived at her cabin, Genevieve was still making notes on a pad. She broke off to let him in. Dillman was eager to hear what had transpired.

"How was dinner?"

"A lot better than luncheon," she replied. "I was stuck next to Father Slattery for that. He was swinging the Bible at us like a sledgehammer. This evening was much more pleasant. I met the notorious Rance Gilpatrick at last."

"I'm still not sure how you contrived that."

"I didn't, George. It was a complete accident."

She told him about the impromptu performance in the Ladies' Boudoir and how Maxine Gilpatrick had insisted she join them for dinner. Since Genevieve had already agreed to dine with Fay Brinkley, she, too, was included in the invitation.

Dillman was pleased. "Having a friend there was a stroke of luck. She gave you some cover. You weren't too exposed."

"Fay is a shrewd woman. She saw through Gilpatrick in a flash."

"What did she say?"

"What we already know—that he's a complete crook. Fay

found him revolting," she said, "and I don't think he was altogether enamored of her."

"He seemed to like you, Genevieve."

"I made sure that he did. And I've certainly got Maxine on my side."

"She has the look of a strong-willed lady."

"Oh, she is, George. Unlike the other women in his life, Maxine actually managed to get him to the altar. There's no question about that. She's his legal wife."

"That will surprise Mike Roebuck."

"Maxine was boasting about it."

"Have you arranged to see her again?"

"It looks as if I'll have to, George. She has this urge to give a song recital in public. I'm supposed to be her accompanist."

"That's wonderful news!"

"Not from where I sit," confessed Genevieve. "I can play reasonably well in private but I'm not a real pianist. I'm terrified of the idea of a public performance."

"They'll be there to hear Maxine Gilpatrick sing, not to hear you play. In any case, you'll have plenty of time to rehearse."

"I'll need it!"

"Think of the opportunity this gives you, Genevieve."

"I'm frightened that I may play the wrong notes."

"It sounds to me as if you've played all the right ones so far."

He pressed her for details of the conversation at the dinner table, and she recounted what she could remember of it. Talk had been light and inconsequential. Gilpatrick's business affairs were not mentioned at any stage, though the other guests seemed to be associates of his. Genevieve tore a page from her pad.

"This is a list of their names," she said, handing it over, "though you'll have to excuse the spelling. Two are Japanese and the rest are Chinese."

"Well done, Genevieve. I'll check these names out with Mike Roebuck."

"They treated Gilpatrick with the utmost respect."

"So I noticed."

"And I think they were going to have a meeting after dinner," she recalled. "Nothing was said between them but looks were exchanged. Nobody was sitting at the table by accident. Except Fay Brinkley and me, that is."

"She sounds like an intelligent woman."

"She is, George. There are hidden depths to Fay."

"How did she get on with the others?"

"She blended in quite well," said Genevieve. "Fay always does. The only person who didn't respond to her was Gilpatrick. She made him uneasy. I don't think he'll try to lure Fay into his harem. His preference is for women like Maxine."

"Does she know the truth about the man she married?"

"She loves him enough not to care."

"What about Gilpatrick? Does he love her?"

"I think so," she replied. "He was very attentive to her. Mind you, that didn't stop him from shooting me a few sly glances. I was grateful that he had a wife at his side. I wouldn't relish dining with Rance Gilpatrick on his own."

"Are you afraid he might offer you a job playing piano in one of his saloons?"

Genevieve laughed. "That would be the least of my worries. While I'm with Maxine, I'm safe. Alone with Gilpatrick, I'd have problems. And I can do without another unwanted admirer."

"Another?"

"Yes, George," she said, opening a drawer to take something out. "Do you remember I told you about that artist, David Seymour-Jones?"

"The scruffy Englishman?"

"That's the one. Fay warned me that I'd made a conquest but I didn't believe her. Then he gave me this." She sighed, handing him the sketch. "He drew this portrait of me."

Dillman scrutinized it. "Very lifelike. The man has a gift."

"Well, I wish that he'd keep it to himself. It was unnerving,

George. I mean, he must have been looking at me for ages and I didn't even know that he was there. Then he thrust this at me and hurried off."

"Was he shy or embarrassed?"

"I'm not sure. All I know is that I felt as if my privacy had been invaded."

"Brace yourself for more of it, Genevieve."

"What do you mean?"

"David Seymour-Jones is not your only unsought admirer," he cautioned. "I sat next to another one this evening. His name is Willoughby Kincaid, and he's the kind of sociable, good-natured English gentleman you must have met a hundred times. Kincaid was very plausible, but there was a whiff of the degenerate about him."

Genevieve was bitter. "In that case, I *have* met him a hundred times."

"He was very taken with you. He even knew your name."

"How did he find that out?"

"You'll be able to ask him. He means to get acquainted with you."

"Then he'll be wasting his time."

"Kincaid struck me as the persistent type."

"That's all I need!" she complained with mock horror. "What have I done to deserve this? We only set sail yesterday, and I'm already saddled with a lovelorn artist and a persistent suitor. I can't think of anything worse."

"Oh, I can, Genevieve."

"Can you?"

"Yes," he said with a grin. "A proposal of marriage from Father Slattery."

When he had put on his pajamas, Father Slattery knelt beside his bunk and put his hands together in prayer. Closing his eyes tight, he thanked God for what he perceived as a successful day and asked for guidance on the morrow. There was no trace of his arrogance now. As he recited the familiar prayers, he was in an attitude of complete submission. He remained on his knees for long time. When he finally climbed into his bunk and switched off the light, he lay in the darkness and congratulated himself on the way that he had rescued the unfortunate stowaways from their incarceration. In his eyes, it was an act of Christian charity. Only utter despair could have driven Wu Feng and his father to flee on the *Minnesota*. Slattery expected to find much more despair when he reached the mission. Saving two Chinese from their plight was a rehearsal for what lay ahead. He was still speculating on the challenges to come when he drifted quietly asleep.

The long day had taken its toll and he fell into a deep slumber. Hours glided softly past. It was the dead of night when the visitor came. Slattery was dreaming serenely of paradise. He did not hear the noise as someone opened the door and slipped swiftly into the cabin. He felt nothing until it was far too late.

Any hopes that Genevieve had of escaping her role as an accompanist were shattered the following morning. To ensure a degree of privacy, she had an early breakfast in a saloon that was almost empty, but she was not alone for long. Maxine Gilpatrick swooped on her.

"Good morning!" she said, kissing Genevieve on both cheeks before sitting beside her. "Well, what a lovely surprise! I didn't expect you to be up just yet."

"I like to make an early start, Maxine."

"So do I. As a matter of fact, I've just taken a turn around the deck to work up an appetite. I'm famished."

"What about your husband?" asked Genevieve.

"Oh, Rance sleeps until midmorning, and I don't want to lie there and listen to him snoring. But I'm so glad that I caught you, Jenny. By the way," she added, "you don't mind me calling you that, do you?"

"Not at all."

"Rance said you were more of a Genevieve, but that's a real mouthful for me."

"I answer to both names, Maxine."

"That's what I thought. You English are always so obliging. Anyway," she plunged on, "I've got some good news. The song recital is a certainty."

Genevieve quailed inwardly. "It's been arranged already?"

"No, but Rance promised to fix it. When he does that, things always happen."

"I see."

"It's wonderful to have a husband who can wave a magic wand for you. And I so want to give this performance, Jenny. We'll have a captive audience. It's going to be a great occasion." She saw the doubt in the other's eye. "What's the trouble?"

"I'd hate to let you down, Maxine."

"There's no chance of that."

"You're a professional and I'm just a floundering amateur."

"Don't be so modest," said Maxine, patting her on the back. "You've got a great touch on that piano. I heard you, remember. You played all those pieces without a note of music in front of you."

"I'd be much more nervous with a big audience."

"Not with me beside you. I got enough confidence for the pair of us."

"That's true," said Genevieve with a smile. "And they'll be too busy enjoying your songs to pay much attention to me. Well," she decided with obvious reluctance, "if you're willing to take a chance with me, then I'll try my best."

"You'll be a star!"

"That's your role, Maxine. I'm the invisible pianist."

"With looks like yours? Not a hope. You'll be as invisible as Niagara Falls."

"What about your repertoire?"

"I've already started working on that," said Maxine. "We know we've got the music for Stephen Foster's songs, so we'll include two or three of those. I have some old favorites that I want to work in and, as a tribute to you, I'd very much like to include something from England."

"We don't have any music."

"We'll rustle it up from somewhere. The orchestra will lend us what we need. I wasn't listening all that keenly last night but I thought I heard them playing 'Greensleeves' at one point. Was I right?"

"Yes, Maxine."

"There you are, then. We have our English folk song."

The waiter arrived with Genevieve's breakfast and took Maxine's order. Other people were starting to drift into the room, but the women were too absorbed in their plans to notice any of them. Maxine's enthusiasm helped to steady Genevieve's nerve. The latter actually began to look forward to the event.

"What about rehearsals?" she asked.

"We need half a dozen," said Maxine. "I'm out of practice."

"We can't just take over the piano in the Ladies' Boudoir."

"Not while the others are around, anyway, that's for sure. Apart from anything else, we don't want to give anything away. When they turn up for the concert, I want them to be surprised by the choice of songs."

"So when do we rehearse?"

"When nobody else is in there," said Maxine. "Before breakfast and last thing at night. We'd have the place to ourselves then. Also," she went on, "there's a piano in the room where the orchestra plays. We can rehearse there sometimes. Rance will speak to the conductor. He'll sort everything out."

"You have a very supportive husband."

Maxine grinned. "He comes in useful sometimes."

"How long have you been married?"

"Only a month, Jenny, but we've known each other for a long time. It was always on the cards. I didn't want to go on singing my heart out in saloons, and Rance needed someone to look after him. So here we are." She made a sweeping gesture with her arm. "This is a sort of delayed honeymoon."

"Where are you going?"

"Tokyo and Shanghai. Rance wants to mix business with pleasure."

"What sort of business is he involved in?"

"Any kind that makes money."

"I see."

"That's what really drives him, whereas I have no head at all for business. Rance will have one kind of honeymoon, I'll have another."

"I hope you enjoy it, Maxine."

"I will now. I know it."

Genevieve felt a sudden lurch. She wished that she did not like the woman so much. Maxine Gilpatrick was investing a great deal of expectation in the concert and Genevieve did not want her to be let down. At the same time, she knew that she was there to quiz Gilpatrick's wife and gain as much information from her as possible. Having met Gilpatrick, she had no qualms about deceiving him, but Maxine was different. She was offering sincere friendship. Sooner or later, Genevieve would have to betray her. Doubt flickered briefly across her face.

"What's wrong?" asked Maxine.

"Nothing," replied Genevieve, forcing a smile.

"You look worried."

"I'll be fine when I've had more time to practice. Until yesterday, I hadn't played a piano for months."

"So what?" said Maxine. "You won't have to play a Beethoven piano concerto. All you have to do is to tinkle away while I sing. You've heard me in action, Jenny. When I turn on the full power, nobody will even hear the piano."

Genevieve shared in her laughter, but her reservations did not disappear. Though she would do her utmost to ensnare Rance Gilpatrick by means of his wife, she did not relish the experience. There could be severe discomfort ahead.

Breakfast with Rutherford Blaine was an excellent way to start the day. Dillman shared a table with him in a corner where he could keep the whole room under observation. Blaine was singing the praises of the *Minnesota*.

"To be frank, Mr. Dillman," he said, sipping his coffee, "I hadn't expected this degree of luxury."

"It can hold its own with most liners afloat."

"The designer is obviously a man of great experience."

"That's where you're wrong," said Dillman knowledgeably. "This vessel was designed by someone with very little practical experience of maritime architecture."

"Oh?"

"His name is William Fairburn. He left school at fourteen to work in an ironworks. He's a remarkable young man. That's why I've taken such an interest in his career. I think that my father had hopes that I might turn out to be like Fairburn, but I went off in another direction." He gave a self-effacing shrug. "I knew my limitations. I could never design a ship of this size."

"Tell me more about Fairburn."

"He went to Scotland to enroll at Glasgow University. It was no random choice. He wanted to study under a professor named J. Harvard Biles. My father used to idolize him. He claimed that Biles was the best naval architect in the world."

"Fairburn obviously profited from his teaching."

"He did more than that, Mr. Blaine," said Dillman, spooning sugar into his cup. "Fairburn saw an advertisement for a competition to design the two largest ships ever to be constructed in an American yard. The *Minnesota* and the *Dakota*. Until that time, the biggest vessel we'd ever built was the *Manchuria*."

"I sailed on the *Manchuria* once," said Blaine. "It doesn't compare with this. But I interrupted you, Mr. Dillman," he added with an apologetic smile. "You were telling me about this contest. Fairburn obviously won it."

"He certainly did. He beat off fierce competition, including an entry from his old tutor, Professor Biles. What an achievement for someone who was still in his twenties!" Dillman tasted his own coffee. "William Fairburn is a genius."

"He designed a fine vessel."

"No doubt about that, Mr. Blaine."

"It's a pity that he couldn't bring his skills to bear on the passenger list," said the other, lifting an ironic eyebrow. "That's the one area where the *Minnesota* has grave shortcomings."

"When you book a passage, you have to take your chances."

"I learned that the hard way, Mr. Dillman."

"What did you make of Mrs. Van Bergen?"

Blaine was discreet. "I've had quieter dinner companions."

"What about Mr. Kincaid?"

"Why do you ask?"

"I wanted to see if your estimate of him matched mine," said Dillman.

"How honest would you like me to be?"

"Completely honest."

"Then the only thing I can say in Mr. Kincaid's favor is that I'd prefer his company to that of a certain Catholic priest. It's a marginal decision," he stressed. "Father Slattery has many defects, but I take him to be a sincere man. I can't say the same of Mr. Willoughby Kincaid."

"Nor me."

"I don't think the word 'sincerity' appears in his lexicon."

"Did you believe that he was educated at Eton?"

"I'm not sure. What about you?"

"Oh, I think he went there," said Dillman, "but I had a strong feeling that he may have left before his time. My guess is that it's not the only occasion when Mr. Kincaid has been expelled. Rolling stones are not always people with wanderlust. They sometimes have good reason to move on."

Blaine was pleased. "I see that we're entirely in agreement here."

"His nonchalance was a little too studied for my liking."

"I found it rather more appealing than Mrs. Van Bergen's life story."

"So did I."

"Her self-concern was worthy of Narcissus. I do hope the lady will inflict herself on another table today. She was very trying."

Dillman's respect for the man deepened every time they met.

While he had a genuine interest in other people, he was highly selective about those whom he allowed close to him. Sufficient trust had developed between them for Blaine to be more open in his comments. Dillman appreciated that. In the same way that Genevieve had found a confidante in Fay Brinkley, he had discovered a sounding board in the older man. Time alone with Blaine was refreshing. He gave nothing away about himself, but his judgment of fellow passengers was astute. Blaine let his gaze wander around the saloon.

"It's very quiet in here this morning," he observed.

"That's surprising when there are so many people here," said Dillman.

"There's an obvious explanation."

"Is there?"

"Yes, Mr. Dillman. That clamorous priest hasn't come in yet. Father Slattery has spared us his boisterous presence. We must be thankful for large mercies. That voice of his could shout down the walls of Jericho." His eyes twinkled. "If only he'd stay in his cabin for the rest of the voyage."

The steward wheeled his trolley along the corridor, then came to a halt. After selecting some white cotton sheets, he put them over his arm and tapped on the cabin door with his free hand. There was no reply. When he knocked harder, there was still no response, so he felt in his pocket for the master key. Light was streaming in through the portholes as he let himself into the cabin. Intending to change the bed, he was startled to see that the bunk was still occupied even though it was noon. He took a step backward.

"Excuse, sir," he mumbled. "I not know you still here."

He was about to leave when he noticed the cord dangling from the pillow.

"Shit!" he exclaimed.

George Porter Dillman responded at once to the summons from the purser. The moment he walked into his office, he could see that a serious crisis had occurred. Mike Roebuck's face was grim. A hollow-eyed Chinese steward was trembling in a seat beside the desk.

"What's happened?" asked Dillman.

"We have a murder on our hands," said Roebuck.

"Are you sure?"

"Quite sure. This is Soong," he went on, indicating the steward. "He found the body about fifteen minutes ago. I've seen it myself, George. He was garroted."

"Who was?" He turned to the steward. "Was this in a first-class cabin?"

"Yes, sir," said Soong. "Number twenty-five."

Dillman was stunned. "Father Slattery?"

"Yes, sir. I sorry."

"It's not your fault, Soong," said Roebuck with a comforting hand on his shoulder. "You were right to come straight to me. Stay here until we get back."

"But I do other cabins, sir."

"Forget those. I'll speak to the chief steward. You've had a nasty shock. You need time to get over it." He turned to Dillman. "Ready, George?"

"Let's go."

While Dillman led the way to the upper deck, Roebuck described how and when the steward had found the body. He saw no point in asking Soong to repeat his story for the benefit of the detective. The steward was still dazed by the experience of stumbling upon a murder victim. When they reached the cabin, Roebuck produced a key.

"I didn't want to leave anyone outside in case it drew attention," he explained as they stepped into the cabin. "The fewer people who know about this, the better."

"I agree," said Dillman. "Apart from us and the steward, who does know?"

"Captain Piercey was the first person I told. And Dr. Ramirez, of course. He established the cause of death." He stared down at the bunk. "Not that it needed a ship's doctor to tell us that."

"Quite."

Still in his pajamas, Father Slattery lay facedown on his bunk with a length of cord trailing down from beneath his throat. Around his neck was an ugly red weal that shaded into bruising. The sheets were in disarray, suggesting a struggle. On the floor lay the priest's Bible with a leather bookmark protruding from it.

"Poor devil!" said Roebuck. "He didn't stand a chance."

"No, Mike. He was up against a professional assassin. First-time killers don't use a garrote as a rule. It's a weapon that needs expertise. The only consolation is that it was not a protracted death. Suffering would have been intense but fairly short-lived." He looked around. "Has anything in here been moved?"

"I made sure everything stayed exactly as Soong found it."

"What about the body?"

"Dr. Ramirez turned him over to examine him, then laid him back on his face."

"Did he give you any idea of the time of death?"

"Somewhere in the small hours. He couldn't be more specific until he's carried out a more thorough examination. Anyway," he said, widening his arms, "this is it. More or less what the steward saw when he came in here earlier."

"Good. I'll want to have a proper search on my own."

"What do we do in the meanwhile?"

"Find somewhere to stow the body, Mike."

"That's what Dr. Ramirez went off to do. We need a quiet room that we can pack with ice." He removed his cap to run a worried hand through his hair. "And we have to work out a way to get him there without being seen."

"It won't be easy."

"We'll manage it somehow. What a way to start a voyage!" he moaned, replacing his cap. "I know we have some shady characters aboard but I never anticipated this. I mean, who would want to murder a Catholic priest?"

"I'm afraid you might have a long queue of suspects."

"Why?"

"Father Slattery didn't exactly make himself popular. He upset a lot of people."

"That doesn't mean they have to kill him."

"Maybe not, Mike, but he won't be mourned in some quarters."

"Was he that unpopular?"

"He brought it on himself," said Dillman sadly. "I've never met anyone who seemed to enjoy ruffling feathers so much. Yet he obviously had so much to offer as a priest. I saw him talking to some Chinese in steerage. He knew how to relate to them."

"Don't forget what he did for those two stowaways."

"I haven't. Father Slattery was a good man who had an unfortunate manner." He glanced over his shoulder. "There was no sign of forced entry. Someone must have let themselves in to do their grisly business. Who has a master key to this cabin?"

"The chief steward. He would have loaned it to Soong."

"Check to see if it went astray at any time."

"I will, George."

"What about your own master keys?"

"They're kept in the safe. Nobody would get in there without dynamite."

"Right," said Dillman. "Look, Mike, I'd appreciate some time on my own to poke around. Something tells me that I won't find much, but you never know. There's usually some clue at a crime scene."

Roebuck handed him the key. "I'll get out of your way, then."

"How will you make sure that Soong doesn't spread the alarm?"

"By speaking to the chief steward. He'll put the fear of death into Soong."

"He'll have to know why he's doing it."

"We can't hide this from the chief steward," reasoned the purser. "He must be told. So must Peter Carroll, my deputy." He counted on his fingers. "With you, me, Genevieve, Captain Piercey, Dr. Ramirez, and Soong that makes eight."

"Nine," corrected Dillman.

"Who else knows about this?"

"The killer."

Expecting gratitude, Rance Gilpatrick was hurt when he met with a loud protest. Maxine was quivering with fury as she stamped around their cabin.

"The end of next week?" she complained.

"I thought you'd be pleased, honey."

"Pleased! We don't want to be kept waiting that long."

"It will give you more time to rehearse."

"A few days is all we need, not the best part of a fortnight."

"It was the only time they could fit the pair of you in," he explained.

"I just don't believe that, Rance. Did you tell them who I was and where I was trained? They're getting real quality in me. Don't they understand that? It's not as if I'm demanding to be paid. I just want to be up there on that stage."

"You will be, Maxine."

"Not at the end of next week. The whole idea will have gone flat by then."

"Calm down, will you?" he soothed.

"How can I be calm when you've ruined everything?"

"I did exactly what you told me, Maxine."

"But you didn't!"

She flung herself into a chair and folded her arms. Gilpatrick let her sulk for a few minutes before he tried to appease her. His wife was not easily won over. It was only when he promised to rearrange her public performance that she softened toward him.

"Try to do it properly this time, Rance."

"I will, honey," he said. "I will."

"There was I, telling Jenny how wonderful it was to be married to a man who waved a magic wand and got things done—and this happens!"

He stiffened. "I made a mistake. How many times have I got to apologize?"

"None," she said, seeing his temper rise and quelling it with a kiss on the lips. "Now that it's been sorted out, we can forget it and go to lunch. By the way, I invited Jenny to join our table."

"As long as she doesn't drag that Fay Brinkley along."

"She won't do that. Jenny could see that the two of you didn't get on."

"Good. I like to eat food among friends."

"Then what are we waiting for?" she asked, slipping her arm through his. "I'm starting to feel hungry again." They left their cabin and walked toward the stairs. "I didn't mean to get so riled up with you just now."

"You had no reason."

"Yes, I did. The truth is that I had a job to persuade Jenny to be my accompanist. She got cold feet, said she wasn't up to my standard. There's no way that I can keep her interested until the end of next week. She'd pull out on me."

"So? Find another pianist."

"I want Jenny Masefield."

"Use the guy from the orchestra."

"We make a better team," said Maxine happily. "Think about it. Two gorgeous women, dressed in our finery. We'll have the men eating out of our hands."

"They're first-class passengers, not patrons in a saloon."

"That's why I want to sing to them, Rance. I'm moving up a few levels." She gave him a nudge. "Don't you like to hear your wife being applauded by an audience?"

"If that's what you want," he said wearily, "that's what you'll get."

"Thank you! We'll have our first rehearsal today."

"You really think Miss Masefield is up to it?"

"Of course," she said confidently. "Jenny needs a spot of practice, that's all. She's good for me, Rance. I like having her around. We had a lovely long talk over breakfast."

"What about?"

"The recital, mainly. But she also wanted to talk about us."

"Us?"

"Yes, how we met. What our plans were."

"Did you find out what *her* plans are?"

"She told us. Jenny's having a long vacation."

"On her own?"

"Why not?"

"Women like her don't stay alone too long, Maxine. They're like magnets. They attract men without trying. What's her game?" he said. "Is she trying to hook some rich guy for the fun of it? Is she looking for a husband?"

"You're always so suspicious."

"With good cause," he said gruffly. "Genevieve Masefield is after something. I want to know what it is."

While he searched the cabin, Dillman was troubled by a profound sense of guilt. He regretted all the criticism he had made of Father Slattery, and he was sickened by the thought that he had been asleep nearby in his own bunk when the priest was murdered. Rutherford Blaine's joking remark also returned to haunt him. Blaine had expressed the wish that Slattery remain in his cabin for the duration of the voyage. That, in essence, was what would happen. The priest would be in no position to upset anyone now. Dillman felt another pang of remorse when he picked the Bible up from the floor and turned to the page with the bookmark in it. He found himself looking at the first psalm and saw that the last verse had been underlined in pencil.

For the Lord knoweth the way of the righteous: but the way of the ungodly shall perish.

As he put the Bible on the table, something fell out of it and fluttered to the ground. It was a piece of white sketch paper that had been folded twice so that it could be slipped into the book. Opening it out, Dillman saw a portrait of Father Slattery. It was uncannily accurate, and showed the priest holding forth in front of a group of Chinese passengers. Dillman had seen the work of the artist before. It was very distinctive. He did not need to decipher the scrawled initials at the base of the drawing. The portrait was clearly done by David Seymour-Jones.

SEVEN

Willoughby Kincaid timed his move well. After watching her throughout luncheon, he waited until it was almost over before he crossed to her table. Genevieve Masefield was sitting with the Gilpatricks and their friends. She looked up in surprise when the tall, elegant, beaming Englishman suddenly materialized at her shoulder.

"Do excuse this interruption," he said, offering a general apology to the rest of the table. He bent over Genevieve. "Miss Masefield?"

"Yes," she said warily.

"You won't remember me, but we met at Lord Wilmshurst's house."

"Oh, I see."

"My name is Willoughby Kincaid," he said, offering his hand. "I could hardly forget you, Miss Masefield. You look as radiant as ever."

"Thank you."

She shook his hand in the hopes of getting rid of him, but Kincaid hovered meaningfully. Genevieve had taken an instant dislike to the man. Even without Dillman's warning about him, she would have kept Kincaid at arm's length. The fact that he knew Lord Wilmshurst was an additional reason to steer clear of him. Her new suitor was sleek and presentable, but she was not taken in by his old-world charm. Maxine Gilpatrick, on the other hand, was drawn to him. Kincaid capitalized on her interest.

"And you must be Mrs. Gilpatrick," he said, turning to her.

"Why, yes, I am, as a matter of fact."

"A famous singer, I hear."

Maxine laughed. "Oh, I wouldn't say that, Mr. Kincaid."

"I would," said Gilpatrick loyally.

"I'm told that you gave the other ladies a real treat in the boudoir," said Kincaid. "Why deprive the rest of us, Mrs. Gilpatrick? A voice as fine as yours should be heard on the stage. However," he went on, taking a step back, "I didn't come to disturb you. I merely wanted to pay my respects to Miss Masefield. Perhaps we could talk later?" he said to Genevieve. "I'm sure we'll have lots to discuss."

And before she could even reply, Kincaid turned on his heel and headed for the exit. Genevieve was annoyed and discomfited. When she lived in England, she had spent years fending off men like Willoughby Kincaid, and thought she would be safe from such overtures in the Pacific. Kincaid was a definite problem. He was not merely persistent, he was resourceful. How he had found out about the song in the Ladies' Boudoir, she did not know, but he had flattered Maxine to great effect and she was still smiling.

"Where have you been hiding *him*, Jenny?" she teased.

"I don't remember Mr. Kincaid at all."

"Well, he remembered you. Where did you meet him? At a party?"

"Probably."

"And who was this Lord Wilmshurst that he mentioned?" said Gilpatrick with curiosity. "I didn't realize that you ran with the blue bloods."

"I don't," replied Genevieve. "Lord Wilmshurst was a friend of a friend."

"You obviously have some pretty classy acquaintances."

"Yes," said Maxine with approval. "Like that Mr. Kincaid. He's a real gentleman. I'm not surprised that he moves among lords and ladies. He's got style."

"Maybe we should invite him to join us for dinner," suggested Gilpatrick.

"Why not, Rance? It could be fun."

"Yes, honey. Someone to talk about old times to Genevieve."

"Please don't ask him on my account," said Genevieve.

"But he's an acquaintance, isn't he?"

"Not really."

Maxine grinned. "I got the feeling that he wanted to warm up that acquaintance into a proper friendship. Is that what worries you, Jenny?"

"No, no," she said. "Of course not."

"So what have you got against the guy?"

"Nothing," she lied, trying to sound unconcerned. "Besides, it's not my place to interfere with your choice of dinner guests. I'd never presume to do that."

"You *do* remember him, don't you?"

"No, Maxine."

"Oh, come on. Don't be shy," said the other woman, nudging her gently. "The guy is crazy about you. I could sense it. Something happen between the two of you?"

"It's not like that."

"Then what is it like?"

"Tell us about this Lord Wilmshurst," said Gilpatrick. "Who exactly is he?"

Genevieve took a deep breath but was spared the embarrassment of a reply by the arrival of a steward. Apologizing for the interruption, he handed a small envelope to Genevieve, then walked away. She took out the card, read the message, and rose from the table with mingled relief and urgency.

"Please excuse me," she said, setting her napkin aside. "I'd forgotten that I made an appointment. I'll have to go, I'm afraid."

There was a flurry of farewells before she swept away from the table. Rance Gilpatrick turned to his wife and spoke in a confidential whisper.

"Well," he said, wrinkling his forehead, "what did you make of that?"

"I think that note was from Mr. Kincaid, suggesting a rendezvous."

"But she didn't seem to like the guy."

"Maybe he's got something on her. Who knows?"

"There's one way to find out. We invite him to dinner."

"No," said Maxine. "Don't do that."

"Why not?"

"Because I don't want to upset Jenny."

Gilpatrick chuckled. "Could be interesting. Watching those two face-to-face."

"She's my friend. Teasing her is one thing, but I'm not having her put in an awkward position. Supposing there was something between them," she went on. "We all have people in our lives we'd prefer to forget. I've got more than most. Jenny Masefield is good company and she also happens to be my pianist. I'm not playing a trick on her."

"It's not a trick, honey."

"She doesn't want him at our table. That's enough for me."

"Well, it's not enough for me."

"Rance!"

"I want to know the truth about her."

"You only have to look at her to see that."

"Do I?" he said skeptically. "No, Maxine. I think she's hiding something and this guy might know what it is. Okay," he added, silencing her protest with raised hands, "I won't invite him to dinner. But there's nothing to stop you talking to him, is there?"

"Me?"

"Well, he's obviously an admirer of yours."

"I think he was just being polite about my singing."

"Mr. Kincaid is a ladies' man. Anyone could see that."

"So?"

"Take advantage of it, Maxine. Speak to him. Find out what he knows."

Seated at the desk in his office, Mike Roebuck looked at the sketch with a morbid fascination. Father Slattery stared back at him. The purser turned to Dillman.

"Where did you find it, George?"

"Tucked away in his Bible."

"What was it doing there?"

"I've no idea, but Father Slattery obviously liked the portrait if he kept it."

"Who is this David Seymour-Jones?"

"An English artist and collector," said Dillman. "He makes a living by writing about Japan and illustrating his work. He also sells artefacts to museums."

"How do you know so much about the guy?"

"Genevieve had dinner with him on the first evening."

"What was his connection with Father Slattery?"

"That's something we'll have to find out." He took the sketch from Roebuck and folded it up again. "But we have more immediate priorities. The main one is to keep the news of the murder to ourselves."

Roebuck shook his head resignedly. "We can't do that indefinitely, George. Our priest was not a man to hide his light under a bushel. He made himself known. People are bound to wonder why such a visible presence has suddenly vanished."

"We'll tell them that he's ill."

"What if someone wants to visit the patient?"

"We'll cross that bridge when we come to it, Mike. Meanwhile, we say nothing. If word gets out, it will create an atmosphere of fear and panic on the ship."

"Captain Piercey wants to avoid that at all costs."

"Then we have to work fast," said Dillman. "If we can solve the crime before the truth leaks out, we'll head off most of the problems. The passengers will still be shaken, but they'll also be reassured that we have everything in hand."

"Do we?" asked Roebuck balefully.

"Not yet."

There was a tap on the door and Dillman opened it to admit Genevieve.

"I came as quickly as I could," she said. "The note mentioned an emergency."

"The worst kind, Genevieve," explained Dillman. "A murder."

Shocked to hear of the crime, she was even more shaken when she learned that Father Slattery was the victim. Genevieve thought about the luncheon she had shared with the priest on the previous day. The dislike she had felt for the man now changed into a deep sympathy. When Dillman had related the bare details, she was full of questions.

"When was he last seen alive?" she wondered.

"Not long after ten," said Dillman. "I noticed him leaving the dining saloon. I assumed that he'd be going back to his cabin, but that isn't necessarily the case."

"Was he alone?"

"As far as I remember."

"What time was the body found?"

"Around noon," said Roebuck. "His steward came to change the sheets and put fresh towels in the bathroom. He walked in on a dead body."

"Where is Father Slattery now?"

"Safely tucked away, thank goodness. It was quite an operation."

"Yes," resumed Dillman. "We moved him when everyone else was in the dining saloon. Dr. Ramirez found an empty refrigerated compartment for us. Mike and I wrapped up the body and carried it down there."

"We felt like Burke and Hare," admitted Roebuck.

"Did anyone see you?" she asked.

"Luckily, no. We had the chief steward and the ship's doctor as lookouts."

Dillman took over. "I don't need to tell you how important it is to keep this to ourselves, Genevieve. As far as the passengers know, nothing has happened." She gave a nod. "Now, let's get down to business. We were invited on this voyage to keep an eye on a particular man. When a serious crime is committed, his name is bound to come up."

"Rance Gilpatrick?" said Genevieve. "I don't think that he could be involved."

"Why not?"

"Gilpatrick wouldn't draw the line at murder," argued Roebuck.

"Maybe not," she replied, "but he'd have no motive. He didn't even know Father Slattery. What possible reason could he have to kill him?"

"Their paths might have crossed," said Dillman.

"That's highly unlikely. I've spent time with him and his wife. Religion doesn't feature very much on their agenda, believe me. Rance Gilpatrick wouldn't let someone like Father Slattery get within reach of him."

"All the same, we can't rule him out. Instinct tells me that Gilpatrick may not be our man, but we have to check him out nevertheless. That's your job, Genevieve. See if there's any kind of link between him and Father Slattery."

"Right. What else can I do?"

"You shared a table with the priest yesterday."

"Unfortunately."

"Give me a list of everyone he upset."

"My name would be at the top, George. Does that make me a suspect?"

"No," said Dillman briskly, "but it means we take a close look at everyone else who was there. I'll try to track Father Slattery's movements throughout the ship. He got around. A lot of people will remember him." He handed her the sketch.

"Take a look at this, Genevieve. I think you might recognize the artist."

She unfolded the paper to study it. "David Seymour-Jones!" she blurted out.

"It's a good likeness, isn't it?"

"Where did you get this?"

"It was in Father Slattery's cabin."

"I didn't realize they knew each other."

"Nor me," said Dillman. "But it's a connection that needs to be explored."

"How?"

"That's up to you, Genevieve. You know the man."

Maxine Gilpatrick did not have to wait long for her opportunity. As she turned a corner on the upper deck, she saw Willoughby Kincaid bestowing a farewell kiss on the hand of a short, stout, middle-aged woman with a puffy face. With a winsome smile, the woman withdrew into her cabin and shut the door. Kincaid saw Maxine approaching.

"Ah!" he said, giving a slight bow. "We meet again, Mrs. Gilpatrick."

"How did you come to know my name?"

"Your reputation goes before you."

"I doubt that, Mr. Kincaid," she said, looking him straight in the eye. "You don't need to flatter me. Until this voyage, you'd never even heard of me."

"That, alas, is true," he confessed, hand on heart. "But I am aware of you now, and I delight in the acquaintance. My spies are very efficient. They keep me well informed."

"I'm not sure I like the sound of that."

"It's not as sinister as it might seem. Yesterday, I understand, you gave the most wonderful rendition of 'Beautiful Dreamer.' Miss Masefield was at the piano."

"Who told you that?"

He pointed to the cabin door. "Mrs. Van Bergen," he explained. "The lady you saw a moment ago. We dined together last night. Mrs. Van Bergen and I discovered a mutual passion for bridge. As it happens, it turned out to be the one way to keep her quiet. She's a dear, warmhearted lady, but she does tend to be rather loquacious, I fear. At the bridge table, however, she's all concentration. We were ideal partners."

"Go on," said Maxine, watching him carefully.

"Mrs. Van Bergen happened to be in the boudoir yesterday when you broke into song. She was so impressed that she made a point of finding out your name. And that," he said, as if producing a rabbit out of a hat, "is how it came into my possession."

Maxine was amused. "Did you think it might come in useful?"

"It already has, Mrs. Gilpatrick."

"What were you doing here?"

"Escorting my bridge partner back to her cabin."

"You spread yourself around, Mr. Kincaid."

"I enjoy making new friends."

"So I see. How well do you know Jenny?"

"Jenny?" he echoed.

"Jenny Masefield."

"Oh, of course. I'm sorry. I was mystified for a moment. I always think of her as Genevieve. It's such a pretty name. And so appropriate."

"That's what my husband thinks."

"He's a shrewd man, Mrs. Gilpatrick. And he has excellent taste."

"You haven't answered my question."

"No," he conceded, "and the truthful answer is that I don't know Miss Masefield very well at all. I was introduced to her at a crowded party. Mine was one of dozens of faces that must have flashed before her. She obviously doesn't remember me."

"Yet you remember her, Mr. Kincaid."

"Do you blame me?"

"Of course not. Jenny is gorgeous." She narrowed her eyes. "Who is this Lord Wilmshurst that you mentioned?"

"A mutual friend of ours."

"Are those the kinds of circles that Jenny moves in?"

"Apparently."

"Where does this English lord live?"

"In London, Mrs. Gilpatrick."

"Which part?"

"Mayfair, probably. It's a wealthy family."

"You went to a party at his house," she pressed. "Can't you recall where it was?"

"I'm afraid not," he said evasively. "Some friends took me there in a cab and I'd had a fair bit to drink by that time. All I know is that it was a splendid occasion and that this vision of delight called Genevieve Masefield wafted past me."

"I can see that she'd make more of an impression than Mrs. Van Bergen."

Kincaid gave a ripe chuckle. "I'd have to agree with you there." He stroked his mustache. "Do you happen to know where Miss Masefield is heading?"

"Japan and China. It's a round trip."

"Capital!"

"What about you, Mr. Kincaid?"

"Shanghai is my destination. If things work out, I plan to stay there for a while."

"You have business interests there?"

"Of a kind," he said easily. "Miss Masefield is on holiday, I assume?"

"Jenny wanted to see something of the Orient. She's a brave woman."

"Why do you say that?"

"I don't know that I'd care to travel so far on my own."

"It's a lengthy voyage," he noted with a smile. "Intense friendships tend to develop at sea. It's inevitable, I suppose, when we're all thrown together like this in the middle of no-where. I don't think Miss Masefield will be alone for long. Do you?"

———

Rutherford Blaine was reading a book in the library when Dillman found him. As a shadow fell across him, the older man looked up. He was pleased to see the newcomer.

"Mr. Dillman," he said. "We missed you in the dining saloon."

"I didn't feel hungry, Mr. Blaine. And I had some work to do. I just wondered if I could have a quiet word with you?"

"By all means. Take a seat."

"It can wait until later, if you'd prefer."

Blaine put the book aside. "Now is as good a time as any."

"Thank you," said Dillman, sitting beside him. "What are you reading?"

"James Fenimore Cooper."

"*The Last of the Mohicans?*"

"*The Pathfinder*. Equally bloodthirsty and with the same improbable plot, but I love his books. They've got such vitality. I just wish his characters wouldn't have such interminable speeches."

"Yes, they do go on at times, don't they?"

"It struck me that Mrs. Van Bergen might have been created by Cooper. She could hold her own with the best of his talkers." They traded a grin. "But I'm sure that you didn't come here to discuss her."

"No, Mr. Blaine."

"So how can I help you?"

"I'm not sure that you can, Mr. Blaine," admitted Dillman, "but it's worth a try. Do you recall the first evening we dined together?"

"Vividly. We had a delightful meal with Mr. and Mrs. Chang."

"That's right."

"I can tell you every item on the menu, if you wish."

Dillman gave a brief smile. "That won't be necessary, Mr. Blaine. All that I want to know is whether or not you saw him as well."

"Saw whom?"

"The man who was watching us."

"I didn't know that anyone was. Are you sure about this?"

"Fairly sure."

Blaine was concerned. "When did you become aware of it, Mr. Dillman?"

"Towards the end of the meal. When we were alone together."

"Did you see who the man was?"

"No," said Dillman. "When I turned around, he'd gone."

"Yes, I remember now. You were distracted for a moment. I thought you were looking for someone. Now I know why."

"You saw nothing, then?"

"Nothing and nobody. I was too preoccupied."

"What about later on, Mr. Blaine?"

"Later on?"

"Yes," said Dillman patiently. "After we parted company that night. Presumably you went back to your cabin."

"Straightaway. I was tired."

"Did you see anyone lurking about in the corridor?"

"Not a soul. Why? Did you?"

"Yes and no," explained Dillman. "I didn't so much see him as become aware of his presence. When I went into my cabin, there was definitely someone outside. I waited a few minutes and opened the door again."

"What happened?"

"I caught a glimpse of someone disappearing around the corner."

"Was it the same man you saw earlier?"

"I think so, Mr. Blaine, but I couldn't be certain. I didn't get a proper look at him on either occasion. Since you have a cabin in the same corridor, I wondered if you'd caught sight of him."

"No, Mr. Dillman. This is the first I've heard of this man." His brow furrowed. "You don't suppose that it could have been Father Slattery, do you?"

"It definitely wasn't him."

118

"He must have been watching us in the dining saloon. He knew when to pounce."

"This was someone else. Father Slattery wouldn't have run away."

"That's true."

"I chased the man for a while, but he gave me the slip."

"How odd! And how disturbing! Have you reported this to the purser?"

"No, I wanted to raise it with you first."

"Why have you left it so long?"

"I was waiting to see if the man would surface again yesterday."

"And did he?"

Dillman shook his head. "Maybe I was imagining the whole thing."

"Or maybe what you saw—or thought you saw—were two entirely different people. Is there any reason why someone onboard should stalk you?"

"None at all, Mr. Blaine."

"Let's hope that it doesn't happen again, then. It must be quite worrying."

"I'd just like to get to the bottom of it. Since you can't help me," said Dillman, rising to his feet, "I'll leave you in peace to enjoy *The Pathfinder*."

"I'm sorry that I can't solve the mystery."

"Perhaps there isn't one to solve."

"I wonder," said Blaine thoughtfully. "You're an observant man, Mr. Dillman. I'm quite certain that you saw somebody. Who he was and why he was there, I have no idea. Do let me know if this kind of thing happens again."

"I will, Mr. Blaine."

"In the meantime, I'll keep my own eyes peeled."

"Thank you."

They exchanged farewells and Dillman went out of the library. Blaine picked up his book and opened it at the page he had reached earlier. He gazed down at the words, but made no attempt to read them. His mind was grappling with something else.

Fine weather enticed the majority of the passengers out on deck. The bright sunlight was deceptive, however, and many people returned to their cabins for warmer clothing when they felt the sharp pinch of the wind. Genevieve Masefield was glad to be outside again. The fresh air was bracing and helped to clear her brain. So much had happened in the past twenty-four hours that she was having difficulty assimilating it. Without even trying, she had been accepted into Gilpatrick's circle, and was now committed to a song recital with his wife as her accompanist. Having unwittingly aroused the interest of an English artist, she was also pursued by another fellow countryman, and feared that Willoughby Kincaid could pose a serious danger. If he knew Lord Wilmshurst, he might also be aware of her broken engagement, and Genevieve did not wish that portion of her life to be resurrected. Fay Brinkley was the one real friend she had made, but she did not sit easily at the Gilpatricks' table and was unlikely to be invited to join them again. Genevieve felt that she was cut off from her true ally.

News of the murder had come like a thunderbolt. She could still not believe it. Whenever she remembered the luncheon with Father Slattery, she was overcome with remorse. There had been moments when she hated the man. All that she felt now was sympathy and deep regret. Whatever his faults, he did not deserve to be killed in such a way. Genevieve had a real sense of loss. It took courage to embark on a mission into the unknown, and Father Slattery had taken on the assignment without a tremor. She imagined how distressed his colleagues in China would be when the dreadful tidings filtered through to them. He would not easily be replaced. The reflection only stiffened her resolve to help in the search for his killer. Until he was found, everything else had to fade into the background.

David Seymour-Jones was elusive. Having established that he was not in his cabin or in any of the public rooms, she ventured out on deck. It took her almost half an hour to track him down. The artist was sitting among the steerage passengers on the main deck, sketching a group of children as they played in the sunshine. Genevieve came up behind him and looked over his shoulder at the drawing.

"That's wonderful!" she observed.

He spun round. "Oh, Miss Masefield! I didn't realize you were there."

Leaping to his feet, he raised his hat in greeting. A change of clothing had not improved his smartness. He wore a crumpled suit of green velvet, a long scarf that was entwined around his neck like a boa constrictor, and a straw hat with random holes in it.

"I didn't expect to find you down here," he said, indicating the crowded deck. "You're rather out of place in steerage."

"I was looking for you, Mr. Seymour-Jones."

He was astonished. "Were you? Why?"

"I wanted to thank you for that portrait you did of me."

"Oh, it was only a quick sketch."

"It was extremely well drawn nevertheless."

"I hope you weren't offended."

"Not really," she said guardedly, "though I would have preferred to know that I was your subject. You took me rather unawares."

"I wanted it to be a surprise."

"It was certainly that."

"A *pleasant* surprise?" he said, fishing for a compliment that never came. "You were such a perfect subject for an artist. Your face has classical lines."

"Thank you."

He was staring at her quizzically as he tried to read her mind. Encouraged by the fact that she had come in search of him, he was disappointed by the coolness of her manner. It made him retreat into an awkward silence. When he tried to produce a friendly smile, it came out as an embarrassed smirk. Genevieve shifted her feet uncomfortably.

"I see that you're keeping yourself busy," she noted.

He glanced at his sketch pad. "Yes, Miss Masefield. Drawing began as a hobby, but it's now a compulsion for me. I've made dozens of sketches already," he said, flicking through the pages. "I like to get a quick outline down first, then put in the detail later. Those children playing, for instance. There was such joy and spontaneity in their movement. If they knew that I was watching them, they'd be stiff and self-conscious."

"Do you always sneak up on your subjects?"

"I'd hate you to think that's what I did to you," said Seymour-Jones with a look of dismay. "I draw what I see in front of me. You happened to be there at the time."

Genevieve did not believe him. "What about your other models?"

"One or two actually asked me to draw them."

"Did they?"

"Yes, Miss Masefield."

"Who were they?"

"The first was a Catholic priest," he said. "I met him down here yesterday. He couldn't wait for me to draw his portrait. He more or less insisted on it. His name was Father Slattery. You must have seen him around."

"I believe that I have," she said tactfully. "Why was he so keen?"

"He's a missionary on his way to China. That's why he made such a point of befriending some of the Chinese passengers. Did you know that he could speak the language?" She shook her head. "Not fluently, perhaps, but he made himself understood. Anyway, he asked me to draw him in the middle of this little group. I think he was going to send the picture back home to his friends."

"Like a photograph."

"Yes, Miss Masefield."

There was another long pause as he searched her eyes for signs of approbation. Genevieve felt sorry for him, but she gave no hint of it. Being forced to talk to him was in the nature of a trial to her. Under the circumstances, however, it was unavoidable. The effort of thanking him for a portrait that had actually unsettled her at a deep level simply had to be made. David Seymour-Jones had information that might prove valuable in the murder investigation.

"Did you talk to Father Slattery at all?" she asked.

"Why do you ask?"

"He looked such an interesting character."

"He was, Miss Masefield. And, yes, we had a long chat."

"Did he say anything about his work in China?"

"A great deal," replied Seymour-Jones. "He was a dedicated man. While I was drawing his portrait, he sat there and told me all about himself. He had a difficult life before he came into the Church, but he didn't whine about it. He was a Stoic."

"What did he do with your drawing?"

"Showed it to everyone else at first. He was so proud of it."

"That's not surprising, Mr. Seymour-Jones. You're a brilliant artist."

"Am I?"

"You don't need me to tell you that."

"Perhaps not," he said shyly, "but I would like you to tell me what you really felt about the picture that I drew of you. Don't be afraid to be critical."

"My only criticism is that I didn't know you were there."

"Supposing you had known?"

"What do you mean?"

"Would you have let me carry on?" he wondered. "If I'd had more time, I could have produced something far better than that. A color portrait with real depth to it." He bit his lip as he studied her. "I don't suppose you'd sit for me properly, would you?"

"I'm afraid that I don't have the time."

"Is that the real reason?"

Genevieve hesitated. "No, Mr. Seymour-Jones," she said at length. "I suppose the truth is that the idea doesn't really appeal to me. That's no reflection on your talent, by the way. I'd just be far too self-conscious as a model."

"That's why I drew the portrait when you weren't looking."

"So I understand," she replied, concealing her resentment behind a polite smile. "In any case," she went on, looking around, "you don't need me when you have so many other people to draw. By the time you've finished, that sketchbook of yours will be like a photograph album of the passenger list."

"It already is, Miss Masefield. I could show you, if you like."

"Another time, perhaps."

"They're not all portraits," he said, eager to secure her interest. "Most of them are just scenes that appeal to me. Children playing, for example. Or birds circling the ship. Or a group of people at the card table." He flicked through the pages. "I even made one sketch of an argument."

"Argument?"

"Yes, Miss Masefield. It went on for a long time. Father Slattery was waving his arms around like a windmill. I don't think he'd want to see that particular sketch. It wasn't very flattering of either of them."

Genevieve's ears pricked up. "When was this argument?"

"Yesterday afternoon. On the upper deck."

"And Father Slattery was involved?"

"See for yourself," he said, finding the appropriate page. "It's rather hazy, I'm afraid, but it does catch the spirit of the moment. There was no love lost between them."

Genevieve looked at the drawing with the utmost interest. Though the figures were only drawn in outline, she recognized Father Slattery's distinctive pose, a finger raised in condemnation. Facing him was a short, neat figure in a suit, waving an arm in anger. A few deft lines from the artist indicated an Asiatic cast of feature.

"Who is this man?" she asked.

"You must tell me that. I don't know his name."

"How can I help you?"

"Because he was sitting at your table yesterday," he told her. "A Japanese gentleman and his wife. That's what puzzled me earlier when I mentioned Father Slattery. You know him better than I do. Why did you pretend that you'd only seen him around when you were seated right next to him during luncheon?"

Genevieve suddenly felt very uneasy. David Seymour-Jones smiled hopelessly.

"I never take my eyes off you in that dining saloon," he confessed.

When he returned to Father Slattery's cabin, Dillman was able to carry out a more thorough search. The presence of the dead man had been inhibiting. As he went through Slattery's belongings, he felt that he was trespassing. There was nothing to hinder him now. He was systematic, working his way steadily through each part of the cabin and putting items of special interest on the table. He was forcibly struck by the lack of any luxuries. Other first-class cabins had wardrobes bulging with expensive clothes and drawers full of costly accessories. Father Slattery owned nothing of real monetary value. His belongings had a sobering simplicity to them. While he might have briefly enjoyed the facilities of first-class travel, he embraced poverty willingly. Dillman noticed how many times his vestments had been repaired and his socks darned. During his short occupation, he had made the cabin his own. A crucifix stood on the table, a framed image of the Virgin Mary hung on the wall, and a pile of Catholic tracts was in a drawer. Another drawer contained a well-thumbed Chinese-English dictionary.

The item that was most useful to Dillman was the priest's diary. It was a large volume, bound in black leather and devoting a whole page to each day. Father Slattery was a conscientious diarist. He not only filled every available inch of space with record and comment, he also noted times of writing.

Dillman saw that the final entry was at 11:15 P.M. The priest gave a summary of what he believed had been a productive day. The fact that it was his last one alive added a poignancy to the account. Dillman was about to read the diary more carefully when he heard a sound outside in the corridor. He tensed immediately, wondering if the phantom observer had come back. Crossing to the door, he unlocked it and inched it open so that he could peer through the crack. Dillman relaxed when he saw that Rutherford Blaine was letting himself into his cabin farther down the corridor. Dillman closed the door and locked it again. He was soon going through every line that Slattery had written since coming aboard.

A tap on the door made him sit up. If someone had come in search of Father Slattery, it was safer to ignore them and wait until they went away. But the caller did not wish to be ignored. The second tap was accompanied by a familiar voice.

"George? Are you still in there? It's me."

Dillman unlocked the door to admit his friend. Roebuck looked harassed.

"What's the trouble, Mike?" he asked.

"Who'd be a purser?" complained the other. "It's a dog's life."

"More problems?"

"I'm afraid so. Someone left a tap running in a bath on the promenade deck and it overflowed like crazy. The couple in the cabin below are livid. They didn't expect to have a waterfall through their ceiling."

"That's a reasonable complaint."

"The next one wasn't," said Roebuck. "A Russian woman on the upper deck reported a missing dog. How do you lose a Borzoi, for God's sake? It's almost as big as her. The worst thing was that she seemed to think I was responsible. She demanded to be taken to the captain. The skipper would have thanked me for that!"

"Anything else?"

"A string of complaints about the smell from the kitchens,

and then the trickiest thing of all. That's why I came in search of you."

"What's happened?"

"Some jewelry's been taken from a cabin on the boat deck. The wife is in tears, apparently. We do advise everyone to leave anything of real value in our safe but some people never listen. Anyway, this man insists on seeing you, George."

"Me?"

"He wants the ship's detective in person."

"How much is the jewelry worth?"

"Over five thousand dollars, apparently."

"What's the passenger's name?"

"Mr. Hayashi. He was hopping mad. That's unusual in my experience. The Japanese have such rigid self-control as a rule. Anyway, Mr. Hayashi won't deal with anyone but you."

Dillman sighed. "Then I suppose I'll have to see him. It's the last thing I want to do when we're in the middle of a murder investigation, but Mr. Hayashi is entitled to our best efforts. We can't let someone get away with five thousand dollars' worth of . . ." He broke off as a memory was triggered. "Wait a minute," he said. "Mr. Hayashi?"

"That's right, George."

"How many passengers of that name do we have aboard?" asked Dillman, taking a slip of paper from his pocket. "There can't be many."

"There are only two, Mr. Hayashi and his wife."

"Then this must be him," decided Dillman, looking at the piece of paper. "This is the list I showed you earlier. The one that Genevieve compiled after she'd dined with Gilpatrick and his cronies. There you are!" he declared, pointing at a name on the list. "I knew it. Mr. Hayashi."

"Even friends of Gilpatrick want their jewelry recovered."

"Do they, Mike?"

"What do you mean?"

"People with that kind of money to throw around know how

to safeguard their valuables. I'm wondering if there really has been a theft from the boat deck."

"Why else would Hayashi report it?"

"To smoke me out," said Dillman. "I detect Gilpatrick's hand behind this. He's using Hayashi in order to make me break cover. When you know who the ship's detective is, it's much easier to dodge him. I smell a rat, Mike."

"What are you going to do about it?"

"Find out the truth."

"How?"

"I take it that you didn't tell Mr. Hayashi my name?"

"Of course not," said Roebuck. "But I promised him that you'd be along directly."

Dillman grinned. "Then let's not disappoint the man."

Needing time to compose herself, Genevieve Masefield went back to her cabin and reviewed what she had found out. The meeting with David Seymour-Jones had been highly embarrassing, but it had yielded one result. The argument between Father Slattery and Tadu Natsuki that had started over a meal had been continued elsewhere. She had seen pictorial evidence of it. Natsuki seemed an improbable killer, but the incident had to be reported to Dillman. The fact that Slattery had some command of Chinese also seemed significant to her. Genevieve made notes of what she had learned, wincing when she recalled the way that the artist had caught her lying about the priest. Though she felt that she had retrieved the situation slightly, it was a bad mistake. More worrying to her on a personal level was the confession from David Seymour-Jones that he watched her so obsessively. It was his clumsy way of making a declaration of love.

When there was a knock on the door, she was startled at first, fearing that it might be him. Slipping her notepad into a drawer, she crossed tentatively to the door.

"Who is it?" she called.

"Me," said Maxine Gilpatrick. "Got a moment, honey?"

"I was about to have a bath."

"This won't take long, I promise."

Genevieve opened the door to see her friend standing there with a pile of sheet music under her arm. Maxine stepped into the cabin and put down her booty on the table.

"There!" she announced in triumph. "The full repertoire."

"Where did you get it all?"

"From the orchestra. I batted my eyelids at the conductor."

Genevieve laughed. "It obviously worked," she said, glancing at the pile.

"I thought you should have a look through it before we have our first rehearsal tonight. I've marked the ones I want to sing. But I'm no prima donna," she went on. "If something doesn't work, out it goes. Is that fair?"

"Very fair, Maxine."

"Good. I'll let you get on with your bath."

"Thank you."

"Oh, I forgot," said Maxine, pausing at the door. "I met your suitor earlier."

"My suitor?"

"The self-appointed one. Mr. Willoughby Kincaid."

"Ah!"

"I'll say this for the guy. He's got the nerve of the devil."

"I gathered that."

"When I met him, he was nibbling at the hand of some woman he claimed was his bridge partner. That's the trouble with him, Jenny. I wasn't sure what to believe about the debonair Mr. Kincaid. He can sure shoot a line."

"What do you mean?"

"Well, he tried to pump me about you, but I gave nothing away."

"I'm relieved to hear that."

"In fact, I turned the tables on him," said Maxine proudly. "I asked him how well he knew you and what sort of a man this Lord Wilmshurst was."

Genevieve became wary. "What did Mr. Kincaid say?"

"Very little. He wasn't even certain where Lord Wilmshurst lived."

"Chelsea."

"He thought it was Mayfair. Is that another part of London?"

"Yes," said Genevieve, "and parts of it are much more exclusive. I'm afraid that Lord and Lady Wilmshurst couldn't afford to live in Mayfair. It's beyond them."

"That proves it! Kincaid said they were very wealthy. Know what I think, Jenny?"

"What?"

"I don't believe that he met either you or Lord Wilmshurst. He only pretended to in order to be close to you. Watch him, honey," she warned. "I reckon that Mr. Willoughby Kincaid was lying his head off."

When Dillman found the cabin, he adjusted his cap before knocking on the door. Voices were heard inside and then the door was opened. Hayashi was a tall, thin man in his fifties with a gaunt face. He peered at the uniformed visitor over his eyeglasses.

"Yes?" he said.

"Mr. Hayashi?"

"Can I help you?"

"I believe that you reported a theft to the purser," said Dillman, deepening his voice to disguise it. "My name is Peter Carroll, sir. I'm the deputy purser and I act as the ship's detective as well. Perhaps you could give me the details of the crime."

Hayashi flashed a toothy grin. "It all a mistake, Mr. Carroll," he said. "My wife to blame. The jewelry not stolen at all. She mislaid it. We find it again. So sorry to give you any trouble. Please to thank Mr. Roebuck for me."

"Of course, sir. I'm glad it's all ended so happily."

"Yes, yes. Good-bye."

Backing into the room, Hayashi closed the door behind him. Dillman stayed long enough to hear a snatch of the conversation from within. He didn't recognize the voices but he distinctly heard the name of Rance Gilpatrick. His suspicions were confirmed. Adjusting his belt, he went off in the direction of the deputy purser's cabin, wishing that the man had a thicker waist. The discomfort, however, had been more than worthwhile.

EIGHT

Genevieve Masefield found the prospect of dinner that evening rather daunting. She would not only be sitting in the same room as a killer, she would be stalked by two wholly undesirable men. Willoughby Kincaid was by far the more cunning of the two, and she knew that he would try to ambush her at some stage. In his own way, however, David Seymour-Jones posed even more of a problem. Genevieve had somehow ignited a spark inside the man and become the unintended object of his passion. Kincaid was patently impelled by a kind of well-bred lust, but the artist was truly infatuated. While she could keep the former at bay, she would find it more difficult to cope with her other admirer. Genevieve was anxious not to hurt his feelings. Seymour-Jones was a sensitive man who would be crushed by blunt rejection, and she wanted to avoid that. At the same time, she could do nothing that might be construed as offering him encouragement. She liked him as a person and admired him as an artist, but his awkward courtship had made any friendship with him impossible. The moment she stepped into the dining saloon, he would be watching her like a hawk. It was disconcerting.

But it was the murder that really preoccupied her. The news that Father Slattery had been involved in a public altercation with Tadu Natsuki had shocked her. When she sat at the same table with them, Natsuki had been a most congenial companion, alert, intelligent, and extremely courteous. Even during the long debate with the priest he had shown immense self-control, though Genevieve did recall the moment when his eyes had flashed with anger. She wondered what had prompted Natsuki, later on, to confront a man whom he could never win over by reasoned argument. Even though Seymour-Jones had sketched at speed, his drawing had caught the ferocity of the exchange. Was the artist providing crucial evidence? Had the enmity between the two men driven one of them to commit murder? It was a chilling thought.

Dillman had told her to look more closely at the people around her table at the time when she sat beside Father Slattery. The women could obviously be discounted as the killer had to be strong enough to overpower a sturdy priest who was bound to put up some resistance. That left three possibilities. Genevieve eliminated Bruce Legge at once. He was too old and inoffensive a man to resort to physical violence. Horace Langmead was far more robust and, being younger, would have the necessary strength, but he lacked any real motive. His were essentially social skills. He was much more likely to snub someone he disliked than seek to kill him. Dillman was certain that they were dealing with a trained assassin, and Genevieve could not believe for a moment that Langmead was practiced in the art of garroting someone. Tadu Natsuki might be a different proposition. A compact figure, he was a man of quiet determination. She was forced to the conclusion that Natsuki had to be a suspect.

Eager to pass on her findings, Genevieve knew that she would have to wait until much later before she could confer with Dillman. He was pursuing his own lines of inquiry. One of her tasks, she reminded herself, was to find out if Rance Gilpatrick was involved in any way in the crime. That meant establishing some connection between him and Father Slattery, and she was not quite sure how to do that. Dinner became steadily less enticing. Her only source of comfort would be the friendship of Maxine Gilpatrick, but that was founded on deception. A relationship that gave her privileged access to Gilpatrick's circle brought severe misgivings with it. When she looked down at the pile of sheet music, she felt a sharp pang of guilt.

An idea struck her. In the hour before dinner, the Ladies' Boudoir would be relatively empty. Genevieve could practice on the piano without interruption. It would keep her occupied and help to relax her. Accordingly, she got dressed, selected a few items of jewelry to wear, then picked up the sheet music. Five minutes later, she was playing her way through "Greensleeves" and humming the words to herself. There were only two people in the room, a pair of ancient German sisters in almost identical evening gowns. They ignored her when she entered and made no objection when she began to practice. Someone else eventually came into the room.

"Oh, it's you, Miss Masefield!" she said, clapping her hands together. "Don't stop playing," she urged as Genevieve broke off. "It's so lovely to hear an English air."

"Not when it's played so badly."

"You're too modest."

"It must be years since I played 'Greensleeves.' "

Moira Legge was wearing a dress of cream satin that was more suited to a younger woman. Its skirt was laid in pleats on the hips and finished with a thick ruche. Draperies of chine ribbon came to a point at the front and crossed with sash ends at the back. The sleeves were composed of a bandage of ribbon tied in a bow at the elbow. The bodice was softened by a chemisette of tiny frills of Indian muslin. Considerable money had been spent on a dress whose style was inappropriate for her and whose color made her already pale face look almost ghastly. Yet she was clearly very pleased with her appearance. Genevieve was tactful.

"What a beautiful dress!" she said.

"Thank you," said Moira. "Bruce thinks that it makes me look youthful."

"It does, Mrs. Legge."

"One has to ring the changes on a long voyage. That's why I always bring a large wardrobe. But don't let me hold you up," she went on, heading for a small table. "I only came to collect something I left in here earlier." She snatched up a magazine. "I never travel without the *Lady's Realm*."

"It's an interesting periodical."

"I brought a dozen issues with me. You're welcome to borrow them."

"Thank you, Mrs. Legge, but I already have plenty to read."

"It's the photographs that I enjoy most," said Moira. "As it happens, I first saw this dress in an edition of *Lady's Realm*. And it was an article on life in Japan that made us want to visit the country." She held up the magazine. "Don't tell Father Slattery, but this is my bible."

Genevieve winced slightly. "I see."

"Oh, incidentally, has that friend of yours made contact yet?"

"Friend?"

"A charming man whom Bruce met at the bridge table. I'm hopeless at cards myself," said Moira with a giggle, "but my husband adores the game. Bruce has a system. It seems to work well. Anyway, he met this fellow and your name somehow came into the conversation. Mr. Kincaid was interested to hear that we'd met you ourselves. Has he been in touch yet?"

"Yes, Mrs. Legge," said Genevieve, hiding her distaste for the man. "Mr. Kincaid made contact with me earlier."

"A fascinating individual, isn't he?"

"I suppose that he is."

"Bruce and I bumped into him on the promenade deck today. He kept us enthralled for ages with his tales. Mr. Kincaid has been all over the world."

"Has he?"

"We're not exactly stay-at-homes, but he made us feel

desperately provincial. And he's such a handsome man, isn't he? I wouldn't admit this to anyone else," she said with another giggle, "but there was a moment when I wished that I was there on my own. Not that I don't love my husband, of course," she added hurriedly, "but it does no harm to a woman of my age to enjoy a little attention. Your friend is a positive delight."

"He's not exactly a friend, Mrs. Legge."

"Then I hope that he soon will be. He'd make such a perfect escort for you."

"Indeed?" said Genevieve, wishing that she would leave.

"We English must stick together," said Moira, lowering her voice and casting a glance at the German ladies, who had now dozed quietly off to sleep. "That's the only thing wrong with the *Minnesota*, isn't it? Too many foreigners aboard. It was so refreshing to meet someone like Mr. Kincaid."

"I'm sure."

"Did you know that he was an expert shot?"

"No," replied Genevieve, showing interest at last.

"He's hunted big game in Africa and India. Lions, tigers, that sort of thing. He must be very brave to do that. Mr. Kincaid shot an elephant once. He's fearless." She looked across at the old ladies again. "Play them a few verses of 'God Save the King,'" she suggested. "That'll wake them up."

"You proved your point, George," said the purser. "Pete Carroll wasn't pleased when he heard that you'd be impersonating him, but it seems to have worked."

"Only because I knew that Mr. Hayashi was one of Gilpatrick's associates," noted Dillman. "We have Genevieve to thank for that. She gave me Hayashi's name."

"I've been doing a little homework on him myself."

"Oh?"

"He's a businessman from Kobe. Some of the freight belongs to him."

"What is he importing?"

"Flour, principally," said Roebuck, "but it's not all going to

136

Japan. It seems that Hayashi has an office in Shanghai as well. Some of the stuff will be unloaded there."

"I wonder why."

"Put that uniform on again, then you can go and ask him."

"No, thanks. Your deputy's waist is inches slimmer than mine."

The purser grinned. "Serves you right. By the way, what happens if Hayashi comes here in search of the real Pete Carroll? Do you play the part again?"

"No, Mike. And the chances of that happening are remote."

"Supposing that Hayashi recognizes you?"

"He won't," said Dillman confidently. "People tend to look at the uniform, not at the man inside it. I learned that during my brief and inglorious time as an actor. Besides, there is a resemblance between me and your deputy. If Hayashi stumbles on the real Peter Carroll, I don't think he'll know the difference."

"I'll take your word for it."

They were back in the purser's office. Dressed for dinner, Dillman had popped in for a chat before going on to the dining saloon. Roebuck looked slightly less harassed. The irate passengers who had found water coming through their ceiling had been moved to another cabin, the missing Borzoi had been reunited with its owner, and the alleged theft of jewelry had turned out to be a ruse. The purser was able to concentrate on the major crisis. He had news to report.

"Dr. Ramirez has been able to examine the body properly now," he said.

"What did he find?"

"All the signs consistent with death by strangulation. There were no other wounds on the body, though there was a large bruise in the middle of Father Slattery's back."

"The killer must have put his knee there to gain leverage."

"That's what Dr. Ramirez thought."

"Did he give you a more exact time of death?"

"Eight to ten hours before the body was found."

"Is that a guess?"

"An educated one. Ramirez is a good man. I trust his judgment. We've had deaths aboard before," said Roebuck, "though they've always been natural ones in the past, of course. The doctor wants to help all he can, George. He has a personal reason for wanting Slattery's killer brought to justice."

"A personal reason?"

"Ramirez is a Catholic. That raises another point."

"Does it?"

"Yes. We're dealing with a priest here. It's a bit unseemly to smuggle his body out of his cabin and hide him in that compartment. I'm wondering whether we ought to let the ship's chaplain in on this. He might add some—I don't know—decorum."

"My advice is to keep him out of it, Mike. The more people we tell, the more likely it is to leak out. I'm sure that the chaplain is a discreet man, but why take chances? Besides," he went on, "I don't think that Father Slattery would want an Anglican priest to start chanting prayers for his soul. He hated Anglicans as much as Baptists."

"What are you?"

"An occasional Episcopalian."

"How did Slattery feel about them?"

"He thought I was ripe for conversion," recalled Dillman with a smile. "Anyway, Mike, for the time being, don't involve the chaplain. Agreed?"

"Sure," said Roebuck. "Any leads in that diary you found?"

"Plenty, if I can dig them out."

"What do you mean?"

"Father Slattery's handwriting is not easy to read," explained Dillman, "and he used some abbreviations I haven't deciphered yet. Also, he had a private code."

"Code?"

"Yes, Mike. He put circles around some names—mine was one of them, as a matter of fact. He drew lines under other names, two or three in some cases. And for some people, he resorted to exclamation marks. In fact, there was one name that had four angry exclamation marks after it."

"Can you remember who it was?"

"A Japanese passenger," said Dillman. "Mr. Natsuki."

The first-class dining saloon was ablaze with color and throbbing with noise. It was difficult for the orchestra to make itself heard above the tumult. Attired in their smart uniforms, waiters guided people to their tables and held chairs back for them. The printed menus gained praise for their design as much as for their contents. Earnest discussions were provoked as diners considered the many tempting choices on offer. Affability was the norm in such a heady atmosphere. New acquaintances were welcomed, established friendships deepened. In the center of it all was the captain's table, where guests of note and distinction were preening themselves. Serene and benevolent, Captain Piercey was the perfect host, talking to everyone at his table in turn and putting them at their ease. The elite members of the vessel were dining in superb style.

Viewing the scene from the comfort of his chair, Dillman wondered how relaxed they would all be if they knew that a ruthless murder had taken place. The knowledge that a priest had been killed in a violent manner would silence much of the shrill laughter and curtail most of the lighthearted banter. Dillman was impressed by the composure of the captain. Though he knew the grim facts, he did not give the slightest hint that anything was amiss aboard his ship. It was only when he caught the detective's eye that Captain Piercey showed that he had not forgotten what had happened in cabin number twenty-five. Dillman read the message in a flash. The captain was asking him how long they could sustain the pretense before the truth leaked out. It was an open question.

When he turned his attention to Rance Gilpatrick's table, Dillman saw that a change had taken place. Genevieve was still an honored guest, but Hayashi and his wife had given way to a couple whom he recognized as the Langmeads. The detective remembered that, like Gilpatrick, they had a cabin on the boat deck. It was only a matter of time before the gregarious Langmeads got to know their immediate neighbors. Genevieve was as poised as ever, though Dillman noticed that she cast an occasional glance across the room to a table on the far side. Following her gaze, he picked out the man at whom it was directed. David Seymour-Jones looked reasonably smart for once. Though everyone else at his table seemed to be chatting away, he remained aloof, his eyes fixed on Genevieve.

Her other would-be suitor was paying no attention to Genevieve. Having somehow engineered a place at a table close to hers, Willoughby Kincaid had his back to her and was holding his companions in thrall with tales of his travels. Kincaid's move had an effect on Dillman's own dining arrangements. He was sharing a table for six once again with Rutherford Blaine and the Changs. Angela Van Bergen was also there, but the absence of her bridge partner had discountenanced her. Hoping to dine with Kincaid, she felt betrayed when she saw that he had deserted her. She lapsed into a brooding silence and offered no welcome when the waiter escorted a new guest to the table.

"I hope that you don't mind my joining you," said Fay Brinkley, taking a seat beside Dillman and looking around the table. "I did want to sit in a smaller gathering."

"Small but eminently civilized," said Blaine.

"Oh, I took that for granted."

Introductions were made and Fay settled down with her new dinner companions. Having heard so much about the woman, Dillman was glad to meet her at last and knew that he could count on her for more interesting conversation than any supplied by Mrs. Van Bergen or by Willoughby Kincaid. Since she was traveling to China, she was very pleased to have Li Chang and his wife at hand to give her advice. Mrs. Van Bergen was polite to her but unusually taciturn. Fay struck up an instant rapport with Rutherford Blaine.

"So you're from Washington, D.C., as well, Mr. Blaine?" she observed.

"Frederick, Maryland, to be exact," he replied. "A little town not far away."

"We're practically neighbors. I live in Georgetown."

"I've been there. It's an attractive part of the city."

"Is your wife not traveling with you?" she asked, noting his wedding ring.

"No, Mrs. Brinkley. She hates trailing along after me when I make a business trip. Marie is a poor traveler, I'm afraid. She'd rather stay at home with the grandchildren."

"How many do you have?"

"Six."

"Heavens!"

"Do you have any children?" he asked.

"Unfortunately, no," said Fay, pursing her lips. "It just never happened."

"I'm sorry to hear that."

"We've got three grandchildren," announced Mrs. Van Bergen, entering the conversation at last. "Alexander, Waldo, and Louise. There may be more to come."

"You have such small families in America," said Li Chang with a grin. "I had five brothers and four sisters. My father bring us up on little money."

"All credit to him," said Dillman.

"You have brothers and sisters, Mr. Dillman?"

"One sister, that's all, Mr. Chang. That's what disappointed my father the most. His only son was not prepared to carry on the family business."

Fay turned to him. "What sort of business was that, Mr. Dillman?"

Conversation ebbed and flowed pleasantly throughout the meal. Though she was keen to hear everything the Changs could tell her about China, her main interest was patently in Dillman. She wanted to know where he was going, when he would return, and what he would do when he got back to America. He gave plausible answers to all of her questions and quizzed her in return. When Fay mentioned her work on behalf of the women's suffrage movement, Mrs. Van Bergen erupted into life like an extinct volcano.

"What nonsense!" she said. "Why on earth should women want a vote?"

"It's a basic human right," countered Fay.

"Then how have we managed so long without it?"

"We haven't, Mrs. Van Bergen. That's the point."

"Politics is a man's world. We should leave it to them."

"And let them get us into even worse messes?"

"Women have no place in government," asserted the other, reddening visibly. "Who would bring up the children?"

"Who brought up yours, Mrs. Van Bergen?"

"I did, Mrs. Brinkley."

"With the help of a governess, I daresay."

"Well, naturally. We do things properly in our household."

"In other words, most of the work was taken off your hands."

Mrs. Van Bergen spluttered. "What else are servants for?" she demanded.

"Most American women can't afford servants," said Fay calmly. "People like you do untold damage to our cause, Mrs. Van Bergen. You collude with those who want to keep us disenfranchised. I don't think that women are a lesser order of creation. I'm sorry that you do."

"Women can have power in China," said Chang softly. "We have a dowager empress and everyone respects her."

"Quite rightly," added Blaine. "Look at England. Queen Victoria ruled over a vast empire for more than sixty years. I know that she was only a figurehead, but she did exert considerable personal influence."

"We're not talking about China or England," said Mrs. Van Bergen obstinately. "We're talking about America, and I'd hate to see an American woman given the vote. We have no experience in such matters." She rounded on Dillman. "You agree with me, Mr. Dillman, surely?"

"I'm afraid that I don't, Mrs. Van Bergen," he replied.

"Why not?"

"I happen to believe in the principle of equality."

She was aghast. "You actually support this ridiculous idea?"

"Let me put it this way," he said calmly. "I've had the pleasure of working alongside women, and that taught me a great deal. Women can do most jobs as well as men and some of them rather better."

"Fiddlesticks!"

"I'm not sure that I'd go that far, Mr. Dillman," said Blaine, "but I do agree with Mrs. Brinkley that women haven't had a fair deal. Their time is yet to come. However," he went on with a conciliatory smile, "this is rather an emotive topic for a dinner party. I suggest that we discuss a safer subject or our digestions will all suffer." He turned to Fay. "How long has your brother been in the colonial service, Mrs. Brinkley?"

"Four years."

"Does he enjoy his work?"

Fay chatted easily about her brother. Her coolness during the argument had come in sharp contrast to the belligerence shown by Mrs. Van Bergen. Sullen and withdrawn, the latter said virtually nothing. When the main course was over, she spurned the dessert and excused herself from the table to retire. Dillman saw the hurt look that she shot Willoughby Kincaid as she walked past his table. Blaine hunched his shoulders.

"We seem to have upset Mrs. Van Bergen," he said regretfully.

Fay was blunt. "She upset herself."

"She no need to get so angry," said Chang. "We all friends here."

"What possessed her to explode like that?" asked Blaine, scratching his head. "It took me completely by surprise. She was almost as bellicose as Father Slattery."

"Father Slattery?" repeated Chang.

"A Catholic priest that Mr. Dillman and I have encountered."

"Oh, yes," said Fay. "I know the man you mean."

"Everyone on the ship must know him by now."

"He is rather memorable, Mr. Blaine."

"It's that crusading zest of his, Mrs. Brinkley," he said. "The odd thing is that I haven't seen him around all day. Have you, Mr. Dillman?"

"No," said Dillman smoothly. "He must be indisposed."

After knocking hard on the door, the man knelt down to peer through the keyhole. He took out a knife, selected a narrow blade, and inserted it into the lock. It was a full minute before he heard a telltale click. He entered the cabin swiftly and shut the door behind him. When he put on the light, he was puzzled by what he saw. The place had an abandoned air about it. He instituted a quick search. Sheets and pillowcases had been stripped from the bed. Towels had been removed from the bathroom. Nothing was on the table or the little desk. It was only in the wardrobe that he found signs of habitation. The meager supply of clothing had been neatly hung up. In the bottom of the wardrobe there was a pile of Catholic tracts beside a crucifix and a Bible.

The man took out one item and held it up. He shook his head in bewilderment. After a last look around the cabin, he tossed Father Slattery's clerical collar back into the wardrobe and closed the door. He had seen enough.

The meal was less of an ordeal than Genevieve Masefield had feared. Some of the credit for this went to Horace and Etta Langmead. At their most genial, the couple befriended everyone around the table and kept the conversation sparkling. There was another bonus. In talking about his business dealings abroad, Langmead aroused Rance Gilpatrick's interest, and the latter talked fondly of the Orient, saying how much he enjoyed trading with both Japan and China. Though he was careful to give no specific details, he did provide Genevieve with some information about his activities. While talking to Maxine, she kept one ear on what Gilpatrick was saying to the others.

Spared any attention by Willoughby Kincaid, she was kept under surveillance by David Seymour-Jones, but his unwavering stare gradually ceased to disturb her. Indeed, once the meal was underway and the conversation bubbled, she forgot all about him. When she did look up, it was usually in the direction of Dillman's table. Genevieve was pleased to note that he had finally met Fay Brinkley, and wanted to see how they were getting on together. However, she did not neglect one of her main duties that evening. Somehow she had to work the name of Father Slattery into the conversation.

"I don't know how I'll be able to sing after this," complained Maxine, finishing her dessert. "I've eaten far too much."

"We could always postpone the rehearsal," suggested Genevieve.

"No, honey. We stick to our schedule."

"It will be rather late before we have the place to ourselves."

"That'll give my food time to go down. Evenings are best for me, Jenny," she said. "Rance will smoke those damn cigars in our cabin. When I wake up in the morning, I croak like a frog. You should hear me."

"There's a concert on tomorrow afternoon," said Genevieve. "It might be an idea to go along to get some idea of the acoustics."

"They'll hear me, honey," boasted Maxine, "don't worry. If you can make yourself heard in a rowdy saloon, you can handle anything. But you're right. We ought to take a look at the competition. Let's go together."

"We will, Maxine."

"Listen, I don't want to monopolize you. It's lovely having you around, but you mustn't feel that we have to live in each other's pockets. Apart from anything else, it cuts down your opportunities."

"For what?"

"Tempting offers from handsome gentlemen."

Genevieve smiled. "I'm happy to forego some of those."

"Has that wily Mr. Kincaid been on your tail again?"

"Not yet, Maxine. I think he's biding his time."

"He can't touch you in the Ladies' Boudoir. And if he does get to be a nuisance, just let me know. Rance will take care of him."

"What do you mean?"

"He has friends aboard who can be very persuasive. They'll get rid of Kincaid."

"I think I'd rather handle it myself," said Genevieve firmly. She looked up as Gilpatrick burst into laughter and slapped his thigh in appreciation. "I'm so glad your husband is getting on with the Langmeads."

"They're nice people."

"They've been very kind to me."

"I like them both," said Maxine tolerantly, "but, then, I like most people. If he wasn't such a liar, I could even like Kincaid. Then there was Fay Brinkley. That woman has such a sharp mind. Rance couldn't stand her, but I admire someone like that."

"So do I. Fay is a good friend. In fact," she said artlessly, "everyone I've met onboard has been very friendly. There's only been one exception."

"Who was that?"

"A Catholic priest called Father Slattery."

Maxine bridled. "Not that guy!"

"You've met him?"

"It was difficult not to, Jenny. He was wandering around the boat deck yesterday, giving out tracts. He had the gall to ask Rance if he was saved." She gave a cackle. "I don't think his reverend ears had ever heard language like that before. My husband is not the religious type."

"What exactly happened?"

"They yelled at each other for a bit, then the priest gave up.

Just as well," she added meaningfully. "If Rance had lost his temper, things could have got out of control."

Li Chang and his wife left the table after coffee was served, but Dillman and Blaine lingered over a brandy. Though she refused the offer of a drink, Fay Brinkley stayed with the two men, supremely at ease in their company. Dillman felt that he had known her for weeks, rather than hours. Blaine, too, was enjoying her conversation. His pleasure was soon curtailed. A waiter delivered a small envelope to him. When he read the message inside, a flicker of dismay appeared on his face, but he swiftly banished it behind an apologetic smile. Finishing his brandy in one gulp, he rose from his seat and excused himself. Fay was surprised at his sudden departure.

"Who can be sending him notes at this time of night?"

"I have no idea, Mrs. Brinkley."

"You don't suppose that it was a billet-doux?" she asked teasingly.

"I doubt that very much. Mr. Blaine is married."

"Mrs. Blaine is thousands of miles away."

"He's a decent man," said Dillman. "I've got to know him quite well. I don't think that he'd dream of being unfaithful. In any case, it's none of our business."

"Quite so." She studied him for a moment. "You're a real enigma, you know."

"Am I?"

"Yes, Mr. Dillman. I haven't quite worked you out yet."

"What is there to work out?"

"All sorts of things. The obvious question to ask is why a handsome young man like you is sitting with a Chinese couple, a staid American, and that rather disagreeable woman called Mrs. Van Bergen."

"Where would you expect me to sit?"

"With a lady of your choice."

"I'm doing that right now, Mrs. Brinkley," he said gallantly.

147

She grinned. "*Touché!*"

"In any case, you're wrong about Mr. Blaine. He's not staid at all. He's a highly educated man with a wicked sense of humor. As for the Changs, I couldn't meet a more pleasant couple. And Mrs. Van Bergen was far less disagreeable than on the first occasion we shared a table." Dillman spread his arms. "I'm where I want to be."

"You're evading my question."

"Am I?"

"I've been on voyages before, Mr. Dillman. Unattached young people tend to seek each other out. It's perfectly natural, after all. And there's something about oceanic travel that does lend itself to that kind of thing."

"You're assuming that I'm unattached."

"Well, you're clearly not married."

"How do you know?"

"Because I've been sitting next to you for the past three hours," she said wryly. "Married men behave like Mr. Chang. Or, if their wives are not there, like Mr. Blaine. Did you hear how many times he worked Mrs. Blaine into the conversation?"

"I thought that rather touching."

"It was. I'm a great champion of happy marriages. I'm the victim of an unhappy one, but I don't feel at all bitter about the institution itself. I envy people like the Changs and the Blaines." She put her head to one side as she watched him. "What about you?"

"I envy them as well."

"Yet you've never married."

"No, Mrs. Brinkley."

"Then you must have someone in prospect."

"Not at the moment," he said. "I'm too fond of my freedom."

"Freedom can be very lonely at times, Mr. Dillman," she said quietly. "Even you must feel the need for company now and then. There are some beautiful young ladies on this voyage. Are you going to neglect them?"

"We shall see."

Their eyes locked for a moment, and Dillman saw something that had not been there before. It was a mixture of curiosity and invitation. He felt he was being challenged. At the same time, there was a hint of vulnerability in her gaze. Fay Brinkley was not making any crude bid for his affection. She was lowering her mask slightly. It was done with great subtlety. Dillman was fascinated. Genevieve had not warned him about this aspect of her friend. He held her gaze.

"I don't think it was an accident that you sat at this table, was it?"

"No, Mr. Dillman," she said. "I never do anything by accident."

It was not the best time for a rehearsal. They had to wait for almost an hour before the room cleared. When they finally started, Maxine Gilpatrick was feeling jaded, and Genevieve Masefield was worried that she would be late for her meeting with Dillman. She had so much to tell him that she was anxious to get away, but the commitment had to be honored. They stumbled their way through a couple of songs before Maxine found her timing. Genevieve, too, improved with practice. Schooled by the vocalist, she learned how to set the pace without forcing it and how to accommodate Maxine's various idiosyncrasies. Doubts still assailed her. She did not feel equal to the task, but she received no criticism from her partner. Maxine was very supportive. When they achieved a passable version of "Jeanie With the Light Brown Hair," they decided to break off the rehearsal. It was well past eleven when they parted.

Genevieve was hurrying up the stairs to the promenade deck, eager to get to Dillman. A man appeared at the top with a smile of greeting. Willoughby Kincaid leaned nonchalantly against the wall as she climbed toward him. Genevieve's heart sank.

"So there you are, Miss Masefield!" he said. "Where have you been hiding?"

"Nowhere."

"I searched for you all over the place."

"I was with friends," she said pointedly.

"Aren't I included in your circle of friends? We did, after all, meet in England."

"Did we, Mr. Kincaid?"

"Of course. That party at Lord Wilmshurst's?"

"Which Lord Wilmshurst would that be?" she asked, confronting him. "The one you think lives in Mayfair, or the one I'm certain has a house in Chelsea?"

He laughed merrily. "You've been checking up on me."

"No, Mr. Kincaid. It's the other way around, and I object very strongly."

"What have I done?" he asked, miming innocence.

"You know quite well. I don't believe you ever met Lord Wilmshurst."

"Then how do I know his name?"

"My guess is that you got it from Mr. Legge," she accused. "According to his wife, you met him at the bridge table. Earlier in the day, I shared a table with Mr. and Mrs. Legge, as you well know. You pumped them for information about me."

"What a suspicious mind you have!"

"I don't like being spied on, Mr. Kincaid."

"A little well-meant admiration never hurt any woman."

"Please don't bother me anymore."

He looked shocked. "Have I been bothering you, Miss Masefield?" He put a hand to his heart. "I'm desperately sorry. It won't happen again, I assure you." He stood aside. "I won't hold you up." He made a gallant gesture. "I bid you goodnight."

"Be honest, Mr. Kincaid. You never set eyes on Lord Wilmshurst, did you?"

"Probably not," he admitted with a laugh, "though I can't be sure. I do like to enjoy myself at parties. Faces all start to look the same after a while. But I did elicit a certain amount of gossip out of the Legges, it's true. I'm not ashamed of that. What else is a fellow to do if he wants an introduction?"

"Behave more honorably."

"Honor has no part in a romance, Miss Masefield. It gets in the way."

His laughter was so disarming that Genevieve found it difficult not to smile. She gave him a nod of farewell and moved off. Afraid that he might follow her, she waited when she turned a corner, but there was no pursuit. For that night at least, she had shaken off her incorrigible suitor. When she got to her cabin, she saw no sign of Dillman and feared that he had gone away. As soon as she let herself in, however, he was tapping on the door. He waved away her apologies for lateness and sat in the chair.

"How have you got on?" he asked.

"Better than I expected," she said, sitting opposite him.

"Did you have a word with your artist?"

"Yes, George."

"Well?"

"Mr. Seymour-Jones not only volunteered the information that he drew that portrait, he showed me another sketch of Father Slattery."

Dillman was intrigued to hear what she had gleaned from the artist. The name of Tadu Natsuki provoked especial interest. Genevieve also told him about the comments she had overheard from Gilpatrick at the table and of his meeting with the priest. It was a remark of Maxine Gilpatrick's that caught Dillman's attention.

"So he has some of his thugs aboard, does he?"

"Maxine said that her husband would set them on to Mr. Kincaid, if necessary."

"I'm wondering if one of them has already been in action, Genevieve."

"Where?"

"In cabin number twenty-five."

"Do you really think that Gilpatrick would have someone killed because he had an argument with him?"

"It sounds unlikely, perhaps," he agreed, "but we have to put

151

his name alongside that of Mr. Natsuki. Both of them crossed swords with Father Slattery. I'm not surprised that Gilpatrick has someone to do his dirty work. It would be helpful to know who it is."

"I'll see if I can find out."

"Check up on Mr. Hayashi while you're at it."

"Hayashi?"

Dillman told her about the alleged theft of the jewelry. She was amused to hear that he had turned himself into the deputy purser for the occasion, but she was also alarmed. It showed how keen Gilpatrick was to identify the detectives on the ship. If he realized that she was one of them, she knew that he would be vengeful. Genevieve began to doubt the wisdom of her friendship with Maxine. She was playing a dangerous game. It was the news about Slattery's diary that jerked her out of her fear.

"Mr. Natsuki's name was in it?" she said.

"With four exclamation marks."

"No other comment?"

"None, Genevieve," he said. "Now that I know about his argument with Natsuki, I suspect the exclamation marks represent a conflict."

"Was Gilpatrick mentioned in the diary?"

"No, but Father Slattery might not have known his name. If it was a chance encounter on the boat deck, introductions may not have been made. And from what you say, the meeting was nasty, brutish, and short."

"That was the impression Maxine gave."

"I need to do more work on that diary," said Dillman. "I'll have to interview the people he met since he came aboard— including Mr. Natsuki. The names are all in the diary. You concentrate on Gilpatrick and his wife. How did the rehearsal go?"

"Badly."

"Why?"

"We were both tired."

"What did Mrs. Gilpatrick say?"

"That we need more practice than she thought."

"It could work to our advantage, Genevieve. I know it's uncomfortable for you, being thrown together with her so much, but she's the best lead we have." He rose to his feet. "It's late. Maybe we should get some sleep."

"You haven't told me about Fay Brinkley yet."

"I was forgetting her."

"The two of you seemed to be getting on well together."

"We were," said Dillman, resuming his seat. "She's an interesting woman. I suspect that's what really upset Mrs. Van Bergen. She was the other woman at our table. When the subject of women's suffrage came up, Mrs. Van Bergen became aggressive. She believes that a woman's place is in the home, even though she doesn't seem to do very much in her own. Fay Brinkley cut her to pieces."

"I can imagine. Fay has progressive views."

"Mr. Blaine shared them. He and Fay had a real affinity. It was a pity he had to leave the table so abruptly. Heaven knows why he dashed off like that, but it must have been something important."

"Are you complaining?" she teased. "It left the field clear for you."

"In a sense. Fay and I certainly had a most intriguing conversation."

"Intriguing?"

"Yes, Genevieve. I felt as if I was being expertly interrogated."

"About what?"

"The life and times of George Porter Dillman."

"What did you tell her?"

"Enough of the truth to satisfy her."

"Fay is a very shrewd woman."

"I discovered that."

"She picks up nuances that most of us never even see. After all, it was Fay who first warned me about David Seymour-Jones. She was horribly right about him."

"Yes," said Dillman with a reflective smile. "Mrs. Brinkley does have a nose for the merest possibilities of romance."

It was almost midnight when he left Genevieve. Instead of returning to his own cabin, Dillman went out on deck to clear his head and to enjoy some solitude. There was nobody about at that time. The night air was chill, but he found it refreshing. A crescent moon shed a dull amber light. Silhouetted against the sky, the massive single funnel belched out smoke as the ship steamed on across the Pacific. Dillman leaned against the rail and stared out across the water. The murder investigation was at the forefront of his mind. Having assimilated all the information he had garnered from Genevieve, however, his thoughts drifted to Fay Brinkley. Their conversation alone had produced a mild frisson that he had been careful not to mention to Genevieve. He wondered why. He did not feel either threatened or tempted by Fay, and took her interest in him as a compliment. He liked her very much. She was not the first older woman to offer him affection, and she would not be the last. But Dillman was impervious to such offers, however discreetly they were made. Since he had met Genevieve Masefield, he had not looked seriously at anyone else. Beside her, even the self-possessed Fay Brinkley was invisible. That made it all the more puzzling that he had deliberately held something back from Genevieve. Was he afraid that she would be disappointed in her friend if he revealed a new side to Fay Brinkley? Or was there another reason?

The wind stiffened and he gave a shiver. It was time to abandon his speculation. Taking a last deep breath of fresh air, he headed for the stairs that would take him down to his own deck. He was still some ways from his cabin when he heard the noise. It seemed to come from a companionway that he had just passed. Dillman stopped to listen. When he heard clear sounds of a scuffle he went to investigate, but he did not get far. No sooner did he reach the companionway than someone came hurtling swiftly down it in a series of somersaults. Dillman jumped back as the man landed at his feet with a thud.

"Are you all right?" he said solicitously, bending over the man. "What happened?"

The victim groaned. He was stocky young man in a dark suit. Blood was oozing from a wound on the back of his head. Dillman pulled out a handkerchief and used it to stem the flow. He was in a quandary. Needing to help the man, he also wanted to pursue the person who had attacked him. He stared up the companionway.

"Who hit you?"

"Nobody," said the man, wincing with pain.

"You were involved in a fight."

"No."

"I heard the noise."

"I fell." The man tried to move and groaned again, clutching his arm.

"Stay here," said Dillman. "I'll fetch the doctor."

"No," said the man. "Leave me alone."

"But you were assaulted."

"I fell down the steps. It was my own fault."

"Someone hit you on the head. It's a nasty wound."

"Leave me alone, I tell you," grunted the man.

Holding his arm and gritting his teeth, he hauled himself up and swayed unsteadily. When Dillman reached out a hand to help, the man shrugged him away and went blundering off down the corridor. He was in great pain and still partially dazed, but he wanted no assistance. Dillman's first instinct was to go after him. Then he noticed an object on the floor and picked it up immediately. In the course of his fall, something had dropped out from inside the man's jacket.

Dillman was holding a revolver.

NINE

Dillman examined the weapon with care. It was loaded. The detective went after the wounded man to question him, but he had already vanished around a corner. Dillman searched for him without success, wondering where he could possibly have gone. He could hardly bang on the door of every cabin in pursuit of him. Abandoning the search, he then went back to the companionway where the scuffle had occurred and climbed to the top. The corridor on the promenade deck was deserted, and there were no indications that a struggle had taken place. Dillman reasoned that it had been short-lived. The fact that nobody had been aroused by the sound showed how quickly the fight had been resolved. When he tumbled down the steps, the noise the man made was partially muffled by the constant hum of the ship's engines. Dillman speculated on whether or not his presence had brought an end to the assault. Had the attacker simply pushed his victim down the steps, or would he have followed to inflict further damage? Whatever the truth, Dillman was grateful that he was passing when he did.

What mystified him was the victim's reaction. Anyone else

who was injured in that way would have welcomed help, yet the man had spurned it completely. He had not even admitted that the fight had taken place. Dillman wondered who he was. It was evident from his clothing that he had not dined in the first-class saloon, and Dillman did not recall having seen him on the ship before. Yet he had disappeared so quickly that he must have had a cabin on the upper deck. Dillman looked more closely at the weapon. It was a Smith & Wesson .38 Hand Ejector with a swing-out cylinder that was opened by a thumb-operated catch on the frame. He noted the locking lug under the barrel into which the front end of the ejector rod was engaged, thus securing the cylinder head at both ends. It was a refinement introduced by the manufacturer some years earlier. Dillman had once carried a revolver of that type in the course of his work as an operative for the Pinkerton Agency. It was an effective weapon, and the last thing he would have expected to find on a passenger.

The sound of footsteps down below alerted him. Thrusting the gun into his belt, he descended the steps at speed. Dillman reached the passageway below in time to see a figure walking casually away from him.

"Mr. Blaine?" he called.

He stopped and turned. "Why, Mr. Dillman. What are you doing about so late?"

"I was enjoying a walk on deck."

"Wasn't it rather cold out there?"

"A trifle."

"I lingered rather longer in the smoking room than I intended," said Blaine with a polite yawn. "I was sorry to desert you and Mrs. Brinkley like that."

"Not at all. You obviously had an important summons."

"It was a false alarm, as it happens," said the other with a bland smile. "I wish I'd stayed to enjoy another brandy. Charming lady, isn't she?" He gave another smile. "Mrs. Brinkley, I mean."

"I didn't think that you were referring to Mrs. Van Bergen."

"Poor woman. I hope that she didn't feel we were ganging up on her."

"We'll know tomorrow when she chooses her table."

Blaine pulled a watch from his waistcoat pocket. "Heavens! It *is* tomorrow," he said, putting the watch away. "I'm far too old to be up this late, Mr. Dillman."

"We all need our sleep."

Dillman followed him along the passageway and around the corner. Blaine paused outside the door to his cabin. He turned to look at his companion.

"By the way," he said, "have you had any more sightings of the gentleman?"

"Which gentleman?"

"The one you thought was watching us."

"My feeling is that he was keeping an eye on me," said Dillman. "But I haven't been aware of him since. He's either leaving me alone or being more careful."

"I hope it's the former. That kind of thing is irritating."

"I take it that you haven't been troubled by him, Mr. Blaine?"

"No," said the other cheerily. "I've had a wonderfully untroubled voyage so far. Apart from being ejected from my original cabin, that is. But one takes that kind of thing in one's stride. Good night, Mr. Dillman. Sleep well."

Their second session was far more successful. It took place shortly after breakfast. Genevieve played the piano in the rehearsal room used by the orchestra. At Maxine's suggestion, they concentrated on only a few songs, working hard on each one until they had refined their performance. When they broke off, Maxine was thrilled.

"We're getting somewhere at last, Jenny," she said.

"*You* are, Maxine," replied Genevieve. "You got better and better. I was more or less the same throughout."

"No, you weren't. You improved each time."

"Did I?"

"Of course," said Maxine, giving her a warm hug. "I'd choose you as my accompanist any day. Apart from anything else," she added with a cackle, "you don't try to pinch my ass like the men who've played piano for me."

Genevieve gathered up the sheets of music. "Look, I hope you don't mind," she said uncertainly, "but I agreed to have luncheon with Fay Brinkley today."

"That's fine by me, honey."

"You must be getting fed up with me by now, anyway."

"Not at all," said Maxine, "but you mustn't feel tied to us. Rance was saying only last night how surprised he was that you didn't spread your wings a little. Give all those single guys aboard a chance."

"Some of them don't need encouragement, Maxine."

"You still having a problem with Mr. Kincaid?"

"Not really. But he did try to waylay me last night."

"We can soon put a stop to that."

"I coped."

"Let me speak to Rance. He'll deal with it."

"No, Maxine. I don't want any violence."

"There won't be any," promised the other. "Rance will get someone to have a quiet word with Mr. Kincaid. That's all it will take. Tommy is an expert at quiet words."

"Tommy?"

"Tommy Gault. He works for Rance."

"Well, I don't want him involved in this, thank you," said Genevieve. "I had my own quiet word with Mr. Kincaid and left him in no doubt about my feelings. I don't think he'll bother me again."

"Good. He'll soon find someone else."

"Men like him always do."

"He's still got that Mrs. Van Bergen eating out of his hand."

"Who?" asked Genevieve, recalling Dillman's mention of the name.

"Some fool of a woman who's been taken in by him," she explained. "They play bridge together, apparently. In fact, it was Mrs. Van Bergen who told him about our little performance of

'Beautiful Dreamer.' That's how he got our names in the first place. Kincaid is a sly old fox."

"He certainly knows how to exploit people."

"Well, he's not going to exploit you, honey."

They left the room and walked along the passageway. Genevieve began to fish.

"I didn't see Mr. Hayashi at our table last night," she remarked.

"No, he was dining with some Japanese friends."

"His wife wears the most beautiful clothes. I loved that jewelry in her hair."

"Hayashi is a rich man and he dotes on his wife."

"What sort of business is he in?"

"I'm not sure but it clearly pays. Rance has had a lot of dealings with him. We'll be staying with Hayashi and his wife in Kobe. They're lovely people. Whenever I ask Rance about Japan, all he can talk about is geishas," she said with a snort. "What I want is one of those kimonos like Mrs. Hayashi. She's got half a dozen of them. Pure silk."

They came to the end of the passageway and stopped. Genevieve pointed.

"My cabin is this way," she said, "so I'll leave you here. Thank you, Maxine."

"For what?"

"Putting up with my mistakes on the piano."

Maxine grinned. "I didn't notice any. We'll have another practice tonight, Jenny. In the meantime, we can have a good rest from each other. Actually," she said, "it's a good job you won't be sitting at our table today."

"Why?"

"Things could get a little noisy. Joe McDade will be there."

"Mr. McDade?" said Genevieve with interest. "I've met him."

"Then you know how he can sound off. His poor wife must be deaf with that voice booming in her ear all the time. Anyway, Rance needs to talk business with Joe, so we'll have to put up with him."

"I thought that Mr. McDade was involved in copper mining."

"He's involved in everything, honey." Maxine grinned. "Just like Rance."

Mike Roebuck stared at the revolver in dismay. He looked up at Dillman with a frown.

"Where did you get this, George?"

"One of your passengers dropped it by mistake."

"We can't have people carrying weapons aboard the *Minnesota*. It's against company rules. Somebody could get hurt."

"Actually, it was the man who owned this who got injured, Mike."

"How?"

"That's what I came to tell you."

Dillman gave him a succinct account of what had happened and Roebuck listened intently. When his friend had finished, the purser had some surprising news for him.

"And this guy vanished, you say?"

"Into thin air."

"Not exactly, George. I had breakfast with Dr. Ramirez this morning. He was called out just after midnight to treat a wounded man. Whoever pushed him down those steps did a good job," he said. "The guy had a broken arm and a couple of broken ribs. Quite apart from heavy bruising, that is."

"What about the head wound?"

"Dr. Ramirez had to put in six stitches."

"Did the man say how he'd come by the injuries?"

"He reckoned he'd had too much to drink and fallen down the steps, but Ramirez didn't believe him. There wasn't the slightest scent of alcohol on his breath. He looked stone-cold sober. Anyway," he continued, handing the revolver back to Dillman, "I can explain how this guy disappeared before your eyes."

"Can you?"

"He popped into a cabin. Not far from yours, as it happens.

That's where the doctor was summoned. Cabin number thirty-seven."

"Thirty-seven?" Dillman was astonished. "That belongs to Mr. Blaine."

When the visitors came, Rutherford Blaine was seated in a chair, reading through a document. The knock on his cabin door made him stiffen. He walked slowly over.

"Who is it?" he called.

"The purser, sir," said Roebuck.

"This is not a convenient moment to call."

"I can't help that, Mr. Blaine. I need to speak to you urgently."

"What about?"

"Last night."

Blaine hesitated, considered the options, then reluctantly opened the door. Expecting to find the purser alone, he was taken aback to see that Dillman was standing beside him. Roebuck led the way into the cabin and the door was shut behind them.

"What are you doing here, Mr. Dillman?" asked Blaine.

"We'll come to that in a moment, sir," said Roebuck. "Is it true that you called the doctor to this cabin last night?"

"Yes. A friend of mine was injured."

"The name he gave to Dr. Ramirez was Poole. Is that correct?"

"Of course. Why shouldn't it be?"

"I'm just confirming details, Mr. Blaine."

"Jake Poole's name is on the passenger list. Check it and see."

"I already have, sir. Mr. Poole seems to have a cabin on this deck as well. Number forty-eight. It's around the corner. I wondered why the doctor was summoned here and not there."

"That's easy to explain," said Blaine calmly. "Jake fell down the steps of that companionway nearby. He was badly dazed.

Since my cabin was nearer, he came banging on my door and I took over."

"Was this before or after you met me?" asked Dillman pointedly. "It couldn't have been before, could it, Mr. Blaine, because you were in the smoking room until midnight. I must say, I find that odd. You told me that you didn't smoke."

Blaine became indignant. "Are you doubting my word?"

"Frankly, I am."

"Why? Look, what are you doing here in the first place?"

"Hoping that you'll tell us the truth, Mr. Blaine," said Dillman coldly. "When I bumped into you last night, you weren't returning from the smoking room at all. You were in that passageway to search for this."

Opening his jacket, he produced the revolver and held it out. Blaine gasped.

"Mr. Dillman found it when the injured man fled," explained Roebuck. "He couldn't understand why someone with a broken arm and broken ribs refused his offer of help. The very least that Mr. Poole could have done was to ask him to fetch you."

Running a tongue over his lips, Blaine looked from one man to another.

"I had a feeling that you were not an ordinary passenger, Mr. Dillman," he said with grudging admiration. "You were rather too observant."

"I'm employed as a detective on this vessel," admitted Dillman, "and I've seen far too much to be deceived. I suggest that you stop lying to us, Mr. Blaine. We mean to get to the bottom of this matter."

Blaine nodded. "You will. First, let me ask you an important question."

"Go on."

"What's happened to Father Slattery?"

"Nothing, sir," said Roebuck, exchanging a glance with Dillman. "I understand that Father Slattery is unwell. That's why you haven't seen him about."

"So he's still in his cabin?"

"Yes, Mr. Blaine."

"Has the doctor been to see him?"

"Of course."

"Now it's you who's lying," accused the other. "There's nobody in that cabin at all. The bed has been stripped and Father Slattery's belongings have all been tidied away into the wardrobe. Don't hide the truth," he demanded. "He's been killed, hasn't he?"

Roebuck paused. "Father Slattery died," he said eventually.

"He was murdered," insisted the other. "There's no other conclusion to be drawn. Jake Poole inspected the cabin last night." He turned to Dillman. "That note you saw me receive in the dining saloon was from him." They stared blankly at him. "You don't understand, do you? It was a dreadful mistake. Father Slattery was not the intended target at all. He wasn't supposed to be in cabin number twenty-five. *I* was."

Dillman thought quickly. He looked down at the gun and remembered the man who had been watching them on their first night. The same man had been lurking in the area of his cabin. The detective was certain that he knew his name now.

"Mr. Poole is your bodyguard, isn't he?"

"He was," said Blaine with a sigh. "Jake is not much use to me in that condition. Neither is that thing," he went on, pointing at the gun. "I wouldn't have a clue how to fire it." He indicated the chairs. "Why don't you take a seat, gentlemen? I think we have a lot to discuss."

When Maxine found her husband, he was sitting in a chair on the boat deck beside a short, thickset man in his thirties with rugged features and a cauliflower ear. As soon as he saw his wife, Rance Gilpatrick hauled himself to his feet and gave his companion an order out of the side of his mouth.

"Make yourself scarce, Tommy."

"Okay, Rance."

"I'll speak to you later."

Tommy Gault greeted Maxine with a gap-toothed grin and a raised hat. She gave him a farewell smile. Gilpatrick waited for his wife to sit down before he joined her.

"Tommy has warmed it up for you, honey."

"I feel sorry for him every time I see that ear of his."

"Feel sorry for the man who gave it to him," said Gilpatrick with a chuckle. "Tommy knocked him out in the next round. The guy was out cold for hours. Still," he continued, patting her thigh, "you don't want to hear about Tommy Gault's boxing career. How did the rehearsal go?"

"Much better."

"Is Genevieve going to be up to it?"

"When she's had more practice. She's still very nervous."

"So am I when I'm around you," he said with a lecherous smirk.

"Behave yourself, Rance!"

"This is our honeymoon, isn't it?"

"Is it?" she complained. "Then why do you spend so much time with your business associates? I'm beginning to feel neglected."

"Well, we can soon change that," he soothed. "Now, why don't you think up some ways in which your loving husband can spoil you?"

"I can give you a hundred at least."

"Hey, don't overdo it, honey."

"Why don't you start with a nice big kiss?"

He leaned over to kiss her. "There! That was a treat for me as well." He settled back in his chair. "Oh, by the way, Maxine, I need to ask you a favor. I want the cabin to myself for an hour or so this afternoon."

"Why?" she teased. "Expecting a visit from another woman?"

"Not unless she goes by the name of Joe McDade."

She was hurt. "You're kicking me out to make way for *him*?"

"Joe and I need to talk."

165

"But we're having lunch with him. You can talk to him all you want—if you can get a word in, that is. Joe McDade just loves the sound of his own voice."

"We need some privacy, Maxine. I never discuss business in public."

"There you go again," she protested. "I'm always in second place. You take me on our honeymoon, then tell me I can't even get into my own cabin. It's maddening. If Joe McDade is so keen to talk to you, why don't you go to his cabin?"

"His wife always takes a nap in the afternoons."

"What about me? Aren't I allowed to take a nap?"

"Not while I'm around." He squeezed her hand fondly. "I'll make it up to you, honey. I promise. But tell me some more about Genevieve. Did you break it to her that there might not be room at our table today?"

"I didn't need to, Rance. Jenny had already agreed to eat with someone else."

"Not that English guy with the mustache?"

"No," said Maxine. "Mr. Kincaid won't be allowed anywhere near her. All that stuff about meeting her at a party was a pack of lies. He never clapped eyes on her until this voyage. Kincaid was chancing his arm."

"So who *is* the lucky man?"

"It's a woman friend. Fay Brinkley."

"That smart-ass!" he said with disgust. "Genevieve can keep her."

"They get on so well together."

"That's what worries me, Maxine. I think they're two of a kind, only Genevieve knows how to hide it better. Underneath, I reckon she's just like Fay Brinkley."

"What do you mean?"

"Calculating."

"No, Rance," she said defensively. "That's not true. Jenny is sweet."

"Oh, she can be very sweet when she wants to be. But I think it's an act."

166

"It's not. I've spent time alone with her—you haven't."

"All right," he said, "what does she talk about when you're together?"

"Music. We've got all those songs to work on."

"She must talk about something else as well. Does she ever mention men?"

"One in particular. Mr. Kincaid. He's been pestering her."

"My guess is that she can handle that. What else does she talk about?"

Maxine shrugged. "You, sometimes."

He became wary. "Me?"

"Yes, she thinks it's wonderful the way you can fix things. Like the concert, for instance. Jenny is interested in what you do. She's asked me about your business dealings more than once. And today," she recalled, "she was talking about Mr. Hayashi."

"Hayashi? Why?"

"She liked him."

"Not in that way, surely?"

Maxine laughed. "Of course not. He's far too old for her."

"So what did she want to know about him?" he pressed. "Come on, Maxine. This is important. Try to remember her exact words. What did she say?"

Genevieve Masefield met him in the purser's office. Dillman was alone. He gave her a kiss of welcome, then offered her a chair. Still mystified, she sat down.

"Thanks for your note," she said. "I came as quickly as I could, though we didn't arrange to meet again until tonight."

"Something came up, Genevieve."

"That's what I assumed."

"I didn't want you to come to my cabin. There are too many people about. You might have been seen. Mike gave us the use of his office. We'll be safe here."

"Where is he?"

"I'll explain that in a moment," he said. "Do you remember

the incident that occurred when I first came aboard? That business with the cabins on the upper deck?"

"Yes, George. You told me about it. Father Slattery was involved."

"To his cost, Genevieve."

"In what way?"

"If he'd taken the cabin originally assigned to him, he'd still be alive."

"How do you know?"

"Because the assassin was not supposed to kill a Catholic priest," said Dillman. "The real target was the man I've talked about before, Rutherford Blaine."

"Are you sure?"

"Absolutely sure. Let me tell you what happened."

Dillman described his meeting with the injured man and his discovery of the revolver. She listened wide-eyed to his account of the visit to Blaine's cabin.

"But why should anyone want to kill him?" she asked.

"For political reasons, Genevieve."

"I don't follow."

"Mr. Blaine is a diplomat. He's on his way to Tokyo to hold secret talks."

"About what?"

"He wasn't at liberty to tell us that, but there's no question about his authenticity. He showed us his credentials. I'm not sure how much you know about the situation in Japan," he said, "but it's not entirely stable. There are certain people there who resent America bitterly. They didn't like the way our president acted as mediator when Japan went to war with Russia, and they've got lots of other reasons to hate us. According to Mr. Blaine, they've stirred up trouble and organized anti-American riots. He's on a highly sensitive mission, Genevieve. It's not difficult to guess one of its objects."

"Closer ties between America and Japan?"

"In all probability. The details don't matter. Mr. Blaine does."

"Is he still in danger?"

"Serious danger," said Dillman gravely. "When he was seen alive yesterday, it must have dawned on the assassin that he's killed the wrong man. He tried to stalk Mr. Blaine last night. Fortunately, the bodyguard got in the way."

"Where is this Mr. Poole now?"

"Recovering in bed. He can't do his job properly while he's there."

"So what's going to happen?"

"We have to take over," explained Dillman. "It's our job to guard Mr. Blaine now. The first thing was to move him from his existing cabin. That's where Mike Roebuck is now. Sorting out the transfer and making sure that nobody else knows about it but the chief steward. Mr. Blaine needs protection. The assassin will strike again."

"So we're not looking for suspects with a motive to kill Father Slattery?"

"Not anymore. We were completely misled there."

"I'm rather relieved," she confessed.

"Why?"

"I don't know, George. I suppose I felt rather ashamed of my suspicions about Mr. Natsuki. He was such a pleasant man. I never really believed that he was a potential killer. I know that he had that blistering argument with Father Slattery," she said, "but I fancy it was more to do with Mrs. Natsuki than her husband. She was cut to the quick by some of Father Slattery's remarks. Mr. Natsuki wouldn't allow that. He went after the priest to confront him."

"He sounds like a good husband."

"He is, George. So polite and decent."

"How discreet do you think he would be?"

"Why?"

"We may need someone in due course who speaks Japanese. That was Mr. Blaine's view, anyway. The man who attacked his bodyguard was not an American."

"Japanese?"

"Jake Poole didn't get a proper look at him because he was

wearing a mask, but he was certain that the man was Asiatic. He was short, quick, and skilled in jujitsu. That's how he got the better of him," noted Dillman. "Mr. Poole is a tough man. He wouldn't be easy to overpower."

"What are you going to do?" she asked. "Check all the Japanese passengers?"

"We already have, Genevieve."

"There must be dozens in first class."

"There are," he confirmed, "And well over a hundred in steerage. We haven't got time to work our way through that lot. There's a much simpler method."

"Is there?"

"We wait until he comes to us."

"How?"

"Mr. Blaine is a brave man," he said admiringly. "He refuses to be shut up with an armed guard outside the door. As long as he's in public, he's fairly safe. Especially if he has company, and one of us will always have an eye on him."

"In other words, you're using him to bait the hook?"

"It was his idea, Genevieve."

"Will it work?"

"I hope so."

"What about me?" she wondered.

"Carry on with what you're doing," he advised. "Just because we're after some political hothead, it doesn't mean that we forget Rance Gilpatrick. I'd like to know more about his business dealings with Mr. Hiyashi."

"I asked Maxine about that. She knew no details. But she and Gilpatrick will be staying with the Hiyashis in Kobe," she said. "So they must be close."

"What else have you learned?"

"The identity of another of Gilpatrick's associates. Joseph McDade."

Dillman wrinkled his brow. "Where have I heard that name before?"

"From me," she reminded him. "Mr. McDade and his wife

dined at my table on the first evening, He was the loud-mouthed man who sprayed his opinions all over us."

"I remember now. What's his connection with Gilpatrick?"

"I haven't a clue."

"Any other progress?"

"Yes," she said, keen to pass on the information. "We knew that Gilpatrick would have henchmen. I discovered who one of them is."

"Well done! How did you manage that?"

"I mentioned to Maxine that Mr. Kincaid had been hassling me."

Dillman tensed. "When was this?"

"Last night, after the rehearsal. He intercepted me on my way back to the cabin."

"You never told me about it."

"We had rather a lot of other things to discuss, George. In any case," she said with a dismissive gesture, "I dealt with it in my own way. But Maxine wanted to bring her husband in on it. She offered to get one of his men to frighten Kincaid off."

"What did you say to that?"

"I wouldn't hear of it. I fight my own battles."

"Or call in me as your heavy artillery," he said fondly, "though I don't think that I'd be needed somehow. Did you ask who might be brought in to warn Kincaid off?"

"I did."

"What was his name?"

"Mr. Gault," she said. "Tommy Gault."

Most people on the boat deck wore coats and hats, but one of them braved the cold wind in a singlet, a pair of shorts, and some boxing boots. Dancing nimbly on his toes, he swished the skipping rope over his head with increasing speed until he built up a steady rhythm. A small crowd, most of them children, gathered to watch him. They had never before seen anyone skip so well or for such a long time. In spite of the wind, the man was soon sweating freely. His face was glistening by the time that Rance Gilpatrick strolled past with his wife on his arm. Gilpatrick waved to his friend.

"That's it, Tommy," he said. "Keep in shape. I may have work for you to do."

When Genevieve spotted her going into the library, she seized her opportunity. Blanche McDade was a rather forlorn figure. She stood in front of the shelves of books as if bewildered by the range of choice. Genevieve came into the room.

"Oh, good morning, Mrs. McDade," she said. "How are you?"

"Fine, thank you," said Blanche, turning to see her. "Are you looking for a book?"

"Yes," replied Genevieve, pretending to scan the shelves. "I was wondering if they had any English authors."

"I like something with romance in it."

"Do you?"

"Yes, Miss Masefield. Joe always sneers at me for reading such books, but I adore them. And I have so much time to read these days."

"Do you know Thomas Hardy's novels?"

"I'm afraid not."

"They're not exactly romances," said Genevieve, "but I think you'd enjoy them. He draws the female characters so well, though some of them do suffer."

"I don't want anything sad."

"Then you're better off choosing your own."

"What about you?"

"I'm rather fond of historical novels, Mrs. McDade. People always seem to have had so much more fun in the old days. At least, that's the impression one gets from the books. The reality, I suspect, was very different."

"Oh, I'm sure it was, Miss Masefield. Life was very harsh. I remember the tales my grandmother used to tell us. They made our hair curl."

"Where did you grow up?"

"In Nebraska."

"Is that where you met Mr. McDade?"

"No, that was in Chicago," she said with a rueful smile. "We were attending the wedding of a mutual friend. I'm Joe's second wife, you know," she explained. "We've only been together for ten years."

Genevieve was surprised. "You seem to have been together for longer than that."

"I know. It feels like an eternity sometimes."

"Is your husband a reader?"

"He never has time, Miss Masefield. The only thing that Joe ever reads is the financial pages in the newspapers. He's a businessman. He always will be. I accepted that when we married. But he's a good husband," she said loyally. "I want for nothing."

"Except his company, I should imagine."

"Joe is a busy man. Besides, I do like to be on my own sometimes."

"Are you enjoying the voyage?"

"Oh, yes," said Blanche, taking down a book to examine it. "It's much more comfortable than I thought it would be. And we've met such interesting people."

"That's the beauty of traveling by sea. You have time to develop friendships." Selecting a book of her own, Genevieve flicked through it. "I understand that you know Mr. Gilpatrick," she said casually.

"Joe does. I've never met him before."

"He's a fascinating man. I was lucky enough to be at Mr. Gilpatrick's table last night. I've never met anyone who's done so much and been so far."

"That's what Joe says about him."

"Are they business acquaintances?"

"Oh, yes," said Blanche sadly. "My husband doesn't have any other kind."

"What about you, Mrs. McDade?"

"I have my books." She replaced one volume and took out another. "You must have met Mrs. Gilpatrick, then."

"Yes," said Genevieve, "she's a delightful woman."

"Joe says I must be nice to her. He needs to talk business with Mr. Gilpatrick after lunch, so he wants me to keep Mrs. Gilpatrick occupied. I'm not very good at that sort of thing, Miss Masefield," she said shyly. "I'm sure that you noticed."

"You'll have no problems with Maxine Gilpatrick."

"Joe said that she used to sing professionally."

"That's right."

"I wish that I could have done something like that," said Blanche wistfully, "but I was brought up in a strict household. My father wouldn't let any of us develop our interests. The only singing I was allowed to do was in church."

Genevieve exchanged her book for another. "What sort of business does your husband do with Mr. Gilpatrick?" she asked, reading the title page.

"They export things together."

"Copper?"

"Oh, no. Something quite different. Joe never talks about it to me, but I think it's to do with those catalogs of his."

"Catalogs?"

"Yes, he brought them with him to show to Mr. Gilpatrick."

"Do you know what's in the catalogs?"

"I haven't a clue, Miss Masefield. To be honest, I daren't look."

Annoyed with himself and in continual pain, Jake Poole was propped up on his bunk. His right arm was in a splint and supported by a sling. Heavy strapping had been put around his ribs. Dark bruises showed on his face and hands. Dillman was sympathetic.

"How are you feeling now?" he asked.

"Frustrated, Mr. Dillman. I want to be out there after that bastard."

"Not while you're in that state."

"He caught me when I wasn't looking."

"You're young and fit," Dillman pointed out. "If Mr. Blaine had been clubbed over the head and pushed down those stairs, he might not be here to tell the tale."

"That's the one consolation. I protected Mr. Blaine."

"Any idea who the man was?"

"None at all," said Poole. "He came out of the blue."

"Were you expecting an attack?"

"Not at the start, Mr. Dillman. I thought this would be a routine mission. It's not the first time I've kept an eye on Mr. Blaine when he's visited Japan. In the past, we had no problems at all."

"Why was that?"

"Because nobody knew who we were and why we were traveling."

"How did they find out this time?" said Dillman.

Poole was vengeful. "I wish I knew!"

The talk with the bodyguard was revealing. Though he knew no details of the discussions that were to take place, he gave Dillman a clear indication of Blaine's importance in diplomatic circles. For some years, Blaine had had ambassadorial duties. Close to the president, he was tried and trusted. Poole also stressed what an easy man he was to work beside. The two of them had been all over the Orient together.

"Why didn't you take advantage of onboard security?" asked Dillman. "If we'd known who Mr. Blaine was, we could have arranged additional protection."

"It's never been needed before," said Poole. "Besides, we were anxious not to draw attention to ourselves. The point about secret missions is that they're supposed to be secret. We assumed that this one was."

"Until you had suspicions about Father Slattery."

"Yes, Mr. Dillman. It was so strange for him to disappear like that. And he was occupying the cabin that was originally assigned to Mr. Blaine. That worried us," he admitted. "When he didn't appear for dinner, I broke into the cabin to see for myself. It was then that I knew we had a real problem."

"Why not go straight to the purser?"

"I thought I could take care of it myself."

"Well, you couldn't," said Dillman reasonably. "If you'd been a little less secret and a little more sensible, none of this would have happened."

Poole was defiant. "I know my job, Mr. Dillman."

"There are times when even the best of us need help. You shouldn't have pushed me away like that last night. I might have saved you a lot of pain."

"I didn't want you to find out what I was doing onboard."

"Well, I know now, Mr. Poole. That's why I've come here. I need your advice."

"Have you protected anyone before?"

"Yes," said Dillman. "When I was with the Pinkerton Agency. I was hired to protect someone who shut the workers out of his factory. It got pretty hectic at times. I can't say that it was a job that I enjoyed."

"Why not?"

"I didn't take to the man I was supposed to protect, and my sympathies were very much with his employees. Still," he said resignedly, "I wasn't paid to take sides. I kept him out of trouble and that was that. But this situation is rather different."

"It is, Mr. Dillman. There's no place you can hide on a ship."

"So what do you suggest?"

Jake Poole's physical injuries had not affected his brain. His advice was clear, practical, and based on experience. Eager to learn, Dillman paid close attention. Most of his own work had been investigative. It was intriguing to listen to a specialist like Poole.

"You're the first guy that spotted me," confessed the bodyguard.

"Only out of the corner of my eye."

"That never happens as a rule. I pride myself on being a

good shadow. Most of the time, Mr. Blaine doesn't even know that I'm there."

"Someone did, Mr. Poole."

"Yes," said the other, wincing as a spasm of pain shot through him. "If they knew that Mr. Blaine was on the ship, they'd figure that he'd have cover of some kind. They must know that I'm out of action now. Be careful, Mr. Dillman."

"I will."

"You'll be a marked man."

"Only if they realize that I've replaced you."

"Are you armed?"

"No, but I'm forewarned."

"Borrow my revolver."

"I don't think I'll need that."

"You might," said Poole. "They made one mistake, choosing the wrong cabin. Don't bank on them to make another."

"Their mistake was to travel on the same ship as me," said Dillman with a determined glint. "Someone had the temerity to commit murder right under my nose. That offended me deeply, Mr. Poole. Like you, I take pride in my job. I won't just be looking after Mr. Blaine from now on. I'll find the person or persons behind this murder," he vowed "When I'm the ship's detective, I like to keep it spick-and-span."

Genevieve Masefield strolled toward the dining saloon with Fay Brinkley beside her.

"What book did Mrs. McDade choose in the end?" asked Fay.

"It was called *The Love of His Life*."

"Well, it certainly wasn't written by her husband," said Fay crisply. "Mr. McDade hardly notices that the poor woman is there."

"She's his second wife," explained Genevieve. "The first one died."

"What of—neglect or humiliation?"

"Don't be so cynical, Fay."

"Some men treat their wives abominably."

"The wives must take a little of the blame for that," said Genevieve. "They should stand up for themselves."

"Wait until you get married," warned Fay. "You'll see how difficult it is."

"I'm sure that you stood up for yourself."

"Of course, Genevieve. I like things my own way."

Fay laughed and led the way into the dining saloon. They were at a table with the Langmeads, Mr. and Mrs. Natsuki, and an elderly man called Vernon Silverstein. He greeted them with a smile, but used a battered ear trumpet when introductions were made. Silverstein had once worked in the Imperial Maritime Customs Service and was returning to China to visit old friends. In spite of his hearing difficulties, he took a full part in the conversation and displayed a gift for anecdote from the very start. The eighth chair at the table remained empty, and Genevieve assumed that nobody would take it. Just before the meal was served, however, a disheveled David Seymour-Jones slipped into the seat and murmured his apologies. He had to repeat his words more loudly into the ear trumpet for the benefit of Silverstein.

Genevieve remained composed but quailed inwardly. Since the artist was seated directly opposite her, she could not avoid his gaze. It was Fay who brought him into the general conversation.

"Are you still sketching the passengers, Mr. Seymour-Jones?" she asked.

"Yes, Mrs. Brinkley," he replied. "I've filled one pad already."

"Do I appear in it?"

"I'm afraid not."

"Don't I appeal to you as a subject?"

"Very much," he said, "but you spend most of your time on the promenade deck and I tend to work elsewhere. Some of my best work has been done on the main deck among the steerage passengers. I have some wonderful group scenes."

"What do you do with your drawings?" said Horace Langmead.

"I keep them as mementos."

"You gave one to Miss Masefield," recalled Fay.

"That was a rather special portrait."

"I thought it was astonishingly lifelike."

"Did you charge for it?" said Langmead.

"Horry!" chided his wife.

"It's a simple question."

"The simple answer is that I didn't, Mr. Langmead," said Seymour-Jones with a glance at Genevieve. "I never charge friends."

Langmead chuckled. "I can see you don't have an entrepreneurial spirit, my friend. If I had your talent, I'd be hawking it around the first-class passengers. Some of them would pay handsomely for a portrait. People are vain. They love to be flattered."

"My portraits are not meant to flatter," said the artist. "They record truth."

"For whose benefit?"

"Mine, Mr. Langmead."

"Well, I don't know that I'd like the truth about my face," said Etta Langmead lightheartedly. "I'd want you to take at least ten years off me."

"You could take forty off me!" said Silverstein, listening through his ear trumpet.

The laughter coincided with the arrival of the waiter, and they broke off to place their orders. Seymour-Jones made a point of ordering everything that Genevieve did, and she was discomfited by that. However, he made no attempt to talk to her. He engaged Natsuki and his wife in a discussion about Japan, tossing in the occasional phrase in Japanese. They were impressed by his intimate knowledge of their country. Silverstein monopolized the Langmeads with stories of his time as a customs official, leaving Genevieve free to converse at length with Fay Brinkley. The latter was delighted to renew their friendship.

"It's ages since we had a proper talk, Genevieve," she said. "I thought I'd lost you forever to the Gilpatricks."

"They let me out on parole, Fay."

"Gilpatrick is such an egregious character."

"I can't say that he's the most prepossessing man I've met onboard."

"Who is?"

"I haven't made up my mind yet."

"Nobody at this table, I suspect," said Fay conspiratorially.

"Hardly," agreed Genevieve. "I seem to attract the wrong people. The latest is a dreadful man who pretended that he'd met me at a party in England. I believed him at first. He was so convincing."

"What was his name?"

"Willoughby Kincaid. Watch out for him."

"Why?"

"He's the kind of man who makes a hobby out of preying on attractive women."

"Nobody preys on me," said Fay bluntly.

"I know," returned Genevieve. "I'm not suggesting you're at risk. I just thought you'd be amused by his seedy charm. Age doesn't seem to be a factor for him. The idea of conquest is everything, however young or old a woman might be."

"What is he? A disreputable English roué?"

"Judge for yourself. He's very plausible on the surface."

"What will I find underneath?"

"A self-appointed man of the world."

"Oh dear!" said Fay. "One of those! I'll give Mr. Kincaid a miss."

"He may not let you, Fay. He seems to be working his way through all the unattached ladies. Your turn is bound to come."

"He'll be wasting his time with me, Genevieve."

"You might enjoy seeing him in action."

"No thanks," said Fay. "I'm not providing target practice for some rake. No disrespect to your nation, but I've never found the English male very appealing."

"Why not?"

"I suppose it's because they're too English."

Genevieve laughed. "I'm not letting you get away with a slur like that."

"I speak as I find, Genevieve. The Englishmen I've met have always been so stiff and humorless. What they learn in those exclusive schools of theirs, I don't know, but they've certainly never been taught how to talk to a woman. Actually, very few men have, whatever their nationality." She gave a confiding smile. "Though I have met one man who passed the test."

"Oh?"

"He was my idea of what a man ought to be. Intelligent, sensitive, attentive."

"What was his name?"

"George Dillman," said Fay. "I sat next to him at dinner last night. He's younger than I am but I'll tell you this: I came dangerously close to flirting with him."

Genevieve hoped that her blush did not show.

TEN

If Rutherford Blaine was feeling nervous in the dining saloon, it did not show in his face. He was as relaxed and urbane as ever. With his back to the wall, Dillman deliberately sat opposite his friend so that he could command a view of the whole room and see if anyone was taking a special interest in Blaine. Joining them at a table for six were their usual companions, Mr. and Mrs. Chang, together with Bruce and Moira Legge. The latter were at their most talkative. Since Genevieve had mentioned them, Dillman knew what to expect by way of an introduction from the English couple.

"We're the Legges," said Bruce jovially. "I'm the right leg and Moira is the left." The others laughed dutifully. "We were on holiday once in Cornwall and we met this couple called Mr. and Mrs. Foot. I thought they were joking at first but that was their real name. You can imagine the fun we had out of that."

"It could have been worse," observed Blaine, reaching for the menu. "Their name might have been Kneecap."

"Nobody would be called that, surely?" said Moira.

"They would, Mrs. Legge. I had a colleague named Louis

Patella. That amounts to the same thing. Ah, crab!" he said, reading the menu. "That looks tempting."

"As long as they don't serve raw fish," she said with a grimace. "That's what they eat in Japan, apparently. The mere thought is revolting."

"They seem to thrive on it, Mrs. Legge," said Dillman.

"It's worse than eating snails, as the French do."

"Yes," said Legge disdainfully. "They've got some deplorable habits, the Frogs."

"Where was that restaurant that served horsemeat, Bruce?"

"There are dozens of them all over Paris, darling. Their standards are different from ours. They'd eat their grandmothers if you let them."

Chang gulped. "French people eat their grandmothers?" he said.

"Only when the snails and the horsemeat runs out," teased Legge.

Amusing at first, the English couple became increasingly tiresome. The Changs were their worst victims. Because they could not understand Legge's sense of humor, they took his facetious remarks seriously. What Dillman objected to was their lordly air. They not only patronized the Chinese-American couple, they shed a few reflex prejudices about the United States. Blaine showed great restraint in holding back from comment.

It was Moira Legge who introduced the subject of religion.

"Does anyone know what's happened to that appalling priest?" she asked.

"Priest?" said Li Chang.

"Be warned, Mr. Chang. He's a missionary on his way to China."

"Most disagreeable fellow," said Legge, fingering his beard. "Father Slattery. That was the chap. He gave the Catholic Church a bad name." He blinked at his companions. "No offense meant if any of you are Roman Catholics."

"I don't believe that we are, Mr. Legge," said Blaine, looking around the table.

"The French are Catholics," noted Legge meaningfully. "That says everything."

"Tell them about Father Slattery," urged Moira.

"I'd prefer to forget him, darling."

"He never stopped talking. Bruce and I hardly said a word."

"No, Moira. You never got a chance to tell your story about China."

"Oh?" said Chang. "You've been to our country before?"

"No, Mr. Chang," she replied, "but my brother has. He's an archeologist. Eric spent two years there before taking up a professorship at Cambridge. He couldn't have picked a worse time to go to the country."

"He not like it?"

"He loved it until he found himself in the middle of the Boxer Rebellion."

Chang sighed and looked at his wife. She gave a little nod.

"Tell them what Eric said, darling," encouraged Legge. "Moira should have told this to Father Slattery," he added, eyes bulging with significance. "It would have put him in his place good and proper."

"I don't know that he needed putting in his place," said Dillman, not wishing to hear anyone speak ill of the dead. "I met Father Slattery and he struck me as very courageous man. Missionary work is always beset by hazards. Hundreds of Catholic missionaries were killed during the rising."

"My brother almost joined them," announced Moira, determined to tell her tale. "When the trouble broke out, he and his team were in the back of beyond, digging up the remains of an old temple. Friends told them to get out quick, but it was too late. Before they could escape in litters, they were set upon by an angry crowd. Eric says they were pelted with stones and clods of clay."

"And jeered at," said Legge. "They were called foreign devils. The crowd wanted to tear them to pieces. They almost did."

"Let me tell it my way," scolded Moira.

"Sorry, darling."

"Eric is *my* brother."

"How did he escape, Mrs. Legge?" asked Blaine.

"By means of his religion. That's what I wanted to point out to Father Slattery." Moira gabbled on. "The leader of the attackers pulled back the straw covering of the litter and ordered Eric to get out and kneel down. Eric refused, knowing that he'd never get up alive again. 'You are Roman Catholics,' said the man. 'Get down!' Eric was not having that. 'We're not Catholics,' he said in a loud voice. 'We abhor Catholicism and all that it stands for. We follow the true religion of Jesus.' Those were Eric's exact words."

"What happened next?" said Blaine.

"The man turned to the crowd and said, 'They're not *T'ien Chu Kaio*.' That means Roman Catholics. 'They're *Ie-su Kaio*,' he told them. That means Protestants. So they let Eric and the others go."

"See what I mean?" said Legge. "That would have shut Father Slattery up."

"I disagree," returned Dillman. "I'm pleased that lives were spared, but you can hardly use that incident as a stick to beat the Catholics. In your brother's position, Mrs. Legge, I'm quite sure that Father Slattery would have proclaimed his Catholicism for all to hear, even though he knew that it was his death sentence."

"There is no killing in China now," said Chang. "All that is past."

Moira was pessimistic. "It could start again, according to Eric."

"Cambridge is rather a long way from China," remarked Blaine. "Unless your brother has remarkable eyesight, I don't think he has any idea what's happening inside the country. Mr. and Mrs. Chang do. They correspond regularly with their family."

"Things are better now," insisted Chang.

"I sincerely hope so," said Legge.

"We even stopped eating our grandmothers."

The unexpected flash of humor from Chang made everyone laugh and brought a natural end to that passage of conversation. Dillman was relieved. He found any mention of Father Slattery very painful. It had been disturbing enough when he had believed that the priest had been murdered by an unknown enemy. Now that he knew the man was the innocent victim of a grotesque error, the death was even more poignant. Blaine shared his disquiet. Though his face remained impassive, his eyes spoke eloquently to Dillman.

The meal was delicious and passed off without incident. Dillman cast many surreptitious glances around the room, but there was no hint of surveillance. Blaine was not being watched. In fact, the only person who caught his eye was Genevieve Masefield. She gave him such a strange look that Dillman wondered what it meant. He had no opportunity to find out. When the meal was over, Genevieve went out with Fay Brinkley. Dillman lingered over coffee, then rose from his seat with Blaine and the Legges. All four of them headed for the exit. Chatting to the Legges, the detective made sure that he kept an eye on Blaine's back. When they got outside, Mike Roebuck was waiting, as planned, to intercept Blaine and escort him away. It was all done with such casual ease that nobody would have suspected collusion.

Dillman gave them fifteen minutes before he made his way to the purser's office. Sipping a cup of coffee, Mike Roebuck was sitting at his desk with the passenger list in front of him. He looked up as his friend entered.

"Is Mr. Blaine safely stowed away?" said Dillman.

"Yes, he likes his new cabin."

"Let's hope they don't find out where it is."

"Nobody followed us today, George, that's for sure. How was I?"

"Perfect. You should go on the stage."

"I already am on it," said Roebuck. "This job is largely a performance. Unfortunately, I never seem to get any applause at the end of it."

"You'll get applause from Mr. Blaine, if everything goes well. And I daresay you might even get a mention in government dispatches."

"I just want to get him to Japan in one piece." He stood up. "Any developments?"

"A few. Genevieve has been very industrious."

"What has she found out?"

"A number of interesting things, Mike. Including the name of one of Gilpatrick's henchmen. I've checked him out on my copy of the passenger list and he seems to have a cabin on the promenade deck."

"Who is he?"

"Mr. Gault. Thomas Gault."

Roebuck was surprised. "I didn't realize that Tommy Gault was aboard."

"You know him?"

"Of course. He was a useful middleweight in his day. I saw him fight in Seattle once. Tommy was very light on his feet. He packed a good punch as well. He was up against a much taller boxer, but that didn't seem to hamper him." He looked down at his own list. "Yes, there he is," he said, pointing. "Mr. Thomas Gault. I didn't spot that. When you've got over fifteen hundred passengers on the list, you can't make a note of them all. Especially the Chinese. We must have dozens called Chang. Don't they have any other names over there?"

"I'll ask my friend, Mr. Chang," said Dillman with a grin. "Tell me about Gault."

"All I know is what I saw in the ring that night and what I read in the sports pages. Tommy Gault had real promise at one time, but I suspect that he may have taken a punch too many. They usually do in the end."

"What does he look like?"

"Short, thickset, plug-ugly."

"He'd be easy to pick out, then?"

"Dead easy," said Roebuck. "Look for his cauliflower ear and his fighter's strut. He stands out a mile. Oh, and be careful, George."

"Why? Is he dangerous?"

"Lethal."

The concert began late in the afternoon. When Genevieve arrived, there was no sign of Maxine Gilpatrick, so she took a seat in an empty row near the back. Maxine was still in a temper when she finally appeared.

"Sorry to keep you waiting, Jenny," she said, sitting down, "but I couldn't get into the cabin to change. Rance was in there with Joe McDade. He *knew* that I wanted to come to this concert. The worst of it was that I was stuck with Joe's wife for half an hour. Blanche is a nice enough woman, but she has so little to say for herself. I was glad when she went off to have her afternoon nap. Anyway," she concluded with a sniff, "when I was finally allowed into the cabin, I had the most terrible rush."

"You're here now, that's the main thing."

"No thanks to my husband."

"They've got a good audience," said Genevieve, looking round. "There must be well over a hundred in here."

"We'll have twice as many as that," boasted Maxine. "We're going to put up posters to advertise it. Maxine Montgomery sings—that's my stage name, by the way. Piano accompanist—Genevieve Masefield."

"Where will you get posters from at such short notice?"

"Rance has fixed it. I told you he was good at arranging things."

"But who's going to do them?"

"He found this artist, making sketches of people on the deck," said Maxine airily. "An English guy with one of those fancy double-barreled names."

Genevieve bridled. "David Seymour-Jones?"

"That's him. He knows you, apparently."

"Yes, Maxine."

"When Rance first asked him, he wasn't interested at all. He got on his high horse a bit and said that he didn't do that kind of work. But Rance talked him around," she said. "When he mentioned your name, this guy suddenly showed an interest."

"That's odd," said Genevieve. "Mr. Seymour-Jones was at my table earlier. He didn't breathe a word about this."

"Maybe he wanted it to be a surprise."

"I've had enough surprises from him already."

Maxine grinned. "Oh, it's like that, is it?" she said with amusement.

"No, Maxine."

"This artist is sweet on you. No wonder he was so keen to do some posters. Hey!" she said with mock aggression. "If he puts your name above mine, there'll be big trouble. I expect top billing."

"You deserve it," said Genevieve, anxious to get off the subject. "But I'm sorry that you found Blanche McDade a little disappointing."

"She was so dull, Jenny. She's an intelligent woman, I could see that, but she's never really lived. Oh, you know what I mean," she said with a nudge. "The woman has no passion in her life."

"Married to Mr. McDade, I doubt if I would."

"Nor me," said Maxine, shaking with laughter. "He's a human walrus."

The arrival of the orchestra was greeted by a burst of applause. Maxine controlled her mirth and watched them take their seats. Genevieve was looking forward to the concert until someone suddenly dropped down beside her.

"I *knew* that you'd share my love of music, Miss Masefield," he said. "Schubert is my favorite composer. I couldn't possibly miss this afternoon." He looked across her and waved a hand. "Hello, Mrs. Gilpatrick. It's lovely to see you again."

"What are you doing here?" demanded Maxine.

"The same as you, of course, dear lady. I came to enjoy myself."

Arms folded, Willoughby Kincaid sat back in his chair and purred contentedly.

George Porter Dillman was in luck. When he tracked down Tommy Gault, the man was on the promenade deck, holding his jacket open so that a small boy could pummel away at his stomach. Two other boys were watching the demonstration.

"Go on," urged Gault, grinning broadly. "Hit me harder."

"I'm trying," said the boy.

"Can't feel a thing."

The children were taking turns to test their strength against him and he was enjoying every moment of it. Coming down the steps toward him was the ample frame of Rance Gilpatrick. Dillman sidled over to him and nodded toward the others.

"That's Tommy Gault, isn't it?" he asked.

"Yes, my friend," said Gilpatrick pleasantly. "Are you a boxing fan?"

"I used to be. I once saw him fighting in Seattle," lied Dillman, repeating what the purser had told him. "A middleweight contest. He was so quick on his feet, I remember that, and he had a mean punch."

"Fourteen knockouts all told."

"He still looks pretty fit."

"Tommy is just showing off for the benefit of the kids," said Gilpatrick. "They watched him skipping earlier on. He knows how to please a crowd."

"Does he still fight?"

"No, my friend. He retired from the ring a few years ago."

"Too much punishment?"

"Too much whiskey," explained Gilpatrick, "and that can be as punishing as anything. It finished his career."

"You seem to know a lot about him, sir," said Dillman, turning to him. "Were you his manager or something?"

"No, just a friend." He stuck out a hand. "Rance Gilpatrick."

"George Dillman," said the other, feeling a firm handshake.

"Where are you heading, Mr. Dillman?"

"I'm on vacation to see as much of Japan and China as I can. What about you?"

"It's a sort of vacation, but I hope to fit in some business along the way."

"How do you find the ship, Mr. Gilpatrick?"

"I like it. I've sailed on the *Minnesota* before."

"Really?" said Dillman, feigning surprise. "Then you have an advantage over me. Mind you, I was there when it was launched. They had a few problems that day."

"So I heard," said Gilpatrick.

"But not so many as its sister ship, the *Dakota*. That fell foul of a group of women reformers from North and South Dakota. They were part of a temperance campaign," he explained, "and objected very strongly to the alcohol that was going to be served at the launch. After all, the ship bore their name. They kicked up a real fuss."

"I seem to recall reading about that, Mr. Dillman."

"It caused a lot of bad publicity."

"People are entitled to a drink."

"That's what Jim Hill thought, and he owned the vessel. He decided to ignore their protest. That really set the cat among the pigeons," said Dillman with a smile. "The women got together and passed a series of resolutions, stating that they hoped bad luck would attend the ship. I guess that you know the rest."

Gilpatrick nodded. "The *Dakota* sank off the Japanese coast."

"I think it was pure coincidence myself, but I daresay some of those women jumped for joy when they heard the news. One paper even talked about witchcraft. Hell hath no fury like a temperance movement scorned."

"It's a pity they weren't aboard the vessel when it sank!"

"The prohibition call is very loud in North and South Dakota."

"Well, I'll never listen to it," said Gilpatrick rancorously. "I'm in the liquor business myself, among other things. Last thing I need is a group of harpies telling me how I should live!" He relaxed as Gault strode across to them. "Well done, Tommy. You gave those kids a lot of harmless fun. Oh, this is Mr. Dillman, by the way. He saw you fight back in the old days."

"Did you?" said Gault, squeezing his hand. "Who did I beat?"

"I can't remember his name," said Dillman. "He didn't stay upright long enough for me to catch it." The others laughed. "That was quite a demonstration you put on."

"Like to take a shot at me yourself?" invited Gault, opening his coat.

"No, no. I'm a bit stronger than those kids. It would be unfair."

"Come on. I can take it."

"Throw a punch, Mr. Dillman," said Gilpatrick, sizing him up. "You look as if you take care of yourself. Test yourself on Tommy. You won't hurt him."

"What if I do?"

"You'll be the first man who did since Whitey Thompson," replied Gault proudly. "He was a champ. Nobody ever had the power in his fists that Whitey did."

The two men continued to encourage him and the children came over to add their exhortations. Having barked their knuckles on the former boxer's stomach, they wanted to see someone get revenge on their behalf. Dillman eventually agreed and slipped off his coat. Tempted to put full power into his punch, he instead pulled it at the last moment. His fist bounced off and Gault laughed derisively. While Dillman pretended to rub his knuckles, the children drifted away in disappointment.

"I did warn you, Mr. Dillman," said the chuckling Gilpatrick.

"What have you got down there?" asked Dillman, indicating Gault's stomach. "It felt like solid steel."

"That's what all the ladies tell me," replied the other.

And he went off into a peal of raucous laughter.

———

In view of the circumstances, Genevieve found it very difficult to concentrate on the music. She was wedged in between the wife of a known criminal and an amorous Englishman with designs on her. Her discomfort was intensified when the pianist took over to play a Beethoven sonata. The sight of a professional musician, sitting at the instrument with such dignity and authority, made her shudder slightly. She could never coax the notes out so smoothly or so crisply. Doubts about the wisdom of agreeing to accompany Maxine Gilpatrick changed into apprehension. There was one source of relief. Willoughby Kincaid made no attempt to touch, fondle, or hassle her. He led the applause at the end of each item and restricted himself to a few knowledgeable comments about the various composers. Franz Schubert was featured most prominently, but work by four others was also included. Kincaid was so well informed that she wondered if he had been doing some research in order to impress her. When she had been in the library, she had noticed a copy of Grove's *Dictionary of Music and Musicians* on the shelf. Kincaid, she decided, might well have resorted to it for factual detail when he saw what the program was that afternoon.

At the end of the concert, he dispelled her suspicions with a polite explanation.

"I'm so sorry if I bored you with my comments," he said to them, "but I grew up in a musical family. My father was a conductor. He gave me my first piano lesson when I was three. I spent years in the school orchestra at Eton. I'd moved on to violin by then. Music is one of the many things I miss, keeping on the move so much. There are not many concerts in the sort of places that I visit."

"I suppose not."

"Anyway, thank you for your company, ladies."

He rose from his seat and led the way to the aisle. The audience was dispersing in a hubbub of satisfaction. The three of them joined the queue for the exit. Genevieve felt less irritated by Kincaid than before. It allowed her curiosity to take over.

"I'm told that you've done some big-game hunting, Mr. Kincaid."

"He's still at it, honey," warned Maxine in her ear.

"Is it true?" asked Genevieve.

"Of course it is," he replied. "Why shouldn't it be?"

"Not everything you tell us has the ring of honesty about it."

He laughed gaily. "You put that so elegantly."

"It was Mrs. Legge who told me about your hunting exploits. Were they real or were you just trying make an impression on her?"

"I'm always keen to make an impression on ladies, Miss Masefield."

"We noticed," said Maxine cynically.

"Mrs. Legge said that you'd hunted in Africa and India," recalled Genevieve.

"Wherever I can," he said airily. "Lions and tigers are my preference, but I've tackled a rhino on occasion. They take some stopping. Mind you, I don't expect to shoot anything larger than duck or quail in China. I can use the Purdy for that kind of thing."

"The what?" asked Maxine.

"A Purdy is the finest sporting rifle in existence, Mrs. Gilpatrick. English craftsmanship at its best. I never travel without it. I've also brought my big hunting rifle with me, but I doubt if I'll ever take it out of its case on this trip. It's the truth, I assure you," he said, stopping as they went out into the passageway. "I *do* know something about music and I *am* a dead shot. Those are two things I'd never dare to lie about. I don't need to, you see." He gave a little bow. "I bid you farewell, ladies."

They wished him good-bye, then turned to face each other. Maxine was skeptical.

"I still think he's making it up."

"We could always call his bluff about the violin," said Genevieve. "We could borrow one from the orchestra and put him to the test. My guess is that he'll come through it with flying colors."

Maxine grinned. "I think he'd prefer you to put him to a different kind of test."

"No, thank you!"

"I have to admit it. The guy was almost bearable today."

"He's clearly had a musical education."

"I'd be more worried about his claim to be a hunter, if I were you."

"Why?"

"He may settle for duck and quail in China," she said, "but he's after something much bigger at the moment. Her name is Genevieve Masefield, and I reckon that he was just stalking her."

"That's the strange thing," said Genevieve. "I didn't feel stalked."

"Neither do the lions and tigers, honey. Until it's too late."

The remark gave Genevieve food for thought as she headed back alone to her cabin. It was not long before she sensed that someone was following her. Kincaid was trying to get her on her own, she feared, separating her from the herd. Her first instinct was to increase her speed, get to her cabin, and shut the door in his face. But that would only give her a temporary respite. It was time to confront him and issue a more forceful rejection. She waited until she had almost reached her cabin, then swung around angrily. Certain that she had been trailed by Willoughby Kincaid, she was astonished to see David Seymour-Jones. A sketch pad under one arm, he gestured apologetically with the other.

"I'm sorry to bother you, Miss Masefield, but I understand that you'll be taking part in a song recital. Mr. Gilpatrick has asked me to do some posters for the event. They'll be in color, of course," he said earnestly. "I have my paints with me. The trouble is that I know nothing about it." He smiled nervously. "I wondered if you could possibly give me some details, please?"

"You should speak to Mrs. Gilpatrick," she replied. "The event is her idea and she's the real star of it, as I'm sure her husband told you."

"I'd prefer to deal with you."

Genevieve was torn. The request was double-edged. Though she was willing to give him the information he needed, she knew that he was only seeking it as an excuse to be alone with her. Seymour-Jones was gentle and unthreatening, but his infatuation with her was causing her some distress. She was unsure whether to provide him with the relevant details or to take the opportunity to distance herself from him.

"This is an inconvenient time," she said at length. "Why don't we meet for ten minutes before dinner this evening? I can tell you everything then."

His face lit up with gratitude. When they had arranged a time, Seymour-Jones went off happily, relieved that he had not been spurned and looking forward to the rendezvous. Genevieve felt only a sense of relief that she had got rid of him. Letting herself into her cabin, she closed the door and put her back against it. Relief soon faded. As she looked around the room, she became aware that certain items had been moved slightly. Even her slippers had been shifted. It was unsettling. When she opened the wardrobe, she could see that her dresses had been rearranged, and there was the same evidence of tampering in the chest of drawers. Nothing had been stolen, but that did not reassure Genevieve. Her cabin had been searched.

George Porter Dillman had to wait for ten minutes while the purser placated an irate passenger. Mike Roebuck was patient and adroit. When the elderly woman left, she had calmed down completely. Dillman stepped into the office.

"What was all that about, Mike?" he asked.

"Complaints about the food. Mrs. Atticus doesn't like meat."

"Then why does she eat it?"

"She likes the alternatives even less."

"What does she live on—fresh air?"

"It's nothing to do with the taste of the food, George," said the purser. "When I worked that out, I was able to suggest an individual menu for her that avoided her embarrassing problem."

"Problem?"

"False teeth. Badly fitted by her dentist. When she tried to bite her way into the beef that was served at luncheon, her top set all but popped out." He gave a chuckle. "I smoothed her feathers and assured her it would never happen again."

"You're as much of a diplomat as Mr. Blaine."

Roebuck frowned. "He's my real headache," he admitted. "Mrs. Atticus is only in danger of losing her teeth. Mr. Blaine's life is at risk."

"Not if we catch the man who's trying to take it."

"That's proving difficult so far, George. We've already got a dead priest and a wounded bodyguard. How many other casualties will there be?"

"None, if I can help it," said Dillman. "By the way, I managed to find Tommy Gault. That ear of his could only have been collected in a boxing ring. I wanted to weigh him up in case he might be our mystery assassin."

"Well?"

"He's strong enough and lithe enough."

"And short. Mr. Poole said his attacker was short and compact."

"I had an unexpected bonus."

"Did you?"

"While I was there," said Dillman, "Rance Gilpatrick came in search of Gault, so I exchanged a few friendly words to see if I could draw him out. Tommy Gault may be the boxer, but it's Gilpatrick who oozes power. When you stand close to him, you can feel it."

"I'm not sure that I'd want to stand close to Gilpatrick. Or downwind of him."

"Why has he brought someone like Gault with him?"

"Not for his scintillating conversation, that's for sure."

"Exactly, Mike."

"So what *is* Tommy here for?"

"It'll be interesting to find out. Is everything set up for this evening?"

"Of course," said Roebuck. "Pete Carroll will see that Mr. Blaine gets safely to the dining saloon, then someone else will walk him back to his cabin. They've been told to make it look natural."

"Where have you put him?"

"Right next door to the master-at-arms. There's a small arsenal in his cabin. At the first sign of trouble, he'll rush to Blaine's aid with two guns blazing. I'm much more concerned about the cabin that Blaine used to occupy," said the purser. "Do you really think you ought to sleep in there tonight, George?"

"I insist on it."

"Suppose the assassin comes calling? As far as he knows, Blaine is still there."

"That's the idea, Mike. We lure him in."

"I'd hate you to end up on a bed of ice next to Father Slattery."

"I won't be caught off-guard like him. I'm a light sleeper."

"Let me put a man in there with you."

"No," said Dillman. "I have a personal score to settle with the killer. I'll tackle him alone. There is one favor I'd ask, though. Don't say anything about this to Genevieve. She'd only worry."

"What about me? You're a good friend. I'm scared stiff for you."

"I'll be fine, Mike."

Roebuck heaved a sigh. "The problem is we don't know

where to look. When we wanted someone with a motive to kill Father Slattery, we found a handful of them. Now we know that Mr. Blaine was the target, we're in the dark."

"Not entirely," argued Dillman. "Whoever is responsible for the attack is very well connected if he has access to government secrets. That narrows the field somewhat. We're looking for a political animal, Mike. Someone committed to derailing the talks that Mr. Blaine is due to have in Japan."

"How could the information leak out in the first place?"

"Spying is the oldest profession in the world," said Dillman.

"The second oldest," corrected the purser. "We've got a couple of members of the oldest profession in steerage, apparently. The chief steward tipped me off." There was a knock on the door. "That may be him now. Come in!"

The door opened and Genevieve Masefield stepped into the cabin. Glad to catch the purser there, she was pleasantly surprised to see Dillman as well. Her face was still flushed. They could see that she was agitated.

"What's the trouble?" asked Dillman with concern.

"Someone's been snooping in my cabin," she replied. "Nothing seems to have been taken but it left a nasty feeling in my mouth. I felt invaded."

Roebuck was alarmed. "When did you discover this?"

"Just now. When I got back from the concert."

"Was there anything that might have given you away?"

"No," she said. "I take great care to leave nothing that would indicate I'm working for the shipping line. That's not the point, however. Somebody has been in there, rifling through my things."

"Are you sure it wasn't the stewardess?"

"She came this morning and had no reason to return."

"How long were you at the concert, Genevieve?" asked Dillman.

"The best part of two hours, I should say."

"Did you go on your own?"

"No, Maxine Gilpatrick came with me."

Dillman nodded. "So her husband would know that you'd be out of your cabin."

"What reason would he have to search it?"

"I'm not sure that he did," confessed Dillman, "and he certainly wouldn't do it in person. He'd send someone else. If Gilpatrick is behind this—and his is the obvious name that springs to mind—then he must be getting suspicious. I met him earlier. He's a wily old bird. Guys like him tend to have a sixth sense."

"I've given him no cause for suspicion, George."

"You didn't have to. He's the sort of man who checks everyone out as a matter of course. Hopefully, his suspicions will have been quelled."

"Supposing somebody else searched the cabin?" wondered Roebuck. "A thief. Was there anything worth taking, Miss Masefield?"

"I left no money or valuables hanging about," she answered. "My jewelry is locked away in your safe. But there were some items that a thief would have taken. My carriage clock, for instance. That was quite expensive."

"Any sign of forced entry?"

Genevieve shrugged. "None. He must have had a key."

"That's worrying," said the purser.

"It shook me, I can tell you. I won't feel safe in there again."

"Would you like the chief steward to find you another cabin?" said Dillman.

"No, George. I'll stay where I am. They're not scaring me off." She brightened. "I didn't think I'd see you again before tonight. I've got some news. Earlier today, I met Blanche McDade in the library. Since her husband is a friend of Gilpatrick's, I tried to find out just how close the two men are."

"And?"

"They've had several business dealings in the past."

"Did she tell you their nature?"

"I'm afraid not," said Genevieve. "Blanche McDade is one of

those obedient wives who are kept on the outer fringe of their husbands' lives. Joseph McDade made his money out of copper, but that's not what he sells to Gilpatrick."

"Go on."

"The two men had a long discussion in private this afternoon. Maxine was seething about it. She couldn't get into her own cabin. But it was a remark of Blanche McDade's that really prompted my interest," she said. "She talked about some catalogs that her husband had brought. He was going to show them to Gilpatrick."

Dillman pondered. "I think this is our chance," he said at length, turning to the purser. "I'm going to need your help, Mike."

"Don't tell me you want to borrow Pete Carroll's spare uniform again."

"No, I'm not posing as your deputy this time. I need you to speak to the chief steward on my behalf. I'm going to need a master key to the cabins on the boat deck and a steward's uniform that will fit me without pinching my waist. Thanks, Genevieve," he said, squeezing her arm. "This might turn out to be our breakthrough."

Marriage to Etta had taught Horace Langmead the virtue of patience. There was no point in trying to hurry his wife. She not only courted the mirror for an hour before dinner, she tried on various dresses and experimented with an array of costume jewelry. Langmead had learned that it was best to ignore the whole process. He buried his head in a magazine until he was called upon to issue his statutory approval.

"How does this look, Horry?" she asked, twirling in front of him.

"Perfect!"

"I want to make people stare at me."

"You still make me stare, honey," he assured her, planting a kiss on her cheek, "and that's an achievement after fifteen years together."

"Sixteen," she said.

"I stand corrected."

He put the magazine aside, offered his arm, then led her to the door. Langmead was not so eager to draw attention to himself. White tie and tails would make him merge into a collective picture of elegance with all the other men in the dining saloon. It was the ladies who would stand out. In spite of her age, Etta Langmead could still turn the occasional head, and she reveled in that power. As they left their cabin, they saw two men at the end of the passageway, deep in conversation. Rance Gilpatrick broke off as they approached and stepped back from Tommy Gault. Eveningdress did not suit the latter. He looked like a demented penguin with an inflamed ear. Gilpatrick dismissed him with a nudge. After a wave of greeting to the Langmeads, the ex-boxer strutted off.

"Maxine will be ready any second," said Gilpatrick expansively. "We can all go down together. My!" he said, arms outstretched as he admired Etta's dress. "You look wonderful, Mrs. Langmead!"

"Thank you, Mr. Gilpatrick," she replied with a titter.

"You'll be the belle of the ball tonight."

"Oh, I don't think I hold a candle to Mrs. Gilpatrick."

"You can compete with anyone, honey," said her husband.

"In the old days, perhaps," she said wistfully. "But not anymore." Maxine came out of her cabin in a beautiful silver evening gown that sparkled under the lights. "Oh, Mrs. Gilpatrick!" said Etta, fingers coming to her mouth. "That's magnificent!"

Maxine basked in her praise. "I wanted to make a special effort."

"You always do."

"Rance chose this dress for me."

"I wish that I could get away with something as daring as that."

"It's not daring," said Maxine. "It's just me."

They laughed and headed for the stairs. The women walked

side by side at the front while the men brought up the rear. Etta Langmead had a complaint.

"Why haven't we been invited to sit at the captain's table yet?" she said.

"You will be, I'm sure," replied Maxine. "Otherwise, speak to Rance. He'll fix it for you." She tossed the question over her shoulder. "Won't you, Rance?"

"What's that, honey?"

"Mr. and Mrs. Langmead would like to sit at the captain's table."

"Hey, hold on," said Langmead. "We'll wait until we're asked."

Maxine was persistent. "Rance has influence. Let him use it."

"If it's no trouble," said Etta, delighted at the offer.

"I'll see what I can do," offered Gilpatrick in a manner that suggested the favor was bound to be granted. "I always dine at the captain's table at some stage."

As they descended the stairs, other couples came into view. Maxine and Etta studied the women's dresses with a sharp eye and exchanged comments. The men showed no interest. Gilpatrick's mind was on someone else.

"What do you make of Genevieve Masefield?" he said artlessly.

"I think she's delightful," said Langmead with a chuckle. "English women don't usually inspire me, but she's the exception. We met her when we were boarding the ship. It's that accent of hers that we love so much. I could listen to it all day."

"Or all night," suggested Gilpatrick with a nudge.

Langmead grinned. "Chance would be a fine thing."

"Someone is in for a treat there."

"Etta wondered if it might be Mr. Seymour-Jones."

"That artist guy in the scruffy clothes? I've met him."

"He was at our table today with Miss Masefield. He never took his eyes off her. Mt wife wanted to do a little matchmaking, but I think she'd be wasting her time."

"Why do you say that?"

"He's not Miss Masefield's type," he replied. "Mr. Seymour-Jones is too shabby and disordered. He's a pleasant guy, maybe, but he seems to grope his way through life."

Gilpatrick was curious. "What sort of man *is* her type?"

"A very lucky one."

David Seymour-Jones was there long before the appointed time. Though he had made considerable efforts with his appearance, he still looked unkempt. He sat in the library with his sketch pad across his knees. When Genevieve finally came in, he jumped up so quickly that he spilled the pad on the floor. He gathered it up with a shy grin. Genevieve was keen to keep the discussion to a minimum.

"It was Mrs. Gilpatrick's idea," she said, taking a seat. "She heard me playing the piano in the Ladies' Boudoir and couldn't resist bursting into song. She has a trained voice. Mrs. Gilpatrick wanted to be an opera singer."

He sat beside her and made notes in his pad. "Her husband said that she'd be appearing under another name."

"That's right. Maxine Montgomery."

"It's where she was born, apparently. Montgomery, Alabama."

"You know more than I do, Mr. Seymour-Jones."

"Is it to be called a concert or a song recital?"

"You'd better ask Mrs. Gilpatrick that. She has very firm ideas."

"What are your ideas, Miss Masefield?"

"To stay very much in the background. I'm only the accompanist."

"That's an important job."

"Mrs. Gilpatrick will take center stage. She has the most superb voice. It takes years to build up that kind of breath control."

"I'll be there to enjoy every moment," he said.

But she knew that he would not be looking at Maxine Montgomery. His gaze would be confined exclusively to the pianist.

Genevieve felt uncomfortable. Eager to terminate the interview, she gave him all the facts that he needed, then stood up.

"That's about it, Mr. Seymour-Jones," she said.

"Not quite," he returned, rising to his feet. "I wanted to ask you how long you'd be staying in Japan."

"Why?"

"I wondered if I might show you some of the sights."

"That's very kind of you, but my schedule is already worked out."

"I'd take you to see the *real* Japan," he promised. "Like the waterfall teahouse in Kobe where I spend my summers. Or the island of Toshi where they dive for pearls. Or bird-watching in the mountains. Have you ever seen a copper pheasant?"

"No, I can't say that I have."

"Their coloring is magnificent. And there are so many other gorgeous birds to look at. I've drawn many of them. Because they know I'm a collector, my friends bring me all sorts of curious things," he said, desperate to engage her attention. "Sword-tailed green grasshoppers, singing toads, and the most amazing butterflies. Last year, one of the fishermen brought me an octopus with fifteen legs."

"I thought that they only had eight."

"This one was a freak. I took it back to England and sold it to a London museum. You can see it on display when you go back. If you read the card beside the exhibit," he said with nervous pride, "you'll see my name mentioned."

"Congratulations!"

"I think you'd love Japan, Miss Masefield."

"I'm sure that I shall," she said politely, "but we ought to be going now. Dinner will be served very shortly." Before she could turn away, he opened his sketch pad to take out a sheet of paper. He thrust it at her. "What's this?" said Genevieve.

"A first idea for the poster."

Genevieve looked down at a drawing of two figures on a stage. Standing beside the piano, Maxine Gilpatrick was easily recognizable, but it was the pianist who stood out. The full-length portrait of Genevieve was so exact in detail and drawn with such obvious affection that she was lost for words.

"Well?" asked Seymour-Jones anxiously. "What do you think?"

Fay Brinkley was delighted to accept the invitation to sit at the captain's table. When she found herself next to Rutherford Blaine, she was even more pleased. She was glad to renew the acquaintance of a man whose intelligence she admired and whose company she found stimulating. As they took their seats, she cast a glance around the room.

"No sign of Mrs. Van Bergen, I see."

"I think that you put her to flight, Mrs. Brinkley. Unless, of course," he added, "you converted her to the cause. In that case, she might be down in steerage, preaching to the women about their rights."

"I doubt that, Mr. Blaine. Unlike anyone in steerage, she enjoys the rights that come with having a rich American husband. That rather blurs her vision of the sufferings of ordinary women."

"I'm afraid they suffer far more in Asia than they do in our country."

"Mrs. Van Bergen won't even notice."

"What about you?"

"Oh, I will. It's one of the reasons I'm going there."

"You have fire in your belly, Mrs. Brinkley."

"I'm just hungry," she said with a laugh, reaching for the menu.

Captain Piercey shared an anecdote with the whole table and they joined in the laughter. Blaine got involved in a conversation with his other neighbor, a Russian aristocrat with a monocle that he had not yet mastered. It was minutes before Fay was able to talk to Blaine again. She made an effort to subdue the curiosity in her voice.

"What's your opinion of George Dillman?" she asked.

"I think he's a splendid fellow, Mrs. Brinkley."

"You and he clearly have an affinity."

"He's a civilized man," said Blaine. "He also has the most extraordinary knowledge of ships. It's an education to sit next to him."

"Yes," she agreed readily, "that's what I found."

"His appearance is so striking. I can see why he was drawn to the theater."

"What do you see him as—Hamlet?"

"Oh, no. I think I'd cast him in a much more romantic role," he decided. "Something like the Count of Monte Cristo."

"You could be right."

"I'm surprised that his theatrical career was such a failure."

"So am I," said Fay. "It makes you wonder how he can afford to travel first class on such a long voyage. Does he have a private income?"

"I've no idea."

"He must have given you some sort of hint."

"Mr. Dillman didn't give it and I didn't seek it. The matter never arose."

"What would your guess be?"

"I'm not given to that kind of guesswork, Mrs Brinkley," he said evasively. "Mr. Dillman is charming company, and that's enough for me. Not everyone aboard this vessel is so personable," he went on, thinking about the murder of Father Slattery. "But that's inevitable, I suppose. In a barrel as large as the *Minnesota*, we're bound to have a few bad apples."

"You sound as if you've bitten into one or two."

"No, no," he affirmed. "I've been blessed in my table companions."

"Even though they included Mrs. Van Bergen?"

"I didn't find her quite as unpleasant as you did, Mrs. Brinkley."

"She wasn't unpleasant," said Fay sharply. "Just stubbornly ignorant." Her eye caught sight of someone entering the room.

"Talk of the devil! Here she is. Right on cue. All we need now is George Dillman," she observed, searching for him in vain. "I took him to be such a punctual man. Where is he?"

Dillman did not make his move until he was given the signal. It was only when the purser sent word that the Gilpatrick party had taken their seats in the dining saloon that the detective moved into action. Dressed as a steward, he had changed his appearance by wetting his hair and slicking it straight back. A false mustache, saved from his days as an actor, also came into use. Dillman moved swiftly. He knocked hard on the door of a cabin on the boat deck to make certain there was nobody inside. Satisfied that it was empty, he used the master key to let himself in. The suite was palatial. It was the character of Maxine Gilpatrick that had been stamped most clearly upon it. The air was charged with her perfume and her possessions were scattered everywhere. Over three-quarters of the wardrobe space was devoted to her. Dillman's search was quick but thorough. Gilpatrick was a careful man. Nothing incriminating was on view.

Taking care to leave everything as he found it, Dillman searched on. He was particularly careful in the bedroom, moving stealthily over the patterned carpet and opening cupboards and drawers with excessive care. It was a fruitless exercise. He was about to abandon it when he thought of the mattresses. Lifting the first, he found nothing at all underneath, but the second mattress yielded its secret. As he raised it up with one hand, he reached inside to pull out a catalog that contained a number of designs.

Dillman was thrilled with the find.

"We've got him!" he murmured.

ELEVEN

The Langmeads had cast their net much wider that evening. Genevieve Masefield was the only person to have dined with them before. Among the newcomers at a table for eight was a young couple from Seattle, patently on their honeymoon. Genevieve liked the Newtons from the moment she met them. They were friendly, kind, fresh-faced, and unashamedly in love with each other. She warmed to Monsieur and Madame Houlier even more. Cultured Europeans who spoke almost flawless English, they had been married long enough to have blended closely together. Subtle signals passed between them all the time. Yves Houlier was a silver-haired man whose handsome features had defeated most of the ravages of time. His attractive wife, Jeanne, ten years younger and wearing an example of the latest Paris fashion, seemed to enjoy it when her husband flirted outrageously with the other women at the table. Myrtle Newton giggled at his flattering remarks but Etta Langmead encouraged him. Genevieve attracted most of the Frenchman's attention. It was pleasant because it was completely harmless. She could not feel the same toward David Seymour-Jones, whose latest portrait of her had caused her more disquiet. Genevieve was grateful that he was not sitting at her table again.

Unfortunately, he had been replaced by her other suitor. Willoughby Kincaid had somehow inveigled his way into the affections of Horace and Etta Langmead. The Englishman was at his most attentive. As soon as wine was poured, he raised a glass.

"I wish to propose a toast!" he announced.

"To whom?" asked Etta Langmead.

"To the four beautiful ladies at this table, Mrs. Langmead. But I'd like to single out, if I may, Miss Genevieve Masefield. I heard the most delicious rumor earlier this evening," he said, gazing at Genevieve. "You not only have the cream of English womanhood siting at your table, my friends. You have a concert pianist. Miss Masefield is to accompany Mrs. Gilpatrick in a song recital." His glass was lifted higher. "Let's drink to their joint success."

Everyone did so with enthusiasm, then plied Genevieve with endless questions. When she finally escaped the interrogation, she found herself wishing that she had never sat down at the piano in the Ladies' Boudoir. The consequences were proving too embarrassing. Horace Langmead leaned across to impart a quiet word in her ear.

"As soon as I met Mrs. Gilpatrick, I knew that she was a performer of some kind."

"Her voice is good enough to sing grand opera."

"Have you seen the dress she's wearing this evening?"

"Yes, Mr. Langmead," she said. "I turned green with envy."

"So did Etta. However," he went on, "her husband was more interested in you."

"Me?"

"Yes, Miss Masefield. The four of us came down to dinner together. When the ladies were walking in front of us, I have to confess that I couldn't take my eyes off Mrs. Gilpatrick, but her husband simply wanted to talk about you."

"Why?"

"Oh, he just asked me what I thought about you. Naturally," said Langmead, "I told him that we were both entranced with you."

"What did Mr. Gilpatrick say to that?"

"He agreed that you were utterly charming. What he couldn't understand was why you were traveling alone." He chuckled merrily. "I did point out that a certain artist was captivated by you but I didn't see much future in that relationship."

"There isn't any, Mr. Langmead," she said quietly.

"Poor fellow! Etta wanted to invite him to our table again."

"To be honest, I'm glad that you didn't."

He probed gently. "Is there any single gentleman you *would* like us to invite?"

"No, thank you," she said firmly. "I don't need anyone to act as my pander."

"That's what I told Etta. It's one of the reasons I suggested that we omit Mr. Seymour-Jones this evening. Though I did see you come in with him this evening."

"That was purely accidental, Mr. Langmead."

"We would have included Fay Brinkley, but she seems to have been elevated."

"Yes," noted Genevieve, looking at the captain's table.

"Etta has been hoping for an invitation on our behalf," he confided. "I must say, I was a little embarrassed when she raised the matter with the Gilpatricks."

"Oh?"

"Mrs. Gilpatrick immediately declared that her husband would arrange it for us. I hate to be beholden to people for things like that, Miss Masefield. I'd much rather be invited to the captain's table on our own account. It would give me no pleasure if I was sitting there merely because I was acquainted with Mr. Gilpatrick."

"I can understand how you feel."

"Not that I don't like the man," he said defensively. "I do. But that's the kind of favor that I'd never have asked from him. Am I being silly?"

"No, Mr. Langmead."

"It's a question of self-respect."

"I agree."

Willoughby Kincaid's suddenly became the dominant voice at the table.

"So," said Yves Houlier, "you've been to China before, Mr. Kincaid."

"Only to the treaty ports," replied the other. "I intend to see rather more of the country this time. Shanghai is the place I know best. It's extraordinary how many English friends I've met there. I must have bumped into at least four chaps who were at Eton with me, and there was a Wykehamist in the colonial service who reminded me that I was once engaged to his sister."

"What's a Wykehamist?"

"Someone who went to Winchester, Monsieur Houlier. It's one of our less distinguished public schools," said Kincaid with mock contempt. "William of Wykeham was a famous Bishop of Winchester who was educated there. He went on to found a college at Oxford. I'm sorry," he continued, looking around the table. "I didn't mean to get diverted into a lecture on English history."

"Tell us about the young lady," encouraged Etta Langmead.

"Which one?"

"The one to whom you were engaged."

"Only briefly," said Kincaid with a grin. "We attended a ball together in London and the excitement got the better of me. When I woke up next morning, I discovered that I was engaged to Cressida Petrie-Hay. It was all a ghastly mistake. Anyway, to get back to China, I'm sure that you'll find it as fascinating as I do, Monsieur Houlier. I heard the call of the East a long time ago."

"What about the call of Cressida Petrie-Hay?" asked Genevieve.

"It fell on deaf ears, I'm afraid. Besides, the engagement was never formally announced in *The Times,* so it was hardly set in stone. I wriggled out of it with as much grace as I could manage. Her brother tells me that Cressida is married to a distant relative of Lord Rosebury's."

"Your former foreign secretary?" noted Langmead.

"That's right. The sixth Earl of Rosebury. Educated at Eton, of course."

"So he was not a Wykehamist?" teased Houlier.

"He'd never have soiled his feet by walking into the place."

"What about Japan?" asked Myrtle Newton. "Have you been there, Mr. Kincaid?"

"I've been everywhere, Mrs. Newton."

"Which do you prefer? Japan or China?"

Kincaid flicked a hand. "Oh, give me China every time. It's bigger, better, and much more mysterious. Its culture is fascinating. I've made quite a study of its philosophy. Yes, I prefer China and the Chinese."

"So does my husband," said Etta Langmead. "He finds the Japanese deceitful."

"No, I don't, honey," he corrected. "I simply think they need watching. But that goes for every nation." He beamed at Genevieve. "Even the English."

"The English don't have a deceitful bone in their body," boasted Kincaid.

Houlier gave him a verbal nudge. "Not even if they're Wykehamists?"

"We don't count those."

"We hope to go to Europe one day," said Myrtle Newton. "What should we see?"

"London and Paris."

"I'd add Rome and Venice," said Yves Houlier. "But avoid Germany."

"Where would you recommend, Miss Masefield?" asked Langmead.

But Genevieve was not listening. She had just seen Dillman come into the room.

Showering them with his apologies, Dillman took his seat at a table for six with the Legges, the Changs, and Angela Van Bergen. He knew about Blaine's move to the captain's table because he had suggested it, wanting to sit apart from the latter so that he would not be identified as a secondary bodyguard. He felt that it was important for them not to be seen together too often. Dillman was far too late for the first course.

"My watch must be slow," he said. "I thought I had plenty of time."

"Didn't you hear that bell they ring to announce dinner?" asked Legge.

"That's what got me out of the bath."

"You must have got dressed very quickly. It would have taken Moira an hour."

"That's not true, Bruce!" she said.

"I'm the one who has to wait, darling."

Having changed out of his steward's uniform, Dillman was in his white tie and tails. His hair had been brushed forward into its usual style, and the false mustache had been removed. Remembering their last encounter, he made an effort to be considerate toward Mrs. Van Bergen. She was wearing a nondescript black evening gown.

"I do admire that dress, Mrs. Van Bergen," he said.

"Thank you, Mr. Dillman. It's my husband's favorite."

"Will he be at the harbor to greet you?"

"Of course," she said complacently. "He'll probably be there a day in advance." She lowered her voice. "I'm glad that Mrs. Brinkley is not with us this evening."

"Are you?"

"I found her intolerable."

"She's a lady of strong convictions, that's all."

"They just happen to be the wrong ones."

"That's a matter of opinion," he said guardedly.

"There was so much bitterness in her."

"I didn't notice it."

"Oh, it was there, believe me. Just under the surface. Mrs. Brinkley is a sour woman. Do you know what I attribute it to, Mr. Dillman?"

"What?"

"Her divorce. Because she made an unfortunate marriage herself, she can't accept that some us have been more successful in our choice of husbands. It never occurs to her that we already have what we want. She presumes to speak for us."

"I don't think that she feels she's representing *you*, Mrs. Van Bergen."

"That's just as well."

"Even if you were given the vote," he ventured, "you probably wouldn't use it."

"I'd throw it back where it came from, Mr. Dillman. What do *I* know of politics?"

"What do most men know? Yet it doesn't stop them pontificating."

"Men were born to pontificate. Women were not."

"Moira pontificates from time to time," teased Legge. "Don't you, darling?"

"No, I don't," she denied.

"I should know. I'm on the receiving end." Legge gave a high-pitched laugh. "One of Moira's nieces is a suffragette," he said. "Damn girl never stops pontificating."

"Well, she doesn't get any encouragement from me," said his wife. "Daisy is going through a phase. I've warned her. If she doesn't grow out of it soon, we'll be forced to cut her dead. Do you know what the suffragettes *do* in England? They're a disgrace to our sex. If she's not careful, Daisy could end up in prison."

"Best place for her," said Legge.

"She had such a lovely disposition as a child."

"I'm sure that Mrs. Brinkley did as well," said Mrs. Van Bergen to Dillman.

Now that he had settled in, Dillman felt able to take stock of the situation at some of the other tables. Unaware of the waspish remarks being directed at her, Fay Brinkley was involved in an intense discussion with Rutherford Blaine, but she somehow sensed that she was being watched. Glancing up, she gave Dillman a secret smile. His gaze shifted to Genevieve. Apart from Kincaid, the only people he recognized at her table were the Langmeads. Genevieve was less engaged than she normally was with her dinner companions, joining fitfully in the conversation but otherwise sitting in silence. There was no silence at Rance Gilpatrick's table. Guffaws came from Joseph McDade as he listened to one of Gilpatrick's stories. Blanche McDade was unmoved but Tommy Gault, promoted to his employer's side for the first time, roared with laughter. Among the other guests, Dillman noted, were Mr. and Mrs. Hayashi.

"Did anyone go to the concert this afternoon?" asked Bruce Legge.

"We did," volunteered Li Chang. "Very nice music."

"First-rate entertainment. What about you, Mrs. Van Bergen?"

"Oh, I was there, Mr. Legge. I particularly liked the Beethoven sonata."

Dillman shook his head. "I'm afraid that I missed it."

"Then you missed a treat, old chap," said Legge.

"You also missed the first signs of a romance, Mr. Dillman," said Moira, closing the lids over her glass eye. "I knew that something would happen between them."

"Between whom, Mrs. Legge?" asked Dillman.

"Have you met that beautiful English lady called Genevieve Masefield?"

"I don't believe that I have."

"You must know her by sight. Bruce and I were at her table recently."

"Yes," sighed Legge, "with that fearful windbag, Father Slattery."

"Tell us about this romance," said Mrs. Van Bergen, eager to snap up any gossip. "Who's the man involved?"

"Who else but your old bridge partner?"

She was hurt. "Mr. Kincaid?"

"We knew that he was interested in her," said Moira, taking over again. "He wanted to know everything we could tell him about Miss Masefield. He's older than her, of course, but I don't think that matters. There's definitely something between them."

"How do you know?" asked Dillman.

"They went to the concert together."

"And sat in a back row," added Legge. "It couldn't be more obvious."

Captain Piercey had endless responsibilities aboard ship, but he was quite prepared to take on another one. When the meal was over and his guests slowly dispersed, he chatted with Rutherford Blaine before accompanying him out of the room, providing him with cover in the event that someone was watching. When the two of them were well clear of the dining saloon, the purser was on hand to escort Blaine back to his cabin and to ensure that they were not followed. Dillman had approved of the plan but he was not concerned with Blaine anymore. His thoughts were directed solely at Genevieve. While he knew that she had no serious interest in Kincaid, he was a little piqued to hear that she had been at the concert with the man and wanted to raise the matter with her, especially as the two of them were now dining at the same table. But there was no rush. He waited until Genevieve left the room, then checked the time. Only Li Chang and his wife remained at his table. Dillman fished for information.

"What do you know about silk, Mr. Chang?" he asked.

"Only that the best kind comes from China," replied Chang.

"The Japanese might disagree."

Chang grinned. "They always disagree with us."

"Silk must be very difficult to transport."

"It is, Mr. Dillman. Last time I sail, I watched them loading bales of silk in Yokohama. Japanese silk, of course," he said, nodding at his wife. "Inferior quality. You are a seafaring man, Mr. Dillman. You must have seen liners being coaled."

"Many times," said Dillman.

"You've seen nothing like what happens in Yokohama."

"Why?"

"Because it's women who do the work," explained Chang. "I not like to say this in front of Mrs. Brinkley in case it made her angry, but she will find out the truth when we reach Japan. Coal barges pull up alongside the ship and the women form chains on a series of ladders. They pass the coal to each other in heavy bags. It is hard, dirty work. They get filthy." He squeezed his wife's hand affectionately. "I not let my wife do anything like that. Women are good enough to load the coal, but men bring the silk bales in special containers."

"What happens when the silk gets back to America?"

"It's checked by customs and railways officials, then put on trains. I know about these cars, Mr. Dillman. I help to design them. They are lined with varnished wood and sheathed in paper so that they are airtight. No dirt or moisture can get into the cars to damage the merchandise. Silk is very costly."

"I know. They obviously take care of it."

"It is strange," commented Chang. "Women will wear most of that silk when it is made into clothing, yet they are not allowed to touch it in the ports. Only men work as stokers, yet it's Japanese women who give them their coal. Something is not right."

Chang was well versed in the movement of silk. After pressing him for more details, Dillman thanked him, then excused himself from the table. Genevieve would have had plenty of time to reach her cabin. He left the dining saloon and strolled toward the promenade deck. Eager to speak with her, he was not as vigilant as he should have been. Though nobody followed him, someone was lurking around a corner near Genevieve's cabin. When she admitted Dillman, the man stepped out of hiding.

Rance Gilpatrick pulled on his cigar and chatted amiably with Joseph McDade. Adjourning to the smoking room after dinner, they had left their respective wives in the Ladies' Boudoir. Gilpatrick was about to start on another anecdote when he saw Tommy Gault come into the room. He listened to the message whispered in his ear.

"Are you sure it was *him,* Tommy?" he asked in surprise.

"I should be. He threw a punch at me this afternoon."

Gilpatrick pondered. "What on earth is Mr. Dillman doing in her cabin?"

"You'll have to be quick, I'm afraid," said Genevieve, taking off her jewelry. "I've got another rehearsal with Maxine in a while and I need to change. I can't play the piano in this dress." She felt the intensity of his gaze. "What's wrong, George?"

"Nothing."

"Then why are you staring at me?"

"I didn't mean to," he said, relaxing. "How was the concert this afternoon?"

"I wasn't really in a position to enjoy it."

"Why didn't you tell me that you went with Mr. Kincaid?"

"But I didn't," she retorted.

"The Legges claim they saw the pair of you in a back row."

"That's true, but I went there with Maxine. I told you that. At the very last moment, Mr. Kincaid slipped in and took the seat beside me. I could do nothing about it."

"Oh, I see. I misunderstood."

"You certainly did, George. I loathe the man. I was horrified when I saw that the Langmeads had invited him to join our table. Kincaid was insufferable."

"I think I owe you an apology."

"So do I."

"I'm sorry, Genevieve."

"What on earth did you think was going on?" she demanded.

"I don't know."

"The simple fact is that I didn't have the chance to explain when I met you in the purser's cabin. Kincaid wasn't on my mind. But while we're on the subject of things we might have told each other," she said with a note of amusement, "why didn't you mention that Fay Brinkley tried to flirt with you?"

"I wasn't sure that she did."

"Come on, George. You're not that naïve."

"Mrs. Brinkley and I had a long chat, that's all."

"It's the looks in between the words that count."

"What did she say to you?"

"That she found you very tempting. Coming from Fay, that's a real compliment. She doesn't hold men in the highest esteem as a rule. And you liked her," she noted. "I could tell that. It's true, isn't it?" He gave a nod of assent. "What would you have done if I hadn't been on the ship?"

"Exactly what I did do, Genevieve. Concentrate on my job."

"You're not on duty twenty-four hours a day."

"Yes, I am. So are you." He gave her a light kiss on the lips. "We ought to spend less time watching each other and more time looking for the killer. I trust you implicitly."

"I thought I trusted you until I saw that light in Fay's eye."

"Genevieve!"

"I was only joking." She became serious. "How did you get on?"

"I may have struck gold."

"Did you find those catalogs?"

"Yes," he said. "They were hidden under Gilpatrick's mattress. At least we know what game he's involved in now. He and his associates are gun runners. My guess is that McDade is his supplier and Gilpatrick is responsible for smuggling the stuff across the Pacific. Those catalogs contained a number of new weapons that are not on the market yet. Some of them had been ticked by Gilpatrick. I think that he means to buy a consignment in the future."

"Does he have a load of guns aboard?"

"I hope so. It's the only way we can nail him."

"How on earth did he get them past customs?"

"People like Gilpatrick always get around the rules. But I didn't only search his cabin, Genevieve. While I was on the boat deck, I had a sudden impulse to pop into Mr. Hayashi's cabin. I'm glad I surrendered to it."

"Why?"

"Hayashi is not as scrupulous as Gilpatrick. He left some interesting things hanging around," he reported, "including a letter from Gilpatrick about this voyage. They're in cahoots together. There's a mention of merchandise from Seattle being exchanged for goods in Shanghai."

"Why there?" she wondered. "Mr. Hayashi is Japanese."

"According to the manifest, he has an office in Shanghai as well. Some of the stuff with his name on it is destined for China. That could be a valuable clue. So could this," he said, taking a slip of paper from his pocket. "What do you make of this?"

Genevieve looked at it. "Is this some kind of hoax, George?"

"No," he assured her. "That's an address of some sort. I took it from a letter heading in Hayashi's cabin. They may not look like it but those are Japanese characters. I copied them down as carefully as I could."

"What use are they? Neither of us reads Japanese."

"We don't, perhaps," he said, "but your friend Mr. Natsuki does."

Back in the safety of his cabin, Rutherford Blaine was able to let his exasperation show.

"How long will this have to go on, Mr. Roebuck?" he asked.

"Until we catch the man who's trying to kill you."

"Supposing he's not alone?"

"Then we'll round up his confederates as well. They'll all

stand trial for the murder of Father Slattery." The purser bit his lip. "He, of course, is another problem. We can't keep the body indefinitely. As soon as this matter is cleared up, Captain Piercey will have to think about a burial at sea."

"It could well have been mine."

"I'm afraid so."

"Ironic, really," said Blaine. "I hate water and never learned to swim. The last place in the world where I want my bones to rest is at the bottom of the Pacific."

"It won't come to that, Mr. Blaine."

"How do you know?"

"Because I have every confidence in George Dillman."

"Does he have any suspects in mind?"

"Yes and no, sir."

Blaine grinned. "You sound like a politician, Mr. Roebuck. The nation's capital is full of them. They're men who can face in seven directions at the same time without ever committing themselves. I call them the yes-no-maybe men."

"Very well," said the purser. "If you want a more specific answer, it's this. We do have someone aboard whom we're watching very carefully. He certainly wouldn't stop at murder, and he has an associate who's strong enough to have killed Father Slattery in the way that occurred. George Dillman is searching for evidence to arrest these men."

"That's the 'yes' part of the equation. Where does the 'no' part come in?"

"The main suspect has been under surveillance since we set sail. We're convinced that he's been using this vessel for the purposes of smuggling. That's the reason we hired Mr. Dillman," he explained. "We know this man is involved in one crime. Whether he committed the more serious one of murder is open to doubt."

"What's his background?"

"He owns a chain of saloons on the West Coast and has been implicated in all manner of illegal activities from prostitution to handling contraband."

"Why haven't the police put him behind bars?" said Blaine.

"He always slips out of their grasp somehow," replied Roebuck. "He's a wealthy man. He can afford large bribes. We know for a fact that he has a number of crooked politicians in his pocket."

The older man tensed. "Do you happen to know the names of those politicians?"

"I'm afraid not."

"But there could be a link with Washington, D.C.?"

"Conceivably."

"What's this man's name?"

"Rance Gilpatrick."

"Means nothing to me," said Blaine, shaking his head. "Thank you, Mr. Roebuck. You've been very honest with me, but I can't say that I feel reassured. Mr. Gilpatrick may or may not be involved in the plot against me. Yet he's your only suspect. The killer may turn out to be someone else entirely."

"We accept that, sir."

"And he may be part of a small gang."

"That, too, is possible."

"Is Mr. Dillman up against them on his own?"

"Don't underestimate him, Mr Blaine. He's a remarkable man."

"I appreciate that, but I do think that he'll need some help."

"He already has it," said the purser. "George Dillman is supported by a partner."

Maxine Gilpatrick had been working on her program in private. Her singing was more assured, her performance more studied. For the first time since they had teamed up, Genevieve Masefield had the feeling that their concert could be a success. She played the piano with more confidence, and marveled at the sheer professionalism of her partner. Though none of the songs would have been suitable for her customary venue in a saloon, Maxine sang them as if they were standard numbers in her repertoire. She put controlled emotion into her work. Her version of "The Old Folks at Home" was so affecting that it brought her accompanist close to tears. They were alone in the Ladies' Boudoir at the end of the day and made excellent progress.

"We're almost there, Jenny," said Maxine, slapping the lid of the piano.

"And we still have two days to go."

"All we need to do now is add some polish."

"You've been doing that, Maxine," said Genevieve with admiration. "I'm amazed at the improvement since the last rehearsal."

"I had a long soak in the tub," admitted Maxine. "That's where I rehearse best."

"Do you want to finish?"

"Let's have one more go at 'Greensleeves.' "

"I'm ready when you are," said Genevieve, playing the introduction.

Maxine took her stance, then launched herself into the song. Genevieve knew the tune well enough to play it without having to follow the music. As she looked up at her friend, she was impressed with the incredible poise that Maxine was showing. The latter was composed, dignified yet totally relaxed. The words seem to come out effortlessly. Maxine sang with the air of a woman who was making one last bold attempt to prove that she should be taken seriously as a singer. Gone were the vocal tricks and movements that she had used during her earlier career. She looked and sounded like a concert artiste at the height of her powers. When she came to the end of the song, it earned warm applause.

"That was terrific, honey," said Gilpatrick, clapping his hands.

"Rance!" she exclaimed, swinging around. "I didn't see you there."

He gave her a kiss of congratulation. "I sneaked in." He turned to Genevieve. "You play that thing well, Miss Masefield.

If you ever want a job as a pianist in one of my saloons, just let me know."

"Don't listen to him, Jenny," said Maxine. "He's only teasing. But you shouldn't be in here, Rance," she went on, giving him a playful push. "This is reserved for ladies."

"I always did like to break the rules," he said cheerily.

"Well," said Genevieve, getting up and collecting the sheets of music, "if that's it, I'll wish you both good night and slip away."

Gilpatrick blocked her way. "Not just yet, Miss Masefield," he said coolly. "Much as I like to listen to my wife's singing, it was you I came in here to see."

"Why is that, Mr. Gilpatrick?"

"I wanted to ask you about a mutual acquaintance of ours."

"Who are you talking about?" asked Maxine.

"Mr. George Dillman."

"I've never heard of the guy."

"Well, I'm sure that Miss Masefield has." He smiled at her. "Haven't you?"

Mention of Dillman's name gave Genevieve a fright, but she concealed it well. Wondering how Gilpatrick had connected her with her partner, she tried to make their friendship sound more fleeting.

"I did meet Mr. Dillman briefly," she admitted.

"Since you came onboard?" he pressed.

"Of course."

"How did you get acquainted?"

"We sat next to each other in the lounge one morning."

"So you wouldn't describe yourselves as close friends?"

"What are you getting at, Rance?" complained his wife. "You've got no right to question Jenny about her private life. Who is this Mr. Dillman, anyway?"

"That's what I'm trying to find out, honey," he replied. "Earlier today, Tommy Gault was showing off in front of a couple of kids, getting them to punch him in the stomach. This guy just happened to be watching, so we started to talk. He gave his name as George Dillman. What I want to know is whether or not it was sheer coincidence that he was there at the time."

"You'll have to ask him," suggested Genevieve.

"Can't you help me out, Miss Masefield?"

"I'm afraid not."

"He hasn't discussed the incident with you?"

"Of course not, Mr. Gilpatrick. Why should he?"

"You tell me."

"I hardly know Mr. Dillman."

"Then what were you doing, letting him into your cabin earlier on?"

Genevieve could not hide her blush. Maxine spared her the necessity of an immediate reply. Torn between annoyance at her husband for putting Genevieve under such pressure and simple curiosity, she veered toward the latter.

"Are you sure about this, Rance?"

"Dead sure."

"How?"

"My informant was very reliable."

Maxine was shocked. "You had someone snooping on Jenny?"

"No, honey. He was just walking past at the time. Keep out of this, will you?"

"Jenny is my friend."

"I'm more interested in another friend of hers. Well," he said, switching his gaze to Genevieve. "Is it true?"

The exchange between husband and wife had given her time to concoct her story. Genevieve met his gaze without wavering and put indignation into her voice.

"I don't have to answer that question, Mr. Gilpatrick," she said, chin held high, "but I will. First of all, however, let me say how disgusted I am at the thought that you felt the need to spy on me. My private life is my own. I can invite anyone I wish into my cabin without seeking your permission."

"Hear that, Rance?" said Maxine. "I endorse every word of it."

"Mr. Dillman is not a close friend of mine," continued Genevieve, "but he did strike me as a very discreet man when I met him. I invited him to my cabin to ask him a favor—and it was not the kind that you imagine," she said acidly. "I don't know who was lurking outside my door but, if he had stayed there, he would have seen how soon my visitor departed."

"What's this favor you mention?" asked Gilpatrick.

Maxine was angry. "It's none of your business, Rance."

"Leave this to me, honey."

"You're upsetting Jenny, can't you see that?"

"It's all right, Maxine," said Genevieve calmly. "I don't mind telling you, but I must insist that it goes no further than this room. What I asked Mr. Dillman was whether or not he'd agree to act as a protective shield."

"Against what?"

"Mr. Kincaid, for one. You were at that concert this afternoon, Maxine. You saw how he crept up on me. And it wasn't the first time. He's so determined to press his advances," complained Genevieve, "that he somehow contrived to sit at the same table as me this evening."

"I noticed."

"However, he's not my only concern. There's someone who's even more of a nuisance and, thanks to you, Mr. Gilpatrick," she said forcefully, "he has an excuse to hound me more than ever."

"How do I come into it?" he asked in surprise.

"Because you commissioned him to do some posters."

"That English artist?"

"Yes," said Genevieve. "David Seymour-Jones. I haven't given him the slightest encouragement, but he's been haunting me since the first day afloat. He drew a portrait of me when I wasn't even aware that he was there and to top it all," she added, working herself into genuine anger, "he followed me to my cabin and pretended that all he wanted were the details of the song recital. The sequel was even more embarrassing. Can you see now why I asked Mr. Dillman for his help? He's my last resort. Because he's married, there can never be anything but friendship between us, so it's perfectly safe. But I need him to be seen with me in public in order to keep the others at bay." Her eyes were blazing now. "Is there anything wrong in that, Mr. Gilpatrick?"

"I guess not," he conceded.

"You should have let Tommy get rid of these guys for you," said Maxine.

"My way will be just as effective," said Genevieve, "but it's not something I care to have voiced abroad. Mr. Dillman would be as outraged as I am to hear that someone had been spying on us. I'm sorry, Maxine," she went on, "but my hand is forced. When I agreed to play the piano for you, I didn't realize that your husband would mount an investigation into my private life. Given the circumstances, I feel that you should look for someone else to act as your accompanist."

Before her friend could protest, Genevieve made a dignified exit. As she strode along the passageway, she could hear Maxine Gilpatrick taking out her rage on her husband. It had been a successful escape.

Dillman was in no hurry to return to his new cabin. After calling on the purser to report his findings, he made his way to the covered promenade on the upper deck. As he looked through the windows, he could see the prow of the *Minnesota* rising and falling with the rhythm of a gigantic rocking horse. It was a comforting sight. With all the problems that had arisen, he had had no time simply to enjoy the pleasure of being on a voyage again. There was something exciting about being so far from land of any description. They were a tiny speck in the largest ocean in the world. He knew that it was also the deepest expanse of water on the globe, and that fact appealed to the sailor in him. The Atlantic might be more dangerous, but the Pacific somehow had more mystery. Dillman was not alone. A young couple was standing a small distance away, arms around each other as they gazed out at the view, lulled into a romantic mood by the steady movement of the vessel and by the beauty of the night sky. When Dillman heard footsteps behind him, he assumed that someone else had come out to savor the atmosphere.

"I wish I was their age again," said Fay Brinkley, stopping beside him.

Dillman turned to face her. "I didn't realize it was you, Mrs. Brinkley."

"Who were you expecting?"

"Nobody."

"Don't you envy them?" she asked, indicating the other couple.

"Not really, Mrs. Brinkley."

"Why not?"

"I prefer to be alone with my thoughts sometimes."

"Is that a polite way of telling me to move on?"

"Not at all," he said with a warm smile. "I'm very pleased to see you. How was dinner at the captain's table?"

"Quite an event, Mr. Dillman. I didn't know we had quite so many important people aboard. We had a Russian princess, a Polish count, and someone who's high up in the Manchurian government. To be honest," she admitted with a laugh, "I'm not sure how I managed to get an invitation."

"They come strictly on merit," he said.

"I think they just pulled my name out of a hat. Still," she went on, "at least I got to sit next to Mr. Blaine. Just as well. I couldn't understand a word that some of the others spoke, especially that Polish count. And whatever you do, please don't ask me to spell his name. It didn't seem to have any vowels in it."

"What sort of a man is the captain?"

"He's a gem. Captain Piercey was the perfect host."

"You were lucky not to be at my table," he said. "Mrs. Van Bergen was there."

Fay laughed. "I daresay she spoke well of me."

"Your name did come up in conversation, I have to confess."

"Well, I hope you defended me like a true gentleman, Mr. Dillman."

"To the hilt."

She laughed again, then stood beside him, staring out across the ocean ahead.

"Have you any idea where we are?" she asked. "I don't. Captain Piercey said that we'd be passing some islands during the night, but I can't recall their name. The wine we drank was very potent this evening."

"How was Mr. Blaine?"

"As engaging as ever. Though I did sense something rather odd about him."

"Odd?"

"Yes, Mr. Dillman. I could be wrong, of course. I did indulge myself ruinously in case it was my only chance to sit at the captain's table. That probably impaired my faculties, but I still had this feeling about Mr. Blaine."

"What sort of feeling?"

"He seemed frightened."

"Of what?"

"That's what I couldn't work out."

"Could he have been frightened of *you,* perhaps."

"It's a delicious thought," she said with a grin, "but I'm afraid that wasn't the case. Mr. Blaine is happily married. His wife's name cropped up more than ever. In fact, it was one of the things that showed his insecurity. He's always been so self-possessed before. But there were moments this evening when he was like an inexperienced swimmer, touching the bottom of the pool with his toe every so often just to make sure that it was there."

"It sounds to me as if he's simply missing his wife a great deal."

"I have no quarrel with that. Husbands *should* miss their wives. You'd be surprised how many of them don't when they're set free. Married men are invariably the worst. Even at my age, I get propositions from husbands on the loose."

"That's hardly surprising, Mrs Brinkley. You're a handsome woman."

"What worries me is that I must look available to them. Do I, Mr. Dillman?"

"I wouldn't have thought so."

"Then why do they come buzzing like flies around a honey pot?"

"I can't answer that."

"Is it because I'm divorced? Does that stamp me as a scarlet woman?"

"Not in the least."

"I can't win," she protested. "I'm shunned by the wives and hounded by the husbands. Divorce carries a social stigma, but I never hide the fact. Actually, I made sure that Mrs. Van Bergen knew my situation in order to scandalize her. Curious, isn't it? Mrs. Van Bergen would cheerfully spurn me because I'm divorced, yet I'll wager that Mr. Van Bergen would be on my tail if he was traveling on this ship without her."

"It's one of the ironies of life, Mrs. Brinkley."

She turned to him. "Why don't you call me Fay?"

"If you wish."

"May I call you George?"

"It sounds like a fair exchange."

"What do you see yourself doing in a year's time, George?"

"I never look that far ahead."

"You don't strike me as a man addicted to idle pleasures."

Dillman laughed. "I can't afford to be, Fay. Besides, I'm too restless."

"For what? Work? Romance? Adventure?"

"Challenges," he said. "Of all kinds."

"Then we have something in common." Their eyes locked. "What are you going to do when we reach Japan?"

"See as much of it as I can before the ship sails on."

"Would you like some company?"

"I'll already have it, Fay," he said, keen to avoid any commitment to her.

She was disappointed. "Oh, I see."

"Besides, you'll be too busy leading a protest at the docks."

"A protest? Against what?"

"The exploitation of female labor," he said. "According to Mr. Chang, the ship is coaled by teams of women who pass heavy bags to each other in a human chain. Can you imagine American women being forced to do that?"

"Metaphorically, they are. But thanks for the warning."

"I don't think China's record is any better with regard to female employment, but Mr. Chang was careful to slide over that. Brace yourself for a few shocks, Fay."

"My brother's already warned me about some of them. Well," she said with a sigh of reluctance, "that wine is getting to my head. Time for me turn in."

"Let me ask you a question first."

"As many as you like."

"How did you know that I'd be out here tonight?"

"I didn't. We met by complete accident."

"You told me that you never did anything by accident."

"Did I?" she replied with a laugh. "That shows how carefully you listen to me, George. I'll take encouragement from that." She gave him a kiss on the cheek. "Let's call it a promising start. Good night."

As he lay on his bunk, Dillman had much to occupy his mind. He had moved to the cabin formerly occupied by Rutherford Blaine, and was determined to remain awake as long as possible. If an attack came, he wanted to be ready for it. While he speculated on whether or not the assassin would try to strike again, he also kept Fay Brinkley at the back of his mind. He had never met a woman quite like her. As soon as they had parted on deck, he resolved to tell Genevieve Masefield about the encounter. Anxious to obviate another misunderstanding, he also wanted to ask Genevieve what she would read into some of Fay's remarks. He suspected that Fay would use Genevieve as a confidante again, and looked forward to hearing what was said between the two women.

But the main question that haunted him was whether or not he was fighting on two fronts or simply on one. If Rance Gilpatrick was involved in the murder as well as the smuggling it would simplify matters considerably, but he inclined to the view that he was up against two quite unconnected villains. That made his job much more difficult. While he was concentrating on one, he was taking his eye off the other. The death threat hanging over Rutherford Blaine had to take precedence, and he was interested in Fay's observation that the man had been frightened. It was hardly surprising. One man had been killed in the diplomat's place, and his wounded bodyguard had been forced to retire from the field. Under such pressure, Blaine was holding up very well. Only someone as acute as Fay Brinkley would spot the quiet tremors underneath the bland exterior.

Fatigue eventually got the better of him. Dillman had been careful to drink very little alcohol that evening, but it had been a long and taxing day. Before he could stop himself, he drifted gently off to sleep. Every so often, he would force himself awake for a few seconds and sit up in the darkness, convinced that someone was there. He was mistaken. Lowering his head to the pillow, he was soon slumbering peacefully again. When the sound came, his eyes were wide open in an instant, but this time he did not sit up. What he heard was the scrape of a key in the lock and the swish of the door as it opened and shut. He did have a visitor this time. Dillman came fully awake.

The man was short, hunched, and stealthy. With a piece of cord held between both hands, he crept toward the bunk and tried to make out the shape of the man lying there. Dillman waited until his nocturnal caller was close before he reacted. He could hear the man's breath and see him in hazy outline. Before the assassin could strike, Dillman flung back the sheets and leapt from the bunk, catching the man with a savage punch to the face. His assailant reeled back, but he recovered with speed. As Dillman tried to grapple with him, a leg shot out to trip him expertly to the floor, and a series of kicks made him grunt with pain. Rolling over, Dillman struggled to his feet and managed to get a firmer grip on the man, hurling him against the wall and landing a punch in his stomach that drew a sharp gasp. Once again, however, the man retaliated, holding one of Dillman's arms and swinging around with speed so that his back was to the detective. He pulled hard. Dillman found himself diving over the man's shoulder to hit his head on the floor.

The fight was over. Realizing that he had picked the wrong man yet again, the assassin took to his heels and fled. Still dazed, Dillman dragged himself to his feet and lumbered out in the passageway. He knew that pursuit was futile. However, two things had been established. The threat to Rutherford Blaine was very serious, but the assassin was definitely not Rance Gilpatrick's henchman. Dillman's stomach punch had inflicted pain. It would have had no impact on Tommy Gault. The detective chided himself for coming off worst in the fight, but at least he had shielded Blaine from the attack. As he stumbled to the bathroom to examine his wounds, he consoled himself with the thought that he had landed a solid punch on the man's face. The bruise would still be there the next day. It was an important clue.

TWELVE

Maxine Gilpatrick's fury had not abated during the night. When she woke up the next morning, she was still as angry at her husband as before. Gilpatrick was not allowed to enjoy his customary lie-in. She shook him until he was roused from his slumbers.

"What's going on?" he mumbled, blinking in the light.

"I want to speak to you, Rance. Wake up."

"Why did you shake me like that? I thought there was some kind of emergency."

"There is," she declared. "It concerns our marriage."

He saw the clock beside his bunk. "It's not even seven yet!"

"Who cares?"

"I do, Maxine. A guy needs his sleep. Get back in your bed."

"Not until we've had this out," she said, hands on hips. "I'm not going to holler at you as I did last night. I just want you to know how upset I am at what you did. I'll never forgive you for that."

"For what?" he asked, sitting up and rubbing his eyes.

"Having Jenny watched like that."

"I thought I had good cause."

"Well, you didn't. You acted outrageously."

"That's not what happened, honey."

"No," she retorted, simmering with rage. "What happened was that, between the two of you, you and Tommy Gault robbed me of the best friend I've made since we came onboard. You also lost me my accompanist for the song recital."

"We'll find another."

"I don't want another. I want Jenny Masefield."

"Then we talk her around. Let me fix it."

"That's the last thing I'm going to do," she stormed. "You keep well away from Jenny in the future. And if Tommy Gault ever gets within twenty yards of her, I'll brain him. Keep him away from her or you'll be sleeping alone in this cabin from now on."

He was hurt. "What do you mean?"

"Exactly what I say."

"Look, take it easy," he soothed. "You're getting this out of proportion."

"No, I'm not, Rance. This is how I see it," she said, folding her arms and glaring her defiance. "Last night, Jenny and I had the best rehearsal so far. It was so good it actually settled her nerves. Before you butted in, we were in a wonderful mood."

"You had every right to be, Maxine. I heard you sing."

"Then why couldn't you just applaud and then take me out of there?"

"Because I came to speak to Miss Masefield."

"You came to accuse her. I know that look of yours. You thought you'd caught her out and bided your time until you could spring your little surprise on her. Jenny is beautiful, unmarried, and over the age of twenty-one," she reminded him. "She can invite the entire crew into her cabin if she wishes to—only she doesn't want Tommy outside the door, counting them as they go in."

He reached out for her. "Maxine—"

"Don't touch me!" she said contemptuously, backing away.

"We can sort this out between us."

"You've done enough sorting as it is. What on earth possessed you to have Jenny watched? She's completely harmless."

"I wasn't sure about that."

"Why not?"

"Oh, little things," he said impatiently. "You knew I had doubts about her from the start. That's why I asked you to find out a little more about her."

"I'm not doing your spying for you, Rance. That's not my idea of a wifely duty. Besides," she insisted, "there was nothing to find out."

"I felt that there was. Especially after that guy Dillman showed up."

"He's a friend of hers, that's all."

"Then why did she deny it at first?"

"Jenny didn't. She merely said she didn't know him all that well."

"She knew him well enough to invite him into her cabin."

"Now we know why. Honestly, Rance," she went on, teeth bared, "I've never felt so humiliated in my life. What you did to that woman was appalling. How would you like it if another man was snooping on me?"

"I thought he might be. Indirectly."

"Who?"

"Nobody," he said, wanting to terminate the discussion. "Listen, honey, why don't we get another hour's sleep, then have breakfast together?"

"I'm not sharing a table with you."

"What do you mean?"

"You still don't see why I'm so riled up, do you?"

"Of course I do. I made a mistake and I'm sorry."

"An apology won't cover the damage you inflicted last night."

"Come back to bed."

"No," she snarled. "I don't even want to be in the same room as you!"

"There's no need to yell. People will hear us in the next cabin."

"Let them hear us!" she shouted.

"Maxine!"

"I still haven't got the truth out of you yet. Why did you want me to keep an eye on Jenny in the first place? And what was it about this Mr. Dillman that aroused your suspicions?"

"It doesn't matter now," he said wearily.

"I want to know, Rance."

"Take it easy, will you?"

"And if you say that to me once more, I'll throw something at you," she said, grabbing a vase of flowers to prove that it was no idle threat. "I'm your wife, or had you forgotten? Married couples are supposed to share things."

"Put that vase down."

"Tell me what I want to know first."

"Put it down," he ordered, getting out of bed to snatch it from her. "And stop pushing me. You're not the only person who can get angry."

"Don't threaten me, Rance. I'm still waiting."

He put the vase back on the table. "You wouldn't understand, Maxine."

"I think I'm beginning to understand only too well."

Gilpatrick turned to look at her. Curbing his anger, he sat on the edge of the bunk with his head in his hands. When he looked up at her again, he made an effort to control himself. He spoke with deliberate slowness.

"Here's how it looked from where I was standing," he explained. "No sooner do we get on the ship than Miss Masefield suddenly pops up out of the blue."

"She was playing the piano. I couldn't resist singing. That's how we met. Jenny made no attempt to seek me out, Rance. How could she when she'd never set eyes on me before? Jenny didn't just pop up. I chose her as a friend."

"You chose her, but I didn't. I confided my suspicions to you at the start. Now," he said, wiping a hand across his mouth, "a few days later, Mr. Dillman turns up on the boat deck. I don't know why. He certainly doesn't have a cabin there. He seemed a pleasant guy and he knew a fair bit about the *Minnesota*. And I admit that I had a good laugh at him when he took a shot at Tommy's stomach and almost broke his hand. Off he went and I forgot all about him. Until—lo and behold!—he's seen slipping into Miss Masefield's cabin."

"By the man you stationed outside."

"I thought I might learn something."

"Why?"

"I told you before. I wanted to know what her game was."

"Jenny is a passenger. She has no game."

"It looked funny to me. Her and Dillman getting together like that."

"What did you think the pair of them were doing?"

"Comparing notes about me."

Maxine bit back a reply. Her rage was slowly replaced by a feeling of disquiet.

"Is something going on, Rance?" she asked.

"No, honey."

"You're up to your old tricks, aren't you?"

"Of course not."

"You swore to me that this was a kind of honeymoon. There might be a little business involved, you said, but it wouldn't get in the way. Well, so far it's been all business and no honeymoon," she said, advancing on him. "Do you know what I think, Rance Gilpatrick? I don't believe you wanted me here as your wife at all."

"I did, Maxine. I love you."

"You just needed a decoy, didn't you?"

"No!"

"What are you up to this time?"

"Some minor transactions, that's all."

"Was that why I was locked out of my own cabin yesterday?" she said with heavy sarcasm. "So that you and the bellowing Joe McDade could discuss a minor transaction?"

"You get the benefit in the long run."

"I'm more concerned with the short run, and there are very few benefits in that."

"Maxine," he protested. "I've done everything you wanted."

"Like insulting my friend and making her pull out of the concert?"

"Who arranged the concert in the first place?"

"You did," she conceded.

"And who fixed it so that you can use the orchestra's piano?"

"You did."

"Then there were the posters I commissioned."

"Don't mention those," she snapped. "Why didn't you discuss it with us before you hire some guy you know nothing about? This David Seymour-Jones may be a terrific artist, but he also happens to be the one man on the ship that Jenny can't bear."

"That's not my fault."

"It's all your fault," she said, crossing to the bathroom and pausing in the doorway. "Now, I want you out of here when I get dressed. Is that understood?"

He was shaken. "No, it isn't."

"I'm not stripping off while you're in the bedroom."

"But I'm your husband."

"No, Rance," she said pointedly. "You're still the same cheap crook you were when I first met you. I thought you'd changed. Now you have money, I thought you didn't need to sail so close to the wind. But you do and you always will. I don't know what's going on this time, but I want no part of it."

"Maxine," he said, crossing to her with outstretched hands.

"Keep away from me."

"Listen," he said, searching for ways to appease her. "I'll make it up to you. I'll fix it so we dine at the captain's table today. I'll have flowers sent to Miss Masefield as an apology. I'll even swallow my pride and beg her to play that piano for you. Just tell me what I can do, honey, and I swear I'll do it."

"Then get lost!" she said.

Disappearing into the bathroom, she slammed the door in his face.

When the purser called on him, Dillman was still in his dressing gown. Mike Roebuck noticed the bruising on his temple and frowned with concern.

"Did he come, George?"

"Yes," said Dillman. "He came and went."

"What happened?"

"His jujitsu was more effective than my boxing skills."

"Tell me all."

Dillman gave him an account of events during the night, admitting freely that his adversary was too elusive for him. The frown on the purser's face deepened.

"Why didn't you come straight to me to report it?" he asked.

"What was the point of that, Mike?"

"I could have started a search."

"Where? By the time you'd rustled up some men, he'd have gone to ground somewhere. On a ship this size, there must be thousands of hiding places. It would've been a complete waste of time."

"The guy tried to kill you."

"Unsuccessfully."

"But he might have come back for a second crack."

"No chance of that," said Dillman proudly. "I gave him too warm a welcome. In any case, he's after Mr. Blaine and not me. I don't think it took him too long to realize that I couldn't possibly be Mr. Blaine. That's why he ran away."

"I think I'd run away if you pounced on me."

"I failed, Mike. I set the trap and he walked straight into it. Then he escaped."

"I did tell you to have someone else in here with you."

Dillman smiled. "I never share a bedroom with another man."

"Not even if he might save your life?"

"I saved it myself last night. And I landed a hefty punch on his face."

"So?"

"All we need to do is to look for a passenger with a black eye."

"If only it was that easy," said Roebuck with a pessimistic grin, "but we can hardly ask fifteen hundred people to queue up so that you can examine their faces. Besides, he might have been a member of the crew. That gives you another two hundred and fifty to get around, and you'll have real problems there."

"Problems?"

"I was thinking of the stokers."

"Yes," said Dillman. "I see what you mean."

"Passions run high down there, George. When you spend your whole day shoveling coal into a furnace, you don't have time for the social niceties. Tempers are short. Arguments start. Fights develop. You'll probably find half a dozen black eyes among the stokers."

"I still think it could be a lead."

"Only if your attacker ventures out into the light of day."

"He can't hide away forever."

"All he has to do is to wait until the black eye fades."

"I'll find him," asserted Dillman.

"Not by putting your own life on the line, George. I'm pulling rank on you. If you want to try this again, you share the cabin with a man or a gun or, preferably, both." He looked around. "Not that there's any chance of him coming here again. He'll try to find out where Mr. Blaine is sleeping."

"Don't tell Mr. Blaine about this, will you?"

"I wasn't going to," said the purser. "He has enough on his mind as it is."

"That's true. Say that nobody showed up."

"How will you explain that bruise on your temple?"

"I banged my head accidentally, didn't I?"

"With a little help from someone else."

"Mr. Blaine needn't know that. Anyway," said Dillman cheerily, "I'm glad you called, Mike. It's not all bad news. I had a productive visit to the boat deck last night."

"Did you get into Gilpatrick's cabin?"

"And into Mr. Hayashi's."

The purser listened to his report and nodded his approval of the find.

"We had the feeling that it might be guns of some sort," he said.

"Gilpatrick gets the silk, Hayashi gets the weapons."

"We'll need more evidence than a few catalogs."

"Don't forget that letter heading I copied in Hayashi's cabin."

"That might turn out to be useless, George. Give me something more solid."

"Then you'll have to trust my judgment."

"In what way?"

"I'm going to need the keys to the orlop deck again," said Dillman. "And I want to take you with me next time I go down there. That's where we'll get hard evidence."

"We can't go breaking into sealed cargo."

"It's the only way."

"The skipper won't sanction that without an extremely good reason."

"Then I'll provide it," affirmed Dillman. "The contraband must be hidden down there somewhere. I'll tell you this, Mike. You won't find any guns in Gilpatrick's wardrobe. There's no room. His wife has filled it to the brim with her dresses."

After waking early, Genevieve Masefield lay in her bunk and considered her plight. She was on the horns of a dilemma. Forced to invent a story about her relationship with Dillman, she now had to give visible proof of it, yet the last thing she wanted was for any link to be seen between the two of them. It lessened their effectiveness. There was also the nagging problem of Fay Brinkley. It was she who had confided her interest in Dillman to her friend. Genevieve could imagine how Fay might react if she saw her with the detective. Fay was an astute woman. Her suspicions would be aroused immediately. However, it was more important to allay Rance Gilpatrick's suspicions. Genevieve had been rocked by his announcement that someone had seen Dillman going into her cabin. There had certainly been nobody in the passageway outside when she opened the door. Someone must have been lurking around the corner, and that thought unsettled her. She wondered if it was the same person who had searched her cabin.

There were two consolations to be drawn from the confrontation on the previous night. Stunned as she had been by Gilpatrick's accusation, she did feel that she had extricated herself from the situation with some adroitness. Genevieve had also used the opportunity to resign from her musical partnership with Maxine. It was a relationship that had been awash with reservations from the start. While it got her close to the Gilpatricks, it also exposed her to danger, but it was at a personal level that the main doubts arose. She was increasingly fond of Maxine, finding, in a woman she expected to be hardened by her experience, a yearning for the recognition as a singer that she had never achieved. Maxine Montgomery sought status. Wanting her to succeed, Genevieve had been dragged along with her, but the anxieties never disappeared. The fact remained that she was using Maxine in order to gain vital information about her husband and his associates. At some stage, when the truth finally emerged, there would have been complications. She felt easier in her mind now that she had withdrawn. Another pianist could soon be found to replace her.

Dillman had to be warned. That was her first thought. After taking a bath she dressed and headed for the purser's office, but he was nowhere to be seen. In view of the fact that she had already been watched, she did not dare to go to the upper deck in search of Dillman himself. Their meeting would have to be postponed. She slipped a note under the purser's door, asking him to warn her partner that something had transpired that he needed to know about. Mike Roebuck would have to act as their go-between. As she headed for the dining saloon, Genevieve knew that Maxine would try to persuade her to reconsider her decision. She might have to cope with the blandishments of husband and wife. Determined to resist them at all costs, she went in to have breakfast.

It was still early and the place was fairly empty. Two friends of hers, however, were already there. They gave her their usual cordial welcome and beckoned her over. Genevieve was glad to join Horace and Etta Langmead. Without knowing it, they would offer her some insulation against a possible swoop by the Gilpatricks.

"You're up with the lark," observed Etta Langmead.

"I wanted to miss the rush," said Genevieve.

"What rush?" asked Langmead. "The place is as quiet as the grave. This is a good time to have your breakfast. The waiters fight to serve you."

"They always fight to serve Miss Masefield," said his wife.

"I don't blame them, Etta."

"I'm so sorry we invited Mr. Seymour-Jones to our table for the second time," she apologized. "Horry told me that you found his attentions rather embarrassing. It won't happen again, Miss Masefield. And we did provide that nice Mr. Kincaid in his stead. He's such an amusing character, isn't he?"

"Yes," said Genevieve, forcing a smile.

"I liked the French couple," said Langmead. "Especially the wife."

"They were such an interesting couple, Mr. Langmead. So sophisticated."

"I wish I knew where she bought that dress," said Etta enviously.

"In Paris."

"Yes, but where? Do you think she'd give me the address?"

"Don't bother, honey," advised her husband. "That's the

trouble with fashion. It changes so quickly. As soon as you got that dress sent over, it would be old hat. Wait until we get to China. They have lovely silk dresses there."

"It's not the same. Horry. I want to look French, not Chinese."

"Wait until you get to Peking," he said. "Chinese women are not all peasants, you know. The wealthy ones dress very stylishly. They can hold their own with the French."

Etta was not persuaded. "Nothing compares with Paris fashions."

"It's a question of personal taste," said Genevieve.

"That's why I'm having breakfast with two gorgeous ladies," added Langmead gallantly. "Ah, here they come!"

Two waiters converged on the table. One took Genevieve's order while the other served the Langmeads. The men went off to the kitchen. Other people were drifting into the room now, but there was no sign of Maxine. Genevieve hoped that she might have finished her breakfast before her friend appeared. Etta Langmead gave her a nudge.

"That was very exciting news that we heard last night, Miss Masefield."

"News?"

"About this song recital you're involved in. I didn't realize you were a pianist."

"Strictly speaking, I'm not."

"You must be if you're able to give a public performance."

"You have beauty and talent," observed Langmead. "An irresistible combination."

"Actually," confessed Genevieve, "there's some doubt about my involvement. I think that Mrs. Gilpatrick deserves a more experienced accompanist, so I decided to pull out of the concert."

"Oh, no!"

"What a shame!" said Etta.

"We were so looking forward to seeing you up on that stage."

Genevieve did not wish to discuss the subject, but there was one advantage. In explaining her position to the Langmeads, she was rehearsing arguments that she might later use against Maxine. She made no mention of Rance Gilpatrick's part in her decision, but she did tell them that David Seymour-Jones had been hired to design posters.

"You poor thing!" exclaimed Etta, a hand on Genevieve's arm. "That can't have been your idea. It's given Mr. Seymour-Jones the excuse to write your name in big letters time and again. That would only feed his infatuation."

"Not now that I've withdrawn, Mrs. Langmead."

"I'm beginning to see the wisdom of that. I mean, every woman likes admiration but not if it's taken to extremes. When he's near you, Mr. Seymour-Jones looks like a lovesick spaniel."

"Spaniels don't get lovesick, honey," said Langmead.

"How do you know?"

"They're dumb animals."

"It doesn't mean that they don't have feelings, Horry."

"Maybe, but they're different from humans."

"Only in the obvious ways."

The marital disagreement continued until breakfast was served. Conversation then moved to other subjects. Genevieve did not enjoy the meal. Every time someone came into the dining saloon, she looked up to see if it was either Maxine or Dillman. Neither of them appeared. Finishing her meal well ahead of the Langmeads, she spurned the coffee and excused herself from the table, relieved that she had escaped a potentially awkward encounter. Her relief was premature. As Genevieve left the room, Maxine Gilpatrick was about to enter it. The newcomer wrapped her in a warm embrace.

"Oh, I'm so glad you're here!" said Maxine. "We must talk."

"There's no point."

"There's every point, Jenny. First of all, I must apologize for what happened last night. What my husband did was disgraceful and I let him know it. Rance stepped over the line. I can't say how sorry I am about that."

"I'd rather forget the whole thing, Maxine."

"It was crazy. He had no cause to be suspicious of you."

"Look," said Genevieve reasonably, "I don't blame you. It's put you in a very embarrassing position, I know, but I have to stand by my decision. I think it best if you find yourself another pianist."

"You're the only one I want."

"I'm no longer available, Maxine."

"Why not?"

"Because of the circumstances."

"They can be changed."

"No, Maxine."

"They can," urged the other woman. "The first thing we do is to get rid of that artist, Mr. Seymour-Jones. We don't need posters. Word of mouth will be sufficient. Rance said that he'd get Captain Piercey to make a public announcement at dinner." She gave a snort. "It's the one bright thing he suggested this morning."

"I still want to pull out."

"But we worked so well together."

"Only up to a point," said Genevieve. "Let's face it, Maxine. You're in a different class. You deserve a professional pianist like the one we saw yesterday in the concert. I could never play as well as that."

"That doesn't matter, honey."

"It does to me."

"The idea only arose because I heard you playing 'Beautiful Dreamer' that day. We blended together instantly. You were in at the start, Jenny. Why throw away all the work that we've done so far?"

"I feel that I must."

"Are you still so mad at my husband?"

"There's a little more to it than that."

"In what way?"

"It doesn't matter now."

"It does matter," insisted Maxine. "If something else is

upsetting you, I want to know what it is. I thought we were friends, Jenny. We are, aren't we?"

"Of course."

"Then tell me what's on your mind."

Genevieve paused to consider how much she should say. Needing to provide a stronger reason to withdraw from the concert, she decided to confide her anxiety.

"Before I tell you anything," she began, "let me say at once that I'm not accusing your husband. He probably had nothing at all to do with this."

"With what?"

"Somebody broke into my cabin and searched it."

Maxine was enraged. "When?"

"Two days ago. Nothing was taken, but someone had definitely been there."

"I'll kill Rance if he was behind this!"

"Don't jump to conclusions, Maxine. I'm sure that he was not involved."

"Did you report it to the purser?"

"Yes," said Genevieve. "He thought it might be a thief. Since I always have my jewelry locked up in Mr. Roebuck's safe, there was nothing worth stealing. I don't really care who it was. The fact remains that someone searched through my things, and that's left me very shaky. I keep returning to my cabin throughout the day to check that he hasn't been back. It's ridiculous, perhaps, but that's the effect it's had on me."

"Sure," said Maxine, with a consoling hand on her arm.

"I've managed to keep up a bold front so far, but underneath I'm scared. It's another reason I can't go through with this concert. That incident is preying on my mind. I may have seemed all right in rehearsal," she said, "but a public performance is much more testing. I'm afraid that the pressure would be too much. I'd go to pieces."

Maxine tried to assimilate the new information. The possibility that her husband had instigated the search made her feel both angry and disgusted. She sympathized with Genevieve, yet she still clung to the hope that they could somehow perform together. She searched desperately for compromise.

"Listen, Jenny. Let me take this up with Rance."

"It might be safer if you don't even mention it."

"I want the truth," asserted Maxine. "If I'm sharing my life with a guy who had your cabin searched, I want to know. For heaven's sake, I'm *married* to him. Rance is no angel," she continued. "I accepted that from the start. Running a saloon is not like being in charge of a cathedral. You have to be tough and ruthless. But he has a softer side to him as well. I knew about his other women. I knew about some shady deals he made. I knew I wasn't marrying Jesus Christ. But heck," she added with a laugh, "it's not as if I was a vestal virgin myself. What I didn't know, however, was that he'd stoop to having your cabin searched."

"We're not certain that he did."

"Putting that aside, how about this for an idea? We postpone the concert."

"No, Maxine."

"It hasn't been announced yet," argued the other. "It would give us more time to rehearse and advertise. And there's another thing, Jenny," she said, gripping her arm, "It'll give you time to get over this business. What do you say?"

"You must look for another pianist."

"I don't want anyone else, least of all that guy in the orchestra. Okay, he's got talent, but he's a man. Don't you understand, Jenny?" she pleaded. "The thing that attracted me most about this whole thing was the fact that we were doing it together, putting on a concert to rival anything the men can do. We'd be striking a blow for women, Jenny. Doesn't that have any appeal to you?"

"A great deal, Maxine. But I've made my decision."

"Good morning, ladies!" said Willoughby Kincaid, bearing down on them. "Discussing your song recital, no doubt?" He offered both arms. "May I have the pleasure of taking the two of you into breakfast?"

"No thank you, Mr. Kincaid," said Genevieve. "I've already eaten."

"What a pity!"

"And I need to go back to the cabin to speak to my husband," said Maxine.

"It doesn't seem to be my day." He beamed at Genevieve. "Can't I even tempt you to another cup of coffee, Miss Masefield?"

Genevieve froze. Over her shoulder, she could see Dillman approaching and saw the bruising on his temple. Her stomach turned. With Maxine beside her, she felt the urge to acknowledge him, especially as the sign of close friendship with another man might help to deter Kincaid. Then she remembered that Maxine would not recognize the detective. She had never met him before.

She turned to Kincaid. "I couldn't touch a thing, I'm afraid. Good-bye."

As she walked past him, Genevieve did not even look up at Dillman.

Rutherford Blaine had a streak of obstinacy in him that they had never seen before.

"I'm sorry, Jake, but I won't even consider the idea."

"Why not, sir?" asked Poole. "It's for your own safety."

"I'd recommend it as well, Mr. Blaine," said the purser.

"I have a duty to protect you, sir."

"You're the one who looks as if he's in need of protection," noted Blaine.

The three men were in Blaine's cabin. Though still nursing his wounds, Jake Poole felt strong enough to offer his services again. In view of the attack on Dillman, the purser was anxious to shield the diplomat even more.

"I may have one arm in a sling," said the bodyguard, "but I

can still hold a gun in the other. We're taught to shoot with both hands, Mr. Blaine. Why take the risk of sleeping in here on your own when I could be in the other bunk?"

"I managed perfectly well last night."

"Only because they don't know where you are yet."

"In that case, there's no danger."

"Yes, there is, sir," said Roebuck. "If they're clever enough to find out what you're doing on this ship, it won't take them long to track you down. Mr. Poole is right. You need protection around the clock."

Blaine gave a wry smile. "Does that mean someone has to hold my hand when I visit the bathroom? No, gentlemen," he said, "I appreciate your concern but it's not necessary. While I'm in the public rooms, I feel perfectly secure."

"This is where the attack is likely to come," argued Poole.

"They still think I'm in that cabin on the boat deck." He turned to the purser. "Were there any problems there in the night, Mr. Roebuck?"

"No, no," lied the other. "Mr. Dillman was undisturbed."

"There you are, then!"

"All that proves is that they know you've moved out of the cabin," said Poole. They'll be searching for this one. I'd like to be here when they find it."

"You've done more than your share already, Jake."

"I feel as if I'm letting you down."

"Not at all," said Blaine. "I'm the one with the guilt. You were attacked because of me. If Mr. Dillman hadn't come along at the right time, your attacker might have finished the job. Imagine how I would have felt then."

"It's my duty, sir. I know the risks."

"Well, you're not taking any more on my behalf. Everything has gone smoothly so far. That door is very stout and it has two bolts on the inside. Even with a master key, nobody can get in at night. I think you should both stop worrying about me," he said confidently. "We must rely on Mr. Dillman to catch this assassin before he reaches me."

Poole had doubts. "What are the chances of that?"

"Much higher than you think," said Roebuck defensively. "George Dillman is an amazing man. Mr. Blaine put his finger on it a moment ago when he talked about that fall of yours down the stairs. Someone came along at precisely the right time. George Dillman has an uncanny habit of doing that."

When he saw Dillman approaching him, Wu Feng's first impulse was to flee, but the detective's reassuring smile made him stand his ground.

"It's all right, Mr. Feng," said Dillman. "I haven't come to arrest you and your father again. I know that you're legitimate passengers now. Your fare is paid."

"This kind man helped us, sir. Father Slattery."

"So I understand."

"You thank him for us? We no see him since."

"I'm afraid not," said Dillman ruefully. "He's been busy elsewhere."

As soon as breakfast was over, the detective had gone down to the main deck in search of the Fengs. Remembering where he had found them, he wondered if they might be able to shed some light on a problem that vexed him. Wu Feng was sitting on the deck among the other steerage passengers. He was still wary of Dillman.

"I want to know how you came to be on the orlop deck," said the detective. "Only crew members have access to the hold. How did you get down there in the first place?"

"By accident, sir. We follow a man."

"What man? One of the crew?"

"No, sir. My father and me, we get aboard the night before the ship sail. We not know where to hide. When passengers come onboard, there are men in uniform who ask everyone to show tickets." He gave a gesture of despair. "We had none."

"So what did you do?"

"We very frightened, sir. When man in uniform come

towards us, we ran away. We go down steps, run as fast as we can. We finish up where you found us."

"But how?" asked Dillman, still puzzled. "The orlop deck is locked."

"The man had a key."

"The one in uniform?"

"No, sir. Another man. He wears a suit and hat. We see him open a door so we sneak in after him and hide. Later," he recalled sadly, "when the ship sail, we find that we locked in. Then you come looking for us."

"Actually, I was searching for something else," said Dillman. "Tell me about this man who let you into the orlop deck. If he was wearing a suit and a hat, he certainly wasn't one of the crew. Can you remember anything about him?"

"No, sir. Nothing at all." A memory surfaced. "Except for his ear."

"His ear?" repeated Dillman.

"Yes, sir," said Feng, indicating with his hand. "It was this big."

Maxine Gilpatrick's anger was no match for her husband's bad temper. He was up, dressed, and ready for her this time. When she accused him of arranging to have Genevieve's cabin searched, he flew into such a rage that she backed off. Gilpatrick denied the charge hotly. His wife came to believe him. A tiny doubt still lingered, however. As she made her way alone back to the dining saloon, she saw the opportunity to clarify the situation. Tommy Gault was descending the stairs in front of her. She hurried to catch up.

"Good morning, Tommy," she said.

"Oh, hello, Mrs. Gilpatrick," he replied. "Sleep well?"

"I've had better nights."

"I went out like a log. They serve good booze on this ship."

"I meant to ask you something, Tommy," she said casually. "When you searched Jenny Masefield's cabin, what did you find?" Gault's eyes darted nervously. "It's all right," she assured him. "Rance told me that you were going in there. What did you find?"

"Nothing," he admitted. "Nothing at all."

It was midmorning before Genevieve finally chanced upon Tadu Natsuki. He and his wife were drinking tea in the lounge. They were both delighted to see her again.

"I wanted to ask you a favor," said Genevieve, sitting beside Natsuki.

"Of course," he said.

"I wondered if you could possibly translate this for me?" She passed him the slip of paper that Dillman had given her. "It's an address that I need to have but I can't make head or tail of it."

Natsuki grinned. "Neither can I, Miss Masefield."

"But you speak Japanese, don't you?"

"Perfectly, but these are Chinese characters."

"Oh, dear!"

"Simple mistake," he went on. "You weren't to know. But you are in luck. I know very little Chinese, but Hisako is an expert. She does translation work for a publisher from time to time. That is why she was so upset by what Father Slattery was saying the other day," he explained. "The last book she translated into Chinese was about Shinto." He handed the paper to his wife. "Hisako?"

"I am happy to help," said Hisako.

Genevieve had thought to bring paper and pencil with her. She handed both to the woman and waited while the latter studied the characters. Hisako's face puckered.

"I'm sorry if it's inaccurate," said Genevieve. "The person who copied it out is not used to writing Chinese characters."

Hisako smiled tolerantly. "I can see that, Miss Masefield. It just seems an odd address for a young lady like you to have." Translating it into English, she wrote it down, then handed the paper back. "There you are."

"Thank you, Mrs. Natsuki. You're very kind." She glanced

at the address and blinked in surprise. "I see what you mean," she said.

Pleased with his discovery, Dillman could not wait to report it to the purser. Mike Roebuck was in his office, locking up the safe. He was intrigued by the latest piece of information, but he still did not find the evidence conclusive enough.

"There has to be something else, George," he warned. "If I go to the skipper and tell him that all we have are some gun catalogs and a cauliflower ear, he's not going to authorize us to tamper with sealed cargo."

"The weapons must be there, Mike. I know it!"

"Find some more proof."

"How much more do you need?" said Dillman with exasperation. "Mr. Feng saw someone with a cauliflower ear on the orlop deck. It has to have been Tommy Gault. There may be more than one black eye aboard, but I bet he's got the only cauliflower ear. Somehow, he has a key to the orlop deck. How did he get it?"

"Who knows? There are far too many keys in the wrong hands on this ship."

"Supposing I search Gault's cabin and find that key. Is that proof enough?"

"No, George. Besides, I don't think he's punch-drunk. Tommy wouldn't leave something like that hanging about. He'd carry it around with him. We're on the right track, I know," he said, "but we need to take just a few more steps along it."

Dillman moved to the door. "I've got an idea," he said. "See you later."

"Hold on," ordered the purser, restraining him with a hand. "When I got back here, there was a note under the door from your partner. She said it's vital to speak to you as soon as possible. I'm to hold you here until she comes."

"Did she give any details?"

Roebuck opened a drawer and took out the note. "Read

it for yourself," he said, passing it to Dillman. "And not just the words. Read between the lines. I smell a crisis."

"So do I, Mike," said Dillman, scanning the note. "What's up, I wonder?"

"Well, she's still able to write neatly so she hasn't been trying to punch Tommy Gault in the stomach. Seriously, though," he went on, "I'm getting worried. I hired the pair of you to catch a smuggler. You've survived an attempt on your life and Miss Masefield is playing piano in the lion's own den."

"We have to take risks in our business."

"That's what Jake Poole said earlier. Look what happened to him."

There was a tap on the door and Roebuck opened it to let Genevieve in. When she saw Dillman, she gave a gasp of relief. It was only the purser's presence that stopped him from putting his arms around her.

"What's happened, Genevieve?" he asked worriedly.

"Lots," she replied, "but let me tell you about that address you found first. No wonder you had such difficulty copying those Japanese characters, George. They turned out to be Chinese."

He grinned. "So much for a Western education!"

"I had it translated and found that it's the address of a firm of gunsmiths in Shanghai." Dillman flicked a glance at Roebuck. "I wanted to find out more about them, so I went to the library to see if there was any business directory of Shanghai. There wasn't, unfortunately, but I remembered someone who might be able to help."

"Who was that?" asked Dillman.

"Willoughby Kincaid. When I went looking for him, of course, he immediately thought that I was finally succumbing to his charms so I had to put him right on that score. However," she went on, "he does know about guns. I didn't tell him how I'd come across this address, of course, but I asked him if he knew of any gunsmiths in the Bund in Shanghai.

The first one he talked about was Telge and Schroeter. Apparently, they furnished most of the Chinese flotilla fleet. Then he moved on to this one," she said, showing the translation to Dillman. "Herzog and Lindenmeier. It's a much more disreputable firm, the kind of place where you can get any gun you want even though some of the other gunsmiths have exclusive licenses for some makes. Mr. Kincaid told me he was offered a Webley and Scott gun there, yet the sole agents are supposed to be someone on Canton Road, Shanghai."

The purser was impressed. "What a memory you have for detail!"

"I couldn't forget the bit about Webley and Scott. They're an English firm. According to Mr. Kincaid, they're small-arms manufacturers from Birmingham."

"We still need a link with Hayashi," stressed Dillman.

"I'm coming to that," she explained. "Though the firm of Herzog and Lindenmeier still retains its old name, it was bought out over a year ago by a Japanese company. Mr. Kincaid said there was a branch in Kobe as well."

"That's where Hayashi lives," commented Dillman.

"There are huge profits involved here. The Chinese army is drilling in Western style and equipping itself with all the latest weapons. But that's only one source of income. The real money, according to Mr. Kincaid, would come from supplying rebel groups who will pay almost anything to get the best guns."

Dillman read the address on the piece of paper before thrusting it at Roebuck.

"There you are, Mike," he said. "Do you have enough to go to the captain now?"

"I'm tempted, I must say," replied the purser.

"Give it a try."

"I will. Thanks, Miss Masefield. You've done wonders."

He let himself out of the cabin. As soon as he had gone, Dillman put his arms around her and gave her a kiss. The first thing she wanted to know was how he had gotten the bruise on his temple. Playing down the danger, he told her about his nocturnal visitor. She was very disturbed, but he managed to reassure her. Now that she had passed on her findings, Genevieve had some more awkward news to impart. He waved her to a seat and perched on the desk beside her. She told him about the confrontation with Gilpatrick on the previous night and how she had been forced to present Dillman in order to talk her way out of the situation. He was pleased to hear that she had also maneuvered herself out of the song recital.

"It could be uncomfortable for you," he observed, "sitting at a piano with a woman whose husband we're on the verge of arresting. Give the Gilpatricks a wide berth from now on. You were getting too close to the fire."

"The flames were certainly licking me last night," she said. "Just think how I felt when Gilpatrick told me you'd been seen going into my cabin."

"It must have been a sticky moment, Genevieve, but there's one compensation."

"Is there?"

"He gave himself away."

"I'm just sorry that I had to use your name like that."

"There was nothing else you could do."

"But it complicates things. How will it look to other people?"

"It will keep Mr. Kincaid and the amorous artist off your back."

"I was thinking of Fay Brinkley."

Dillman sighed. "Yes, I'm glad you mentioned her. We had a chance encounter last night. Except that I don't believe there was much chance involved."

When he related what had happened, she was amused and intrigued. Genevieve was also glad that he was so honest about it and held nothing back. Anxiety returned.

"Fay will be hurt if we walk into the dining saloon together."

"There may be a way around that," he said thoughtfully. "Leave it to me. But if we are going to be identified as a couple, there's something we can do at once, Genevieve."

"What's that?"

"Issue a challenge." He moved to the door. "I'll explain on the way."

When he got back to his cabin, Rance Gilpatrick was given a severe jolt. After the row with his wife, he had seen no sign of her. Maxine, he assumed, was keeping out of his way unless he lost his temper again. He prided himself on having rebuffed her accusation about the search of Genevieve Masefield's cabin. It had enabled him to gain the upper hand again. He soon discovered that that was an illusion. When he stepped into the cabin, he sensed at once that something was awry. It was markedly tidier than it usually was. None of Maxine's possessions were scattered about on the table or chairs. Going into the bedroom, he had the same experience. There was a sudden emptiness. Gilpatrick dived for the wardrobe and flung open the doors, hoping to find it filled with his wife's dresses. He stepped back in alarm. They had all disappeared.

Tommy Gault's fame as an entertainer had spread. Over a dozen children had gathered on the boat deck to watch his displays of strength. Though wearing a jacket and pants, he stood on his hands to amuse them, let them punch him in the stomach, and lifted each of them in turn by getting them to hold their elbows tight against their sides. Cupping the tips of their elbows in his hands, he lifted them right above his head in one fluent move. The children loved it. When Dillman arrived with Genevieve, the children were laughing with glee at Gault's antics. Recognizing Genevieve, he was a little shamefaced at first, fearful that she might have come to accuse him of searching her cabin, but it was Dillman who had sought him out.

"I wondered if I could take another crack at you, Mr. Gault?" he asked.

"Sure, Mr. Dillman," said the ex-boxer. "Wear a knuckle duster, if you like."

"No thanks. I just want to be certain that you've got nothing hidden away under your shirt." He removed his jacket and gave it to Genevieve. "Take your coat off. Let me see the target properly."

"I'll put on a singlet and boxing shorts, if you prefer," boasted Gault, slipping his coat off. Genevieve took it from him. Gault slapped his stomach. "See? Nothing there except hard muscle. Whitey Thompson said it was like hitting a brick wall."

"In that case," said Dillman, flexing his right hand, "I'll take a small precaution."

Retrieving a handkerchief from the top pocket of his jacket, he wound it around his knuckles. The children were agog. Dillman was tall and fit. He looked as if he might trouble Gault. Some of them egged him on while others, who had seen his earlier attempt at throwing a punch, sided with Gault. As Dillman got himself ready, the little audience cheered them on. Nobody noticed that Genevieve was slipping a deft hand into the pocket of Gault's jacket.

"Ready?" asked Dillman.

"Give it all you've got," goaded the other man.

"Here goes!"

Dillman did not pull his punch this time. Putting much more power into the blow, he struck Gault in the middle of the stomach and saw a faint glimmer of pain in his eyes. Dillman shook his hand, then removed the handkerchief to blow on his knuckles. The children laughed and Gault grinned in triumph.

"You're welcome to try any time, Mr. Dillman," he said.

"No thanks. I think I've learned my lesson."

"It was my fault," said Genevieve. "I wanted to see if what he told me was true."

"It's true, all right," said Dillman, taking his jacket from her. "I've never felt stomach muscles like that before. I'll need to put my hand in cold water."

"Congratulations, Mr. Gault," she said. "The professional wins the day."

Gault put his chest out. "I was a good fighter. Fourteen knockouts."

"It shows."

After helping him on with his coat, she went off with Dillman and left Tommy Gault to entertain the children. They were out of earshot before Dillman spoke.

"Did you find anything?"

"Yes, George," she said, slipping a key into his hand. "In his right pocket."

"I had a feeling it would be on him somewhere."

"What now?"

"I'm going down to the orlop deck to see if it fits."

THIRTEEN

Rance Gilpatrick's anger was tempered with embarrassment. Though he demanded to see the purser instantly, he was more subdued as he explained the situation. Mike Roebuck was fascinated by the latest development, but his face remained motionless.

"Where is Maxine hiding?" asked Gilpatrick.

"I have no idea, sir."

"She must be on the ship somewhere. If my wife intended to jump over the side, she'd hardly take her entire wardrobe with her."

"I agree with you there."

"So where is she, Mr. Roebuck?"

"I don't know. Did Mrs. Gilpatrick leave no note for you?"

"No," complained the other. "She just vamoosed."

"Don't worry too much about it, sir," said the purser, trying to reassure him. "It's not the first time this kind of thing has happened. What usually occurs is that the lady in question storms out, goes off alone to brood, and gradually calms down. It's not my place to offer advice where disputes of this nature are involved, but I've noticed how valuable a cooling-off period can be for both parties. Why not wait for a few hours?"

"Because I don't want to wait."

"At the moment, I suspect, your wife doesn't wish to be found."

"She ran out on me. I want her back."

"Did you have some sort of disagreement, sir?"

"That's between her and me."

"Of course, sir."

"So stop offering me advice and find out where my wife is hiding."

"I'll have to speak to the chief steward," said Roebuck. "If she wanted another cabin, Mrs. Gilpatrick may have gone straight to him. He'll pass on the information to me so that I can make an adjustment in the passenger list. When he does—"

"Where will I find this guy?" interrupted Gilpatrick.

"The chief steward has quarters on the main deck, sir."

"Give me the number of his cabin. This is my wife we're talking about, damn it! I can't hang around until the chief steward decides to report to you."

Mike Roebuck soothed him, gave him the details he wanted, then held the door open for him. As Gilpatrick surged out, Dillman was coming along the passageway. The detective offered a polite greeting but the other ignored him, heading for the staircase and plunging down it. Dillman joined the purser at the door of his office.

"What's got into him, Mike?" he asked.

"His wife has left him."

Dillman was astonished. "Left him?"

"Yes, George. When he went back to the cabin just now, she'd cleared out all her things. Gilpatrick has been searching everywhere for her."

"What prompted all this?"

"Who knows? But it must be something serious. I wonder if it has some connection with this projected concert."

"It does, Mike. Let's step inside and I'll explain." They went into the office and closed the door. "Genevieve was forced to pull out. That really upset Mrs. Gilpatrick."

He told the purser about Genevieve's confrontation with Gilpatrick the previous night and how she had taken the opportunity to withdraw from the song recital.

"That's not enough reason for a wife to leave her husband," said Roebuck.

"There's more," said Dillman. "When Mrs. Gilpatrick cornered her this morning and tried to persuade her to change her mind, Genevieve confided that someone had searched her cabin. She hinted, very subtly, that Rance Gilpatrick was involved. My guess is that he was and that his wife has found out about it. She's a spirited woman. Maxine Gilpatrick would be outraged."

"She got her message across to her husband, I know that."

"It obviously stunned him. He didn't even see me when he rushed past. Still," he went on, "let's forget his marital difficulties for a moment, shall we? Did you speak to Captain Piercey?"

"We had a long talk, George."

"And?"

"He wants to think it over."

"You mean, he won't give us permission to open some of the cargo?"

"I'm afraid not."

"But he must."

"Not without more evidence."

Dillman thrust a key at him. "Show him this."

"What is it?"

"The key to the orlop deck. It fits, Mike. I've just tried it."

"Where did it come from?"

"Tommy Gault's pocket."

"You *stole* it?" asked the purser.

"We borrowed it," replied Dillman. "I played a little trick on him. While Genevieve was holding his jacket, she searched the

265

pockets and found the key. How did a passenger come to have something as valuable as this in his possession?"

"The skipper will ask the same question."

"Go back to him. Tell him we must examine that cargo."

"I will," said the purser, taking the key. "But what will happen when Tommy Gault finds the key missing? He'll guess who must have stolen it, surely?"

Dillman smiled. "I doubt it. Genevieve and I have arrested enough pickpockets to know how they work. When she found the key in his pocket," he said, "she replaced it with a similar one. Genevieve took a selection with her. My feeling is that Gault went down into the hold on the day we sailed to make sure that all of their cargo was aboard. He'll have no reason to visit the orlop deck during the voyage."

"You're a genius!"

"Tell that to the captain. Oh, and while you're at it, Mike, I need a favor."

"What is it?"

"Genevieve and I have to be at the captain's table tonight. Arrange it, please."

When he found the cabin, Rance Gilpatrick banged on the door with a bunched fist.

"Maxine!" he called. "You in there?"

"Go away!" she answered from inside.

"Open this door."

"No, Rance."

"Open this door!" he shouted. "I'm not standing out here."

"Then take yourself off. You're not coming into my cabin."

"We already *have* a cabin. On the boat deck."

"That's all yours now," she said coldly. "You can have as many meetings in there with Joe McDade as you like. I've got my own place now."

"Let me in!" he ordered.

"Never again. You're done with pushing me around."

He tried to control his ire. "Maxine, *please*," he begged.

"Good-bye, Rance."

"Why are you doing this to me?"

"You know why."

"There's no need to get sore with me, honey. I told you. I'll fix everything. You want Miss Masefield to play the piano, you'll have her. I guarantee it."

"Save your breath. Jenny guessed that you were behind it."

"Behind what?"

"That search of her cabin."

"I swear to you that I had nothing to do with it!"

"Tommy Gault sings a different tune."

He gulped. "Tommy?"

"According to him, he went in there but found nothing. Tommy's not very bright. When I told him I knew he'd carried out the search, he confirmed it. One of you is lying, Rance," she concluded, "and it's not him. Now disappear, will you?"

There was a long pause. "Maxine," he said at length.

"Are you still there?"

"We have to talk."

"No, Rance," she said vehemently, "you have to learn to listen. We're finished. I've walked out on you. I can't share my life with a cheat and a liar. You spied on my friend and had her cabin searched. Why? What were you expecting to find? It's a dreadful way to treat your wife's friends."

"I'm sorry. It's not the way it sounds. Let me explain."

"I'm sick of your explanations."

"Maxine!"

"This conversation is over."

Gilpatrick was near despair. "We've got to sort this out. I can't spend the rest of the voyage with my wife in a separate cabin. I've got business associates aboard. We have to be seen together, honey," he pleaded. "Think how this will make me *look*."

From the other side of the door came the sound of mocking laughter.

———

Luncheon found Genevieve Masefield back at the same table as Fay Brinkley. Their hosts, the Langmeads, had also invited the Newtons, along with Yves and Jeanne Houlier. It was an inspired selection. Everyone got on extremely well with one another and the repartee was witty and free flowing. Genevieve had finally shaken off both of her admirers. David Seymour-Jones adored her from a distant table and Willoughby Kincaid ogled her from a much closer one, but she was unperturbed. She could talk with friends instead of having to fend off unwelcome attentions. Seated next to her, Fay contrived a private word during the main course.

"What's all this about a song recital?"

"I've had to withdraw, Fay."

"I didn't know you were involved in the first place," said Fay. "Why didn't you tell me? You're a dark horse, Genevieve. How many other secrets are you holding back?"

"None."

"So why did you pull out?"

"I just wasn't up to it," said Genevieve sadly. "Maxine Gilpatrick is a seasoned professional while I'm just someone who can play the piano fairly well."

"I think you're being modest."

"No, Fay, I'm being a realist."

"Mrs. Gilpatrick is a very interesting lady," observed Fay. "I wish I'd been able to get to know her better. Etta Langmead says that she trained to sing opera."

"That's right, but Maxine took a wrong turning somewhere."

"She did that when she married her husband."

"You disliked him, didn't you?"

"That's an understatement," said Fay bitterly. "Anyway, I was in here having a late breakfast when Gilpatrick came stamping in. He treated the waiter appallingly. I can't bear it when people bully servants like that. The waiter did nothing wrong, but Gilpatrick was taking his anger out on the poor man. Anyone who marries him is in for trouble. Gilpatrick is violent and uncouth. What's your opinion?"

"Pretty much the same as yours, Fay."

"You know him better than I do."

Genevieve nodded. "It wasn't exactly a salutary experience."

"What about his wife?"

"Maxine is a lovely woman. She's had a tough life but has come through it well. I like her very much. That's how I got drawn into this song recital."

"Will the event still go ahead without you?"

"It's in the balance," said Genevieve tactfully. "But what about you, Fay? I haven't seen you for a while. What have you been up to?"

"All sorts of things. The most important one occurred last night." Her eyes sparkled at the memory. "I had what you might call a little adventure."

"Did you?"

"Yes," said Fay, making sure that nobody else was listening. "I went for a walk on the upper deck and who should I bump into but George Dillman? I told you about him. That handsome man I met in here one day. When I saw Mr. Dillman there, I couldn't believe my luck. The setting was so romantic."

"What happened?"

"We talked and talked and got steadily closer. It was wonderful."

"Did he ask to see you again?"

"Oh, no. Mr. Dillman would never do that. He's in no hurry, Genevieve. It will take a few more sessions on deck at night before we get to that stage. But I'll ease him gently along. It will come to fruition in time."

"I see," said Genevieve, giving nothing away. "What else have you been doing?"

"Upsetting Mrs. Van Bergen whenever I can. Oh, and I was able to vent my spleen on Joseph McDade as well. Do you remember him?"

"Yes. He launched that terrible attack on President Roosevelt."

"He caught me in the lounge when I was enjoying a coffee,"

said Fay, slicing her salmon. "For some reason, Mr. McDade thought I needed the benefit of his ignorance, so he started to lecture me on the defects of our president. I saw red, Genevieve. I told him that if he hated the way the country was being run, he should do every American a favor by emigrating. You should have heard him rant and rave. That pallid wife of his was so embarrassed by it all."

"I do feel sorry for her."

"Yet the funny thing was this," continued Fay. "Later on, she came looking for me on her own to apologize for the way that her husband had lost his temper and to thank me for what I said. Nobody has stood up to the old walrus before."

"I don't think Blanche McDade ever will."

"She's terrified of him, Genevieve. When he found that he couldn't browbeat me, McDade went back to his cabin, swearing that he'd get his own back somehow. He was in such a rage, according to his wife, that he even took a gun out of his case at one point. I didn't like the sound of that, I must admit," said Fay worriedly. "What's he doing with a gun in the first place? Intelligent people are supposed to win arguments with reason, not with a loaded weapon."

"Did his wife know that he had a gun?" asked Genevieve with interest.

"No, she was as shocked as I was."

"Don't get too upset about it, Fay. I don't think it was a serious threat."

"That's what Blanche McDade said. When her husband calmed down a bit, he told her that there was no real danger. He had no ammunition. I thought that was so peculiar," said Fay. "Why should a man carry a gun when it has no bullets?"

Genevieve kept the answer to herself. Fay Brinkley had unwittingly given her another piece of evidence. Yves Houlier began to talk about a holiday that he and his wife had spent in England, and Genevieve was called in to pass comments. Half an hour slipped by in the most pleasurable manner. Everyone at the table seemed to be having an enjoyable time except Horace Langmead. With a fixed smile on his face, he spent most of the time listening rather than contributing. For an extrovert like Langmead, it was highly uncharacteristic behavior. When he excused himself early from the table, Genevieve was concerned about him. She turned to Etta Langmead.

"Is your husband unwell?" she asked.

"Horry? No," said Etta, "he's never unwell."

"He seemed rather distracted."

"It was that row he had earlier on."

"Row?" said Genevieve.

"Yes, Miss Masefield. Don't ask me what it was about because I don't know, but it really shook Horry. I've never seen him so angry."

"He's so even-tempered as a rule."

"I know. Horry is a dear."

"Did he tell you why he was upset?"

"All he'd say was that the man was never to be invited to our table ever again."

"What man?"

"The one he had the row with," said Etta. "David Seymour-Jones."

Rance Gilpatrick did not stand on ceremony. Grabbing him by the throat, he pushed Tommy Gault against the wall. Gault's eyes widened in alarm.

"What's the matter, boss?" he asked.

"Did you tell my wife that you searched that cabin?"

"Mrs. Gilpatrick already knew."

"Of course she didn't," snarled Gilpatrick. "But she does now—thanks to you."

"She asked me what I found, that's all."

"What did you tell her?"

"The truth," said Gault. "Nothing."

"Did you say *why* I sent you into that cabin in the first place?"

"No, boss. I'm not that stupid."

"Oh, yes, you are. You've ruined everything."

Gilpatrick started to belabor him and Gault immediately went into the defensive posture he used in the ring. Not daring to strike back, he took most of the punishment on his arms. Gilpatrick soon tired. Breathing heavily, he stepped back.

Gault lowered his guard. "I'm sorry, boss."

"It's too late to say that."

"I don't see what I've done wrong."

"Because of you, my wife has left me."

"On a ship? How can she do that?"

"By moving to another cabin," said Gilpatrick, taking another swipe at him. "Why did you have to open your big mouth, Tommy? I warned you to tell *nobody*."

"I didn't think that included Mrs. Gilpatrick."

"Maxine was at the top of the list."

"Has she really left you, boss?"

"Yes. Genevieve Masefield is a friend of hers. She was also going to play the piano for Maxine in the concert. That blew apart when I told Miss Masefield that George Dillman was seen sneaking into her cabin at night." He ran a desperate hand through his hair. "How was I to know that she simply wanted to ask the guy to offer her some protection? I thought they were working together somehow."

"They are," said Gault.

"What do you mean?"

"They came looking for me earlier on the boat deck. Mr. Dillman decided he wanted to throw another punch at me. I'll tell you this, boss, he hit me much harder this time. I didn't show it, of course, but he hurt."

Gilpatrick needed a moment to absorb the information. "They came *together*?"

"Yes, boss."

"Dillman and Miss Masefield?"

"I think he wanted to show off in front of her," said Gault. "He made me take my coat off so that he could have a proper

272

look at the target. Then he took off his own coat. Miss Masefield held them for us."

"She held your coat?" Gilpatrick's mind was racing. "Where
do you keep the key, Tommy?"

"The one to my cabin? In the pocket of my trousers."

"The *other* key, you imbecile! To the orlop deck."

"Oh, that's in here," said Gault, patting his coat pocket. "You
told me to keep it on me at all times. I even have it tucked
into the top of my boots when I do my skipping."

"Is it still there?"

"Of course, boss."

"Let me see it."

"Why?"

"Let me see it, Tommy. Now!"

"Sure," said Gault, taking the key from his pocket to hand
it over. "Here it is."

Gilpatrick examined it. "You were duped," he said angrily.
"This is not the same key at all. They must have switched it
with the other one."

"It looks like the same key to me."

"Oh, it's similar, I grant you. But it's not engraved like the
other one. I paid a lot of money to get hold of that key, Tommy.
And you let them take it off you."

"But what would they want it for, boss?"

"I've got a nasty suspicion about that."

"Mr. Dillman and Miss Masefield are only passengers," argued Gault, scratching his head. "Why should they steal a key
to the orlop deck?"

Dillman inserted the key and unlocked the door. He turned to
the purser with a smile.

"See? I told you it fit."

"It was the one thing that persuaded the skipper," said Roebuck. "I just hope that we find what we're looking for down
here or we could end up with red faces."

Dillman was confident. "We'll find it."

"How do you know?"

"Why would Rance Gilpatrick and Joseph McDade sail over four thousand miles if they didn't have some merchandise aboard?"

"I can't speak for McDade," said the purser, "but Gilpatrick has a good reason to book a passage on the *Minnesota*. He's on his honeymoon."

"Not anymore, Mike."

The purser had a torch and a copy of the ship's manifest while Dillman was carrying a crowbar. They made their way to the hold where the goods being imported by Mr. Hayashi were kept. Some were destined for Japan, but most were going on to Shanghai. Lighting in the hold was patchy. Roebuck shone the torch on labels affixed to the sides of the various boxes and barrels.

"Where do we start, George?" he asked.

"With something relatively small."

The purser tapped a box. "What about this one?" he suggested. "It's supposed to contain copperware."

"Then it probably does," said Dillman. "Look at the label. It's being unloaded at Yokohama. Hayashi has legitimate imports for Japan down here. We need something that's going on to China." He searched among the boxes. "Shine your torch over here."

Roebuck obliged and they saw that the label indicated Shanghai as the destination. According to the manifest, the box contained only leatherwear. Dillman waited for a nod from the purser, then went into action, using the crowbar to pry open the wooden lid of the box. Roebuck thrust his hand through a layer of straw and pulled out some decorated leather belts with silver buckles on them. He looked disappointed.

"Dig deeper, Mike," advised Dillman.

"I can feel the bottom of the box," replied the other, thrusting his arm into the consignment. He held up another handful of belts. "We've drawn a blank."

"Let's open another."

"Hold on, George. I'm starting to have second thoughts."

"Why?"

"We could be making a mistake."

"How many times have you been to China?"

"Dozens of times."

"And how many Chinese have you seen with belts like these? Most of them wear those pajamas, Mike. You don't need expensive leather belts with them. What's the point of importing this lot?"

"There are plenty of foreigners in the treaty ports."

"I know," said Dillman, studying a large box, "but there's a limit to how many belts they'd buy. Look, here's another load. Hayashi Imports. I'll bet my bottom dollar that it doesn't contain what it says on the label."

Before the purser could stop him, he used the crowbar again and the wood splintered. The nails groaned in protest as they were levered out. Dillman put the lid on the ground and gestured to his friend.

"Be my guest."

"I hope we strike oil this time, George."

"Start drilling."

Putting his torch down, Roebuck used both hands to lift the straw insulation out of the box. Leather belts were coiled up and neatly packed in rows. The purser reached in to pull some out. With a baleful expression, he showed them to Dillman.

"I think we're out of luck," he said.

"Not necessarily," said Dillman. "Let me have a go."

Thrusting his hands into the box, he got no farther than the top layer. He grinned.

"What have you found?" asked Roebuck.

"A false bottom." Getting his fingers under the edges, he lifted out a piece of wood that fitted into slots near the top of the box. "Hold that, Mike," he said, giving him the tray of leather belts. Additional straw was used to cover the rest of the contents. He felt through it and pretended to be disappointed. "Oh, no! I just don't believe it."

"More leather belts?"

"I'm afraid so," said Dillman, "but these are a different kind, Mike. Look!"

He pulled one out with a flourish and held it up. Roebuck let out a cry of triumph. What the detective was holding was a cartridge belt filled with live ammunition. There were dozens of others just like it in the box. The purser was thrilled.

"Give me that crowbar, George," he said. "I'll open the rest."

The meal had been an unqualified success. Genevieve Masefield had not only shared a delicious luncheon with a congenial group of people, she had learned something of great interest from her friend. Fay Brinkley's argument with Joseph McDade had produced a startling consequence. So irate had McDade been after his defeat at the hands of Fay that he had rushed back to his cabin and pulled out a gun. Genevieve was not surprised to hear that it was not loaded. She suspected that it was not kept for protection at all but a new model that McDade had brought along to show to Rance Gilpatrick. If she and Dillman could somehow get hold of the revolver, it might help to link the two men even more closely. The other information gleaned at the table had left her in two minds. Fay's account of the late night encounter with Dillman was very different from his. While she believed the detective, she still found Fay's declared interest in him a little worrying. As she hurried back to her cabin after luncheon, she was not sure whether to be amused or piqued by the whole business. If Dillman was going to be on deck in the moonlight, Genevieve wanted to be the person who was with him.

Her mind was still grappling with the notion as she let herself into her cabin. An unexpected sight made her gasp with fear. Seated in the chair was the ample figure of Rance Gilpatrick, waiting patiently for her return.

"What are *you* doing here?" she demanded.

"I wanted a little chat, Miss Masefield," he said with quiet menace.

She tried to escape but Tommy Gault had been waiting behind the door. Slamming it shut, he grabbed her with one arm and put the other hand over her mouth to stifle her scream. Gilpatrick got up from the chair so that Genevieve could be forced down into it. Standing behind her, Gault held her in a firm grip.

Gilpatrick took an object from his pocket and held it inches from her face.

"We brought your key back," he said. "What have you done with ours?"

Rutherford Blaine enjoyed another meal with the Changs and the Legges. Angela Van Bergen was the sixth person at the table, but she was more reserved this time. When it was all over, Blaine found himself sweeping the room with a nervous gaze. The fact that he was the designated target of an assassin was starting to unnerve him. He wondered how much longer he could keep up the pretense of being unconcerned. Deprived of his bodyguard and indirectly responsible, in his view, for the murder of Father Slattery, he was feeling the cumulative effects of anxiety. Making his way to the exit, he did not have the usual measured confidence in his gait. The deputy purser was waiting to engage him in conversation. After a short while, as on a previous occasion, they strolled off together as if chatting casually. In fact, the deputy purser had been assigned to escort him safely to his cabin while making sure that nobody followed them.

They took a circuitous route, going up a flight of stairs to the promenade deck before descending down two flights to the main deck. After going along a bewildering series of passageways, they finally came to their destination. Walking toward them was a steward with a tray of food in his arms. They waited until he went past, then carried on until they reached Blaine's cabin. The diplomat thanked his escort before letting himself into the cabin and locking the door behind him. The deputy purser continued on his way and turned a corner. From the other end of the passageway, the steward reappeared. He sidled back to Blaine's cabin and made a mental note of the number. When he walked away, there was a smile of satisfaction on his face.

The first person to be arrested was Mr. Hayashi. Supported by armed men, George Dillman and Mike Roebuck went to Hayashi's cabin and confronted him with the evidence that they had found in the cargo hold. The Japanese businessman was fervent in his denials, but he was hauled off nevertheless. Joseph McDade protested his innocence even more loudly when they found him and his wife in their cabin. Dillman waved a sheaf of papers in his face.

"How do you explain these, Mr. McDade?" he demanded. "They're invoices bearing your name along with that of Mr. Gilpatrick. We found them hidden away inside boxes that turned out to contain rifles, revolvers, and an extensive supply of ammunition."

"I know nothing about those things!" yelled McDade.

"We have reason to believe that you do, sir."

"I export copperware and leatherwear. Those invoices were planted on me."

"Do you have business dealings with Mr. Gilpatrick?"

"No, he's just a friend."

"Then why did you give him catalogs from some gun manufacturers? I saw them with my own eyes when I searched his cabin," said Dillman. "The game is up, Mr. McDade. Smuggling is a serious crime. Gun running is particularly obnoxious."

McDade caved in. The purser ordered one of the men to take him off to the master-at-arms to be locked up. Dillman was more concerned about Blanche McDade. Stunned by the revelation, she sat in a chair and stared in front of her. Dillman knelt down beside her.

"I'm sorry about this, Mrs. McDade," he said softly. "I'm sure that you had nothing whatsoever to do with it. I could see that from your reaction. Your husband will have to face charges, I'm afraid, but you can continue to occupy this cabin." He put a comforting arm on her shoulder. "Would you like us to call a stewardess?"

"No, thank you."

"Is there anything else we can do for you?"

"Look in his case."

"What?"

"Look in his case," she whispered. "My husband keeps a gun in there."

It was one more piece of damning evidence. When he had searched the case and taken possession of it, the purser thanked her for her help, then led the others out. When the door closed behind them, he turned to Dillman.

"She needs help, George."

"I know."

"This has knocked her senseless. Do you think I should call the doctor?"

"Let's send a nurse of sorts instead," suggested Dillman. "Genevieve knows Mrs. McDade well. She'll be happy to talk to her. Besides, her cabin is just around the corner. Let's see if she's there, by any chance. She deserves to know what we found in the cargo hold. It was Genevieve who got that key for us."

They moved off swiftly. Reaching the cabin, Dillman knocked on the door.

"It's me, Genevieve," he called. "Are you there?"

Muffled sounds came from within, followed by a taut silence. Dillman knocked again but there was no reply. Sensing trouble, he took a master key from the purser and inserted it into the lock as quietly as he could. Mike Roebuck and two armed men stood ready. When Dillman flung open the door, they charged in after him. Genevieve was tied to the chair with Tommy Gault behind her, one hand over her mouth. Rance Gilpatrick glared at the newcomers. Seeing the hopelessness of their position, Gault made a dash for the door but Dillman intercepted him. He was seething with anger that rough hands had been laid on Genevieve. Bunching a fist, he swung a punch that caught Gault on the ear and sent him reeling. When the boxer recovered and came back at him, he had the barrel of a gun thrust at his chest. He backed away, cursing under his breath.

"Get him out of here," said Roebuck. "Lock him up with the others."

"What others?" asked Gilpatrick.

"Mr. Hayashi and Mr. McDade. Your fellow gun runners."

While the two men dragged Gault out, Dillman undid the ropes that held Genevieve and embraced her. She was frightened but not hurt, explaining how the two men had been in her cabin when she returned there. Dillman turned on Gilpatrick.

"You need some lessons in how to treat a lady with courtesy," he said, squaring up to him. "No wonder your wife ran out on you."

"Shut up!" howled Gilpatrick.

He hurled himself at Dillman, but he was no match for the detective. Pushing him away, Dillman delivered a relay of punches that sent him staggering back against the wall. Blood was streaming from Gilpatrick's nose. He had had enough.

"It's my duty to place you under arrest, Mr. Gilpatrick," said the purser.

"On what charge?"

"Smuggling. We have invoices that bear your name and catalogs found hidden beneath your mattress from gun manufacturers. They were given to you by Joseph McDade, who is already behind bars."

"This is nothing to do with me, Mr. Roebuck," said Gilpatrick, dabbing at his nose with a handkerchief and changing his tack completely. "Look, we're all adults here. I'm sure that we can sort this out between ourselves." He reached for his wallet. "I can see that I've put all three of you to considerable trouble and you deserve compensation. What would you say to five hundred dollars apiece?"

Dillman bristled. "I'd say we should add a charge of attempted bribery."

"McDade and Hayashi are the real criminals here."

"Save your lies for the courtroom, Mr. Gilpatrick," warned the purser. "The jury won't believe them any more than you do. The evidence against you is overwhelming."

"Take him out, Mike," said Dillman.

Roebuck moved to the door. "Come on, Mr. Gilpatrick."

Gilpatrick stared first at Dillman, then switched his gaze to Genevieve.

"I *knew* that there was something fishy about you," he said, his voice dark with rancor. "All the time you were making friends with my wife, you were really after me. You were too good to be true, Miss Masefield. Now I can see why."

"Out!" snapped the purser.

Grabbing the prisoner by the neck, he dragged him off. Dillman shut the door after them, then went to wrap Genevieve in his arms once more. She was able to show her emotions now, clinging tightly as her eyes began to moisten.

"Thank heaven you came when you did, George. He was terrifying."

"Did he touch you at all?"

"No, but it was only a matter of time."

"How did they get on to you?"

"Gilpatrick realized how we'd tricked the key out of Gault."

"It must have been a nasty moment," said Dillman, "finding them both in here."

"It was dreadful. I thought that they were going to kill me."

He hugged her even harder. "You're safe now, Genevieve. They can't hurt you. Mike and I broke open some boxes in the cargo hold and found them full of weapons. Paperwork inside the boxes ties Gilpatrick with Hayashi and McDade."

"That's something I found out," she said. "McDade has a gun."

"His wife told us about it. Mike Roebuck has confiscated it."

Genevieve was surprised. "Blanche McDade told you?"

"She was in the cabin when we arrested her husband. It all came as a terrible blow to her. In fact, she was so shocked, I thought she needed a friend in there to offer solace. That's why we came looking for you," he explained. "But it turned out that you were the one in need of assistance."

"I'm much better now," she said, giving him a kiss of gratitude. "It was a kind thought, George. If she's in her cabin, I'll see if I can comfort her."

"Are you sure?"

"She's a nice woman. I want to help."

"Mrs. McDade will appreciate that. But don't stay in there indefinitely."

"Why not?"

"You have a date with me this evening, Genevieve," he said proudly. "We're dining at the captain's table, and the invitation couldn't come at a more appropriate time. I think we have a lot to celebrate."

When he tied his tie that evening, Rutherford Blaine noticed that his hands were trembling. The suspense was telling on him. While he had every confidence in the ship's detectives, the fact had to be faced that they seemed no nearer to apprehending the man who was trying to kill him. The task was daunting. On a ship carrying almost eighteen hundred people, it was extremely difficult to pick out the would-be assassin. Time was on his side. There was over a week before they reached Japan and, no matter how vigilant his guards, opportunities for an attack were bound to arise. Blaine was frightened. He was on a secret government mission, yet his thoughts were not about affairs of state. All that he could think of was his wife, Marie, sitting innocently at home as she awaited his return from diplomatic duties. He could imagine how her world would crumble if she received news that her husband had been murdered.

A tap on the door caught him unawares and made him jump.

"Who is it?" he asked through the door.

"George Dillman," came the reply.

"I'll be with you in one moment, Mr. Dillman."

"There's no hurry, sir."

Blaine put on his tailcoat, then checked his appearance in the mirror. After brushing a stray hair back into place with his hand, he decided that he was ready. He opened the door and saw Dillman waiting for him. He noticed the bruising on his temple.

"What happened to your head?" he asked, shutting the door behind him.

"I had to subdue someone in the course of an arrest."

Blaine's face ignited with hope. "The assassin?"

"Unfortunately not, sir," said Dillman, falling in beside him as they walked toward the stairs. "It was a parallel investigation that ended very successfully. A gang of smugglers is now under lock and key."

"I'd feel more secure if the killer had been caught."

"He will be, Mr. Blaine."

"When?"

"Very soon."

"Do you have any more clues as to his identity?"

Dillman took a deep breath. "We're working on the case."

"In other words, you've made no progress."

"Be patient, sir. These things can't be rushed."

"I'm just wondering how long I have to put up with being escorted everywhere."

"Until we've got the person or persons responsible for the murder of Father Slattery," said Dillman. "It's only a matter of waiting. The vital clue will fall into our laps when we least expect it."

———

Since she was dining at the captain's table, Genevieve made a special effort. She put on her favorite dress, an evening gown in ivory-colored taffeta, simply trimmed with ruches and a round-shaped silver band. The skirt was rather full on the hips, the attractive frou-frou at the feet secured by broad flounces that were trimmed with pleated ruches, arranged in festoons. A pearl necklace and pearl earrings completed the outfit. After twirling in front of the mirror, she was satisfied. Genevieve was ready to cut a dash in the dining saloon. Knowing that Dillman was on escort duty elsewhere, she set off alone. Waiting for her at the top of the staircase was David Seymour-Jones. He saw her hesitate.

"I only came to apologize, Miss Masefield," he said quickly, surging forward. "I hadn't realized that I was being such a nuisance."

"You're nothing of the kind, Mr. Seymour-Jones," she lied without conviction.

"Yes, I am. When I first met you, we were two of the few English people on a ship full of foreigners. Actually," he confessed, "I think of Americans as even more foreign than the Japanese and Chinese. Don't ask me why. But I have distressed you without meaning to in the least. Mrs. Langmead scolded me for it."

"Mrs. Langmead?"

"That wasn't the reason she came looking for me," he went on. "I upset her husband earlier today, and she wanted to know why. He's such a placid man, she said, though I didn't find him very placid on the main deck."

"What was he doing down there?"

"That's what I asked him, and he got very angry with me."

"Why?"

"I still don't know, Miss Masefield," he said. "After all, it was Mr. Langmead who suggested that I ought to start charging for portraits. When I saw him on the main deck, I was sketching an interesting group of passengers and the two of them were on the very edge of it."

"The two of them?"

"He was talking to one of the stewards. A Chinaman with a hideous bruise on his face. I was just drawing them in outline when Mr. Langmead saw me."

"What did he do?"

"He went wild," said Seymour-Jones. "He accused me of spying on him and tore the sketch up. The steward disappeared in a flash. Mr. Langmead warned me that if I ever tried to draw him again, he'd report me to the purser. Then he charged off."

"That doesn't sound like Horace Langmead."

"When he tore up that sketch, he destroyed an hour's patient work."

"This steward you mention," she asked. "Was he from steerage?"

"Oh, yes. You could tell from his uniform. Perhaps that's why Mr. Langmead went down there. The man wouldn't have been allowed in first-class areas of the ship. Anyway," he continued, "that isn't why I came to speak to you, Miss Masefield. I simply wanted to apologize and to say how disappointed I am that you won't be playing the piano at the concert. Mr. Gilpatrick told me that when he sacked me."

"Sacked you?"

"Yes, I won't be designing any posters now. Not that it matters," he said with an admiring smile. "If you're not involved, I wouldn't do the posters anyway."

Genevieve was touched. The artist's attentions had troubled her in the past, but he seemed so innocuous now. She felt sorry for him. Before she could say anything else, however, her other suitor suddenly materialized beside her. Willoughby Kincaid frowned.

"My goodness!" he exclaimed. "You already have an escort, Miss Masefield."

"Not exactly, Mr. Kincaid," she said. "Do you know Mr. Seymour-Jones?"

"We've seen each other around."

The artist shook the proffered hand. "How do you do, Mr. Kincaid?"

"I'm a little crestfallen, to tell you the truth," said Kincaid. "I'd hoped that Miss Masefield—resplendent as she is this evening—would finally recognize me for the splendid fellow that I am and choose me as her beau. But you got here first, sir."

"I simply wanted to speak to Miss Masefield," explained Seymour-Jones.

"It doesn't matter," said Genevieve happily. "As it happens, I'm dining at the captain's table this evening with a certain gentleman. But there's no reason why the two of you shouldn't escort me to the dining saloon." She offered both arms. "Well?"

All three of them were soon descending the stairs together.

George Porter Dillman was never off duty. While he savored the pleasure of being at the captain's table, his eyes scanned the room constantly. Rutherford Blaine was still under threat of death and the chances were that someone in the dining saloon was involved in the plot to kill him. No matter how often he looked around, however, Dillman could discern nobody who was taking a particular interest in Blaine. Seated between Fay Brinkley and Moira Legge, the diplomat was comfortable and relaxed. He never even glanced in Dillman's direction. Fay Brinkley did, however, on more than one occasion. There was mingled surprise and resignation in her eyes when she saw Dillman beside Genevieve Masefield, but there was no hint of chagrin.

When her gaze shifted to Genevieve, it was compounded of affection and disappointment, an older woman's acceptance of a friend's superior beauty and charm. Genevieve caught her eye and collected a smile from Fay. She was relieved. Being seen by Kincaid and by Seymour-Jones was an advantage to her. They identified her and Dillman as a couple and saw that their own hopes were doomed. Fay was a different matter. Her interest was in Dillman, and she flattered herself that she was slowly engaging his emotions. Genevieve admired the bravery and lack of bitterness with which she seemed to acknowledge defeat. It meant that their friendship would survive.

In a dining saloon that was almost full to the brim, some people were conspicuous by their absence. Rance Gilpatrick, Tommy Gault, Joseph McDade, and Mr. Hayashi were all being held in custody. In the circumstances, neither Blanche McDade nor Mrs. Hayashi felt able to be seen in public and they were dining in their rooms. Maxine Gilpatrick, by contrast, was unabashed. The news that her husband had been arrested neither shocked nor upset her. It was something that she knew would happen one day, and she responded to the situation with fortitude. Instead of skulking in her cabin, therefore, she put on her most spectacular evening gown and sailed into the room as if making an entrance onstage. Sharing a table with the Langmeads, she was eating heartily and joining in the animated conversation. When she realized that Genevieve was watching her, she looked up, flicked a glance at Dillman, then grinned in approval at her friend.

But it was Horace Langmead who attracted her attention most of all. Sleek and jovial, he sat among friends and chortled merrily. He was the same man Genevieve had met on her first day aboard. But the one who intrigued her was the person who had been so incensed by a harmless artist that he had torn up his drawing. Some of Langmead's comments echoed in Genevieve's ears. One of the first things he had said to her was that Japan was too good for the Japanese. Had it really been the joke that it had sounded? His wife had confided that Langmead thought the Japanese deceitful and preferred the Chinese. He had certainly championed Chinese fashion over Parisian. But it was something else that triggered suspicion in her mind. When the name of Lord Rosebury had been mentioned at the table, Horace Langmead had known instantly who he was. Many English people would not be aware of who the former foreign secretary was. An American who identified him at once must have known of his visits to the Far East.

"George," she said after long contemplation, "I've got some news."

"What's that?" he said, enjoying the excuse to lean in close to her.

"I think I might know who the killer is."

When the meal was over, Dillman waited until the captain had left before he escorted Genevieve toward the exit. On their way, they paused beside Fay Brinkley's table. She was disturbed by the sight of the bruising on Dillman's temple. It was something she had not noticed in the subdued lighting on the previous night. Fay thought that it gave him a more rugged look. She squeezed Genevieve's arm and spoke in a whisper.

"I saw him first," she complained with a smile.

"Not quite."

"I said that you were a dark horse."

"I'll explain everything tomorrow, Fay."

"You already have. I'm not blind."

Dillman had detached Blaine from the table and walked toward the door with him. After being introduced to the Changs, Genevieve stayed to chat with them and with the Legges. It was Moira Legge who could not contain her excitement.

"And we thought you'd end up with Mr. Kincaid!" she blurted out.

"That was never a meeting of true minds, Mrs. Legge," said Genevieve.

"He was terribly keen on you," noted Legge.

"Who isn't?" said Fay with envy. "Genevieve can take her pick."

"It looks as if she's done just that," said Moira Legge, staring after Dillman.

The detective was unaware of her scrutiny. Standing at the door, he was talking to the purser while Blaine chatted with Mrs. Van Bergen as she was about to leave. With so many people around, the diplomat felt secure while he awaited his escort. Dillman passed on the information that Genevieve had given him. Mike Roebuck reacted with interest.

"A steward from steerage?" he asked.

"With a face that was badly bruised," said Dillman.

"So you didn't give him a black eye, after all."

"We're not sure that this *is* our man, Mike, but it's a possibility that has to be looked at. Genevieve is fairly convinced about it."

"We have quite a few Chinese stewards aboard."

"How many of them have been in a fight?"

At Dillman's suggestion, the two of them led Blaine back to his cabin, taking a new route and ensuring that nobody was trailing them. When they turned onto the passageway on the main deck, Dillman called them to a halt and held out his hand.

"Could I borrow your key, please, Mr. Blaine?" he said.

"Why?" asked the diplomat. "I'm perfectly safe now. There are bolts on the inside of the door. Once they're in place, you'd need a battering ram to get in."

"The assassin knows that, sir. By now, he may have discovered where you are. Since he can't get at you once you're inside, he may try an alternative strategy."

"Alternative?"

"Gain access while you're not there," said Dillman, "and lie in wait."

"How would he get hold of a key?"

"We have reason to believe that he may be one of the stewards. He'd know where the key to this cabin was kept."

Blaine handed over his key. When Dillman put it in the lock, Roebuck stationed himself directly behind him to shield the diplomat. Entering the room, Dillman switched on the light and closed the door behind him to give the impression that the real occupant had returned. The place was empty, but he sensed danger. Its most likely source was the bathroom. Slipping off his coat, Dillman tossed it on the bunk and went into the bathroom. When he flicked the switch, the light did not come on. Someone had removed the bulb. Dillman knew the attack was imminent. As a figure came hurling at him out of the gloom with a length of cord in his hands, he got a firm grip and used the man's momentum against him, swinging him around in a semicircle until he collided with the wall. The attacker was winded. Before he could recover, Dillman threw a series of punches to his head and body. Weakened even more, the man still had the strength to aim a kick at Dillman's leg that made the detective wince. He flung himself on the interloper and they grappled violently. When they fell to the ground, Dillman managed to stay on top.

Alerted by the noise, the purser used a master key to open the door in order to come to Dillman's aid, but it was not required. Sitting astride his opponent, Dillman pounded away with both fists until resistance slowly faded. He dragged the man into the cabin so that he could see him in the light. Wearing a mask, his attacker was dressed in the uniform of a steward from steerage. Dillman tore the mask away from the man's face to reveal the bruising he had inflicted earlier. The Chinese steward did not even have the breath to curse Dillman. Turning him on his front, the detective used the piece of cord to bind his hands. He was still panting from his own exertions as he hauled the man upright. Blaine took a few tentative steps into the cabin.

"Have you got him?" he asked.

"Yes, sir," said Roebuck grimly.

Blaine inspected the prisoner. "Who is he?"

"The man who killed Father Slattery," said Dillman.

"Why was he after me?"

"We'll know that when we arrest his boss, sir."

Acting on Dillman's orders, Genevieve followed the Langmeads into the lounge and kept them talking. Horace Langmead had regained all of his conviviality. It was difficult to believe that such an amiable man could be involved in a murder plot, and

Genevieve was troubled by doubts. Had she made an appalling error? It would be highly embarrassing if they accused Langmead of a crime when he was completely innocent. Dillman seemed to be taking an inordinate time and the wait began to vex Genevieve. Etta Langmead was as curious as anyone to know about her dinner companion.

"Who is he, Miss Masefield?" she wondered.

"A friend," replied Genevieve.

"Why have you been keeping him to yourself?"

"He's rather shy."

"There's no room for shyness onboard ship," said Etta. "You must invite him to join our table tomorrow. Mustn't she, Horry?"

"Yes, yes," he agreed heartily. "Any friend of Miss Masefield's is always welcome."

At that moment, a steward came into the lounge with a message for Langmead. Getting up at once, Langmead excused himself and followed the man out, wondering why the purser had asked to see him in his office. Etta Langmead took advantage of her husband's absence to clasp Genevieve's arm.

"Good," she said with glee. "Now that he's gone, you can tell me *everything.*"

Horace Langmead approached the office with apprehension, but it did not show in his face. When he was invited in to see the purser, his smile was intact. It broadened when Roebuck introduced him to Dillman, who was standing in the background.

"Pleased to meet you, Mr. Dillman," said Langmead, shaking his hand. "We were just talking about you to Genevieve Masefield. You're a fortunate man, sir."

"Thank you," replied Dillman.

"We hope the pair of you will join us at our table."

"That won't be possible, I'm afraid, Mr. Langmead."

"Why not?"

"I didn't introduce Mr. Dillman properly," said the purser.

"He's not a passenger. He's one of the ship's detectives." Langmead's smile congealed. "So is Miss Masefield." The visitor was visibly shocked. "Tell me, sir," Roebuck went on, "does the name Ho Ni mean anything to you?"

"No, it doesn't. Never heard of the fellow. Who is he?"

"He's the man who gave me this," explained Dillman, pointing to the bruise on his temple. "I was able to repay the compliment this evening in Mr. Blaine's cabin. Mr. Ni is a steward in steerage. At least, he was. He's now under arrest for the murder of Father Slattery and the attempted murder of myself."

Langmead shrugged. "What's this got to do with me?"

"You were seen talking to Mr. Ni on the main deck earlier on. We have a positive identification, sir. Mr. Seymour-Jones was most obliging. Though he was only able to peer at Mr. Ni through the bars of his cell, he picked him out instantly as the man he tried to sketch along with you. Now we know why you tore up that drawing."

"Mr. Seymour-Jones had no right to do that sketch of me."

"Perhaps not, Mr. Langmead, but did you have to pounce on him like that?"

"Do you still deny that you know Mr. Ni?" added the purser.

"Categorically. I did speak to a Chinese steward," admitted Langmead. "It's true. But I had no idea what his name was. I simply asked him how his face had got that terrible bruise on it."

"Yes," resumed Dillman. "Mr. Seymour-Jones did overhear something of what you were saying to him but he couldn't understand you, could he, sir? You were speaking in Chinese to Mr. Ni. You obviously know the language," he said, producing some letters from his pocket. "I found these in your cabin just now when I searched it. That's why Miss Masefield was keeping you and your wife talking in the lounge, you see. We needed time to gather our evidence."

Langmead started to bluster, but he knew it was futile. Opening the door, he tried to make a run for it but he went straight into the arms of the deputy purser who had been waiting outside. Struggling in vain, Langmead was forced back into the purser's office.

"Now, sir," said Roebuck, "supposing that you start telling us the truth?"

It was midnight before George Porter Dillman had finished. The long interrogation of Horace Langmead had been revealing but exhausting for all concerned. However, Dillman could not retire to his cabin. He had agreed to a rendezvous. Genevieve Masefield was waiting for him on the covered promenade of the upper deck, gazing out to sea. Steady rain was beating at the windows. The prow was plunging low as it came down from the crest of a wave. Embracing her warmly, Dillman apologized for keeping her so long and explained what had happened. Genevieve was thrilled.

"What a day!" she observed. "We netted four smugglers and a killer."

"Don't forget Horace Langmead," he said. "He was the key figure. Ho Ni was only a hired assassin. It was Langmead who gave him his instructions."

"Why, George? What did he have against Mr. Blaine?"

"Nothing, personally. But Langmead was working for the Chinese government, and they were not pleased at the idea of closer links between Japan and the United States. That's what Mr. Blaine is trying to negotiate," he said. "It's all to do with the balance of power. President Roosevelt wants Japan to act as a buffer against Russia and China. That's why he favored Japan when he mediated between the two countries after the Russo-Japanese war."

"In what way did he favor them?"

"He sacrificed Korea to the Japanese. You'd have to live in the Far East to appreciate the significance of that. It really angered the Chinese. They have their own fears of Japan," he went on, "so they don't want it strengthened by closer relations with the United States."

"Why are they afraid of Japan?" she asked. "China is so much bigger."

"Japan has a very effective army, Genevieve. Russia discovered that. And did you know that Japan has the fifth most powerful fleet in the world?"

"A small country like that?"

Dillman grinned. "Think of the small country where you lived," he reminded her. "The British navy ruled the waves at one time. Being small hasn't stopped Britain from building the largest empire ever seen. Japan is a very ambitious nation," he stressed. "They have imperial designs. The Chinese are right to keep a wary eye on them."

"How did Mr. Langmead get involved in all this?"

"His business dealings brought him to China. He liked the country. They sensed that he could be bought, Genevieve, so they worked on him. They paid him very handsomely. Langmead has political contacts in Washington, D.C."

"So he set up a small network of spies."

"Yes," said Dillman. "Now that we've caught him, it can be smashed."

"And I thought that Mr. Langmead was such a nice man."

"Spies usually are. They have to be plausible in order to do their work."

"Just like us."

"Yes, Genevieve." He slipped an arm around her. "Just like us."

"But things will have to change now, George," she pointed out. "Different methods will be needed. We've been seen together in public. Everybody realizes that we know each other."

"So?"

"They think that we're involved in a romance."

"Then we'll have to give them every reason to go on believing that, won't we?"

Genevieve turned to him. "How do we do that?"

"Oh," he said, pulling her to him, "we'll find a way somehow."

POSTSCRIPT

The Minnesota *did well at first, but a sharp fall in freight rate put an end to the owner's dreams of huge profits. The ship began to lose money but was nevertheless kept in service for over a decade. In October 1915, she was withdrawn from service and became the target for a group of companies eager to make war profits out of England's food crisis. After repairs that lasted a year, the* Minnesota *arrived in New York in February 1917 via the Panama Canal. She was renamed* Troy *and carried cargoes of record proportions across the Atlantic for the remainder of World War I. After the war, she was converted to burn oil. She lay idle for three years. In November 1923, she left New York under tow for a scrap yard in Germany.*